BURGUNDY DOUBLOONS

BOOK ONE: WAKE

TJ SPENCER JACQUES

NOVELS BY
TJ SPENCER JACQUES

NINE NOTCHES

BURGUNDY DOUBLOONS

INFALLIBLE SERIES

This is a work of fiction created by author TJ Spencer Jacques. All the characters, organizations, and events portrayed in this novel are either products of the author's imagination or used fictitiously.

This book is dedicated to my dad Dwight Elton Weaver who died in 1977 when I was a little boy, but I never for got his love.

BURGUNDY DOUBLOONS

BOOK ONE: WAKE

TJ SPENCER JACQUES

ACT I

CHAPTER 1

Desperate arms reached for him with open palms and importuned fingers, as if he were a returning messiah who had decided to make good on a promise. Afloat, he careened through a river of multicolored faces as far as his eyes could see. A few looked familiar, but only a few. Though he wished he could shower them all with the desires of their hearts, he ignored them. Charity wasn't his to give. Nonetheless, they reached for him with great need, only to receive a smile and a wave as he floated by in all his grandeur.

But he wasn't cruel or selfish; nothing could be further from the truth.

All their needs would get addressed eventually, but for now - if just for the moment - his only purpose was to hoard their eyes and tease their expectations. The same was true of the woman who trailed behind him, draped in everything that glowed, gleamed, and glittered. His wife. *The Queen.*

She was a Queen, but nothing like Elizabeth or Mary. Her husband was King, but he wasn't in the House of Tudor - not even close. Nor was the duration of their reign anywhere near those of the famed British royals. He was in the House of Fuller, as in the Fullers from New Orleans. After ten unsuccessful years of campaigning, he and his wife had finally been voted King and Queen of a Carnival parade.

As King, his job was simple: Wave at the crowd of parade-goers and make eye contact with as many cell phones as possible. And so, he smiled just as he had rehearsed and waved like a royal.

All but four people smiled back as he passed. The grim faces stood along the first row of the barricades, on the left side of the King's float. *Such conspicuous faces in a throng of joy.* A woman, a teenage girl, and two little girls stared at him as if he'd drove down a one-way and rolled over their puppy. The King wondered what was wrong.

Are they not happy to see me after waiting hours for the parade to roll down Canal Street?

Their stares bruised his skin and caused a mishap in his only duty: To smile and wave.

A sudden jolt caused by the street debris underfoot jostled his float. It disrupted his focus on the four who didn't appear entertained; the hard sway nearly caused him to fall. The King regained his balance and remembered to smile and wave. The floats that trailed him - sixty-five in total - had more than enough beads and throws to guarantee that everyone caught something. Even the police who guarded the route, even the branches of the trees. As his parade rolled into the night, he felt like a real king, and from the few glimpses he caught of her, his Queen was feeling her role, as well. Not even on their wedding night had she smiled for so long, so perfectly.

The reign of the Fullers.

A reign of exactly one day, but a lifetime of memories.

They were lovers, in the sense that they loved the solitude of being together. The opposite sides of a plush leather sofa, under a thick wool blanket comprised their special place, perfect for Sunday afternoons. He begged her to read mystery novels aloud, just to souse in the musical serenade of her voice - so soothing it cradled him to sleep. In a dreamlike state, he still absorbed every word as he drifted through metaphorical wonderlands and sailed away from the greatest subtext God ever created: New Orleans.

. . . But not for long.

Their love-hate relationship with the city during Carnival was bipolar. No other holiday mattered as much because they were practitioners of the Greatest Free Show on Earth. They were both lifelong members of krewe: the orthodoxy of the Crescent City. Their krewe's monthly meetings, dues, budgets, costume debates, elections . . . and all their year-long preparation for one day - one parade - consumed them for 364 days out of every year. Surprisingly, after each year's Mardi Gras, they quickly re-enlisted.

But the Fullers had developed a coping mechanism that aided in their recovery from the Carnival parade: they hauled ass out of New Orleans the following day.

Once the last bead was tossed and the final toast was lifted at the ball, the Fullers blended into the herds of departing tourists and boarded a noon flight out. It was their annual thing; the way they celebrated their marriage, a yearly revival that bonded them. Kelsey and Rhonda Fuller tied the knot on Mardi Gras Night in 1984. Then, they left one party and flew to another; the desert paradise of Las Vegas, Nevada.

They didn't go because Vegas was better than New Orleans, but it provided them a way to avoid the gloom of the following morning. Kelsey and Rhonda wanted no part of Ash Wednesday: the guilt or the pending invasion of credit card statements. Evacuating to Vegas was their way of delaying the hangover - at least for another week.

He still enjoyed walking behind her four paces or so - far enough to appreciate her seductive prance, but not too distant that she would feel alone. Kelsey was still very much in love with Rhonda. Even after decades of marriage, she could still seduce him with a nice pair of jeans and heels.

As they walked through the Southwest Airlines terminal at McCarran International, Kelsey spotted their driver - the same driver from last year and the four previous years. He was a slender African-American man with a military cut; no more than thirty years old, in a black suit that hadn't felt a steam iron since last year, when he had waited for them in the same place.

His name was Quincy. He stood in front of a black limo that gleamed like plastic - or better yet, like the glass on a downtown skyscraper reflecting the noon sun. Directly below his chin was a cardboard sign: *Welcome to Vegas, Mr. and Mrs. Fuller.*

Kelsey handed Quincy two of the carry-on bags. "Whenever I see your face I know the party is about to start." Kelsey placed the large rolling suitcase into the trunk.

"And whenever I see you and your beautiful wife I dream of living in New Orleans for the rest of my life! How was your reign as King and Queen?"

After a fifteen-minute drive, they arrived at the same hotel they stayed at every year. Kelsey tipped Quincy the same as last year: a crisp fifty-dollar bill.

"Why thank you, Mr. Fuller! What time would you like me to pick you up for dinner?"

"Same as usual, Quincy."

"Great, then I rest a little from all of the Mardi Gras fun and I will see you for five o'clock."

Even the front desk clerk remembered them, because Rhonda always presented them with Mardi Gras gifts like beads and cups, items they used to welcome other tourists from New Orleans.

The elevator ride up was swift, but the hallway commute to their room was a country mile to Kelsey. He wobbled down the hall like one leg was suddenly shorter than the other. The luggage - two carry-on bags on each shoulder and Rhonda's over-stuffed rolling suitcase - was unforgiving.

His breathing labored like he was a kid with severe asthma who had left his inhaler at school on his desk.

His two-pack-a-day Little Debbie habit became more evident as Rhonda outpaced him and arrived at room 1968 nearly a minute ahead of her husband. She waited for him at the door. From down the hall, her eyes lectured, but there was no way for him to tune her out.

I am out of shape, I know it. Okay.

The air that escaped his lungs brushed her tapered bob cut.

Rhonda waved a card in front of the electronic door lock; the light turned green. They entered a beautiful, luxurious room - one that appeared as a glossy page in pitch-book for a timeshare.

Kelsey dropped the two bags that hung off each shoulder and released the plastic handle of the suitcase. Shortly after that, he collapsed, right up the center of the bed like an old Calgon commercial, as if a lumberjack had yelled *Timber!*

In little over a year, he had managed to gain twenty-five additional pounds but lose two inches from his hairline. A hopeless case of coastal erosion, more of his forehead gleamed, while the sandy-colored hair he loved receded. The good news was the pillow-top-mattress was firm enough to support all 275 pounds of his six-foot-tall body. His head slowly turned at the exact time his wife opened the drapes that blocked the money-shot: that majestic Vegas skyline.

Rhonda exhaled. "God . . . I love this view of Vegas." Her arms extended with clutches full of drapes. "And that looks like the same street magician from last year. He has a crowd this year. You should come see this."

He wanted to, but the dribbling in his chest wouldn't allow it.

"I think I will chill here for a moment and appreciate the view of you."

Though they were the same age, Kelsey looked more like her sugar daddy. From the outside, their relationship may have appeared as an illegal fling with the office receptionist. She was the type of woman a man cheats with just to experience a particular body type. But Rhonda wasn't an office romance gone wrong, nor was he a married man battling through the final stage of a midlife crisis. They were legally together for all the right reasons, and loving every second of every day.

Rhonda's focus on the street magician was broken by her cell phone. She answered it.

"Yes Reese, we have landed." She shot Kelsey a look. "He's right here . . . stretched across the bed, faking another heart attack." Rhonda took a seat next to her husband on the bed. ". . . Other than that, Vegas is just as beautiful as last year, and not as hot as I expected."

She returned to the window and continued her conversation

with their daughter. The sweat on Kelsey's shoreline dried as his heart rate slowly returned to normal. Rhonda was near the end of her call.

"Reese, my spies have clocked in!" Kelsey yelled. "And if I get any word of a party, we're on the next plane smoking to New Orleans. Understand?"

"She heard you," Rhonda replied.

Rhonda ended her call and heaved the large suitcase onto the bed, inches from his head. She hung the evening wear in the closet and unpacked several pairs of heels.

From the floor of the closet she looked over her shoulder. "So, are you going to lay there like a log this entire vacation?"

"Yes . . . that sounds like a good idea. Why not?"

"If you would've followed Dr. Mohammad's instructions and marched in place just thirty minutes a day, you . . ."

He interrupted. "I know, if I would have stepped in place thirty minutes a day then I wouldn't be an out-of-shape piggy."

"Well . . . I didn't call you an out-of-shape piggy; those were your words."

"But I know what you're thinking . . ."

"Okay—Mr. Piggy!" Rhonda chuckled.

"Oh. Oh, I see how this goes, now I'm Mr. Piggy, but when I was ripped and chiseled . . ."

"Chiseled? Oh, my . . ."

"Yes, you heard me." He flexed his biceps. *"Chizzzzzeled.* Ripped. Shredded like lettuce. Remember?"

"Hmm, no."

"Seems like you have lost weight and memory, my dear. You couldn't keep your hands off me . . . so you seduced me into getting you pregnant. Remember?" he laughed.

The unpacking of luggage ceased. She stood still as a mannequin. Both of her arms rested on her hips. Her head tilted to the right.

"Seduced you . . . ha! I was the sexiest girl at LSU and the prettiest on the cheerleading squad - all four years." Her arms formed an L as she re-enacted a cheer. "I seduced you into getting me pregnant? Now I have heard it all!" Her laughter grew louder. Rhonda leaped and high kicked, taunting him with her timeless agility.

"Yeah, you seduced me all right . . . and I didn't know any better, because I was just a little virgin . . . saving my virginity for marriage." He finally sat up and placed praying hands below his chin.

"Virginity?! Ha!"

Rhonda grabbed a pair of her perfectly folded jeans from the suitcase and started whacking Kelsey on his back. He laughed as Rhonda leaped on the bed behind him and pulled him back in a headlock chokehold.

Her voice lowered to a growl. "I was the *Last American Virgin* and don't you ever forget that," she whispered in his ear.

"Okay, okay . . . I wasn't a virgin. You're ch-choking me."

"And don't you forget it."

"Uncle . . ."

Rhonda released her grip. "Now lift up . . . you're starting to smash me."

"How about you use your brand new CrossFit muscles and push me off?"

"Kelsey!"

"Nope . . . Mr. Piggy is comfortable right here."

Laughter filled the room.

"For real Kelsey, you're smashing me; I can't breathe."

Slowly, he lifted himself off Rhonda's slender body and turned to face her. He moved downward to her lips; they kissed. Then he raised and lowered again to her lips; another kiss.

"I am doing push-ups just for you."

"Aww, that is so sexy. But you can't quit in mid rep. Eight more push-ups to go—my lips will wait for you down here."

"If you would do this more often, I might just get in shape."

"I might consider that . . . but for now you owe me eight more kisses." She smiled at him and puckered her lips.

"I love you."

"I love you too, Kelsey."

"Thank you for every year of this marriage. Thank you for every novel you read to me. Thank you for being my best friend. I am the luckiest man . . . in Vegas."

As he lowered down to kiss her again, there was a knock at

the door.

"Who could that be?" she muttered.

"I placed the *Do Not Disturb* hanger on the door!"

"Well . . . go see who it is and hurry back," Rhonda said as she unbuttoned her jeans and slowly unzipped. Her lip color matched her auburn hair, which highlighted a pair of wide, caramel eyes. Their love story was a romantic script unlike any other novel. She was his Grace from *Will & Grace,* and he was her Mike from *Mike & Molly.*

Their exchange was interrupted by another knock on the door.

"I'm coming . . . hold your horses!" he yelled.

"Please hurry back . . ." she purred.

After three grunts and a sciatic stretch, Kelsey arrived at the door. He surveyed the hallway through the peephole. "It's a bell-hop!" he yelled over his shoulder. "Did you forget a bag in the lobby?" he asked as he reached for the twist handle.

"No dear, we have all of our bags."

The door swung open.

The bellhop was gone.

In his place stood a woman who looked no more than thirty-five years old. She was dressed in a white nightgown, and had blonde, tangled hair and chapped lips. Kelsey's nose detected the stench of fish guts. Decayed. Rancid. Around the woman's neck was something he was very familiar with: a string of Mardi Gras beads. Hanging from the beads, resting in the center of her chest, was a round, red medallion: a doubloon.

At her side were three girls. The taller of the girls appeared no older than fifteen. The other two were much younger.

"Ma'am . . . can I help you?"

She didn't reply.

From the bed, his wife called out, "Honey . . . who's that at the door?"

The faint sound of evil giggling from the two little girls caught his attention. Between their blonde locks of hair, he noticed that the girls wore masks of thick, yellow pus, caked on like a pink-eye infection. The teeth appeared rouge; a hue more commonly left behind by cheap lipstick.

Feeling uneasy, Kelsey retreated a couple steps into the room.

That's when he recognized them. It was the woman and the three girls from the parade route.

"Kelsey, who is that at the door?"

He finally acknowledged his wife. "If you give me a moment, I am trying to figure that out."

As he turned to address the woman again, she smiled. "The unborn has returned and the glass has shattered."

"Excuse me?" His brow wrinkled. "I think you have the wrong room."

"The unborn has returned and the glass has shattered," she said again in a voice that ground his nerves like a pencil sharpener. Kelsey looked over her shoulder to the left and right for the usual hotel staff who veered like ants in and out of rooms, but the hallway was desolate.

"The High Priestess sent me to find you!" one of the little girls said in a giggle that was stolen from Vincent Price.

"Excuse me? Ma'am, I think you have your room numbers confused . . ."

"No confusion, Mr. Fuller. It is you and your wife I come for - it is time to make atonement."

"Atonement? Lady, it's too early in the day to be this wasted." Kelsey began to close the door. "Do you, and your kids, a favor - go sleep it off."

"The unborn has returned and the glass has shattered," the lady said again. The little girls with pinkeye joined in.

The unborn has returned and the glass has shattered.

The unborn has returned and the glass has shattered.

The unborn has returned and the glass has shattered.

Kelsey tried to close the door, but the youngest of the three girls put her arm inside the door frame where the lock clicks into the bolt slot.

"Hehe, we're so happy to find you!" the teenage girl laughed. All three girls continued to giggle until the woman took a step toward Kelsey.

"It is time to fulfill the prophecy."

In the center of her chest, the red doubloon pulsated like a beating heart. The girls also wore the same pulsating doubloon. "The High Priestess sends her regards."

Kelsey tried to push the little girl out of the doorway, but he couldn't. "Look, woman, I don't know what the fuck your issue is, but I am asking you nicely to back your child out of my door."

"It shall be fulfilled as it was spoken over your life . . ."

"What was spoken?"

A hand with razor-sharp nails swooped across his throat. Blood oozed through his fingers as he clutched at his neck. Kelsey staggered backward into the room. The woman followed. The girls followed. They closed the door behind them.

Kelsey was unable to warn his wife as he bent to the floor. In a single motion, the woman grabbed him by the back of the head and gouged out his eyes. Kelsey fell to the carpet. In full view of Rhonda, the woman punched her fist through his chest plate and tore out his heart.

Rhonda screamed, but the sound-proof walls she loved so much worked to perfection.

She hurried to retrieve her cell phone as the woman lifted her husband off the floor and held him over her head. With his blood pouring over her like a warm shower, she slowly bit off his lips and feasted. With trembling hands, Rhonda Fuller tried to call 911 while keeping her eyes on the woman. Suddenly, her husband's lifeless body slammed to the floor. The woman stepped over Kelsey and moseyed toward Rhonda.

It took less than a minute for Rhonda to meet the same fate as her husband. Both were placed in the bed, nose to nose, toes to toes, as if sound asleep from a night out on the Vegas Strip.

The Fullers had long been doomed but didn't know it. Sentenced to death, but oblivious. Their grace period expired had yesterday. Yesterday was Mardi Gras.

The woman in the bloody, white nightgown led the three girls out of room 1968. Seconds later, they disappeared down the hall. It was only yesterday that Kelsey and Rhonda had fulfilled their dream of reigning as King and Queen of their Carnival parade. It was their guilt by association that cost them their lives.

CHAPTER 2

Four Weeks Earlier
1524 Toledano St.
New Orleans

Helen McGowan could hardly contain her excitement and pride; her husband was finally going to walk in his father's shoes as Captain of the Krewe of Ares. Just when she'd lost hope that it was going to happen, all the members voted overwhelmingly for her husband after one of the most controversial campaigns they had ever experienced. Mud was slung. Rumors were created. Every imaginable innuendo, both true and false, traveled from tongue to ear faster than the devil could keep track. But her husband, Jack McGowan, had emerged the victor, and would sit as Captain until he decided to retire - or until the Good Lord called him home, whichever came first.

On the kitchen table was a custom coffee mug she had ordered in anticipation of his victory. In bold letters on the front, it read *Captain of Ares.* As lifelong members of the organization, Helen and her husband knew that *Captain* - or *President,* as it's known in some other krewes - was the only leadership position remaining. As a couple, they'd worked their way up the ranks. The knock many of the members had against her husband was his age, but Jack always quickly remind them that many voters also felt JFK was too young to be President.

Helen could still feel the kiss on her lips when it was announced that her husband was the new Captain; she could also still hear the small cacophony of boos from those who supported his rival, Edward Perrier. As her husband made his way to the podium through a pathway of supporters, those who opposed his win were quickly drowned out by the members who felt the club needed younger, more progressive leadership. After he concluded his gestures of thank you, she watched as Jack McGowan cleared his throat and began to speak, uniting their krewe behind one leader.

"I would like to thank all of you who voted for me, and also embrace those who didn't. I promise to make the Krewe of Ares the best Mardi Gras krewe the City of New Orleans has ever seen. I only wish my dad was here to see this moment—but liver cancer took him away from us less than nine months ago. With his vision and determination inside of me, I will continue to grow this organization until the day we reign as the King of Mardi Gras, dethroning those snotty bastards once and for all!"

The crowd erupted in cheer.

In the oven was his favorite: hot cinnamon rolls. Across her forearm she held his gray pinstripe suit and purple satin tie. A yellow clock shaped like a kitten hung on the kitchen wall. The kitten's nosey eyes moved from left to right as if he were searching for mice. His tail wiped the wall from morning to night, back and forth until morning again. The trusty kitten notified her that it was 7:50 a.m. Her husband only had a few minutes to eat and be on his way. Helen called for Jack again.

"Jack, are you shaving?" One foot rested on the first step, one hand on the banister ball. "Please hurry Jack, your meeting with the treasurer and Attorney Ray Igelhart is set for 8:30!" Her body leaned slightly to the left, as if the angle would allow her to look around the wall past the top of the stairs and into her bedroom. "I have your suit pressed, and it's hanging on the banister."

"Thank you, pumpkin, I will be right down."

Back in the kitchen, Helen heard the sound of the oven alarm. She hurried. Just in time, she removed the hot cinnamon rolls and placed the tray on top of the stove. Remembering that her husband hated when the bottom of the rolls baked hard, Helen relocated them one by one onto a plate. She walked over to the table and placed the cinnamon rolls next to the morning paper she had retrieved earlier that morning. Finally, she poured hot coffee into her husband's brand-new mug, then poured some into her shiny, new mug adorned with bold letters: *First Lady*.

"Pumpkin have you seen my black shoes? I can't seem to find them."

"I have them down here. I will set them on the stairs."

". . . okay, thanks. I love you . . ."

"I would love you more if you would hurry up! You are going to be late."

According to the kitten, the time was exactly eight o'clock. The room to the right of the kitchen was the formal dining room, and on the dining room table sat a pair of freshly shined black leather Brooks Brothers shoes. Treating them with the gentleness of glass slippers, Helen was careful not to smudge his shoes. After shining the shoes, she trotted back through the kitchen, across the living room, and back to the base of the stairs, where she softly placed the shoes on the third step - just above his suit, which patiently waited on the banister.

"Jack! Oh, Jack! It's eight o'clock. You're going to be late," her voice was weighted with anxiety.

At the base of the wall that led up the stairs, there was a picture she had somehow never noticed. The picture captured her husband speaking with several police officers; in the background was a float. Helen took a step closer to the photo, puzzled at how she had never noticed it before. The date on the picture was February 27, 1968.

"Jack, when did you hang this picture?" she called out, but he didn't reply.

Just as she was about to remove the picture to inquire about it, there was a knock at the front door.

"Just a minute! Jack someone is at the door, but everything is right here," Helen called, hanging over the banister." She heard a *thump* just above her head. Good . . . *he's finally coming down*

Just then, there was another knock on the door. "Helen, it's me," a voice called out.

"Okay, Frieda, hold your horses."

Helen unlocked the door to welcome in her younger sister Frieda. Frieda was carrying a food tray with a plastic oval-shaped cover. She entered the living room and made a right toward the kitchen to place her plate on the table. "Helen . . . you baked cinnamon rolls?"

"Hmm, yes."

"But last night I called you . . . and we agreed on oatmeal and wheat toast. Your doctor asked you time and time again not to bake anything. That's why I went through all the trouble of driving through all that rush hour traffic . . ."

"Frieda, today is a special day - and one that was fitting for cinnamon rolls. And we can still enjoy the oatmeal."

Helen made eye contact with the kitten, then hurried back to the base of the stairs.

"The time now is 8:15 and you suit is still hanging on the banister. With the drive time, you are officially late. Jack! For heaven's sake, I still have to help you dress, just like you were one of our boys."

Just as Helen McGowan gathered the gray pinstripe suit and the shoes, Frieda grabbed her by the arm. Turning Helen to face her, she removed the suit and shoes from her arms.

"Frieda, I know my knees are bad, but he's just like a child sometimes. He is easily distracted. I bet he's on the phone up there and has lost track of time. On his first day as Captain, he's late. That's not a good example to set."

"My dear sister, we have discussed this several times . . ."

"Thanks for your help, but I can make it up these stairs. Hand me the suit, please. Jack is late."

"Helen, Jack isn't late . . ."

"Yes, he is! His meeting time was set for eight-thirty, and I bet he's on that phone . . ."

"Helen, he's not on the phone . . ."

"Well, you don't know my husband as I do . . . the man can procrastinate with the best of them."

"Helen, Jack is not up those stairs; he's not in this house. Jack has gone to be with the Lord. Please, come walk with me back to the table."

"What?! That's nonsense. Hand me that suit right this second. My husband is upstairs." Helen leaned to the left again and called out for her husband. "Jack, my silly sister seems to think you're dead. Will you please come down these stairs . . . and get this suit?"

Helen waited. Frieda stood perfectly still, wearing a smile of empathy.

"Jack?"

"Helen, Jack is not up there. Jack hasn't been up there in five years. He's gone to be with the Lord."

"He has not! He has not, I tell you. My husband is upstairs . . . on the phone. I'm going up there to help him get dressed, and when I come back down, I don't want to see you."

Before Frieda could stop Helen, her sister gripped the railing and started to pull her body up the stairs. One foot after the other. *Thump-thump, thump-thump* she went until she made it to the second floor. Out of breath, she paused for a moment before disappearing right down a short hallway that lead to her bedroom.

"Jack? Jack? This is not funny!" Helen yelled out as she walked into the master bedroom and through to the bathroom.

"Jack?"

Helen veered into each bedroom as she called out for her husband, each time with the expectancy of seeing him. With each room she exited, more panic began to take root. Slowly, she made her way back down the stairs. *Thump-thump, thump-thump, thump-thump.* "Maybe he's in the backyard, and I just didn't see him walk by."

As Helen turned in the direction of the back door, Frieda grabbed her by the arm.

"L-Let go . . . of . . . me!"

"Helen, Jack is dead . . ."

Helen's rage was sudden and hot. "Get out of my house, right now! Get out before I call the police. How dare you speak like this about my husband, how dare you?!"

"Helen I am not letting you go down that hall. Jack is not in the backyard. He's not in this house . . ."

"Then who in the hell answered me? Who called me 'pumpkin' this morning? Only Jack. Only my husband. He said 'I love you,' I heard him . . ."

"Helen, Jack called you 'pumpkin,' and he loved you and the boys very much, but he is deceased. So are your sons, Craig and Steven. All three died of liver cancer. Helen, I know this is confusing, but I am here to help you cope. I've never left your side. Helen . . . please have a seat with me, and I will call your boy. Just come have a seat."

"My Jack is dead? B-But, he was just elected Captain . . . of Ares . . . yesterday. I was there . . . there is no way my husband is -"

"Helen, Jack was elected Captain way back in 1968, nearly fifty years ago."

"No . . . that was yesterday. Why are you saying these things?"

Helen became winded and dazed. As Frieda walked her to the kitchen table, her body twisted toward the stairs, her arm extended, and her index finger aimed at the second floor. Frieda sat Helen in the chair nearest to her purse and gently restricted her mobility. She had her nephew's number on speed dial, so she called Helen's youngest son Trent, who lived in Bristol, Connecticut with his wife and kids. His phone went immediately to voicemail, so she left a hurried message.

"It's me. Your mom is having another episode. Please call me back and help me calm her while I call the home health agency and her doctor. There was no one with her when I arrived."

CHAPTER 3

After leaving a voicemail for Trent, Frieda administered Helen's morning medication regimen. She found Helen's plastic seven-day container, snapped open the section for Tuesday, and removed one single ten-milligram capsule of Donepezil. After Helen swallowed her Alzheimer's medication, Frieda suggested they head into the living room and watch *The Price is Right* together. Helen agreed.

As she assisted Helen to the living room from the table, Frieda noticed a tan and pink Coach purse on the counter - one she knew wasn't her sister's because it was far too flashy in design for Helen's taste. Frieda gently lowered Helen onto her cloth-covered La-Z-Boy rocker. While Helen was distracted by one of her favorite game shows, Frieda took the opportunity to inspect the purse. She held it up to the light with one hand underneath and the other grasping the leather handle straps. *Oh my, this is a really nice bag, I must have one just like it, but in white.* The overnight nurse had left in a hurry. Her cell phone, wallet, and credentials were still in the purse. Frieda called her nephew Trent again.

"Where is Bob Barker?" Helen called from the living room.

"I don't know this guy. Why does he wear those God-awful glasses? Frieda, where is Bob Barker?"

"Helen, Bob Barker is on vacation. That's Drew Carey. He once had his own sitcom, remember? Drew is only filling in, but Bob Barker will return tomorrow," Frieda yelled from the kitchen as she waited for Trent to answer.

Helen objected to the sight of Drew Carey. "Bob Barker wears nice suits and is very handsome. Not this guy. Frieda, where is Bob Barker? Are you sure this is The *Price is Right*?"

After the fourth ring, Trent finally answered. "Hello? Frieda? Is everything okay?"

"Hi, Trent . . . Wait, Trent excuse me for one second. Helen, that is the same *Price is Right* you're watching . . . Bob Barker is on vacation, remember?"

"When is he coming back? I don't like this man. Where is Bob Barker . . ."

Frieda covered the phone to prevent yelling in her nephew's ear. "Tomorrow, Helen, he'll return tomorrow! Trent I am back, thanks for holding -"

"Aunt Frieda, are you telling that little white lie about Bob Barker again?" Trent chuckled. "At some point, Mom is going to catch on."

"Trent, I don't have the heart. She's seventy-two years old but strong as Hulk Hogan! She might toss every damn television out the front door if she ever discovers Bob Barker retired."

"You're right, she might."

"So every morning, I come over for breakfast, and we repeat the same routine. As crazy as it sounds, this is our normal - but over the past two months things have been a little haywire."

"Haywire? How so?"

"Well, for starters, I called the home health agency to get an explanation for why there wasn't a nurse here when I arrived, and they informed me that the overnight nurse was here on time and worked most of her shift, but left around four a.m."

"Without giving us any notice?"

". . . Trent, I didn't know how to tell you this, but the nurse that quit this morning was the third nurse in two months. At first, I thought they were exaggerating . . ."

"Exaggerating about what?"

"Exaggerating about . . . well, how can I say this . . ."

"Just let it out, Aunt Frieda . . . exaggerating about what?"

Something caught Frieda's eye. A time-worn Polaroid held in place on the refrigerator by a thirty-year-old strawberry magnet. It showed Frieda and Helen seated together at the Krewe of Ares Ball back in 1968.

Frieda peeked around the partition wall that separated the kitchen from the living room, comforted to know Helen was still resting in her La-Z-Boy. Her face still wore the same confused look as she stared at Drew Carey. It was hard for Frieda to see Helen in this condition. The moment she turned seventy, the Alzheimer's disease had invaded her mind and body.

Helen was a retired elementary school teacher, but long after she wiped her board for the last time, she dressed and presented herself appropriately for leading a class of twenty students. Her daily attire was still fitting for tea with Nancy Reagan and Margaret Thatcher. Helen looked a lot like Margaret Thatcher. Everything mattered to Helen. Her hair, her clothes, her family, her landscaping, her reputation, her organizations, and her church: Our Lady of Prompt Succor.

A woman who once read three romance novels a week, *The Times Picayune*, and the *New York Times* Sunday edition, who once actively engaged in local politics and was a daily caller on WWL870 AM radio, had been reduced to a caricature of her former self. Trapped in shuffled memories. Hunted by depleting recollection. Tormented by gray hair that would have never seen the light of day if she were still in her right mind. The visible gray was the hardest for Frieda to accept.

"Aunt Frieda! You there? Did the call drop?"

"Sorry, Trent, I'm here."

"You were saying before the phone cut out that you thought

the nurses were exaggerating. What about?"

"Yes, that's right . . . I lost my train of thought for a second." Frieda moved across the kitchen diagonally, coming to rest in the far corner by the stove. It was there that her voice lowered to a whisper. "The director at the nursing agency has it all documented. Back in November, the first nurse complained about your mother and the conversations she was having; outbursts about people and events from years ago. At first, I wrote the complaints off simply as the symptoms of her illness. Then the nurse described the sounds . . ."

"Sounds? Like things going bump in the night? That house is over 150 years old - it's to be expected."

"Yeah, I thought the same thing, but those weren't the types of sounds the nurses filed in their complaints. These were sounds that came from full-blown conversations your mother was having with someone."

"Conversations? My mom has full-blown dementia. It's what people who have dementia do - they talk to themselves and hallucinate. Aunt Frieda, that is still not an excuse for that nurse to leave my mother alone and not notify us."

"But they heard Jack -"

"What! M-My dad . . . ?"

"Yes. All three nurses reported that the person your mother conversed with answered back. They heard entire conversations. They heard him speaking as though it were just another day - speaking as if he were alive and well. When they entered the room, they saw no one else but Helen, but after they closed the door - before making it halfway down the stairs - they would hear his voice again. Trent, all three nurses confirmed what they heard. All three said it was Jack McGowan, based on how your mother addressed *The Voice*. Some way, somehow, Helen is communicating with your father."

"Aunt Frieda . . . you do realize how ridiculous this sounds to me . . ."

"I know, and that's why I didn't want to bother you and Marci about it - I figured I could handle it on my own. But this morning, the nurse that ran out of the house at four a.m. was one of the owners of the agency. Trent, she didn't even grab her purse; it's right here on the counter. The nursing agency asked if they could send someone over to pick it up, and if I could meet them outside of the front gate."

"Aunt Frieda, are you kidding me? They are that afraid of the house?"

"I thought the same thing at first - that someone must be pulling my leg - but when I arrived this morning and saw her purse sitting there on the counter, I knew something went terribly wrong."

"Aunt Frieda, you're there every day. Have you witnessed or heard anything strange? Have you heard any of these conversations Mom is having?"

"No, I haven't. But this morning, Helen had one of Jack's suits pressed, and cinnamon rolls fresh out the oven . . ."

"My dad loved cinnamon rolls…"

"I know. And I have observed your mother in various stages of confusion, but today was different. Helen was convinced that your dad was going to walk down those stairs. At one point, she almost convinced me."

"So we no longer have service to care for my mom? It was challenging to find another trusted home health agency. I trusted them; they came highly recommended. Aunt Frieda, this is very frustrating and disappointing."

"I am sure it is -"

"Being up here in Bristol only adds to the helplessness."

"Trent, there is one more thing . . ."

"You mean that's not the sum of it?"

"I'm afraid not . . . are you sitting down?"

"Oh boy. Yes, I am."

From the living room came the sounds of "Nadia's Theme," more commonly recognized as the theme music for *The Young & The Restless*. Frieda took another peek at Helen; she was sound asleep.

"Aunt Frieda, I am sitting down . . ."

"Sorry, I was turning down the television. I never thought I'd see the day when your mother would doze off during *The Young & The Restless*. Seeing her like this breaks my heart."

"I know it's hard, Aunt Frieda; it breaks my heart that I am not there with you. But before you put me on hold you were going to share something. What else is going on?"

"It's like . . . when I arrive in the morning for breakfast, I never know which Helen I'm going to meet." Frieda took a seat at the kitchen table. "On some days, it's like we're reliving our lives in discussions we had years ago, but in real time, if that makes sense -"

"It does . . ."

"Yesterday, it was a memory from the day she met your father - in 1962. Today, it was 1968, when your father was elected Captain of Ares. After she took her meds, Helen said something that troubled me." Frieda stared off into the corners of her mind.

"Like what . . . what did she say?"

Frieda took a deep breath. "She said: *I've repeatedly apologized to that woman, but she still took my boys, and then she came for my dear old Jack. Frieda, I apologized over and over again, but it fell on deaf ears. But she didn't get my baby boy, not yet at least.*"

"Woman? What woman? Did she mention a name?"

"Trent, she never mentioned a name, but I can tell my sister is worried about you. Even in her illness, she is deeply fearful something will happen to you and her grandbabies."

"Well, Aunt Frieda, there is the only thing left for me to do. I have to relocate. I have to come home."

"Trent, I didn't want to suggest it, and Lord knows I've tried everything to keep you from having to uproot Marci and the kids, but Helen needs you - she needs to see your face. I think it might help reduce these episodes."

"Thank you, Aunt Frieda. I appreciate everything you have

done in caring for my mother, but Marci and I will have to take it from here. It's hard to believe that out of three boys, I am the only one remaining. The only one left from the McGowan household."

"Believe me when I say I think about your dad and your brothers every single day. Cancer is so cruel. So evil . . ."

"And our family has endured more than most families could stomach. Being in Connecticut helped me escaped 1524 Toledano Street for a while, but no longer. I can't run from my grief anymore. My kids will hate me for it - and Marci might threaten me with a divorce for even suggesting it, but we have to say goodbye to Bristol. My mother needs me. If you can keep an eye on things for a little while longer, I will make my way down there as soon as possible. I will call you later today with the details. Love you, Aunt Frieda."

"I love you too, Trenton."

CHAPTER 4

S he didn't want to leave, but her husband had no choice, which also robbed her of all options. However, Marci spared him the hard-sell on relocating to New Orleans - for some time now, she had known it was inevitable. Leaving the house at 43 Cricket Hill Road in Bristol, Connecticut was difficult. It was the only house they had ever owned, and the only home her kids had ever known.

As her husband slowly merged the twenty-six-foot Penske out of the driveway and onto Cricket Hill Road, ten teary eyes caught a final view of a snow-covered residence they would never awake in again. Now, they would only visit in dreams and family photos.

It was less than two months ago that Marci and Trent had watched the kids open their Christmas gifts - soon after, they all welcomed the New Year. Now, only a few weeks later, Marci watched her husband lock the lift gate on a truck that contained everything they owned. Even her rare ceramic doll collection was on board - the one her daughters knew was off limits.

Her face rested on her fist as she drove. From the back seat and to her right, the alternating sniffles dissolved into a chorus of deep sighs. The only words she spoke were *thank you* to each tollbooth cashier as they waved her through an endless line of tolls.

Whereas Trent had the solitude of his empty passenger seat, Marci was sentenced to mile after mile of *Are we there yet?* and *I have to use it now!*

Marci knew that most of the urgent restroom breaks were nothing more than the kids needing to escape the confinement of her Honda Pilot, yet she obliged and understood their need to pause their endless Southern expedition.

To stretch.

To reload the snacks.

To breathe the air of unknown lands.

Her youngest was Zoe. She mentally escaped the Honda by playing *Minecraft* on her iPad, talking on a headset to the second-grade friends she had left in Bristol. Her naturally red locks were on loan from her grandmother and provided the perfect cover for a habit she struggled to quit. Marci had noticed her daughter's thumb in her mouth fifty miles ago, but decided to allow Zoe the soothing pleasure as a severance of sorts.

In the rearview mirror, Marci glanced at a display of unquenchable sorrow. The only cure was to turn around, but she couldn't turn around. Next to Zoe was Maggie - the one that sniffled the most, wept the most, and protested the most. In a low-wave frequency only a mother could detect, Maggie whispered *I hate you* at every rest stop. Marci heard her every time.

Less than three weeks ago, Cole Reichert had asked Maggie to the Sixth Grade Winter Formal. He was her first heartthrob crush. She had said yes, then screamed *NO* at her parents when they informed her of the move to New Orleans. In the back seat, Maggie hid under one of her mom's UCONN Volleyball sweatshirts and never made eye contact with anyone, her eyes fixated on Cole's picture on her cell phone. Her hands were damp from tears. The preteen was reduced to a murmuring coquina clam washed onto on the wrong shore.

And then there was Amarah, sitting silently in the passenger seat. She was an alternate cheerleader who had just gained a permanent spot on the squad after Rene Collins broke her leg. The signs of her grief were visible and unavoidable. Not in tears, but in darkness. Gone was her perkiness and loud voice, gone was her interest in who was dating whom and who broke up with whom and why. Gone were her crystal blue irises that smiled as she chattered away. They had been replaced by two topaz nuggets treading in a crimson tide.

Gone were her blonde pompom hair and raspberry lips. Last night, she had dyed her hair black. It shone as black as the midnight side of the moon, matching her lips, which she had tinted the shade of West Virginia coal.

But Marci refused to look at herself, no matter how many times she gazed into her rearview mirror. Her tear ducts had long since parched. Marci was not only leaving Bristol but leaving her younger sister. Their births were only ten months apart, and they were carbon copies of one another. The two were inseparable by choice, and although they had different interests, they never grew tired of each other.

Their mother had stopped dressing them alike around eight years old, only to have Marci and Evie re-sync their wardrobes in high school just to confuse classmates. Marci had a love for art and Evie had a passion for literature. Marci collected things, and Evie wrote stories about the things her sister collected. Evie had received a Master's in Fine Arts from the University of Connecticut, and for no other reason than to be close to her sister, Marci had done the same.

Evie idolized Katie Couric, and even evolved into her idol in dress and appearance. Marci mirrored the style because the transition was seamless due to their resemblances. Evie later entered into journalism, and like Couric, worked her way up to an evening anchor desk. Marci found her passion in the buying and selling of Colonial-age real estate in Bristol, and in the hoarding of antiques. For the first time in her life, Marci didn't live within a mile of her sister. She was on a highway headed to a city that sat five feet below sea level; a place great to visit, but only to party. They were traveling south to live in a land far, far away, as Zoe had described their voyage. The description proven accurate by their estimated time of arrival: twenty hours left to drive.

Marci followed her husband as he trekked down I-84 and weaved through Connecticut. They slowed down on snow-layered I-81, which took them through Pennsylvania and down to Nashville. It was there they had decided to sleep for the night. Up early the next morning, they cruised through Birmingham, didn't remember Meridian, then passed Picayune only to cross Lake Pontchartrain on the Twin Span and drop down into east New Orleans.

Their bodies felt the dramatic decrease in altitude. For the first time, the view outside the window caught their attention as an urban metropolis emerged in the distance. The interstate delivered on its promise as they careened closer and closer to downtown New Orleans.

"Mommy, have we arrived in a land far, far away?"

"Yes, Zoe, we have arrived in that faraway land, but the food is unbelievably delicious, and they have the best parades."

"Parades?! I love parades! Can we go to one?"

"I am sure your father is looking forward to taking you guys to your first Mardi Gras. You can count on it."

"Wow, Mommy, what is that? It looks like a big, gray ball . . ."

"Zoe, that is the Louisiana Superdome, and you're right, it does look like a really giant ball. As a matter of fact, your dad took me to a football game there, and it was a lot of fun . . ."

"Why didn't you take me with you to see the big, gray ball?"

"Because I didn't know you then, sweetheart."

"Whaaaaaat?"

"Meaning, it was before you were born. It was before any of us were born," Maggie piped up.

"That's correct, Maggie, your father and I were married in Bristol, and part of our honeymoon was here in New Orleans."

"Why did you come all the way down here?" Zoe wondered.

"Well, we stayed here for the weekend, enjoyed the football game, and then your dad gave me a tour of the city. That Monday, we boarded a flight to Jamaica."

"I wish I could have gone on that trip with you and daddy. Can daddy take us on a tour?"

"I hope not," Maggie grumbled.

"Maggie, it's not that bad, you have to give New Orleans a chance -"

"I want to go on the tour. Can you ask Daddy to take me?" Zoe pleaded.

"You should ask him. I'm sure he would be delighted to introduce you to the French Quarter and the aquarium."

"There's an aquarium? Mommy can we go . . . today? Please, please, please can we go -"

"Not today, Zoe. I am tired of driving, and I know your father is just as exhausted, but we will definitely bring you to the aquarium."

"I'll pass."

"Maggie . . ."

"Mom, I have no interest in visiting Fish Jail or any other form of captivity. I have just relocated to a jail . . ."

As Maggie spoke, her mom slammed on the brakes. Trent had been forced to a sudden stop to avoid hitting a car that cut him off. *I thought we had bad drivers in Bristol; nothing compares to New Orleans.*

A text from her husband read: *That asshole cut me off.*

Marci replied: *I know, stop texting and keep your eyes on the road.*

A few minutes later, the large Penske truck turned onto Toledano Street. *Your destination is on the left*, assured the calm, female voice of the GPS.

"Thank God - we made it," Marci sighed as she parked.

Only then did Amarah remove her headphones; her eyes had been fastened shut since Birmingham. She looked to the right at the house across the street, then left at her new home. A deep sigh escaped her dark-tinted lips.

"Amarah, this will be a huge adjustment for all of us. We did this for your father; he had no other choice."

"There was a choice, but he didn't consider it. He didn't consider any of us . . ."

"Amarah, your grandmother has sensitive needs, and this home is much larger to accommodate all of us . . . and all of our stuff."

"I still can't rationalize how moving five people could have been less stressful than relocating one little old lady? But whatever you say." Amarah stuffed her headphones into her bag. "In three years when I graduate, I am moving back to Bristol. This is day one - only 1,094 more days to go!" Amarah grabbed her book bag, then slammed the passenger door.

Next out of the Honda was Maggie. Her exit was punctuated by another slammed door, leaving Zoe and Marci alone in the car.

"Zoe, after we unpack, get comfortable, and take our baths, let's say we paint our toes?"

"Yes, let's paint our toes and eat ice cream."

"That sounds like a plan. Let's go greet Daddy." Marci reached behind the passenger seat for her purse, which had tilted over and spilled its contents.

"Mom, is that Grandpa waving at me?"

Marci recovered the last of her items and put them back in her purse. "Zoe, your Grandpa is no longer with us; he's in Heaven. Remember?"

Zoe waved back. "Hi."

Marci turned to see Zoe waving at the second floor of the house, but didn't see anyone.

"Zoe, let's get out of this car; we're suffering from cabin fever."

"Mommy . . . do I have a fever?"

"No Zoe, cabin fever is when you have been trapped in a small space for a long time. Not like a fever when you have to stay home from school."

It was February in New Orleans, but there was no snow on the ground to shovel, and no wintery gusts of air to freeze their cheeks. It was barely even winter as compared to Bristol; the air felt more or less like an unseasonably warm autumn. Marci could hardly picture life without snow - then she was reminded of the seasonal headaches she had left behind. Her longing for snow-capped homes moved to the recycling bin of her mind.

Marci took little Zoe by the hand and they headed along the sidewalk toward the front gate. Zoe waved again.

CHAPTER 5

She wanted to enter the house but couldn't; the exterior was too beautiful to ignore. Like a warm pacifier to an infant, Marci instantly saw her new home in New Orleans as truly the next best thing to Bristol. And so she stood, motionless, in admiration. The anterior view of 1524 Toledano Street was a perfect collaboration of meticulous renovations with a teaspoon of modernization.

The huge oak trees provided a perfect curtain of shade, without suffocating the drive-up view. Though it was far away from everything she knew, it immediately felt like home - like the perfect ending to a turbulent journey.

Hello gorgeous, she whispered.

Before caressing the knob on the wrought iron gate that led to the porch, Marci took a moment to appreciate her new home up close. The house was much larger than their old home on 43 Cricket Hill Road in Bristol. The magniloquent terrace was first to hold her attention. A matching set of railings cloaked the second story balcony. She briefly stepped out of her body to lounge and enjoy the critically acclaimed novel *Nine Notches* on the terrace. From her luxurious reading nook, imaginary Marci glanced down at the real Marci and winked.

The house on Toledano Street was a domicile of privilege, yet it somehow remained humble. It retained all its character and mystique, both timeless and tested. It had a soul and a voice, a tree and a mind of its own. It was big enough to welcome all, but intimate enough to settle. Homes like this were the reason Marci became a merchant of antiquities. Her weakness? A house with a beating heart and a dossier of tales.

A cottage of comfort.

The epitome of her passion.

Her passion was the sole reason she'd opted out of selling new construction, though she could have scored tremendous profits. To Marci, few things compared to driving by real estate that had been entrusted to her, knowing she had matched it with the most loving of parents - those who would pass it on with care to the next generation.

La douceur du foyer: Home, sweet home.

On the entrance gate to the property, there was a doorknob that gave way to ascending levels of cement steps; two sets in total. The balcony rested upon four inviting white columns that by design bulged slightly in the center, but effortlessly supported the upper level.

Even the porch was deliberately monotonous, as if reflecting a stormy sky.

I think I love you.

The floor of the porch stretched out from an olive-colored back wall, which featured dollar-green-colored window shutters. To her delight, a white picket banister wrapped around the edge of the portico. It veered in and out of the four white columns, only separating to allow guests the opportunity to knock on the front door.

My new obsession, from this moment on.

Marci greeted the front view of her new home with a gentle smile; it was old but playful. An acre of grass stretched to the right of the house, where an oak tree waited patiently for a child to swing. Though she'd visited the home many times before, today, Marci McGowan saw 1524 Toledano Street for the first time as her home, with all its hidden treasures waiting to be explored. *I cannot wait to converse with you and listen endlessly.*

From the rear of the house came a waving gesture, an invitation to come and explore. Zoe noticed, but the curbside view held Marci in a trancelike state, locked and focused on every minute detail of the residence. Zoe accepted the invitation.

"Mommy, let's go see the backyard."

"Not now, Zoe, not now."

CHAPTER 6

Trent had hired a local moving company called Tou Brothers Movers to help with the unpacking - the company came highly recommended by Aunt Frieda. Tou Brothers Movers was comprised of a total of four African American men. Three appeared to be in their twenties, and one older gentleman appeared around sixty years old. Despite being considerably older, one couldn't help but notice that he was in incredible shape.

Dude is built like a machine for his age, Trent thought to himself. The older man's name was Earl, and from the metal chain around his neck, Trent could tell he was retired military. He resembled Don Cheadle, only older. Fully developed muscles rippled every part of his upper body, but both of his arms showed painful-looking scarring - the kind that could only come from a horrific fire. Even his neck showed the same deep scars, and though Trent's curiosity cried out for satisfaction, he couldn't bring himself to ask Earl what had led to his injuries.

The men formed a conveyor system of moving the boxes from the back of the truck to the front porch, where Earl and another man carried them to the second floor. It was then that Trent joined in. On the second pass, Earl stopped in the middle of the front room holding a medium-sized box.

"Mr. McGowan, I think you need to check this box right now. When I picked it up, I could hear what sounded like broken glass. Sir, I did not drop it. We found it toward the back wall of the truck. Whatever is in this is shattered."

"Thank you, Mr. Earl, just sit it right there."

"Just call me Earl."

Earl handed Trent a cutter to slice through what seemed like an inch of tape Marci had plastered across the top of the box. Inside, all three of her dolls were in pieces.

"Earl, I was forced to jam the brakes on the interstate, and I guess everything slid forward. At that exact moment, I knew it: something was broken."

"Man, I hate when this happens. Some situations you can control, some you can't."

"Tell me about it."

"I'm no expert, but they appear to be pretty expensive."

"Of all the things in this truck, why did it have to be this box?"

Earl shook his head in pity. "While your wife is showing the girls the house maybe you should a make a run for it - I think I can buy you a thirty-minute head start. My wife was also into collecting glass dolls. One time I broke one. If I remember correctly, I woke up in the hospital."

"Marci is going to kick my ass something awful."

"I'll just leave you alone with this box. Rest in peace, Mr. McGowan."

"Great, just call me Trent."

"Okay, nice knowing you, Trent." They shared a laugh.

"I appreciate that, Earl. Looks like I have to face the music on this one. I'll wait until tomorrow to break the bad news."

"I totally understand. Would you like me to tote this one upstairs?"

"No, you can leave it right there; I have to re-tape it."

"Okay, make sure you don't forget to tuck it away," Earl warned. "If you need a place to stay just give me a call - I have extra rooms."

Trent chuckled. "Thanks, Earl, I appreciate the offer."

Marci wanted to have her expensive ceramic dolls - some valued as much as seven thousand dollars - shipped separately, but Trent had insisted that he could transport them safely with the rest of the furniture.

From the corner of his eye, Trent noticed that Earl was enthralled by the photos that led up the staircase. He focused on one black and white picture more than the others, to the point that he freed his hands of the box and walked slowly to the wall. The picture captured flambeaux carriers guiding a Mardi Gras parade through the night as they twirled kerosene lanterns above their heads.

Trent walked over to Earl's side. "I see you have an appreciation for Mardi Gras of old. Before it became so commercialized. This picture was a few years before my time. I was born in 1971, and this was taken in . . . I believe . . ."

"1968." Earl answered.

"That's pretty good. I grew up in this house and never knew that -"

"Trent . . . please excuse me for one second."

Trent could tell something about the photo had made Earl very emotional. The older man jogged out of the house and continued across the street. He then began to pace in a circle along the sidewalk, his hands covering his eyes.

"What's the deal with Pops?" one of the movers, a man named Kaleb, asked as he groomed his dreads.

"Not sure, but I think one of the photos on my wall took him to a sad place," Trent replied.

After about fifteen minutes, Earl returned, clearly in no mood to talk. Trent did not bother to press the issue. Suddenly, he heard Marci coming down the stairs with Zoe - the box of shattered dolls was still in the middle of the floor. Trent quickly picked it up. It sounded like a container full of Christmas tree ornaments. He compressed the box into the hall closet.

"How's it coming along?" Marci asked as she released Zoe's hand and watched her run down the hall toward the backyard.

"We're just about done," he said as he leaned on the closet door. "Have the other two made any comments about the house? I haven't managed to get a word out of either one."

"So far Zoe loves it, but Maggie . . . is Maggie. She's in her new room complaining to anyone online who will listen. Amarah was just face chatting with her soon-to-be ex-boyfriend, Justin. In her mind, she feels they will survive a long distance relationship. They're doomed."

"That's good news to me, because those two were getting too close way too fast. That Justin kid seemed like the eloping type. New Orleans probably saved him from getting choked to death with my bare hands."

"Maybe so, but I think you'd better sleep with one eye open; she's angry enough to choke you, too." They laughed for the first time since leaving Bristol.

"Honey, I know I asked a lot of you, leaving your sister and the real estate firm. I love you so much for supporting me through this. If there was any . . ."

She finished his sentence. "There wasn't any other way. We didn't have the room in our house; it would have been a nightmare of congestion and clutter. And I didn't want us separated, so it is what it is. We're family; we stick together, we move together."

Trent grabbed Marci, and they kissed.

For the next two hours, Trent and the movers unloaded and positioned their belongings into his mother's home, which was big enough to consume it all with room to spare. Once the last item was tucked away, he thanked the movers, gave Earl and his crew a four hundred dollar tip, then collapsed on the living room sofa. The only thing left to do was to figure out a way to tell Marci that all her dolls had been crushed into little pieces.

For now, it would have to wait.

From down the hall that led to the backyard, the pitter-patter of little feet approached.

"Daddy, this is a really big house."

"I know, but do you like it?"

"Daddy, I love it, and my new dollhouse. It's huge."

"Zoe, what dollhouse?"

"The dollhouse back there, the one Grandpa made for me.

Marci entered the room. "I have to hand it to you," she kissed him again. "You out-did yourself. That's a really nice touch."

"I'm glad you like it," he said, puzzled.

Trent casually walked to the backyard, and there it was: a beautiful, six-foot-tall pink and purple dollhouse. The only problem was, he hadn't ordered it. *I'll have to thank Aunt Frieda for this precious gift for my daughter.* Right as he reached for his phone, it rang.

"Hi Trent, it's your Aunt Frieda. Are you guys finished with the move? Your mother is getting very cranky; she can only stand my house for three hours, and that's it."

"Yes, we're all done."

"Great. We're headed your way."

"I really appreciate you sitting with her while we moved everything. Lord knows I would have never been able to get us situated with Mom trying to micromanage us."

"It's not a problem at all, that's why I suggested it. Helen is stubborn as a mule."

"And another thing - thank you for having this beautiful dollhouse built for Zoe. You didn't have to do this. She loves it."

There was silence on the other end on the line.

"Hello . . . Aunt Frieda? You there? Did the call drop?"

"Hmm . . . Trent, I did not order a dollhouse."

"Aunt Frieda . . . no need to be modest . . ."

"Trent . . . I didn't order it. Where would I have found the time? Helen has been a handful. One minute she's sitting perfectly still watching TV, and the next, she has my car keys in hand and is headed out the door. Trust me. I am still trying to catch my breath, not ordering anything like a dollhouse."

Zoe's voice echoed in Trent's head: *The dollhouse over there, the one Grandpa made for me.*

"Aunt Frieda, now that I think about it, Zoe said Grandpa built it for her." Trent walked over to his dad's old tool shed. On the floor was fresh saw dust, and the chemical scent of latex paint.

"Trent this is that thing we spoke about."

"That thing?"

"Yes, that thing - the thing with your dad."

"But why is this happening . . .?"

". . . that's why you're here—to figure out why."

CHAPTER 7

Frieda pulled into the driveway with Helen; the street view facing the kitchen window showed Maggie and Zoe seated for dinner. They also caught a glimpse of Marci at the stove. Across the room walked Trent, but there was no sign of Amarah. When Helen entered the house, she nearly jumped for joy at the sight of her two granddaughters seated at the kitchen table; she remembered them all.

"My Lord, there's my Bristol Police Officer! And look at my precious babies! If only Jack was alive to see this."

"Sweet Jesus, that baked chicken smells delicious!" Frieda yelled as she followed Helen into the kitchen. An outbreak of hugs ensued.

"Mommy you got your wish, I am home for good, and I returned with many."

"I rejoice - thank God!" Helen McGowan reached up for a hug from Trent. Next in line was Marci.

"Trent, this house was always too big for me. I wanted something small, like our family home in Chalmette, but Jack - God bless the dead - insisted. Sometimes I can still hear him in here . . ."

"Okay, Mom, no need to scare the girls with stories of their pappy walking around the house, it was hard enough to get them down here!" Trent laughed. "Aunt Frieda! How have you been?"

"You already know!" Frieda laughed as she hugged Trent and Marci. "Can I have a word with you on the porch?"

Trent and Frieda stepped outside and took a seat on the bench swing that his father had hung to perfection in 1998. She worried if the old swing would hold them both without falling, and to her surprise, it held. Frieda was sixty-four years old but had the mentality of a forty-year-old. Her style was reminiscent of Blanche Devereaux from *The Golden Girls*, and like the fictional Blanche, she enjoyed dating as often as possible. With her sister drifting in and out of reality, however, Frieda had become the unwilling matriarch of the family.

"Trent, I am so happy that you came home. I have been worried sick about you since your dad and the boys passed away. By the way, how are you holding up? Any issues with your liver?"

"None at all, Aunt Frieda, I took a preventative step to make sure everything functions as normal."

Frieda was delighted. "Well, I'll drink to that! Promise me you will continue to get regular checkups and stay on top of it?"

"I promise - you have my word. So, what do you want to talk to me about? I get the feeling it doesn't have anything to do with liver cancer."

A couple walked their dog along the sidewalk; both waved hello. Trent and Frieda returned the greeting. The night air was fidgety - the type of air that freezes words in front of your lips. Frieda tucked her thick wool coat tighter within the inner seams and buried her ears beneath the collar.

"So, lay it on me," Trent requested.

"First I wanted to say that even though you and Marci have moved home, you can still count on me to help care for Helen. She is my only sister left out of seven. Her doctor says it helps her condition if her routine remains the same. With that in mind, I will still show up here every morning and have breakfast with her."

"That means a lot to me - you are my angel."

"The other thing is, on the way over here, your mother said a few things that disturbed me deeply."

"Like what?"

"I never mentioned to Helen that you were moving back because I wanted it to be a surprise . . ."

"Yes, I remember, we discussed that in detail."

"Trent, somehow she knew."

". . . You don't think she overheard your phone conversations with me?"

"No, I don't. I was meticulous to keep all aspects of your relocation a secret, but Helen knew the day and time. She knew. Not sure how, but it was no surprise to her!"

Trent stood from the swinging bench and looked through the kitchen window. Zoe noticed him and waved. He blew her a kiss.

"None of this makes any sense to me. I'm struggling to process it all. Nurses hearing my dad, this enormous dollhouse in the backyard . . . My wife thinks I ordered it when I assumed it was you, and now this."

"Freaky, isn't it?"

"Very."

"I think I will write a book called *Freaky Shit at Helen's House*. What do you say?"

"I would love it if it wasn't a true story based on my life."

"Then you may want to have a seat for my first chapter."

"Oh boy."

"As you can tell from driving in, Mardi Gras season shifts gears this weekend, and all of the major krewes are rolling, including your dad's old krewe."

"I know, I am a part of the Facebook page, and I'm looking forward to connecting with old friends."

"I don't know about that." Frieda's face tightened and contorted like she'd bitten into a fat lemon. "On the drive over here, Helen started going on and on about not taking the kids to any parades. She said Jack told her to keep his grandkids home."

"But Mardi Gras is a major part of our family tradition. I already promised Zoe I would take her . . ."

"You may want to consider canceling those plans—your dad sent word through Helen to avoid all parades this Carnival season."

"My dad died five years ago . . ."

"Not according to Helen - he's in this house."

"Aunt Frieda, please don't go there . . ."

"I am just the messenger, don't shoot me, Officer McGowan." The swing slowed to a stop.

"Aunt Frieda, our family krewe rolls in on Thursday - I have already notified the Fullers. Kelsey and Rhonda are King and Queen this year; they wanted to pay tribute to my dad with a toast. I can't back out now. Aunt Frieda, even you said my mom pulls you into conversations from years ago. I think that is the case now."

"If you say so, but Helen mentioned your daughters by name. I am not saying it's accurate, but taking into account all the other wacky things . . . I just thought you should know."

"Thank you. I will get to the bottom of all this, but my daughters will experience their first Mardi Gras. They grew up in Bristol with stories of Carnival in New Orleans, but this is the first time my stories will come to life. I want my kids to have the same childhood I enjoyed, and create new memories - and I didn't drive twenty-two hours to miss Mardi Gras."

"Trent, you know your mother. She is adamant about skipping those parades, so expect more arguments. Anyhoo, if she starts to act up around bedtime, grab the remote and switch to Turner Classic Movies. Anything Betty Davis or Joan Crawford will calm her down in seconds."

"Not sure how I would have made it without your help. How can I ever repay you?"

"No need, just have Marci fix me a plate, and I will head on home."

Trent requested that Marci fix the plate to go, then walked his aunt to her car. Frieda started the engine, then rolled down the window.

"Trent, I know you're set on going to the parade, but Helen wasn't hallucinating when she warned me. I know the difference. I am not one to tell someone what to do with their kids, but I have a bad feeling as well. Just sleep on it, okay? Love you." She backed out onto the street and drove into the night.

CHAPTER 8

Later that night after dinner and soothing baths, the entire family settled in for the evening. Marci made her usual bedtime rounds, but in a different house. Her first stop was Amarah's room, where she found her daughter submerged in a video chat with Justin. Seated in the middle of the bed on pretzeled legs wearing a high-beam halogen smile, the happiness in Amarah's eyes riddled Marci with guilt. In that brief moment, she was reminded of her first boyfriend Carlton Jeffers, and how horrible it would have been to leave him in the early days of their courtship.

Marci had later discovered that Carlton was the typical high school jerk, but only after losing her virginity. He dumped Marci for another virgin two weeks before the prom, leaving her shattered and humiliated. Ever the resourceful one, Evie corralled a ban of dateless friends, and they went to the prom as a group. Despite having a great time that night, it was many moons before Marci trusted another man - Trenton McGowan was the next guy she dated after Carlton Jeffers. Marci had been a few days away from sharing that story with Amarah when Trent informed them about the move to New Orleans. Shortly after that,

Justin ascended into boyfriend martyrdom. To Amarah, he was *The Greatest Guy on Earth.*

With the softness of silk-wrapped feet, she entered the room. With the stiffness of whiplash, Amarah offered a cheek, and Marci accepted her crumbs of affection.

In the next room was Maggie, who Marci found submerged in social media long pass her eight o'clock curfew. She startled her middle child as she entered the room and extended her hand. Maggie surrendered the cell phone. In their old home, Marci and Trent's bedroom was downstairs, past a squeaking staircase that served as an early detection alarm for their daughters—but not the house on Toledano Street. All bedrooms were on the second floor, directly across from Marci - zero time to recover from mischievous behavior.

A kiss on the forehead.

A pout.

"Goodnight, Maggie," Marci called softly as she turned to leave the room.

"I hate this house, and I hate New Orleans."

"I know Maggie, I know."

A quick peek at Zoe. She was sound asleep, still tightly tucked under her *My Little Pony* blanket with her favorite thumb in her mouth. Her toenails shone bright pink from their after-bath pedicure session. Another kiss for Zoe. *Goodnight, my little princess.* Marci half-turned to leave the room when her foot collided with a box stuffed with summer clothes and sandals.

"Shiiiiit," she winced as she leaned against the wall, trying her best not to wake Zoe. "Dammit, I keep forgetting to move that box."

A tidal wave of pain traveled from her little toe straight to her chest; the kind of pain that throbs even more when you touch it, but touching it is the only way to caress the nerves. After about five minutes, when her foot had cooled enough to walk, she dragged the box out into the hall and placed it in front of a large utility closet. The closet was full. She searched for available space to store it, but the second level of the house was at full capacity. Then she remembered another downstairs closet - in the hall that led to the den.

At first, Marci planned to drag the box into her bedroom until Trent was finished with his shower, but then she was reminded of how hard he had worked during the unpacking. She nearly fell twice, but after a great struggle, Marci made it to the first floor with the bulging box of clothes. Gasping for air that bobbed and weaved, she was forced to take a seat on the stairs. Like a car out of gas, she got behind the box and pushed with all her might until it slowly arrived in front of the closet door.

Immediately after opening the door, she spotted a familiar box - the one that contained her ceramic dolls.

CHAPTER 9

Trent opened the bathroom door, allowing the steam and heat to escape. With a towel over his face, he dried his hair and blindly walked toward the bed. Suddenly Trent stopped. The pain felt as if he'd stepped into a box of knives, which were now cutting and slicing into the bottoms of his feet. He immediately removed the towel from his face. Directly in front of him stood Marci. Under his feet were the remains of her ceramic dolls. There was nowhere he could step without feeling glass syringing into his skin. Glass was everywhere.

"Not even the fucking courtesy of letting me know my dolls were destroyed," she said in a flat, monotone voice as she watched him hobble through the glass.

"Marci I was going to tell you tomorrow. Did you have to dump the glass all over the floor?"

"Yes, I had to."

"Look, Marci, I am sorry."

"Sorry my ass, Trent. How could you . . ."

"How could you dump glass all over the floor, knowing it would cut my feet?"

"Fuck your feet."

"Marci, don't go there, I will replace the dolls. Okay?"

"Sure you can purchase more, but you can never replace them - they were priceless to me. Evie had the dolls blessed by Father Murray. Not only were the dolls very expensive, but they represented each one of our daughters. They were priceless!"

Delicately, Trent pinched the sole of his foot to remove the fine white particles hiding beneath his skin. *I can't believe she found that box that fast. Then again, I can.*

Trent had never witnessed this level of anger from Marci. Her tears could not compete with the frown on her face as her bottom lip dissolved into her upper teeth. Trent sat silently, knowing that any word he uttered at this moment would only add gas to the inferno.

"Trent, I would have respected you more if you would have come to me with the box full of broken pieces instead of trying to hide it in the closet. I was going to find them eventually."

"And I was going to tell you."

"Lies." Marci stormed out of the room and down the stairs. A few seconds later, the front door slammed.

It was 9:30 p.m. and Trent did not want Marci to leave the house, but he dared not stop her. In the end, it wasn't the burglary that launched President Nixon into Watergate - it was the subsequent cover-up. *She's right; I should have confessed when Earl discovered the dolls were destroyed.*

"Daddy, did you cut your feet?"

"Yes Zoe, Daddy stepped in glass and cut his feet. Now go back to bed, please sweetheart."

"Is Mommy angry with you?"

"Yes Zoe, Daddy did a bad thing."

"Grandpa said he taught you better than that. Lying is bad. Bad Daddy. Bad Daddy."

His tweezers stopped mid-pinch. "Zoe, lying is bad, and we should always do the right thing even when no one is watching. I apologized to Mommy—now go back to bed, please."

Did she just say 'my Grandpa'?

Zoe ran from the door and leaped into her bed. "Nite-nite, Daddy!"

"Nite-nite, Zoe."

"Hey, what's all of the screaming about?"

"Maggie, I broke your mother's dolls."

"Not the ceramic dolls? Please tell me you didn't break those dolls!"

"Yes, I shattered her little babies, the expensive ones, the dolls that represented each one of you."

"You know she may never speak to you again? You do know that, right?"

"She'll be angry for a while, but we'll get through this."

"Keep thinking that."

"Goodnight, Maggie."

"You're doomed."

"Goodnight, Maggie."

"She may never come back."

"I said . . . goodnight, Maggie.

Trent couldn't follow Marci even if he wanted to. His pressure points revealed more ceramic splinters; the pain returned the moment he attempted to walk. Suddenly he saw a hoodie race past his room and down the stairs. It was Amarah. Seconds later, the front door slammed again.

CHAPTER 10

In the car, Marci leaned back in the driver's seat and cried. There was more she wanted to say to Trent, but she needed some fresh air. *If he would lie about something that simple, what else has he lied about? I wouldn't be this pissed off if he would have only handed me the box with a heartfelt apology. But no, he tried to hide it from me. Trent knew how precious those dolls were to me.*

The light from the front porch distracted her emotional rant; it was Amarah. Marci rolled down the passenger window but didn't unlock the door.

"What is it, Amarah? I came out here to be alone for a moment."

"I wanted to have a word with you, alone."

"This is not the time, Amarah - can it wait until morning?"

"Mommy, can we please take a ride? I need to talk."

"I will unlock the door, but I don't know my way around here, so you will have to settle for the driveway."

"Fine, just open the door."

Marci sighed and granted her daughter's request. Amarah slid into the passenger seat and turned to face her mother.

"Mom, I wanted to get you alone to ask you if I could move back to Bristol and live with Aunt Evie. I hate this house, I hate this city, and I am not looking forward to this new school. What's the name of it again?"

"For the fourth time, it's Ursuline Academy."

"Ursuline. An all-girls Catholic school, with pleated uniform skirts - you can't do this to me."

"Amarah, it's one of the premier schools in the city. Unfortunately it is all-girl, and they wear uniform skirts. Sorry."

"This city will be the death of me."

"You're overreacting . . ."

"Mom, you just dumped shattered glass all over your bedroom carpet. If I'm overreacting, then I got it from you."

"We, he had it coming." A partial smile crawled across Marci's face as she dried her eyes.

"Aunt Evie said if it's okay with you and dad then she would love to have me finish out high school with her. Mommy, can I please go back to Bristol? Please?"

"You would leave us to be with Justin?"

"Mom, it's not just Justin, my life is in Bristol. Everything that makes me who I am is in Bristol."

"Cut the bullshit, Amarah, Justin is in Bristol."

Though she saw right through Amarah, Marci understood the feeling of wanting to go home: she felt the same way. She wanted to go back to Bristol just as bad. Though she loved their new house, everything else felt foreign. As a matter of fact, Marci wanted to leave at that very moment and never look back, but she loved her husband.

"Amarah, you have to believe me when I say this; I understand how you feel. I did not want to move here either, but your father needed to be here for your grandmother . . ."

"We're going to be miserable."

"Amarah, don't say that..."

"Mom it's the truth, and you know it. I feel like the needs of one person outweighed everyone else's - so we all have to suffer.

There is no reason to keep me down here other than to trap me in misery with you."

It crushed Marci to hear Amarah say those words, but she could relate. Amarah spoke everything that she felt but couldn't say, because she wanted to be supportive during Trent's time of need. But Amarah was right; she was miserable. She hadn't spoken to Evie since yesterday because the conversation was too painful to stomach. Marci knew she would miss her sister, but she didn't anticipate just how much.

"Amarah, your father deserves to be surrounded by his family as he supports your grandmother during these difficult times. As angry as I am with him right now, it still gives me great comfort knowing I have a husband who would drive across the country just to care for someone he loves. I know he loves all of us the same way. We need to be here for him."

"But Mom -"

"Amarah, I need you to be a big girl. We cannot leave him here and go back to Bristol because we are a family. Whatever is happening in the life of your father is also happening in your life—and he needs you right now. No, you cannot go back to Bristol to live with my sister, because we cannot go back to Bristol with you - at least not right now."

Marci and Amarah sat in the driveway until eleven o'clock before they decided to call it a night. Entering the house, they tried their best to make the least amount of noise, but they were surprised to find Grandma McGowan seated in the formal dining room - fully dressed. She wore a pink ball gown with elbow-length white gloves and luminous pearls. Marci also noticed that she was wearing three-inch heels and her face was completely made up. There she sat in near darkness, illuminated only by the dinner candles on the opposite end of the table.

Marci walked slowly toward the dining room to confirm whether Grandma McGowan was okay; that's when she heard her reply to someone.

"Jack, it's 1978, stop beating yourself up over what happened ten years ago and enjoy this fantastic ball. No one remembers what happened in 1968 anyway, so just let it go. Will you?"

To Marci and Amarah's amazement and concern, Grandma McGowan talked to the candle for another twenty minutes without one break in conversation. They stood in the doorway silently, now fully understanding why they had to come to New Orleans. Guilt overcame both of them at the same time for fighting Trent over the decision to move home; even Amarah felt selfish after witnessing her grandmother's condition firsthand.

Then, without notice, Grandma McGowan stooped on her tiptoes to give someone a kiss goodnight. Marci and Amarah stepped back into the darkness. They watched from the hall closet area, where Marci's dolls had been hidden, as the pink satin gown gracefully moved toward the stairs. The clacking of Helen's heels on the tile floor only ceased once they made contact with the padded staircase. They trailed behind her across the living room trapped in a cumulous cloud of Chanel No. 5, floating her up toward her bedroom.

Once she made it to the second floor, Marci and Amarah felt the temperature of the room drop dramatically to the point that they could see their breath. Something else was still in the room with them - or better yet, someone. Only then did Trent appear at the top of the stairs. Gingerly, he descended to the first floor.

"I had no idea things were this bad, Trent! I would have never allowed our children to come down here at night!"

"Marci, I am truly sorry about the dolls -"

"Trent, this is not about the dolls right now, this is about your mother. Amarah and I just witnessed her at a ball in 1978, right here in the dining room."

"Dad, it was super creepy."

"Guys, now you understand why I had to come here; her symptoms are getting worse."

As they spoke, a picture on the wall behind them fell as if someone had spiked it like a football. More glass slid across the floor. Trent dove for the sofa. Amarah ran to the kitchen to retrieve a broom and dust pan while Marci approached the fallen photo.

It was the black and white picture from 1968. Next to the photo near the shattered frame lay two old newspaper clippings. Marci brushed away the glass and stood inspecting all three items. She tried to make sense of it all; it helped when Amarah clicked on the living room light.

"Trent, are you familiar with these?" Marci handed Trent the newspaper clippings.

"No, I'm not, but one of the movers - the older gentlemen name Earl - became very emotional earlier today when he viewed this same picture."

Marci took a seat next to her husband. "Trent. Trent! What the fuck is going on in this house?"

"What are you asking me?"

"We just overheard your mother in the kitchen. She was trying to convince your dad - she specifically said 'Jack' - to forget about what happened in 1968 at a parade." Marci's eyes frantically scanned the clippings. "These newspaper clippings were hidden behind this picture; they're from that same year. They're about the Krewe of Ares."

To free up his hands, Trent placed one of the timeworn clippings on the end table near the lamp, then delicately unfolded the old *Times Picayune* article. As he read the article, Amarah took great care to sweep up the glass.

"Oh my God, I don't believe it," Trent winced as he rose to his feet. "I must have a word with my mother. Please excuse me."

Marci and Amarah followed him. "Trent what is?" Marci called. "I would like to know first."

As soon as he placed his foot on the first step, Marci noticed his mother at the top of the stairs, still dressed in her pink ball gown, pearls, and white satin gloves. Marci grabbed her husband and daughter by their arms as they focused their eyes on Helen McGowan. As they gazed at her, she spoke.

"Trent, your father said it wasn't his fault. It was out of his control. The glass has shattered."

With that, Helen McGowan about-faced and returned to her bedroom.

CHAPTER 11

February 2, 1968

From under a single street light on the corner of Louisa and Rocheblave Street, a three-part harmony reverberated beneath a soulful solo. An alto in the key of C, a baritone in lower B, and a melodic soprano blended acoustically behind a silvery falsetto. They were the NOLA Hearts, and the song they were rehearsing was "Ooo Baby Baby" by Smokey Robinson and the Miracles.

On every porch and through every kitchen window, families enjoyed the weekly gift of live music performed by four teenagers from the neighborhood.

Martin Robichaux.

Tyrone Barabino.

Freddie Franklin.

Orrin Toussaint.

One such neighbor was Bridgette Banks, who sat on the tailgate of her father's 1963 green Buick station wagon, swinging her legs with her best friend, Phyllis Narcisse. Their boyfriends were members of the NOLA Hearts, but it was Bridgette who had won the heart of the lead singer.

"My boo-boo should be the lead - I think he's too cute and fine for the background," Phyllis said as she blew a kiss at Martin.

"He was the lead singer before Tyrone and Freddie asked my Spuggie to join the group," Bridgette poked her tongue out at Phyllis.

"That's only because Orrin is the tallest - that's all."

"Tall, and sexy. And he could sing a nun out of her black dress."

"Like he did you?" Phyllis smirked.

"No, not yet. But soon. Real soon."

"Gurrrl, keep making him wait if you want to, but one of those horny heifers at Carver gonna put it on him."

"There isn't a heifer at Carver who can steal my Orrin! Now shush, Phyllis! You're making me miss my favorite part of the song."

With cuffed hands, Orrin pretended to sing into a microphone, his long hair flowing around him. His voice dipped her between each verse of the ballad. Bridgette knew she was the microphone he held as he aimed every note in her direction.

Her dream was to become a doctor and open a family practice in her neighborhood. His dream was to get discovered by a major record label like Motown, but the one dream they shared was to get married right after they graduated from Carver High School.

Bridgette was the middle child of three girls, and had a mother obsessed with the preservation of their wholesome reputations. In their neighborhood, if a girl was labeled as *hot* or *fast*, it wasn't a reference to track and field, but to the perception of promiscuous behavior. Quite often there wasn't any truth to the rumors; most were created out of envy by a jealous rival who wanted a guy like Orrin and branded someone like Bridgette as *fast* or *hot*. Many girls fell victim to tarnishing rumors such as these, and regardless of their merit, the effects were the same.

But not the BG Girls, as they were known - not Betsy's Girls.

Betsy Banks didn't give an inch when it came to dating and hovered over her daughters like a kite. All Bridgette's interactions with Orrin were limited to watching the NOLA Hearts rehearse under the streetlights and one-hour monitored phone calls. Orrin was also granted the privilege of carrying her books home from school; that was all the freedom BG Girls were allowed. Her mother's salty undercurrent regarding Orrin was not helped by the fact that he had declined all invitations to church. Betsy Banks didn't care for people who didn't regularly attend Sunday services.

The NOLA Hearts ended their Motown cover with a perfect pitch crescendo. *Ooh, ooh, ooooooooooOOOOH.* A bouquet of applause fell from ever porch as they took a bow.

While the group was still in the act of bowing, Bridgette's father, Lawson Banks, came outside to watch the end of the performance. "'Ain't Too Proud to Beg' - that's my song!" Mr. Banks yelled, drawing laughter from the surrounding porches.

"Daddy, please go back in the house," Bridgette blushed.

"If they sing 'Ain't Too Proud to Beg,' one time, I bet they win that talent show."

"Mr. Banks, what makes you so sure?" Phyllis asked.

"Because I have an ear for music, like Berry Gordy. I know what the people like."

"Daddy, please go back inside."

"Hey, you boys got a manager?"

"No sir, Mr. Banks," Orrin replied.

"WELL, YOU DO NOW! I'm bout to quit my job!" he laughed.

"Mr. Banks!" Phyllis chimed in. "Now you know you wouldn't quit that good job at the post office . . . to manage the NOLA Hearts. And even if you tried to quit, Mrs. Banks would chase you back to work."

"I would quit it before God got the news, and by the time my crazy wife found out . . . we would be halfway to Detroit!" Mr.

Banks chuckled as he took a seat in his rocking chair.

"Daddy!"

"Don't *Daddy* me, those boys . . . can sing!"

Reddened with embarrassment, Bridgette slid off the tailgate. "DADDY, GO BACK IN THE HOUSE! You're interrupting my concert."

"It's a talent show rehearsal," her dad replied.

"No," Bridgette pointed at her smile, "it's my private concert with songs just for me."

Phyllis rolled her eyes at Bridgette. "And me too - my little boo-boo is right there on the end." Phyllis winked at Martin. "Heyyyyyy boo-boo."

Distracted by her father, Bridgette failed to notice that Orrin was standing directly behind her. His voice suddenly sent tidal waves of soul through her body.

I KNOW YOU WANT TO LEAVE ME BUT I REFUSE TO LET YOU GO!

The entire neighborhood provided an on-beat clap as the NOLA Hearts performed her father's special request. Like Orrin, Bridgette was also a singer. Unlike him, however, she was forced to sing because her mother was the choir director. Every member of the Banks household was in the choir - like the after-dinner dishes, singing was a chore.

One of the many reasons Bridgette loved Orrin was because he serenaded her every day. The endless range of his voice always left her in awe, and though Mrs. Banks would never admit it to Bridgette, she knew her mom was also impressed with Orrin's vocal talents.

As he had with "Ooo Baby Baby," Orrin nailed "Ain't Too Proud to Beg" to the amazement of all who sat on their porches, those who sat on the tailgate of the Buick station wagon, and most of all, Bridgette's father, who relished the number from his rocker.

The NOLA Hearts' background singers struck every move in the Temptations choreography while Orrin's voice traveled from a depth of pain his young heart had never experienced. The song came to an end with another thundering applause from the porch audience.

"See there. I told you dem boys could sing! Didn't I tell you?" Mr. Banks ejected from his rocker. "The post office can kiss me goodbye because we're about to go on the road!"

"We're ready whenever you are, Mr. Banks," Martin laughed.

"I'm ready right now, *let's go!*"

"Mr. Banks, we would be honored to have you as our manager," Orrin said right before ending the rehearsal. "That's a wrap, fellas, let's do it again. Same place same time tomorrow." Bridgette watched as the rehearsal concluded and the members with congratulated each other with bro-hugs and dap.

It was the same ending to every rehearsal; Martin would bend an elbow, Phyllis would interlace her arm inside her reserved space, and once they were woven together, he would escort her home as they launched into a duet. Their song tonight was "Precious Love" by Tammi Terrell and Marvin Gaye.

Bridgette wanted to kiss Orrin, but not in front of the porch audience, and not in front of her father. So, she waited and watched until the audience members moseyed into their homes; the sound of clapping screen doors provided the final adulation of the evening. Only her father and two little old ladies across the street remained outside, but Bridgette's cup of patience poured empty. I wish Mrs. June and Mildred would take their nosey asses inside!" she mumbled.

To her left, her father was still humming his favorite tune in his rocker as he waited for an encore. Bridgette turned halfway toward her dad. With kitten-like eyes, she nudged him toward the screen door.

"Young man, did you know I was an ordained minister? I have a Bible right on the front seat - we can do this thing right now."

With a grin as wide as Lake Pontchartrain, Orrin replied, "Mr. Banks, if I didn't think your wife would skin us alive, I would take you up on that offer tonight!"

Once the screen door closed, Bridgette's finger invited Orrin down to her strawberry scented lips - he accepted her invitation. Her head barely reached the middle of his chest, and the size of one of his hands equaled two of Bridgette's. Orrin towered over her, and she loved every six feet and four inches of him. His skin was the color of a perfectly wrapped Cuban cigar, but felt more like a satin ribbon to the touch.

"My dad loves you so much," she said as their lips parted slightly from their union.

"And you?"

"What about me?"

"Do you love me as much as your dad loves me?" he smiled.

A low Eartha Kit purr escaped her lips. "Prrraawww, after the talent show next month, you will know how much. Maybe sooner . . ."

"Oh, really?"

"Yes . . . really. I'm ready."

She could never look him in his oak wood eyes for long; they rendered her helpless every time. His style was torn out of the Sam Cooke catalogue of cool, with a magnetic personality and smile that charmed every girl at school. Surprisingly, he was humble, and like Bridgette, had earned multiple academic honors.

Orrin wasn't Bridgette's first attempt at dating. For a summer two years ago there was Alfred, but Mr. Banks wouldn't allow him inside the front gate. That wasn't the case with Orrin - it helped that both families lived only three homes apart on Louisa Street.

"Those talent show judges won't know what hit them next month. You guys sound great," she complimented.

"You think so?"

"I do . . ." Bridgette slid her fingers between his. "How you change your voice like that from song to song I will never know. It's like one minute you're Smoky Robinson, and the next you're

David Ruffin. That's why my mother has never given up on you joining her choir. She always says, *One day you will let the Lord use you the right way."*

"Thanks, baby! I wish I could join the choir. The two of us singing together would turn that church inside out."

"Speaking of which, my mom's birthday is in two weeks. You should consider surprising her with a solo."

"I may consider that -"

"Just a thought, since you're planning to ask for her blessing. That church solo would soften her up a lot."

"You think?"

"Baby, you are the most talented person I know. My dad is dead serious about the NOLA Hearts. He thinks you have what it takes to be a star."

"And that's all I dream about - getting picked up by a record label like Motown - but first I need a look."

"A look? You look just fine to me. What are you talking about, a look?"

He kissed the strawberries again. "You know, like the outfits worn by Sly and the Family Stone." He wiped the stars with both hands. "Stage presennnnnnccce. Something that sets us apart from the other doo-wop groups."

"Where is all of this coming from? Orrin, I love the look you have."

"I appreciate that, I do. But I'm tired of performing in dusty shoes and rag-tag suits from the thrift store. That's how I feel when I am on stage; like a singing hobo."

"Orrin, baby, don't say that . . ."

"That's how I feel. Then there's this new thing I heard about called funk music, and when it becomes the next Big Thing, I want to be in the front of it. I'm tired of singing Motown songs."

"Well, I am not sure about this funk music you're talking about, but your clothes are perfect. With the voice you have, the moment you start singing, the audience will love you, too."

"I know that, but -"

Bridgette interrupted. "But nothing, Orrin! I watch you all the time as you move through the halls at school - I watch them part for you like Moses. You have an effect on people. They admire you - not the clothes. Baby, it's you."

"But I feel bland . . . like I am missing something. It's hard to explain."

Bridgette rolled her eyes slowly to the left. "This is Martin's idea, isn't it?"

"What makes you say that?"

"It's Martin; I know it is. The moment Phyllis gave him that pompadour like he's James Brown, I said to myself, *here we go* . . ."

"It's not Martin . . ."

She huffed. "It is Martin. Deep down, you feel like he's trying to upstage you from the back. And he's always talking about designer suits and patent leather shoes, not to mention he's high yellow like Smokey Robinson and you're -"

He cut her off. "It's not Martin or his ridiculous hair -"

Her necked hula-hooped. "YES IT IS!" Her arms folded in a tight tuck. "And if you think I'm putting a perm in your hair, you're crazy. I like your slick bald-fade and natural waves. I like your clothes, even if they're not name brand. I love you, Orrin."

"And I love you too . . ."

"But when are you going to love Orrin as much as I do?"

"Bridgette . . . Bridgette . . . Bridgette," Orrin sighed, exasperated. He placed his hands on the sides of her face. "It doesn't have anything to do with Martin, or Tyrone, or Freddie . . . It's about wanting to perfect my presentation, that's all. I didn't tell you, but I have been looking for a part-time job because I'm tired of asking my mom and grandmother for money. I'm too old for that. It's time for me to contribute. Even you have a part-time job . . ."

"Orrin, I don't see anything wrong with getting a part-time job to help your mom, but you guys don't need multicolored suits. Baby, just sing, and your amazing voice will take care of the rest. Just sing, Orrin, and stay as you are. I love this version of you."

"So in other words, if I get a pompadour, it's over between us?"

She snickered. "Hmm, now where did I put Alfred's phone number?"

Orrin laughed. "Unless you're sending a pigeon with a message for him to call you, I'm not worried about Alfred. Mr. Banks chased him with a rake the last time he came around."

"That's a lie, and you know it . . . it was a broom," she chortled.

"By the way, it's a good thing your taste in men improved; your future was looking pretty grim with Alfred the Dropout."

"Put'em up," Bridgette growled as she punched him in the stomach. Whack!

"Ouch!" he laughed as he shielded his ribcage. She shuffled her feet like Muhammad Ali, then slugged him again on the shoulder. Her punches felt like tickles to him.

"Oh, you think it's funny, huh?"

Before Bridgette could throw another jab, Orrin bear-hugged her and lifted her off the ground. As her feet dangled, their eyes eclipsed at the perfect time - at that precise moment when a couple is wrapped together in a euphoric bond. In a frequency only her ears could detect, he crooned her favorite song.

Cupid, draw back your bow
And let your arrow go
Straight to my lover's heart for me, for me
Cupid, please hear my cry
And let your arrow fly
Straight to my lover's heart for me.

Abruptly, without the slightest pardon or courtesy, their perfect moment in time was interrupted by the two remaining members of the porch audience. "Yes, Innnndeed!" a voice drifted from across the street. "This lil' gal is bold - she knows her mammy don't play that shit!" Mrs. June laughed out loud from her porch.

"I know that's right; it's just a matter of time, honey," Mrs. Mildred chimed in, looking over the top of her eyeglasses.

As Orrin was about to kiss Bridgette, the front door swung open with the force of a hurricane - so violent it rattled the white wooden panels on the exterior walls.

"BRIDGETTE MARIE BANKS! What in the name of Jesus is going on out here?! Have you lost your cotton-pickin' mind?"

It was Mrs. Betsy Banks.

CHAPTER 12

Bridgette's mother leaned halfway out the screen door with her right hand on her hip. Even the way she cleared her throat was a threat; even her poorly placed wig warned of a pending altercation. As if Bridgette were a carton of fresh eggs, Orrin gently lowered her to the ground. He knew every verse in Betsy's rule book regarding public affection - according to chapter one, he was in violation.

"Good evening, Mrs. Banks."

"Good evening, young man," she replied abrasively.

Orrin could feel the heat of her breath from the sidewalk, so he tried to redirect her rage.

"Sooooo . . . how did we sound tonight, Mrs. Banks?"

She didn't answer him immediately; only after several deep breaths.

"You're getting better," she said, then paused as if to indicate the performance had been average. "You still need to work on your breathing, you're cutting the notes off too soon. And that little Martin is trying to sing lead from the back, you know? That's why it's called a *background singer,* they sing in the back. Not the front. Other than that, you're getting better. And one more thing -"

The entire time Mrs. Banks unfurled her critique, Bridgette faced Orrin, silently mocking her mother with crossed eyes and a tongue that flapped out the side of her mouth. Orrin struggled not to burst into laughter. Bridgette was a master of comedic impressions - she mouthed her mother's words in perfect sync. To Orrin, Bridgette was beautiful and silly; a prankster and pretty. *This girl don't know when to quit.* Right on the verge bursting into laughter, Orrin pinched Bridgette on the arm until she stopped the impressions.

". . . And another thing, on that song, 'Ain't Too Proud to Beg,' you're not going up high enough on 'Ain't too proud to plead.' That's three notes up the scale. Either get up there or leave that song alone. You hear me?"

"Yes, Mrs. Banks."

"Bridgette, these dishes ain't gonna wash themselves. Get on in here."

"I'm coming, Momma," Bridgette replied while still facing Orrin. He watched as the pupils of her eyes disappeared under her lids. Watching her interact with Mrs. Banks was too much - Orrin tried to hide his laughter in a cough.

"Well hurry it up then," Mrs. Banks ordered.

"Ahhhhh, she makes me sick," Bridgette said in a whisper to Orrin.

"Bridgette . . . you said something?"

"Momma, give me a minute to say goodnight."

"Well say it then, and get on in this house. Tonight is your dish night and you gonna wash'em."

Orrin's coughing stopped. "Before you go, thank you so much for the advice Mrs. Banks. I will work on my breathing."

"If you would join my choir then you wouldn't have that problem, would you?"

"No ma'am," Orrin said as Mrs. Banks closed the front door and flicked on the porch light.

"You know she's waiting for you in the living room," Orrin

warned.

"Ooooh, she gets on my nerves!" Bridgette sighed.

"Guess you better head on in before Mrs. Banks beats us both with a switch." He planted a quick kiss on her cheek. "Call me after you wash the dishes."

"I will if I can get through and the phone isn't busy. Your brother talks on the phone more than a bill collector. When the phone rings, I bet he jumps off the toilet with a stinky booty . . . huh?" Bridgette said as she backed into her yard.

"Go inside, Bridgette, and call me. I will make sure my brother is off the phone."

"Okay, but make sure you wipe that phone first!" Bridgette yelled from the porch. "I love you, *Orrinnnnnn*."

"I love you, *Orrinnnnnn*," Mrs. June and Mrs. Mildred teased. "That's just how it's going to happen to her." Mrs. June said. "She gonna get her lil' issue in her belly. Watch what I say."

After a short stroll to the middle of the block, Orrin arrived home to 2337 Louisa Street. His grandmother's house was originally a double shotgun home, but after his father was killed in Vietnam two years ago, Grandma Ellen had cut a door in the middle, and Orrin, his mom, and his brother had moved into the newly enlarged residence.

His mother worked in housekeeping at the Howard Johnson hotel on Canal Street. Teresa Toussaint would leave at six in the morning right after waking her sons for school and would not return until six in the evening. During the day and often late into the evening, his grandmother constantly cooked, and the house was always as hot as her oven.

Orrin's grandmother cooked for the sick and shut in, the construction workers who wanted a hot meal, the local homeless, and anyone who was hungry. Grandma Ellen was the unofficial Red Cross for the entire community, the Queen of Benevolence, and the one who always received a call from local pastors whenever there was a family in need.

His grandmother was also a very resourceful woman who placed a great deal of value in having a paid off mortgage, and the first son in the neighborhood to graduate from college. Orrin's uncle Donald worked as a math professor at Dillard University and lived around the corner. In fact, their backyards fences touched.

As often as she could, his grandmother harassed their mother about going back to college and getting her degree. Every evening his mom entered the house drop-dead tired from cleaning, his grandmother would remark. *"One day soon you gonna get sick of cleaning up after white folks and take your ass back to school."*

Grandma Ellen was comfortable in her segregated world; she despised the entire integration movement. As long as the schools and clinics were staffed at the same level as those in the white community in Chalmette, as long as Charity Hospital provided emergency care on Tulane Avenue, his grandmother saw no need to integrate.

Her greatest joy was that she had saved Orrin and his brother from the latch-key lifestyle, and was able to pass down family traditions, recipes, and their native tongue. Orrin was less than enthused to learn the ways of his grandmother, and his brother never attempted.

As Orrin made his way to the kitchen, the aroma of okra gumbo moved around him like fog and was thick enough to chew. In a straight line, he jogged through the house, because he knew how much doing so agitated his grandmother.

"Boy, stop running through my damn house before you knock my pictures off the wall!" Grandma Ellen yelled.

"Good evening, Grandma."

"Good evening. Go check the mailbox."

"I did, only one letter today."

Grandma Ellen sat at the kitchen table cutting a batch of sugarcane roots and bay leaves. Her hair was always braided in two cornrows above her ears, from front to back. Her body was inflated with high blood pressure long before many knew the dangers of hypertension, but her constant sweating and shortness of breath should have been reason enough for concern. To Orrin, however, her sweating was normal. Across her left shoulder was a full-length towel that she used to dry her hands, with the other end reserved for her face and neck.

"Grandma, it's from the Orleans Parish School Board," Orrin told her as he approached.

"What it say?" she asked as she diced a bell pepper.

"It's addressed to my momma."

"Boy, open it and read what it say." The sound of a knife colliding with a wooden board grew louder.

Orrin ripped open the envelope and unfolded the letter. He read it aloud.

Dear Mrs. Teresa Toussaint,

On behalf of the entire New Orleans Public School Board, I'm writing you to inform your family that Orrin Toussaint has been selected for enrollment in Francis T. Nichols High School. This bussing initiative is part of our ongoing efforts to fully comply with the Supreme Court Ruling Brown vs. Board of Education, which makes segregated schools in the State of Louisiana illegal. This change will not go into effect until the fall school year starting in September 1968, but for your convenience, we have already provided the principal at Nichols with a copy of your son's transcripts and shot records . . .

"Well, I be damned. You can stop reading right there because you ain't going." Grandma Ellen grunted her way up from the table and swayed in her mumu over to the stove, where a pot roast hid in the oven. Her pot roast matched the color of her forearm, so she removed it and placed it on the counter.

Her kitchen was also her court. From within its walls, she handed down her rulings. It was a place where you either accepted her decisions or fled if it was too hot. But it was always too hot; a personal sauna where her thick, carpet skin was heat resistant while everything around her baked, including the wallpaper that bulged at the seams, the faded linoleum floors, and even the table and chairs.

Orrin yelled toward the rear of the home for his brother. "Oh, Cap, come read this."

"I'm on the phone!" he yelled back.

"Put Ola Mae on hold - she'll live. It's important."

After five minutes or so, his brother thumped his way into the kitchen from his room in the rear of his grandmother's side of the house. He resembled Orrin, only shorter and more athletic. Everyone called him *Cap* because he was the captain of the football team for three consecutive years - and a highly recruited running back.

"This better be important," his brother said.

Orrin handed him the letter and watched his eyes scroll through every sentence.

"Wow . . . they're sending you to integrate Nichols . . . for your senior year?"

". . . And just like I told Orrin, you can throw that letter in that trash bucket right over there because he ain't going," his grandmother said as she arranged a shelf in the refrigerator.

"Grandma from the sound of it, it doesn't seem like we have any choice. They have already sent my records to Nichols High," Orrin pleaded.

"Throw that letter in the trash now! You ain't going nowhere! You will finish high school at Carver, then go on over by your Uncle Donald at Dillard."

Orrin's brother stood. "This letter says it's only fourteen colored kids getting transferred."

His grandmother banged on the counter. "They're going to get somebody child killed sending only fourteen *coloreds* over there to Nichols with those hateful-ass white folks. And a lot of boys from Chalmette go to Nichols, too. You have one more year to go, and now they wanna integrate? They can kiss *my black ass*. You will be at Carver!"

"Who are you fussing with?" their mother asked as she entered the kitchen and slung her purse on the table.

"Good evening, Momma," the boys greeted Teresa. Orrin handed his mother the letter as she took a seat. Her uniform still reeked of exhaust from pushing a Kirby vacuum cleaner for eight grueling hours. As usual, her hands were bone dry from

Ajax powder, and she had just enough energy left to wave for something to drink.

Teresa read the entire letter. "Well, it's about time."

"About time for what?" Grandma Ellen asked.

"Momma, it's about time that these schools came out from under these Jim Crow laws. I want my sons exposed to an integrated society - to compete with all races in the classroom and the workforce. It's better they learn the ways of the white man now than to get on the job and have to figure it out."

Orrin listened as he poured his mother a glass of lemonade.

"Well, ain't nobody told you to get a job cleaning after white folk all damn day - you came up with that plan. I told you take your ass over there to Southern University."

"Momma, I have said it over and over again, once the boys are in college and I have their costs covered, I will go back to school. But I can afford to -"

"Teresa, that ain't nothing but an excuse."

"It's not."

"Goddammit, it is. They have plenty of young girls just like you - with two and three babies - graduating. With babies on their hips, they're graduating. And getting good jobs downtown on Poydras. Off-on-the-weekend kind of jobs."

"Momma, I know! So please stop throwing it in my face." Teresa opened her purse and retrieved a pack of Kool cigarettes.

"Don't light those things in my house . . ."

While his grandmother and mother argued over the letter from the school board, Orrin followed his brother back to his room. Once there, his brother picked up the phone. "Ola Mae, you still there? I need to have a quick conversation with my lil' brother . . . I'll call you right back . . . I love you too."

"I love you toooo, Ola Mae," Orrin heckled.

As his brother hung up the phone, Orrin took a seat on his bed. "I don't have a problem with going to Nichols - in fact, I have always wondered about it."

"Well, a friend of mine was bussed from Booker T. Washington to JFK High, and he loves it. He said everything is better over there. Even the textbooks are brand new."

"Grandma will never allow me to go. In her mind, no school

is better than Carver High."

"Orrin, Grandma's greatest fear is one of us getting lynched - she thinks every white person's goal in life is to hang a black man."

"Cap . . . tell me about it. Grandma is just as racist as the folk in Chalmette, but you didn't hear it from me," Orrin chuckled.

"I know, and there's no way to convince her otherwise. That's why some things I tell her, and some things I don't." His brother opened his book bag and handed Orrin what appeared to be a large greetings card; it was a letter from the USC Athletic Department. "The counselor asked me to visit her after lunch, and when I did, she handed me that card. Orrin, I have a scholarship offer from the University of Southern California."

Orrin leaped in the air. "USC! Wow! Cap, this is awesome!"

"*Shush!* Keep it down; I don't want Grandma to know just yet. I was going to tell them tonight, but that was before you read your letter. Grandma will never let me go to USC - especially since the great coach Eddie Robinson sat at her kitchen table and ate red beans and rice. She gave him her word I would attend Grambling University and when she gives her word, it's kept -"

". . . until her last breath," Orrin finished.

"But I think I want to go to USC. I heard L.A. is nothing like the South - no racism out there. Black and white people get along like Dr. King's Dream."

"There is no way Grandma is letting you attend a school in Los Angeles," Orrin reminded him. "But I want you to go. I want you to follow your dreams straight to the NFL."

"And I want you to go to Nichols High for your senior year. Maybe we should have a talk with Grandma after Mardi Gras; she's always in a better mood."

"You're right - for about three days, she's a completely different person. Let's have this conversation with her on Wednesday."

"Sounds like a plan, little bro."

CHAPTER 13

O rrin awoke the next morning to the sound of a heated argument in the kitchen - as did his brother on the other side of the house. It was Grandma Ellen versus his mother fully engaged in Round Two. In an attempt to mute the wall-trembling screaming match, Orrin pressed a pillow across his face, but to no avail. His grandmother's voice was too loud, deep, and raspy.

"Orrin is my child, and I want him to get the best education possible. Even if it means sending him to a school named after a Confederate general."

"Teresa, you sound foolish! He's learning just fine at Carver - you think they're going to teach him the same as white kids? You crazy and a fool," Grandma snapped back.

A few moments later, Orrin heard the thunder of the front door colliding with the frame as his mother stormed out of the house to catch her bus. But the argument didn't stop there - not for his Grandma Ellen.

Everything she touched was abused and battered; pots were violently stuffed into cabinets, utensils were slung into a yellow dishrack that sat on the counter. One after the other, *PLACK* . .

. *PLACK . . . PLACK* went the cabinet doors, refrigerator door, pantry door, back door, and everything else that featured a door.

That's when Orrin heard the sound of a fatality.

From the kitchen came the violent sound of a large glass item shattering on the linoleum floor. That, too, was his mother's fault, even though she was miles away. But no tantrum was complete without one of his grandmother's mountaintop declarations.

"What ya'll not going to do is run all over me in my house," she told the mixing bowl.

Looking down into the mixture of flour, "I'll be damned if she thinks she's going to send my boy up there to *Nichols High School*. I be damned. That lil' job with them white folk has gone to her head. Ain't nobody gonna have my boys hung up in a tree somewhere in Chalmette. That ain't gonna happen!"

Orrin entered the kitchen but didn't say a word; he knew to keep quiet whenever Grandma Ellen was locked in an argument with the appliances and cabinets. When it came to his grandmother, just because you may have left the room didn't mean the argument was over - she often continued it alone until you returned. The one thing that was for sure was the fight was going to continue until Grandma Ellen was the victor.

From the floor, in the space between the table and the counter, sharp pieces of a white dinner plate reached for Orrin in agony. He picked up a broom and a dustpan and swept as his grandmother moved like a tornado around the kitchen.

"That's the problem with some of these Negroes: white man say jump, they jump. They put no value in their own community. They think just because it's white, then it's better. Well, it ain't better to me. Some of the best teachers in the State of Louisiana are at CARVER HIGH SCHOOL, and a lot of those kids from Carver are going to college, becoming doctors, lawyers, and everything."

The trade-in for affordable housing is the loss of environmental control. In exchange for a place to live, his mother had yielded over her parental control to his grandmother. As long as they lived in her house, they were forced to obey her rules, and when it came to Orrin, Grandma Ellen was beyond strict.

She poured the last of the whipped cake mix into four baking pans. Holding a salad bowl filled to the rim with cornflakes, Orrin tried to tiptoe out of the kitchen before she noticed him, but it was too late.

"Have you been getting your lessons?"

Orrin answered without turning around. "Yes ma'am, and I'm still on the honor roll."

"That's good and keep it that way, but you know what lesson I'm talking about. Don't play crazy." The mouth of the oven exhaled hot breath throughout the kitchen as she arranged the last of the four baking pans on its tongue.

"*Jiwe la kwanza?*" she asked.

Orrin quickly swallowed two spoons of cereal to buy some time. Searching his mind, he only recognized the *jiwe*, but the meaning of the other words escaped his memory. He also knew that if he failed to answer correctly, he could kiss Saturday morning goodbye. Wrong answers meant hours on end in front of her foul-mouthed oven. But any answer was better than none at all - so he took a swing.

"I have the stone?" he winced.

"You asking me or telling me?"

"Grandma, I can't believe this . . . I was just studying this the other day -"

"You must take me for a fool!" she snapped.

"No ma'am, I don't take you for a fool. I know I know this . . ."

"If you spent half the time studying like I told you and less time showing off for those lil' gals up the street you would know what it means."

"Well, I got part of it right, didn't I?"

Her thick, callused hand slapped the table. "*Jiwe la kwanza.* The first stone! If you don't know what I'm asking, then there is no way you're going to respond correctly."

The light bulb above his bald fade switched on. "That's it, I knew I knew that one. The first stone is: *A soul cannot be removed to acquire wealth that wasn't earned.*"

"That's right! Now say it in the correct tongue."

He needed more time, so Orrin gulped down four large spoons of soggy cornflakes while his brained scanned for the correct verbiage. She was correct in her assessment of him. For the past three weeks, he had been consumed with the NOLA Hearts, Bridgette, and finding a part-time job. He'd skipped his lessons, like she'd guessed, and now it was obvious. But the wrong answer was still better than no answer at all, so Orrin took another swing at it.

"*Roho haiwezi kuondolewa ili . . . ili . . . ili . . .*" He ran out of guesses.

"*Roho haiwezi kuondolewa ili kupata utajiri ambao haukupatikana,*" Grandma Ellen repeated six times until Orrin was able to recite the entire rule. "Do you think I'm teaching you this because I have nothing else better to do?"

"No ma'am."

"Do you think I'm gonna live forever?"

"Well . . . I would love you to . . ."

"But do you think it's gone happen?"

"No ma'am."

"Then I need you to get off your ass - get serious and learn your lessons. Do you understand?"

"Yes, ma'am . . ."

"Now the next time I ask you to name one of the twelve *Mawe ya maisha* and you give me some mumbo-jumbo, you can kiss that singing group goodbye and that lil' Bridgette better not ring this phone. Do you understand?"

His Adam's apple sunk to the bottom of his throat, then slowly inched back into place. "Y-yes, ma'am. Grandma, I promise to study more." With a bowl half-full of soggy cornflakes, Orrin meandered out of the kitchen, through the middle door, and back to his room.

Grandma Ellen was the boss of everyone who lived on 2337 Louisa Street, but the black stove was her boss. The stove was like an overbearing lover; she couldn't go too far or stay away too long. He was extremely possessive. On the burners, three pots of various sizes puffed and steamed. In the smaller pot, she cooked rice. In the medium-sized pot, she simmered stewed chicken legs, and in the larger pot was jambalaya.

As he sat on his bed slurping down the last of his breakfast, Orrin absorbed everything as his grandmother opened the squeaky pantry door and continued her original argument with his mother - with shelves of canned goods standing in as surrogates.

"... All it took was one letter and she done made up her mind to ship my grandson up the road. Just one letter. They didn't have to beg her - she just handed the boy over. Knowing how important he is to this family! If I didn't watch her come out of me, I wouldn't believe she is my daughter. She just foolish!"

PLACK went the pantry door.

Tiptoeing back to the sink to wash his bowl, Orrin interrupted, "Grandma do you need anything before I head outside?"

"Other than you learning your lessons, no, I'm fine!" she replied bluntly.

"Okay, I'll be on the porch studying my lessons if you need me," he said as she opened the mouth of the oven and released a sweet breath of moist baked cakes. She placed the cakes on the counter, where they sat butt naked as they waited to get draped in creamy chocolate frosting.

After a Friday of back-to-back exams all day, Orrin was in no mood to do any additional studying, so instead of his lessons, he decided to read the Saturday newspaper on the porch in the cool of the morning. After flipping through several pages of the *Times Picayune*, he scanned the entertainment section. That's when it caught his eye.

The *Billboard* Top 100 R&B full-color insert. The feature that morning was Sly & the Family Stone's debut album cover for *Dance to the Music*.

"Oh brother!" Orrin said with excitement. "Wait until I show Martin . . . this!"

His hypnotic trance on the Family Stone was broken by the arrival of a shiny, red Ford pickup that parked in front of Martin's house. Orrin didn't recognize the truck, but the man who drove it was known throughout the neighborhood as Pananie (Pah-nanie) the Junk Man. He was an older light-skinned guy who could easily pass for Latino, but he was very much African American. A half-white.

Today was Orrin's first time seeing Pananie dressed in business attire. He always wore dirty overalls, and on a normal day, he drove a loud, rusty truck that hauled a trailer used for collecting metal scraps. But not today. Orrin could tell Pananie was returning from a meeting, and his assumption was confirmed when Martin's father, Mr. Gary Robichaux, exited the house to greet him. Moments later, several other men arrived, and they all convened in the rear of Pananie's truck.

About ten minutes later, Martin yawned out of the front door and greeted each man gathered in his driveway. Never one to intrude, Orrin sat patiently on his porch and waited for the ideal moment to get Martin's attention. After about thirty minutes, he was successful. Martin plowed across the street to Orrin as if each step required great effort and labor.

"Bro, what's the meeting about?"

"My dad and uncle are taking over the flames from Mr. Lawson, who's gotten too old."

"The flames?"

"Yeah, the flames. You know, the torches."

"What the men carry in the night parade?"

Martin answered in mid-yawn. "Ahhhhh . . . yes. My dad and his brother have been carriers since they were teens, and this Mardi Gras night will be my first time walking with them."

"I can dig it, but why?"

"It's sort of like your grandmother is always on you about family traditions. Sort of like that, but without the African crap you have to learn."

"It's not African crap, but I get where you coming from - I am sick of tradition."

"That's because there's no money in that stuff with you and Grandma Ellen, but I will get paid to carry on our tradition. I am only in it for the money. I need clothes."

"You mean the men who twirl those lanterns?"

"Yup."

"You mean the brothers in the white clothes - who march in the white folk parades?"

"Yup, they're called flambeaux carriers, and people at the parade are so happy to see you, they pitch money. It's like being a stripper on Bourbon Street, but you get to keep your clothes on."

"But to get the money, you have to collect the coins off the ground?" Orrin asked

Martin yawned again. "Ahhhhhh, yes, my cousin said he made almost a hundred dollars last year before the parade made it to Canal Street."

"All from walking in one parade with a torch?"

"And I plan to spend all of it on clothes for the big show," Martin replied, wiping the sleep from his eyes.

"Clothes like this?" Orrin asked as he handed Martin the *Billboard* R&B ad with Sly & the Family Stone.

Suddenly Martin woke up. "Ya see; that is what I'm talkin' bout RIGHT HERE! This is cold blooded! Sly is a *bad, bad* man - check out that cape."

"I said the same thing to Bridgette; we need to have a signature look like the Isley Brothers and Sly if we expect people to take us seriously."

"This right here, Orrin," Martin slapped the page repeatedly. "This should be our new look. Well, I can't speak for the entire group, but it will fa-sho be mine."

"Mine too . . . but I have had the hardest time trying to find a part-time job. Do you think your Uncle Pannie will let me carry a flambeau torch? I really could use the money."

"You want to be a flambeaux?"

"If it will help me buy a new outfit for the talent show - you bet I'll do it."

"Well, he has extra flambeau torches, so let's go ask him."

Orrin and Martin stepped to the rear of his Uncle Pananie's truck, where the gathering of men was now up to sixteen. One by one, they were handed flambeaux to carry. Some of the men were in their early to mid-thirties, others were only a few years older than Martin and Orrin.

To Orrin, the flambeau looked more like a protest picket sign, but made entirely of metal. In the front of the flambeau were four cups that resembled candle holders. The stem of each flambeau was a two-inch pole; sturdy like a galvanized water pipe.

Orrin and Martin listened in on the conversation for a while as Pananie shared stories of what it was like for them to carry the flambeaux back in the 1920s. He talked about how drunken white women would play a game of titty flash while the flambeaux carriers did their best to ignore them.

"Keep the nipples but give us the nickels," Pananie laughed in a nostalgic moment. "Mighty fun time we had back then - it wasn't all bad." In story after story, Pananie shared precious memories of Mardi Gras gone by as the men listened in reverence.

After the flambeaux carriers departed with their torches, Martin approached his uncle.

"Uncle Pananie, Orrin wanted to know if he could march with us in the parade?"

"Let's see; I have two more torches left. If it's okay with Sister Ellen, then it's just fine with me. But you need to clear that with Sister Ellen first - before I hand you the torch."

"Okay, will do. I'll be right back," Orrin said as he sprinted home to his grandmother.

"What Sister Ellen cooked today?" Pananie asked.

"Stew chicken and rice—and she made a big pot of jambalaya with potato salad. Oh, and some chocolate cake," Orrin shouted over his shoulder.

"Then ask Sister Ellen to send me a plate!" Pananie yelled.

"Yes, sir!"

Orrin ran across the street, leaped over three porch steps, and flashed through the front door toward the kitchen. About halfway in, Orrin heard, "Boy, stop running through my damn house before you knock my pictures off the walls."

"Grandma, Mr. Pananie asked for a plate."

"A plate of what?"

"Your chicken, jambalaya, and potato salad. Oh, and some chocolate cake."

"How Pananie know what I cooked?"

"He asked, and I told him . . ."

"What did I tell you about putting my pots in the street? People don't need to know I cooked."

"Grandma, everybody from here to Canal Street knows you cook every day."

"That old Pananie always begging. Got all those white folks fooled like he's so *PO*, picking up the trash they throw out. Beulah told me just the other day that Pananie done build the biggest house in New Orleans East, right off Morrison Road. He's the only black person over there, and the white folks don't bother him."

"Wow! Pananie made that much money hauling trash and scrap?"

"Some say the only people around here with pockets deeper than Pananie are Negros who own funeral homes and that mafia man. Now, what's his name again?"

"Carlos Marcello."

"Yes, Marcello. But you ain't heard none of this from me because I like to mind my business."

"You? Mind your business? I have heard it all!" Orrin joked.

"Look-a here, I don't go around asking people's business like nosey Mildred down the street. People tell me *thangs*. Like, Pananie built that house in the East with cash. Made all that money in scrap - and don't give a dime. Stingy like a Jew in the bank!"

"I never knew that. So Pananie is well-off?"

"Yes, he is."

Once the plate was stacked with stewed chicken, potato salad, and jambalaya, Grandma Ellen wrapped it tightly in a sheet of aluminum foil, then used a separate sheet of foil for the chocolate cake.

"Go on take that to *PO*-mouth Pananie and tell him Otis Redding said my light bill could use a little 'Love & Tenderness.'"

Orrin held the plate from the bottom. "Grandma, there's one more thing I wanted to ask you."

His grandmother wiped her face with the long end of the bath towel. "What is it, boy?"

"I wanted to know, well . . . Pananie said if it's all right with you . . ."

"If what is all right with me?"

"Pananie has a walking crew in the parades, and he said if it's okay with you then I can walk with them this year . . ."

"Walking in the parade doing what?" She turned from the sink. Sweating. Nostrils flared. Head tilted down to the left. Even her two cornrow braids wanted to know.

"You know . . . walking. In the parade."

"Walking in the parade doing *whaaatah*?"

At that moment, Orrin's brother entered the kitchen, went straight for the same salad bowl, and filled it to the top with cornflakes.

"From what I understand, they carry those torches and make pretty good money."

"As a flambeaux?!" his grandmother yelled. "Are you standing in my kitchen asking me if you can be a flambeaux carrier?"

"Yes, ma'am."

The scene from that morning began to replay; she turned back to the sink where two of her pots soaked in water hot enough to boil a sack of crawfish. With a wire pad, his grandmother proceeded to scrub one of the pots so hard Orrin heard the screams beneath the dishwater. Suddenly, both pots were slung into the plastic dish rack without care or concern for their lives - that's when she turned back to Orrin.

"I wish I would catch a grandson of mine out there cooning like a monkey for those white people. I'll break that flambeau over your ass. You hear me?"

"Yes. Yes, ma'am."

Cap buried his face in the cereal bowl and convulsed in laughter. A spoon of cornflakes went into his mouth and then fell back from where it came. When their grandmother moved around the table and backed Orrin against a shelf that held her fig preserves, his brother started coughing up cornflakes. Only her toes fit inside her purple house slippers; her ashy heels dragged across the floor. With her right hand on her hip and a long bath towel across her shoulders, her left hand proceeded to tell Orrin exactly how she felt about his request.

"Do you see any of us out on the street corner begging for handouts?"

"No, Grandma . . ."

"Have you ever seen me on Canal Street tap dancing for pennies?"

"No, Grandma -"

"Then what in the hell makes you think I would allow you to disgrace this family like that?"

"Grandma, I just looked at it as a way to get extra money for clothes so I wouldn't have to bother you and my momma."

"Boy, listen to me." Her purple slippers slid two more paces toward the fig preserves. "I will only say this one time. We don't coon for no damn body. Do you hear what I say?"

"Yes, Grandma," he replied as the glass jars of figs behind him rattled in fear.

"When your brother asked me if he could shine shoes on Canal Street, what did I tell him?"

"Our family don't coon."

"You got-damn right - we don't coon! That's your answer. Hell no!"

In the corner of Orrin's eye, his brother continued to hide in the bowl of cereal, his spoon in his hand, laughing into a soggy, cream-colored mush. Orrin moseyed out of the house with his head buried in his chest and the plate for Pananie securely in his hands. Once he made it to the porch, he saw that Pananie was seated in his truck, waiting for the plate while he puffed on a carved tobacco pipe. Just right of Pananie's truck, resting on the chain-link fence in front of Martin's house, were two flambeau torches.

Orrin jogged to the truck with the plate of food and handed it to Pananie. Under the carport in a lawn chair sat Martin, still enthralled in the photo of Sly & the Family Stone.

"Tell your grandmamma I said thank you kindly for the food, beause Lord knows I love that woman's cooking!"

"Yes, sir," Orrin said.

"Did you ask your grandmother if you could walk as a flambeaux?"

Orrin looked over at the two torches resting on the fence, then glanced at Martin. Martin met his eyes, then jumped out of his trance in excitement.

"I'm buying this outfit right here! Watch how the girls scream when I step on stage in this suit - and when the NOLA Hearts hit that spin move, I'm going to whip with that cape! *FLAP, FLAP* - I'm gonna be *CLEEEEAN* as the Board of Health!" Martin bragged.

"Young man, what did Sister Ellen say?" Pananie inquired a second time.

Orrin's eyes cut away from Martin as he cleared his throat. "My grandmother said . . . yes. Yes, I can march with you."

"You sure?"

"Yes, sir, she even gave the okay for my brother. He can carry that extra flambeau."

"Okay then. That works for me. We have a lighting of the torches on Monday the twenty-sixth at seven p.m. over in the parking lot by Carver. I will see you then."

"Yes sir, we'll be there."

CHAPTER 14

Carver High School
Monday, February 26, 1968
6:45 p.m.

It was the flambeaux custom to have a brief lighting ceremony the evening before a parade to test the torches - a ceremony that Orrin eagerly anticipated. The stadium parking lot at Carver High was peacefully asleep. Suddenly, the sound of metal dragging across concrete caused an abrupt awakening. Moments later, about fifty flambeaux carriers all gathered in a huge circle around Pananie - grateful for the opportunity, festive in their mood.

Orrin watched as Martin's father demonstrated how to light the torches for the new guys, while many of the veteran carriers shared memories about flambeauxs who had passed away over the years.

A few feet to his right, Orrin listened in as one of the experienced carriers named Willie Love demonstrated how to entertain the parade crowd for his younger brother. He appeared to be no more than thirty-five years old and wore a green military-issued jacket with matching boots. Other than the jacket and the boots,

Willie Love lacked the polished appearance more commonly associated with someone who was active army personnel.

"This is how you get that money - dem white folks like to see you dance when that parade stops, so watusi while you spin that flame. That's how I make five dollars every time at parade rest," Willie explained. "And another thing - some white men ain't gonna want you watusing in front of their women. They get jealous real quick if that wife smiles at you, so keep your distance from that kind."

Orrin took a mental note of how to make at least five dollars during every parade break - he was a natural entertainer, and the watusi dance was also a part of his act with the NOLA Hearts.

Locked in a near shoulder-to-shoulder oval, Orrin experienced a moment of spiritual connection with his metal torch and gained a sense of brotherhood unlike anything he had felt in his doo-wop group. The base of the galvanized pole stained the insides of his hands the color of sweet potatoes as he became one with the light, familiar with every dent along the surface. The skin on his face, neck, and arms was threatened by four scorched containers that held the liquid thermal substance as tea bag-sized flames parachuted from above his head and dawdled toward the ground.

With a swift twist of his wrist, the torch completed a full rotation. Then, it went around a second time as he became hypnotized by the illumination. A third twist confirmed his command of the flames. Next to Orrin was Cap, who held his torch with the ease of a broomstick. It didn't take much arm-twisting to convince his brother to become an accomplice: a chance to earn enough for a new pair of Converse All Stars was too much to resist.

The lie?

A Mardi Gras night party at Phyllis's house.

Phyllis's home was the perfect cover because her mother, Mrs. Gail Narrcisse, was known for having bi-weekly card parties and a monthly fish plate supper. She used the money from these events to help neighbors with light bills or past-due rent. No matter how perfect the scheme appeared, the weight of Orrin's flambeau felt like a fist of feathers compared to his colossal anvil of self-condemnation.

He had lied to Martin.

He had lied to Pananie.

He had lied to his mother.

He had lied to his grandmother.

The life span of a lie is but a second unless there is a second lie. To buy one outfit cost Orrin's integrity a total of five lies - which was three more than he expected to spend. But in his mind, the opportunity to woo the talent show judges with his voice and appearance justified his fall into falsehood. And so it slowly fell to the ground, where it crackled and popped alongside the molten droplets of tar from the torch: his integrity.

After this, I will never lie to my grandmother again - or to anone else.

The stadium parking lot was ablaze with an orange hue that warmed the evening air inside the ring of torches. It was then that a deep, heavy voice interrupted his trance.

"It is time!" Pananie called out from the middle of the circle. Like a Civil War lieutenant preparing a regiment of slaves, Pananie called all the men to attention; particularly Orrin and his brother.

"A few of you are here tonight for the coins we collect along the parade route, but money is not the reason we gather here every year," Pananie said as he stood in front of Orrin and Cap.

"There was once a time when black men were forced to haul the flambeaux - our ancestors didn't have much choice back then. But today we do . . . and here we are . . . again. Folk always ask me, why do I still carry this flame? My answer is simple - I do it to pay honor to our fathers, uncles, brothers, and friends who were forced to carry the flame before us." Pananie's eyes searched the soul of every man in the circle.

"So tonight, we prepare to light up another parade route because the spirits of our ancestors are watching. On Mardi Gras night, I want you to hold your head up high and know that you are continuing a tradition that has passed down from the slave man to the free man of color, and despite how those aristocratic Negros feel about us, we know our purpose. All hail the flambeaux!" Pananie yelled.

"All hail the flambeaux!" the men replied.

Once Orrin and his brother arrived home, they hid their air-cooled torches under the house, then took a seat on the front porch. After about ten minutes of silence, Orrin recognized that something was bothering Cap, because he never lifted his head. Then came the mumbles.

"I-I . . . don't think we should do this," his brother said, oscillating his head back and forth.

"Cap, we have already received out torches - we've already taken part in the lighting ceremony . . ."

"I know but we lied to Grandma Ellen. It just feels wrong."

"You know what else feels wrong?" Orrin stood above his brother and spoke a few inches from his head. "Watching Momma struggle to buy you football cleats."

Cap shot him a look. "That was one pair of cleats, and you beg Momma way more than I do, with the hair dos and the stage clothes."

"That's why we're walking in the parade tomorrow - we need to start making our own money. Momma wouldn't have to work half as hard if we had part-time jobs."

Cap stood to face Orrin. "Why do you think I train so hard? Why do you think I wear out so many pairs of tennis shoes?" His lips compressed, his finger that punched Orrin in the chest. "I am busting my ass trying to make it to the NFL so Momma will never have to work again. It feels wrong. I'm sorry, but I can't go along with this . . ."

"I need you to go along with this because if we're not together, then Grandma will worry."

"Orrin, she worries when we're together, she worries in her

sleep, she worries when she's cooking . . . that's what she does twenty-four hours a day - she worries."

"Not if she knows we're at Phyllis's house . . ."

"Phyllis lives around the damn corner, not uptown -"

"Cap . . . I know where she lives!"

"Do you . . ."

"I realize this is risky . . . but it's the best plan I've got. It's this or nothing."

"Well . . . nothing sounds good to me."

Cap wanted no part of his plan no matter how much Orrin tried to sell him on earning enough money for a new pair of football cleats. Orrin also knew Cap was right. It would take little effort for Grandma Ellen to confirm their whereabouts, especially considering that she and Phyllis's mother would often have after-dinner conversations about what they planned to cook the following day or which corner store had the best meat special.

"Look . . . I don't like lying any more than you do, but the talent show is next month, and I need this money - you also need this money. Just like that scout from USC discovered you on the football field; record labels also use talent scouts." Orrin's voice lowered to nearly a whisper. "Cap . . . this could be my big break if we win this talent show. I am asking you to go along with me this one time - that's all I'm asking."

With fingers interlocked above his head and eyes that searched for the moon, Orrin could tell his brother was conflicted.

"Okay . . . I will go along with it because you're right, I am tired of asking Momma for money. But if something goes wrong, just remember . . ."

"I know. I know. You told me so."

"Damn right . . . I told you so."

CHAPTER 15

O rrin and his brother entered the house and made their way toward their respective sides of the home through the middle door frame in the kitchen. His brother veered left toward the stove as Orrin took long, quiet steps to the bathtub. About thirty minutes later, there was a gentle knock at the front door. Turning off his bath water, Orrin jogged through the house to answer.

"Somebody get the door!" his grandmother yelled out from her bedroom.

"I got it!" Orrin replied.

"That's Gail's daughter." Grandma Ellen never referred to Phyllis by her first name; it was always *Gail's daughter* or *Gail's gal*. "She's come for that pot of butter beans and pan of cornbread on the top of the stove."

Orrin swung open the door, and there she stood. Alone, wearing a suspicious grin, under a beam of light.

"Hey, Phyllis."

"Hey Orrin, my momma sent me for the pots for the Mardi Gras cookout."

"You plan to carry those huge pans by yourself?"

"No, that's what I have a man for," Phyllis said as she glanced across the street toward Martin's house.

"I should have known that lovesick puppy was going to jump at any opportunity to walk you home."

"Well, a lovesick kitten used me to come see you." Her suspicious grin was confirmed, but there was no one with Phyllis, nor anyone walking in his direction from the Banks residence.

"Around this time of night? Bridgette has that smelly cream on her face and just snapped the last of her sponge rollers. I know her - she is done for the night." As Orrin held the door open so could Phyllis walk past, he heard the faint sound of a cat.

"*Meow, meow,*" it called from the darkness of the alley on the side of the house. Then the cat called out again.

"Meow, Orrin, I am a lovesick little kitten with no one to kiss. It so cold down here. *Meow,*" a hidden voice beckoned Orrin.

Instinctively, he stepped to the edge of the porch on the side of the house, and there she was - hiding in front of the alley gate.

An airy whisper. "Pssst . . . hop down here. Meow."

"Bridgette, what are you doing down there?"

"Well . . . I was hoping to sneak a kiss from a certain person. What does a girl have to do to get a little action around here?"

"All I know isszzz, you two better not get caught kissing on the side of that house - you know how fast rumors spread around here," Phyllis giggled as she closed the door.

Ignoring Phyllis, Orrin leaped off the side of the porch into the dark alley that separated his grandmother's shotgun house from Mrs. Dorothy's. It was there that he kissed her. Softly. Repeatedly. Until her breath stretched into whole notes, and he could feel the rhythm of her heart in the small of her neck

"Hi, baby," Orrin said as he perused deeper into her hazel eyes.

"I needed to see you." Bridgette wrapped her arms around his waist and pretended to fall asleep on her favorite pillow - his chest. The wintery moon provided the perfect amount of light in their lover's lane, that narrow alley where they had shared their first kiss. It was the place they always retreated to after every argument, the mecca of everything that mattered to them, the place where they dreamed the impossible, the tight place that swathed their every emotion.

His fingers combed through the hair on the back of her neck as every exhaled breath froze inches from her berry-scented lips. They shared an amorous sigh, the kind that says *I could lie here forever* . . . but forever was interrupted by an unknown.

"Orrin, can I ask you a question?"

"Bridgette, you can ask me whatever you like," a romantic baritone replied.

"Why do you smell like smoke?"

"Oh . . . it's nothing. I was just about to take a bath when Phyllis knocked on the door."

She lifted her head from her favorite pillow. "I understand that, but why do you smell like you just ran out of a burning house?"

"Bridgette, I'm just covered in exhaust from Pananie's truck. We were standing directly behind it, and . . . I guess . . ."

She backed out of his arms. "You do know, that *I know* you're lying to me?"

He tried to pull her back to him, but her stiff arm wouldn't budge. With her other hand, she blocked his attempt to sidestep her demand for the truth.

"Bridgette I am not lying to -"

"You are."

"I'm not."

"Orrin!"

"It's just smoke from . . ."

"Orrin!" her voice raised a pitch higher than his assertive baritone.

"We-we were standing near his truck while it was idling, and I guess . . . all of the smoke got in my clothes - I was just about to take my bath. Why are you making a big deal out of this?"

"I believe you were running your bath water. What I can't understand is why do you feel the need to lie about why you smell like a FLAMBEAUX CARRIER?" Her eyes narrowed into a single matchstick, while his eyes grew as wide as two boiled eggs.

"How? How . . . did you find out?"

"How do you think?"

"Phyllis?"

"Yes, Phyllis! Do you know why? Because *sheeeee*, has an honest relationship with Martin. He tells her everything - and she tells me everything. I have known since Friday, when Pananie gave you those funky-ass torches, but I waited for you to tell me."

"Bridgette, I was going to tell you . . ."

"When? After you humiliated yourself on Canal Street? When were you going to tell me? Huh? When?"

She no longer gazed at him but rather down to the right, at the base of the chain-link fence that cut the alley into two halves. Those hazel eyes he loved so much suddenly became reddish and watery. Bridgette had compared him to Martin, but in the worst way - as if he didn't measure up.

"I was going to tell you before the parade tomorrow, and that's the honest truth."

"Orrin, don't . . ." Her stiff arm turned into a pointed finger. "The only reason we're discussing this now is because I caught you in a lie."

"Okay. All right! You got me - but you know exactly why I didn't tell you. It's conversations like this."

"Oh, really?"

"Yes, really," he said as he backed away. "You're just like your mother . . ."

"My mother?" Her arms instantly folded.

"Yes . . . your mother. Judgmental!" Orrin's finger pointed down at Bridgette. "Between you, my momma, and my grandmother, I am tired of people telling me what to do. It's time for me to be my own man and make my own decisions . . ."

"So being your own man means looking me in the face and lying?"

"I didn't say that, but why do I have to get your approval for every little thing? This is not that complicated - I'm going entertain some children in a parade and make a few dollars . . ."

"Entertain children? Orrin, I think you know full well what the problem is - it's degrading and humiliating."

"Oh, I get it now! You don't want me to march as a flambeaux carrier because it will make *YOU* look bad. Too afraid word will get back to you from one of your girlfriends."

"If it's as simple as entertaining children, then have you told your grandmother about this new career you have?"

It was then that his eyes honed in on the bottom of the chain-link fence, and he ignored the question. A porch light had clicked on. Mrs. Dorothy stepped out onto the porch draped in a pink plush housecoat with a matching hair wrap that concealed her rollers. She veered down at them in the dark of the alley.

"Everything all right out here?" She held her housecoat together in the clutch of her hand.

"Yes, Mrs. Dorothy," Orrin answered. "Sorry to bother you."

"Ain't no bother. I just needed to see where the humbug was coming from, that's all. You two better get out of this cold before they have to rush you to the Charity Hospital with the pneumonia. You hear me?"

"Yes, ma'am," Orrin and Bridgette replied.

Once Mrs. Dorothy reentered her house, Orrin's eyes reconnected with that interesting area at the bottom of the fence, but it was too late. In that dark, narrow alley, Bridgette had him cornered.

"You haven't told her, have you? You planned to pull this off without any of us finding out?"

"Bridgette, this conversation is over . . ."

"No, it's not." She grabbed him by the arm. "So let's hear the complete lie - where are you supposed to be on Mardi Gras night while you're making a fool of yourself?"

Before Orrin could answer -

"I hope not with me! I want no part of it."

At that moment that Phyllis and Cap exited the front door carrying pots of food. Orrin and Bridgette lowered the volume on their argument. In one swift motion, Bridgette clasped Orrin by the hand, and inside her grip, he felt something.

She stood on tiptoe to whisper in his ear. "Here is all of the money I have saved up from babysitting for Pastor Prevost. Take it. Go buy the clothes you want for the talent show."

When Orrin opened his hand, he held $125. He closed the money back into her grip. "I can't accept this from you. I am tired of taking from the women in my life." He pushed the money deeper into her hand and softly closed her fist.

"Orrin, please take it," she whispered again.

"Bridgette, I can't."

In a silky voice, "Didn't you say I was going to be your wife one day? Your help-mate?"

"Yes, I said that, but . . ."

"Well, I'm practicing."

"Bridgette, I can't take money from you. How does that look that you had to buy my clothes?"

"Orrin, it doesn't make you any less of a man to accept money from me. We are a couple. There are times I am going to have more than you and sometimes you will have more than me. It doesn't matter as long as we take care of each other. You are my Prince - it's the least that I can do."

"Hmm, this pot ain't getting no lighter while you two alley-cats suck face down there," Phyllis interrupted.

Orrin kissed Bridgette on the center of her forehead. "I have to earn my own money." He took her by the hand and escorted her to the front of the porch.

"Would you like us to carry the pots home for you?" Cap asked Phyllis.

"No, because my honey-boo is coming now to help us."

Almost on cue, Martin exited the front door of his house with a toothy grin that was visible from across the street. The conversation between Orrin and Bridgette continued in their eyes as Cap handed Martin the large pan of cornbread.

Suddenly, the front door swung open. "Gail's daughter gone yet?" Grandma Ellen called out.

"She's leaving now, Grandma - Martin is going to walk her home."

"Well, Gail just called looking for her. Phyllis, hurry up and get on around that corner. You hear me?" Grandma Ellen slammed the screen door.

"Yes, ma'am," Phyllis and Martin replied.

Orrin watched as Martin, Phyllis, and Bridgette walked along the pavement toward her home. Bridgette turned with both hands begging *please*, but he flew her a kiss from his porch and declined for the final time. Once her door closed and the porch light dozed off for the night, Orrin continued to gaze at Martin and Phyllis as they approached the end of the block before making a left out of view. Orrin turned around and went back into the house.

On the coffee table sat that radiant insert of his favorite artist, Sly & the Family Stone, in that outfit. With the insert in hand, he continued to the rear of the house until he heard his grandmother call out from her bedroom.

"Orrin, where you at?"

"In the bathroom."

"Step in here."

CHAPTER 16

O rrin entered his grandmother's bedroom to find her stretched diagonally across the bed with her head resting on the inside of her arm. The carpet in her room was a thick, grassy texture; her bedroom and the living room were the only grass floors in the house.

On the nightstand on the farthest side of the bed were three large, flickering candles that cuddled a picture of Jean Pierre Chauvet, Orrin's grandfather. Every night, right before she went to bed, his grandmother would light the three candles that stood guard behind the photo of her husband. Every morning, she would blow them out. Orrin figured it was her way of enjoying his grandfather's presence in the bedroom, since it had been several years since he passed away.

His grandfather was a painter; not the kind who painted houses, but the kind who captured smiles on canvas. It felt like only yesterday that Orrin would watch his grandfather pack his brushes and paint tubes, his century-old easel and folding chair, and depart for the French Quarter.

"Time to go capture the souls," his grandfather would always say on his way out the door.

Sometimes, late into the night, his grandfather would sit down and duplicate every portrait he had painted that day. He said a little prayer over each, then stored them away. In many ways, Orrin felt his grandfather was more than just a street merchant who peddled art. He was more of a therapist for those who needed advice, a man involved in the transference of joy to those who were depressed. Some also believed he was a healer of the sick people who posed for his canvases.

Only a few had experienced it, and most of them were children, but those that he had affected swore they were healed of their afflictions, so he became a legend. Orrin's grandfather was known from the river to the sea as *Dr. Brushes: the one who healed me.*

Selling smiling faces back to the faces that smiled was how he made his living, until the day a massive stroke left him unable to paint or talk. At first, Dr. Brushes was only a shell of himself, but Orrin was grateful for that shell. Then the stroke returned, demanded all, and took all. Dr. Brushes was loved and remembered by the generations of families he had painted.

To the right of Grandma Ellen's nightstand, cut into the paneled wall, was a closet that was just as wide as her queen-sized bed. Stuffed inside the closet from end to end were his grandparent's clothes, with all his grandfather's shoes perfectly shined underneath, and all the tools of his trade tucked away. In the corner of the room, near the closet, stood Grandma Ellen's long wooden walking cane, which accompanied her when she left the house. Her gait was stable enough to get around the kitchen and hallways unassisted, but when making a significant trek, she used her trusty old cane for balance and support.

Bare walls wrapped the room, with the exception of a stack of prayers, which was tacked behind some dried sweet potato skins. The prayers were little strips of paper, all timeworn like old obituaries. The top of each prayer slip read like the prescription for an illness - providing instruction and purpose.

• *Kwa Wasiwasi* (For Worry)

- *Kwa Hofo* (For Fear)
- *Kwa Ugonjwa* (For Sickness)
- *Kwa Uponyaji* (For Healing)
- *Kwa Ustawi* (For Prosperity)
- *Kwa Upendo* (For Love)
- *Kwa Huduma* (For Providence)
- *Kwa Huzuni* (For Grief)
- *Kwa Uhuru* (For Freedom)
- *Kwa Haki* (For Justice)
- *Kwa Kulipiza Kisasi* (For Revenge)

At the end of her arm, folded in the grip of her fingers, Orrin's grandmother held one of those prayer slips - *Kwa Wasiwasi*.

"Orrin, what are your plans for tomorrow?"

His first thought: *Bridgette ratted to her mother, and her mother called the house.* His second thought: *Cap got cold feet and spilled the beans.* As he searched his reserve bin of possible lies, his grandmother followed up her question with additional detail.

"The reason I ask is that we're heading out at four in the morning to watch the Zulu Parade. I plan to meet up with my sister Beulah on Claiborne and Iberville this year because they say it's still muddy on Orleans from that interstate construction." Then a secondary thought merged into the original reason she had called her grandson. "It's been three years since that developer. What is his name?"

"Robert Moses, Grandma."

"Yeah, that's him. Uprooted all those beautiful oak trees up and down in Treme to build that damn elevated interstate. I told Beulah years ago that we Negros better keep it down on this side of Rampart Street, before the white man realize we're having too much fun. Well, they realized it. Looks like I spoke that into life, didn't I? Didn't I?"

"Grandma, I don't think it's your fault. From the look of it, the choices were to run it through the French Quarters or cut it through the black neighborhood. The blacks will lose that one every time."

Orrin hated the elevated interstate just as much as his grandmother, because it had destroyed the Mardi Gras he once knew for black people. The bend of Claiborne and St. Bernard Avenue, all the way up to the Central Business District, had once been shaded with swollen oak trees, making up a green space area known locally as the Nutra Ground. This green space was wide enough in the middle of Claiborne Avenue to allow the Zulu parade to roll on both sides of the road. Before the city killed the trees, Treme, the oldest black neighborhood in New Orleans, considered by many to be the heart and arteries of the black community, was the ultimate Mardi Gras experience for African American families who camped along the route.

Countless historical homes and jazz funeral processions once made up the backdrop of Treme. This was the place where men dressed in skeleton costumes and grown women dressed as baby dolls walked together in unison with the Social Aid and Pleasure Club. If Harlem was in the South, they would call it Treme. It was an inscrutable place where thousands of rapturous families would meet up every year at the same time as if someone were taking an attendance roll, but no one person was in charge of Mardi Gras. In Treme, they shared everything during Mardi Gras, from good food to cold beer and endless laughter, without a stressful care in the world.

In the air, you could once hear the sounds of Motown mixed in with local legends like Fats Domino, Ernie K. Doe, and Al "Carnival Time" Johnson. Professor Longhair wrote a song about the area in his anthem, "If You Go to New Orleans." This was also the same Treme that Louis Armstrong talked about in an interview during his reign as King of Zulu in 1949. This was Treme.

And just like that - the Mardi Gras Orrin and his family were accustomed to celebrating changed, with very little advance notice to or consent from the black community. The overpass project not only destroyed the greenery, it also displaced about five hundred African American families. Despite the unwelcome concrete overhaul, families continued to meet on Claiborne in the same spot for the Mardi Gras parades, and the overpass was incorporated into the current tradition.

"Well, Grandma, I plan to spend Mardi Gras day with you. But later that -"

"But later what?" she huffed. "I know you're not planning on hanging around Bourbon Street."

"No ma'am, that's not what I'm saying."

"I know you're not. When we leave from down there you and your brother will leave with us. You hear what I say?"

"Yes . . . Grandma, we will leave with you but . . ."

"But . . . what?"

"But we wanted to go to a party at Phyllis's house later that night."

"At Gail's house? They havin' something over there?"

"Yes, ma'am."

"Well I just talked to Gail, and she neva said nothing bout no get together after we done got together all day."

"That's because it's a teenage party. Just a few of us singing and dancing. That's all, Grandma."

There it was - another lie to go with the original lie. For a brief moment, Orrin began to wonder if it was all worth it. For tomorrow to go according to plan would require a miracle - but he also felt he had come too far to turn around now.

"You talked to your momma bout this party?"

"Yes, ma'am."

"What she say?"

"Well, she said she didn't have a problem with us going because we would be right around the corner and that was better than hanging out downtown."

"Well, I don't have a problem with it either - much rather you there than running the streets in dem French Quarters. Anything can happen down there."

It was at this point that Orrin knew another story about a lynching was coming, because she sat up on the bed and started fanning the prayer slip like she was on the front pew of a Baptist church. Her prayer For Worry - *Kwa Wasiwasi.*

"I will never forget, long as I live, how two of Vesta Mae's boys and her nephew got caught down there on Mardi Gras about six years ago. You remember what happened to them, don't you?"

"Yes ma'am," Orrin quickly answered in hopes that the recurring horror story would end there - but it didn't. Grandma Ellen rocked in sorrow as if the horrific incident had just happened yesterday.

"Why they went down there foolin around with them drunk white women? That oldest boy got to *smellin his-self.* No one could tell him nothing - wouldn't listen to Vesta Mae at all. But she did tell them right - but that oldest one head was too damn hard."

Grandma Ellen's mattress became a rocking chair as she fanned her face. The temperature in the room was more fitting for a sweater, but fanning was the way she calmed her nerves. Then, on some days when her nerves were beyond a calming point, she would leave the English-speaking population completely - and drag Orrin along for the ride.

"*Kukaa na yako mwenyewe.*"

"Stay with me?" Orrin guessed.

"NO!" Her eyes scolded him from head to toe and back. "Now say it with me: *Kukaa na yako mwenyewe.*"

"*Kukaa na yako . . . mwenyewe,*" Orrin repeated.

"Yes, *Kukaa na yako mwenyewe:* stay with your own kind. I even warned her oldest boy that morning . . . stay with your own kind. But he didn't listen. No! He didn't listen, and that's how it happened to them. Caught up! Every year those hot lil' white girls come down from Natchez and Jackson wearing those little masks, thinking they can do whatever with whoever, but when it comes to black men and white women - ain't enough masquerade masks in France to cover that up. People saw them kissing and everything with those girls - then the wrong people saw it."

Then came silence.

Then came the squeaking of an old box spring hidden beneath her indented cotton mattress.

Then came the anguish, then came the heartache and the heartbreak, then came the low mumble from years of living in fear of the lynching gangs.

"When they found Vesta Mae's boys, all three of them were cut in half. They tied them to the train tracks right at the end of Canal on the riverfront - near that liberty monument. That's their favorite place, you know - where they like to kill young Negroes who develop a liking for white women. Those devils left them out there three days and dared anyone to move them."

Orrin digested every word as his grandmother struggled to clear the tribulation out of her throat, but she couldn't. The loss of Vesta Mae's boys was a sore that showed no signs of healing, a woe that his grandmother was determined to carry. For the first time, he understood the reason for her possessiveness; his grandmother was connected to Vesta Mae, therefore she shared her grief.

"When the funeral home got Vesta Mae's two boys and her nephew, wasn't much they could do with them but close the casket."

Then came more silence.

Then came the wind that danced between the center blocks, the ones that lifted their shotgun house two feet off the ground.

Then came the fluttering of that prayer slip for worry—Kwa Wasiwasi.

Orrin tried to snap his grandmother out of the memory of what happened to Vesta Mae's sons and nephew. "Grandma, it hurts me too - what happened to Mrs. Vesta Mae's boys and her nephew, but I don't believe all white people are out to kill us. Since the Civil Rights Bill passed, it seems to me that some white people are ready to leave the past in the past. I know what happened to Mrs. Vesta Mae's sons was evil, but all white people are not the same - they don't all think that way. And the ones who do think evil - I forgive them. That's all I'm saying."

"Part of me prays your eyes never see the things I saw with my eyes. I pray your heart never feels the pain my heart has felt. But then the other part of me wants you to see and feel all of it - because it makes you *kulala na jicho moja wazi*."

"Grandma . . . I'm sorry, but I don't understand . . ." His lack of study was obvious.

"The right amount of pain will make you sleep with one eye open. *Kulala na jicho moja wazi*."

"I understand, Grandma, but I am still hoping for a better day. Like Dr. King's Dream."

"And that's why Dr. King called it a *dream* - because when he woke up he was back in Birmingham, back in the real world of hate. That's where we live—in the real world. It is for that reason I need you to study. Did you get your lesson at all today?"

"I did, Grandma." Another lie.

"At some point, the precious gifts of knowledge I'm pouring into your head have to stop sliding out of your ears like honey. Orrin, we're running out of time; your eighteenth birthday is less than two years away. Do you understand?" Her voice returned to the same somber tone she had used to retell the story of Vesta Mae's sons. "Soon I will pass down to you everything that was passed down to me, as your grandfather demanded before he closed his eyes for good. He handpicked you - and it's my job to make sure you're ready."

"I will not let you down. After Mardi Gras, I will get serious. I promise." Orrin walked over to the side of her bed and held her tight. "Can I get you something out of the kitchen before I take my bath?" He kissed the top of her head between her two cornrow braids.

"No. I'm fine. I done put up all the food for tomorrow. Just make sure you and your brother are up early to load everything when Donald gets here. He should be here around four in the morning. You hear me?"

"Yes, ma'am."

Then came silence.

Then came squeaking.

Then came more fanning and mumbling.

"Goodnight, Grandma." Orrin turned to leave his grand-mother's candlelit bedroom, but there was no reply.

Kwa Wasiwasi.

CHAPTER 17

Mardi Gras
February 27, 1968

T he only hiccup of the day was that Uncle Donald over-
slept and missed Grandma Ellen's four a.m. load-up
time. This worked in Orrin's favor because for most of
the morning, his grandmother was busy fussing at his uncle. She
never mentioned a word to Teresa about their conversation the
night before. So far, his plan was going according to plan.

It wouldn't have mattered if there had been an approaching
hurricane; Grandma Ellen would rather die than miss her favorite part of Carnival in New Orleans - the Mardi Gras Indians.
The title of the group was misleading; the Mardi Gras Indians
were not actually Native American tribes who joined in the festivities. Rather, they were African American families who cos-
tumed on Mardi Gras morning to pay tribute to the indigenous
tribes that once hid runaway slaves.

Having a front-row seat in Treme to see the beautiful multicolored tributes was of the utmost urgency on Mardi Gras morning, but they did not make it until seven-thirty, which was the

latest Grandma Ellen had ever arrived on Claiborne Avenue.

"Something told me to call around there and make sure you got up! We damn near missed everything!" Orrin's grandmother tore into his uncle.

"Ma, we haven't missed a thing. Will you please calm down before you give yourself a heart attack?" Donald pleaded with his mother.

"What's gonna give me a heart attack is I can't get none of you to do what I ask you to do. If I could drive myself, we would have been out here hours ago. Got-damn-it!" she yelled at the back of his head as they approached the agreed-upon location. Once Donald parked the car, he, Orrin, and Cap began unloading the food. With Orrin's help, Grandma Ellen stepped out of the car, took hold of her walking cane, and began to amble toward their viewing spot, still huffing and fussing as her cane propelled her forward.

Tat.

Tat.

Tat.

Tat.

Tat.

Even once she joined her sister Beulah, Vesta Mae, and her sister Florence Collins, Grandma Ellen continued to fuss. Even though it was clear that they had made it in time to see the Mardi Gras Indians and the King of Zulu, Orrin's grandmother pressed on his uncle like a hot steam iron.

In fact, her rage against his uncle only subsided when it was time for the Krewe of Zulu to pass by; only then did the sun begin to smile. Then the parade took a brief pause in the front viewing area where Grandma Ellen sat, and one of the members tossed a decorative coconut toward all four ladies. With a gold and black coconut in one hand and a can of Dixie beer in the other, Orrin watched as Grandma Ellen's mood lifted with the morning sunshine. For the rest of the day, his grandmother enjoyed her Mardi Gras. For Orrin, it was good to see her enjoying life - even if it was only one day out of the year.

While she was engulfed in a conversation with Vesta Mae, Beulah, and Florence about why his mom couldn't attend Mardi Gras because she took that horrible job in housekeeping, Orrin took the window of opportunity to inform her he was headed back to Louisa Street to get ready for the dance party.

A simple kiss on the cheek was all that was required to slip away into the crowds of parade-goers. Orrin and his brother migrated from the all-black carnival on Claiborne Avenue across the segregation line - Rampart Street. Then, they traveled up St. Charles all the way to Napoleon Avenue. Once they reached the starting point of the parade, Orrin noticed that they had arrived an hour earlier than Pananie had requested. It had been the only way to keep the timeline of his lie in order.

Shortly afterward, Pananie and Martin arrived with their torches, which Orrin and Cap had handed Martin earlier that morning - a seamless handoff. That part of the plan also worked to perfection. Within the hour, as the sun disappeared for the day, the rest of the flambeaux members arrived with their torches, wearing smiles that appeared rehearsed. It was then that Pananie assigned Orrin and Martin to march behind the Captain's float. His brother and flambeaux veteran Willie Love were assigned to the rear.

Pananie and Martin's father's roles were to trail the parade in his truck filled with kerosene refills, refreshments, and a chamber pot should any of the carriers face a sudden need. In cases of emergencies, the carriers were instructed to pass the word back to Pananie from the front to the rear of each float, and he would make his way up within ten minutes at the most.

As Orrin stood in between the floats waiting for the parade to roll, his eyes panned through the hectic scene around him. Several members of the krewe were running late and scrambled to their float with bags of throws and food. In front of each float were black guys who either drove the tractors or guided the mules, in cases of the smaller floats. All were seasoned professionals of several Mardi Gras parades, and all were unphased by the chaos around them.

For an additional thirty minutes, the krewe members scrambled about until they heard the sounding of a bell coming from the float behind him. The Captain was ready to roll, with or without the members who were tardy.

After the sounding of the bell, Pananie and Martin's father made a pass by each section and ordered the flambeaux carriers to light their torches. Following Martin's lead, Orrin immediately lit his torch. The base of the pole was cold to the touch, mirroring the evening air, but above his head, where the flames crackled in their four canisters, the air quickly began to warm.

As soon as his torch was ablaze, Orrin noticed a fragile-looking elderly lady just on the other side of the barricade. She tried desperately to get his attention - and it worked. She greeted him with a smile that was as bright as the burners on his torch and invited him with a wave over to where she stood. Orrin accepted her invitation. The elderly lady was assisted in standing by a much younger woman, who gleamed with the same gracious smile and warm eyes.

"This is our favorite place to be on Mardi Gras night. My mother would bring me to this spot every year, and now I am bringing her," the younger woman yelled over the tractor-trailer motors and disorganized krewe members. "It has become our family tradition to stand at the start of the parade and be the first to thank the men who carry the flambeaux torches. Here is a little token of our appreciation." The woman's elderly mother placed ten dollars into Orrin's hand.

"My husband is Captain this year, and my sons are riding on float number four, so today is pretty special," the daughter said as she held open a string of gold commemorative beads with a Krewe of Ares 1968 doubloon medallion attached. The doubloon sparkled in the slightest amount of light. As she held the beads open with both hands, Orrin slowly lassoed his head inside.

He stared at the doubloon in awe; it was unlike any of the plastic beads normally tossed into the crowds - this was collector's item for sure. Slowly, his head raised. "Thank you. Thank you so much, ma'am . . . and Happy Mardi Gras!"

"Before you leave, can I please take a picture of you as you twirl your flambeau? I plan to capture every precious moment of my husband's first ride as Captain."

Orrin agreed. After the photo was taken, the elderly woman turned to Orrin. "Happy Mardi Gras to you, too," she said with praying hands in front of her lips.

With pep in his step, Orrin strutted back into formation, fanning his face with the new ten-dollar bill and brandishing his new piece of jewelry. Martin jokingly held out his hand - only to have Orrin dap him off.

"You have to be the luckiest guy in the world!" Martin yelled over the noise from the tractor. "Stuff like that always happens to you!"

"If this keeps up, I will have all the money I need before we make it to Canal Street."

"No more small talk with the parade folk - remember what Pananie and Willie Love said," Martin advised.

Orrin wrote off Martin's advice as mere jealousy because he had collected ten dollars before the parade rolled ten feet. It was no secret that the two competed at everything - including girls. Martin was first to like Bridgette and had tried for years to get her attention, but she ignored every attempt he made to date her - only to have Orrin steal her heart by singing one song. Her favorite song.

He hates that I have money and he don't, Orrin thought to himself as he walked back to his side of the float.

Horns began to blare on the tractors, and the Krewe of Ares slowly moved down St. Charles en route to the French Quarter. It didn't take Orrin long to realize that everything Willie Love had described was true; the crowds showered him with hands full of quarters, dimes, nickels, and pennies. On each block, Orrin estimated that he was collecting anywhere from one dollar to three-fifty, and he was elated. So was his brother, who was in a state of constant coin collecting every time Orrin managed to catch a glimpse of him.

Orrin and Martin twirled their torches and danced down St. Charles so intensely that Orrin hardly noticed they were less than a block away from the largest crowd of the night - the parade goers who waited on Canal Street.

As he collected coins, Orrin reflected on how wrong his grandmother was about night parades, and certainly how wrong she was about the people who greeted him along the route. The more he smiled at them, the more they returned his smile with coins; on occasion, a dollar or two. Martin fared just as well.

As the Krewe of Ares turned right off St. Charles and onto Canal Street, Orrin became overwhelmed by the roar of the waiting crowds. In some cases, the people appeared seven rows deep, but huge crowds didn't equate to more coins.

Though the number of smiles was about the same, the parade goers downtown were more appreciative and approachable than the groups they had encountered on Napoleon Avenue. Gone were the crowds who loved the tradition and pageantry - both qualities were lost on crowds on Canal Street. It didn't take Orrin long to realize that this group appeared more concerned about receiving than giving. Many of them hardly noticed Orrin at all as he twirled his torch, wanting no part of the dripping tar.

After slowly traveling a few blocks on Canal Street towards the Mississippi River, the parade made a U-turn and proceeded up for several more blocks. Orrin noticed a few black parade goers sprinkled into the crowd, but often toward the back. The only angry stares he encountered didn't come from the people that his grandmother had warned him about - they came from two black men dressed in business attire. Their eyes said things that were cruel, hurtful, and unforgiving. One appeared to take a few notes as Orrin twirled past him, while the other aimed his camera directly for Orrin's face.

Orrin tried to avoid the flash, but it was too late - he knew he was going to be featured on the cover of a magazine like *The Lousiana Weekly, Ebony*, or even worse, *The Jet*. His grandmother loved *The Jet* and always picked up a copy on her frequent trips to the meat market.

Panic and anxiety rushed up his body like a bottle rocket. Thoughts of his grandmother seeing that photo dominated his mind to the point that he didn't notice the parade was no longer traveling down Canal Street. It had made a hard right into the French Quarter.

Everything in the tiny French Quarter was smaller, tighter, and far less friendly than on Canal Street. It was then that Martin instructed Orrin not to twirl his torch, but to lean it in front of him. After about two blocks, the parade came to one of the few stops of the night - a complete halt known as a Parade Rest. Orrin calculated that he had collected less than a dollar from the moment the parade turned onto Canal, and nothing since they veered off. Not only that, the family atmosphere had dissipated completely, leaving a row of compressed drunks and agitated tourists.

Orrin turned to get a visual of his brother, who appeared locked into conversation with Willie Love. He wondered how much Cap had earned, and hoped he'd fared better on Canal Street, but he was doubtful. The good news was his belt now struggled to hold his pants, which could only mean he was well above his hundred-dollar goal. Martin was confident of the same. The only problem now was, there was no sign of the parade moving, and with each minute that ticked away, his legs grew heavier and heavier.

On the float behind him, Orrin saw several men huddled around the gentlemen who rode on the Captain's float. From that conversation, Orrin overheard that the tractor that pulled the King's float had overheated and stalled, but they were hitching an alternate tractor and the parade would roll again in about ten minutes.

"The night was almost perfect! Next year I want all new tractors - our own tractors - no more of these farm vehicles! It ends this year!" an irate Krewe Captain screamed at several krewe members. The same krewe members worked with great haste to get the parade moving again.

Following Martin's lead, Orrin begin to stomp on the flickering patches of tar that lit the ground in front of him with the heels of his sneakers. His torch was nearing the end of its kerosene supply, which was perfectly fine because after forty-five minutes of Parade Rest, his adrenaline was depleted and replaced with fatigue.

After his second yawn of the night, which came a little past nine p.m., Orrin noticed two couples parallel to his left shoulder. They all appeared to be in their twenties. The two girls shared a cigarette while their boyfriends faced each other in conversation as they sipped beer out of long-necked Budweiser bottles. Suddenly, one of the girls tried to get Orrin's attention.

"Did you have to carry that thing this entire parade?" one of the girls asked. She wore burnt orange-colored pants, a pinstripe orange and white jacket, and a *Gidget* smile. Her dark black hair was pinned on top with a burnt orange ribbon, which sat in front of her bun.

The blonde hair girl next her wore a dark brown suede skirt that stopped right above her knees, matching knee-high suede boots, and *I Dream of Jeannie* eyes.

"Oh, it's not that heavy," Orrin replied. Martin tried to get his attention by banging his flambeau pole on the ground three times, but Orrin never noticed.

"Well, it looks mighty heavy, but I'm sure a big boy like you can carry that thing with no problem," the girl in the suede skirt said.

"Hey Orrin, come see this," Martin called.

Once Orrin made his way over to the other side of the float, he noticed that Martin appeared very concerned.

"What up, bro?" Orrin asked as he extinguished the tar droplets with the heel of his shoe.

"What did those girls ask you?"

"She asked if I had to carry this torch the entire time, I told her yes."

"Don't talk to them. Okay?!"

". . . Okay . . . but they seem pretty friendly. Just shooting the breeze while we wait for the parade to roll."

"Orrin, just don't talk to them."

"Okay, okay . . . bossman," Orrin replied in a facetious tone as he back-paced to his side of the float. As soon as he made it back, the questions started again.

"Geeeeeee-whiz you're tall. I bet you play basketball?" the girl in orange asked.

"No, he looks more like that singer . . . what is his name? Gosh . . . you know . . . the song we listened to in the car earlier today?"

"Sam Cooke . . . 'Cupid'!" the girl in orange yelled.

"Yes, that's it, you look just like Sam Cooke. I bet you can sing, too," the girl in the mini-skirt implored, but Orrin didn't reply.

"Wow, he does favor Sam Cooke, he does. Do you know that song?" the girl with the *Gidget* smile asked.

Orrin couldn't resist nodding his head.

"Could you sing a little of it for us? It's not like this parade is moving anytime soon. Please?" orange pants asked.

It was then that Martin banged his flambeau on the ground six times. Once Orrin looked in his direction, Martin placed a finger over his lip like a kindergarten teacher leading a class to the library. Orrin shot him a look back.

I am not talking to them!

Suddenly, without notice, one of the boyfriends pushed his way in front of the two girls. He wore a maroon-colored letter-man jacket with a large, white, commercial-carpet C stitched on the upper left side. The C was short for Chalmette High School, located in Chalmette Louisiana - the place his grandmother had warned him about during her many rants at the kitchen table.

CHAPTER 18

The guy in the letterman jacket asked. "Nigger boy, what did you say to my girl?"Orrin didn't reply. "Nigger, are you hard of hearing?" he yelled again. The girl in the orange tried to turn his head to face her, but he shoved her hand away from his face.

Martin stepped in front of Orrin. "Sir, he didn't say a word. Not one word. Please pardon us, and we will be out of your way."

"Nigger, don't you *Sir* me - I heard him say something to my girl and I want him to say it to me."

"He didn't get out of the way with me - I simply asked him about the torch, that's all," the girl in the orange pants explained.

"That's not all I heard. I could have sworn I heard this nigger boy say he likes white women!"

"He didn't say that - I swear he didn't. Now if you just let us be, we will be on our way," Martin tried to calm the situation.

The second guy also caught Martin's attention; the one who wore the black leather jacket and blue jeans. Martin watched as he whispered in the ear of the irate boyfriend, and just like that, he instantly calmed down. Moments later, the two couples backed away from their float and began to walk along the side-walk, then headed down St. Phillips Street. It took less than a minute for Martin to lose the two couples in the crowd up ahead. They vanished, and not a minute too soon - the entire ordeal had left Orrin visibly shaken.

"*I told you not to talk to them!*" Martin yelled out of the corner of his mouth.

"I didn't . . . it was those two who asked me a million questions, but I never said a word."

"Well, I am glad that's over. It looks like this parade is finally starting to move again."

Martin was correct - the parade had started to move again after the alternate tractor was hitched to the King's float. Above his shoulder, Martin could tell the Captain was thrilled once again, because a huge smile returned to his face as he waved to the crowd of drunks.

It was 9:35 p.m. and Martin's feet cried out for freedom. His flambeau flames appeared as birthday candles after a wish. He wanted out of the parade, and the last six hours were the longest he'd gone without talking to Phyllis. Annoyingly, two of the four canisters on Orrin's flambeaux were still crackling in the night as the Krewe of Ares approached the intersection with St. Phillips Street. Then suddenly, the parade came to another halt.

"What in the hell is going on up there?" The Captain yelled out to his tractor driver. "Otis!"

"Yes, boss?"

"Run up there and find out what's going on! We should have already made it to Esplanade by now!"

"Oz headed up there now, boss." Otis leaped off his tractor and ran as fast as he could to the stalled tractor.

The pole of Martin's flambeau became a pillow as he rested, making sure to keep Orrin in his sight at all times. Not only did his feet have the blues, but intense muscle spasms pounded on his lower back like a bass drum. Martin wanted out of the parade - Mardi Gras 1968 was over as far as he was concerned - but they still had four more blocks to go before they reached the end.

There he stood in the center of the intersection on a street that was far too narrow for a parade, in an abnormal neighborhood that was unimpressed and imposed upon . . . but hope was running in his direction. Up ahead, Martin spotted the driver of the

Captain's float making his way back with an update. No sooner did he explain the reason for the delay did Martin notice the King's float pulling off - followed by the Queen's float. The Captain's float was next in line.

"Martin, pick up your flambeau!" Orrin called out to him, but his back refused to straighten. With the ounce of strength left in his body, Martin lifted his flambeau and slugged his body forward. Suddenly, out of the corner of his eye, he saw the two guys from the recent argument running toward them on St. Phillips Street carrying a red metal can.

"Don't do it, son!" Martin heard the Captain call out.

"Oh lawd!" Otis yelled.

Orrin look out!

Is what Martin tried to say, but the words didn't come out in time. The guy who wore the maroon letterman jacket doused Orrin's flambeau with something volatile, causing a curtain of fire to wrap his body from head to toe. The gasoline converted the controlled flame into a raging inferno. It was the gas caused that caused Orrin to scream in agony. He fought the fire but missed on every punch. Before Martin could react, Orrin was down on his knees.

Martin dropped his torch and ran over to help Orrin, who was now engulfed, but there was little he could do other than pat at his friend's head and face.

"Somebody please! Help! Water - we need water!" Martin cried out as Otis slammed the brakes with such force it ejected the Captain into the crowd.

As Otis looked around for help, Martin, Cap, and Willie Love arrived in a sprinter's haste. They all removed their jackets and tried their best to smother the flames, but as soon as they extinguished one section of Orrin's body and diverted the flames from his face, the fire re-ignited around his legs. Once they extinguished his legs, it burned again in his face. The fire burned through his brother's jacket and shirt, leaving Cap with only bare hands and arms to smother the fire.

For nearly five minutes, Orrin burned.

Inaudibly screaming at first.

Then silently.

Then came the loud screams. Not from Orrin, but from Cap. Screams that rushed through Martin's soul like a tsunami through a broken dam. Screams that could only come from someone connected by blood, birth, and bosom.

"My brother! My brother!"

Were the only two words they heard, but they were a sufficient enough pair to convey the totality of his loss. In a frantic search for water, Willie Love knocked on each door that sat on the corner of St. Phillips Street, but no one answered.

Martin wrapped his arms around Cap, who continued to kneel over his brother's simmering body. Ignoring his own burnt arms and hands, he tried as best as he could to hold Orrin's lifeless body. Minutes later, the crowd parted as the police finally arrived with four EMS workers. Two rushed to Orrin's side while two tended to his brother, but Cap was more concerned about Orrin.

"My brother - they killed my brother! THEY KILLED MY BROTHER!" Cap screamed at the crowd in rage and sorrow. He charged all who looked upon his brother's body as an accessory, because no one had offered to help but the driver, Martin, and Willie.

By this point, the guys who had poured the gas and the two ladies who had asked the questions where nowhere to be found - but the red can once filled with gas remained.

"Young man, what is your name?" asked an officer with a pen and a miniature notebook in hand.

"Martin Robichaux."

"And what did you see?" the police officer asked.

Still suffering from shock, Martin gathered just enough composure to answer the officer's question as the EMS worker placed Orrin and his brother in the back of the ambulance. Martin attempted to climb in the back of the ambulance with the lead singer of the NOLA Hearts, but the officer held him by the arm. "Where are they taking them?"

"Charity Hospital." The Officer replied.

"I have to go with them - please let me go," Martin pleaded.

"As soon as we're done I promise to get you to Charity if you don't have a ride, but you appear to be the primary witness to this entire incident," the officer told him as the ambulance raced away.

CHAPTER 19

It was then that the entire attack pixelated, then spooled into fragmented shudders. It felt like a bad dream where it was up to him to pull a lever that would prevent a collision of two approaching locomotives - if only he had the strength. The torment of watching the two men hurl the ten-gallon gas can through the crowd and lacking the reaction time to warn or save Orrin had already started to take its toll on Martin.

"I will make this fast - what did you see?"

"Sir, we were standing here waiting for the parade to continue when these white guys started harassing us. One of them started accusing my friend of flirting at his wife. I told the guy he wasn't flirting with his wife, but what I had to say didn't matter - he was set on picking a fight. Then they left, and we thought it was over -"

"When you say 'they,' who are you referring to?"

"The two men, and I guess the other two were their girlfriends or their wives, I am not sure. But it was four of them all together."

"And which one poured the gas?"

It was then that the entire attack pixelated, then spooled into fragmented shudders. It felt like a bad dream where it was up to him to pull a lever that would prevent a collision of two approaching locomotives - if only he had the strength. The torment of watching the two men hurl the ten-gallon gas can through the crowd and lacking the reaction time to warn or save Orrin had already started to take its toll on Martin.

"Both men carried the can. The guy in the black leather jacket helped the man in the maroon jacket lift it high in the air, but it was the one in the maroon jacket who doused Orrin . . ."

It was then, as Martin treaded through a rip-current of contrition, that the captain of float number three walked over and introduced himself.

"Officer, I am the Captain of the Krewe of Ares," he said in a tone of authority that was laced with an air of possessiveness.

"Did you see what happened?"

"Officer . . . before I answer that, I just wanted to let you know that I have sent for the attorney for the Krewe of Ares. He is riding on the last float and will make his way up here shortly to give an official statement."

"But if you witnessed the entire incident, why not simply give me your account of what happened?"

"Because it is our policy that any and all public statements regarding incidents of this nature must have approval from our attorney first."

"And what is his name?"

"Attorney Morris Igelhart, he's about thirty floats back so if you don't mind?"

"The sooner I can get a statement, the sooner we can piece this thing together, but if you say your attorney is on his way, then I guess I will interview a few other witnesses. Like the driver of your tractor. What is his name?"

"Who me? My name is O -"

Before Otis could answer, the Captain cut him off with a wave. "This is my driver and he has worked for this krewe for well over twenty years - our attorney will also have to approve his statement."

"Your attorney . . . this Morris Igelhart guy has to approve his statement as well?"

"Yes, Officer, he'll be here any minute and we will gladly answer any questions you may have."

Martin watched as the police officer shuffled through the crowd of parade-goers seeking eye witness statements, but most of the people who were there at the time of the attack had long since migrated back to Bourbon Street.

To Martin's disappointment, the NOPD Officer lacked the thoroughness of Joe Friday, one of his favorite characters on *Dragnet*. Over the past four seasons of *Dragnet* and all of the syndicated re-runs that followed, Martin had developed an intermediate knowledge of how police investigations were supposed to go. He knew the officer was not only botching the investigation, but barely had enough information to send out a BOLO (Be On the Look-Out).

The NOPD officer just happened to be first on the scene because the incident had taken place in his zone along the route. Martin also noticed that the officer appeared no older than the guy in the maroon letterman jacket - only days out of the police academy, with a stench of conceited cockiness that was difficult to stomach.

"Sir, the guys who attacked my friend ran down St. Phillips toward Rampart. There is a chance you could catch them if . . ."

The officer cut him off. "We have units searching for them now."

"But I haven't given a complete description of the two women who are with them."

"Boy, I am asking the questions here! Do you understand?" he growled.

"Yes, sir." Martin walked over to where he had dropped his flambeau and stood next to Willie Love as if they were waiting for the parade to resume.

"I told all of dem boys not to talk to white woman, I said it over and over. Why didn't he listen to me? This would have never happened!" Willie agonized.

"Willie, he didn't talk to them - they were talking to him . . ."

"Young blood, that is the same as talking to them. When they ask you something you have to walk away. I know I said it. I know I did," Willie repeated in the way a person does when they can't find their car keys and someone asks if they've searched in the most obvious of places.

Moments later, a local news reporter from WDSU and his cameraman arrived on scene. Shortly after that, Martin watched the Captain do an about-face once he heard the voice of his attorney calling out to him from the rear of his float.

Morris Igelhart approached accompanied by five other men. As soon as they reached the Captain, they called a huddle. After five minutes of what appeared to be a debriefing, Martin noticed the Captain shaking his head left to right in complete defiance to the attorney, but in the time it took a scoop of ice vanilla ice cream to melt in July, his defiance turned into compliance. Attorney Igelhart stepped forward to give a statement first as the Krewe Captain stood behind him with his eyes focused on the ground.

That's when Martin's attention shifted from the huddle in the rear of the float to the rapid approach of two men he needed now more than ever. From nearly a block away, Pananie and his father raced towards him at an aerobic pace. Fret and distress enveloped their faces.

They arrived winded, panting in urgency. It was then that Martin broke the tragic news as best he could, and allowed Willie to fill in the details during his interludes of grief and dejection.

Once the officer had gathered the statements from the Krewe of Ares, he moseyed back over to Martin. "Now, you say your name is Martin Robichaux . . . correct?"

"Yes-yes, s-sir." Martin replied.

"Now, which one of you is homeless?" he asked.

Martin's father interjected. "Homeless? None of these boys are homeless."

"And you, what's your name?"

"I am Gary Robichaux, and this is my son. I am one of the leaders of the flambeaux carriers."

The officer made an entry in is notebook, then shifted back to Martin. "Earlier you mentioned that the argument started because your friend flirted with the man's wife?"

"No, that's not what I said." Martin cleared his throat and took a step closer to the officer. "I said the man accused Orrin of flirting with his wife. They left and came back with a can of gas

- and poured the gas on his torch, face, and legs. Before I could make it to him, before I could, could . . ."

With both arms around Martin "take your time son."

Martin took several deep breaths. "Orrin was spinning in pain. He tried to cover his face, but . . . but . . ." Martin collapsed in his father's arms.

"Sir, this was a calculated attack," Mr. Robichaux said. "How were they able to retrieve that much gasoline in the French Quarters?" he asked as he pointed at the gas can.

"That gas can has to have their fingerprints on it," Martin suggested.

"I am aware that the can is evidence - don't tell me how to do my job!"

"Officer, we're not trying to tell you how to do your job, but my son has provided you with enough information to leave now and track down these people."

"And we plan to do just that."

"Well, if you're done then we need to get to the hospital in a hurry," Pananie requested.

"You're free to go. If I have any additional questions, I will pass by the hospital or call you."

Before the officer could finish his sentence, they all departed as if sucked into a vacuum tube. They raced back to Pananie's truck, then onto Charity hospital to check on Cap and perhaps see Orrin for the last time.

CHAPTER 20

10:05 p.m.

G randma Ellen beached across her bed; her head rested on the cushion of her arm. In between periodic smiles, she dozed off to sleep, only to reflect on the day and smile before dozing off again. Today was a good day. The morning had started earlier than most. The day was long, but tonight marked the end of a successful Mardi Gras, so the fatigue was well worth it.

Did I leave the TV on?

I need to get up and take my bath.

Did I put all of that food in the refrigerator?

I wonder if Bridgette is pregnant? Her hips seem wide.

One thought after the other whaled in her mind, but her body was done for the day, and all of it would have to wait until tomorrow. Then, one of her questions was answered when she heard the intro music for the ten o'clock news airing in her living room. Moments after that, she heard the sound of someone moving around in the kitchen.

"Orrin? Cap? Is that you?"

"No Momma, it's me," Teresa replied.

"How long you been here?"

"I just walked through the door about ten minutes ago."

"The boys made it in yet?"

"No, but once I fix my plate, I will call around there by Gail and ask her to send them home."

"Go on and eat your food. She has two of my good pots, and I need her to send them with the boys. Gail will keep your stuff unless you borrow it back." Grandma Ellen was exhausted, but she needed to call Gail and ask her to return her grandsons and her good pots.

On the other side of the dividing wall, she could her Teresa relocating her dinner to the living room, where she could enjoy her meal and the evening news.

With a series of painful grunts and several deep breaths, Grandma Ellen managed to sit upright. She slid into her slippers and swayed her way into the kitchen. In the kitchen, the phone was mounted on the wall next to the refrigerator. It had a coil cord that could stretch eight feet, which allowed her to sit at the table and talk. She dialed. After the fifth ring, a low, raspy voice answered.

"Hel . . . lo"

"Gail?"

"Yes, this Gail. Who this?"

"Gail, this Ellen, when your party is over do you mind sending my pots with the boys? Please tell them their mother said it's time to come on home."

"Ellen, I can send the pots in the morning, but there's no party over here. I was sleep."

"Excuse me?"

"We did all the partying we needed to do this morning. Everybody in here sleep 'cept Phyllis."

"Gail, I know I'm hard of hearing, but did you just say there's no party over at your place?"

"I promise there's no party over here."

Grandma Ellen felt her blood pressure spike like sliced bread popping out the toaster. Her body felt like someone had connected her to a helium tank.

"Well . . . Orrin told me you were having a party tonight."

"No party over here, but I overheard Phyllis and Martin talking about a parade or something. You know they talk under their breath like no one can hear them, but I don't miss a thing."

"Well, I be! Is Phyllis in the house?"

"In the house? Phyllis don't play with me. I hear her in the den fiddling around. I'll ask her if she knows they whereabouts. Hold on, Ellen . . ."

As Grandma Ellen sat on hold, she could hear Gail call out to Phyllis in the den and ask her if she knew where the boys were. After a brief back and forth, Gail returned to the phone.

"She said something about they were in a parade tonight."

"A parade? Did she say going to a parade, or in a parade?"

"Hold on, let me ask."

Gail placed her on hold again to confirm, but Grandma Ellen knew. Orrin had lied to her, and she knew it - she'd felt it three days ago but was too busy cooking to address him. Carnival season marked - and still marks - the beginning of a series of local celebrations, and the demand for her food was non-stop until after Mothers' Day. So, she'd ignored that soft voice in her spirit which told her to address Orrin.

"She said in a parade. You may want to call over there to the Gary Robichaux house, because sounds like they all together."

"I'm bout to do that right now . . . thank you and sorry to call so late."

"Ellen, you ain't neva no bother to me. We're all raising teens, and you know like I know, they will look you in the face and tell a bald-mouth lie before the spoon hit the floor."

"Gail, you ain't never lying!"

"I will walk the pots round there myself first thing in the morning. Okay?" Gail yawned.

"That's just fine with me, and if Phyllis hears anything, please have her call us."

"I sure will, bye bye."

In one single motion, Grandma Ellen ended the call with Gail and immediately dialed across the street to the home of Gary and Sandra Robichaux. As the phone rung, she yelled out to the living room. "TERESA! Did you give the boys permission to march in a parade tonight?"

"What?" Teresa replied.

Before Grandma Ella could respond, a woman answered the phone. It was Sandra in the key of C - for crisis.

"HELLO, HELLO!"

"Sandra, this Ellen, do you know the whereabouts of my boys?" Before Sandra could answer, "Because I just spoke with Gail and she said they're with Martin at the parade." Before Sandra could respond, "Is that true?"

"Ellen, I just hung up with my husband. He called from Charity, and there has been a terrible accident. I'm on my way to you."

CLICK.

DIAL TONE.

She had to get to her daughter to prepare her for the hospital before Sandra barged through the front door, but her legs were no more stable than two links of sausage. By the time Grandma Ellen hoisted herself from the kitchen table and placed the phone on the receiver, she heard Sandra opening the front door. Seconds later, Grandma Ellen heard the sound of a dinner tray and dishes crashing to the floor, followed by a dreadful squall.

"Oh, Lawwwd! No! No! Mommma! Momma! Momma!" Teresa screamed "That can't be my babies! That can't be!"

With one hand on the wall, Grandma Ellen braced her way down the hall - directly to the source of the anguish. At a pace faster than she was accustomed to moving, she arrived in the living room, where broken dishes littered the floor. Then came the voice of a news reporter.

Yes, parade-goers who lined the streets of the French Quarters to see the King and Queen of the Krewe of Ares described an horrific scene tonight.

Sandra wrapped her arms around Teresa and locked her fingers while they stared down at the RCA floor model television.

New Orleans Police Department has confirmed that two flambeaux carriers were injured something awful after a malfunction with a flambeau torch. The two flambeaux carriers were identified as Orrin Toussaint and his brother, Earl Toussaint.

Suddenly the screaming ceased - the only sound was a deep *thump* followed by shorter *thumps* as Teresa's lifeless body slid through Sandra's arms and hit the wooden floor.

"Help me get her over to the sofa," Grandma Ellen called to Sandra.

With much effort, they lifted Teresa off the floor and stretchered her on the sofa. They worked to revive her, which proved unsuccessful at first, but slowly, she churned back to consciousness. Over their shoulders came the voice of the reporter as he continued his coverage.

I am also joined by two officials for the Krewe of Ares: Attorney Morris Igelhart and the Krewe Captain, Jack McGowan. They have issued the following statement:

The reporter then placed the microphone below the chin of Jack McGowan, who appeared lethargic as the words oozed into the microphone.

From time to time we get these . . . these little Negro boys who slip into our parades, and normally we don't mind them because they entertain the crowds with their lanterns. And though they beg for coins, they have never been a problem until now.

Grandma Ellen watched in rage as Jack McGowan searched for his words - coached on by his attorney, who whispered in his ear.

Tonight, there appears to have been an accident involving two homeless kids who accidentally set themselves a fire. Though it is a tragedy and our prayers are with the family, the Krewe of Ares is in no way responsible for the accident that has occurred, nor did the victims, Orrin and Earl Toussaint, have permission to march in our parade this evening.

Moments later, the reporter signed off from his coverage, and the anchorman transitioned the evening news to other sights and sounds from Mardi Gras morning. Around that same time, Teresa was revived in a full panic.

"My babies! I have to get to the hospital now!" Still in her housekeeping uniform, Teresa hurried to the kitchen and returned with her coat and purse.

As Sandra and Donald helped Teresa into the back seat of his vehicle, Grandma Ellen stoically walked to her room and opened a nightstand drawer on her husband's side of the bed. Inside the drawer was a red candle wrapped in a dingy sheet of sackcloth and tightly tied with an old piece of rope. After removing the wrapping, she lit the red candle and place it in front of the photo of her late husband.

Grandma Ellen turned from the photo of her husband. From the closet, she pulled her coat off the hanger and grabbed her purse. It was then that her son leaned halfway into her bedroom.

"Hurry, Momma! We're waiting for you. We have to get to the hospital."

"I'll be right behind you, son," Grandma Ellen said as she walked around the room to the adjacent wall that held her batch of prayer slips. Once there, she folded two slips in her hand.

• *Kwa Uponyaji* (For Healing)
• *Kwa Kulipiza kisasi* (For Revenge)

Uncle Donald quickly arrived at the emergency entrance of Charity Hospital. Grandma Ellen wasn't surprised to see that there were no news reporters seeking the truth, nor did she see one NOPD detective. On the way to the hospital, Sandra shared everything her husband and Martin had told her. Grandma Ellen knew the truth.

From the ER waiting room, they made their way to the burn unit, where Grandma Ellen spotted Willie Love and Gary trying to console Pananie. On either side of him, they held him up. It was then that Teresa bolted down the hall in a sprint.

"I'm so sorry - I'm so sorry!" Pananie cried as Teresa ran by him, "I thought they had permission from you!" Teresa ran past him and entered the room.

Grandma Ellen watched as her daughter frantically entered the burn unit room. Then she looked across the hall to the nurses' station. It was at the nurses' station that she found the attending physician. Realizing she had left her cane standing in the corner of her bedroom, she called for Donald. With the assistance of Donald on one arm and Sandra on the other, Grandma Ellen made it to the burn unit room to find only one bed. In the lone bed was Earl Touissant, who everyone called Cap.

Earl lay bandaged on both arms up to his shoulders, and across his chest. The bandages wrapped around his neck and face gave his grandmother a clear indication of the intensity of the fire. At the foot of his bed, face-down on the mattress, was Martin. He never lifted his head as he wept.

From the nurses' station, Grandma heard several bellowing squeals, all the same in length and equally dreadful. Horrifying and distressful sounds she hadn't heard since she'd accompanied Vesta Mae to identify her two boys who were tied down to the train tracks.

Needing no assistance this time, Grandma Ellen pulled her daughter out of the arms of Willie Love and walked her back into the room that was designated for bad news. Orrin Toussaint, the lead singer of the NOLA Hearts, was pronounced dead at

11:15 that night.
   The cause of death?
   Accident.
   Status of NOPD Investigation?
   Case Closed.

CHAPTER 21

It was around midnight when Gary and Sandra decided it was time to leave. The only problem was, Martin refused leave Earl. With each attempt to escort him out of the room, Martin held tighter onto the bed rails.

Martin didn't budge until Grandma Ellen walked over to him and whispered in his ear: *Show me the exact place where my grandson's soul stepped out of his body.* Only then did Martin release his grip on the rail, and the two walked down the hall.

His father, Pananie, and Willie Love followed them to the truck, while Donald and Sandra elected to remain behind to console an inconsolable Teresa. Due to the nature of Earl's injuries, the doctors predicted a five to nine-day stay. Earl was still in grave danger of septic infection, and tomorrow would be the first of several experimental skin-grafts.But Grandma Ellen had to leave. Immediately. Not because she couldn't handle the sorrow of the situation and needed to escape - not in the least. She needed to see something - to touch something . . . and Martin was the person she needed to take her there.

In the bed of the truck sat Gary and Willie Love. In the front seat sat Martin, his Godmother, and Pananie. Grandma Ellen sat in silence; not even a sniffle, not even a tear. The only sound of weeping came from Pananie and Martin, the hum of the engine, and the roaring thunder from an approaching winter storm.

After a short ten-minute drive back to the French Quarter, Pananie's truck came to a rolling stop.

Martin pointed to mark the spot where Orrin fell.

Willie Love knuckle-tapped the back window.

Pananie folded into the steering wheel.

Gary Robichaux cried into his lap.

It was Willie Love who leaped over the side of the truck bed to open the door for Grandma Ellen. With Martin on one arm and Willie on the other, they ushered her to the exact place where Orrin had collapsed in flames.

And there it was.

A place that was the cause of death, the reason for death, and the explanation of death. A place she had warned about for obvious reasons, all of which her grandson ignored. But she had to touch the place before the rains washed away the evil stain and the morning sun chased away the darkness of those who had murdered Orrin.

Lest they forgot her grandbaby.

Gone were the crowds that lined both sides of the street. Gone were the carnival floats that showered gifts upon anyone who asked. The only bits of evidence from yesterday were the roaming herds of intoxicated tourists and their unquenchable appetites for adult entertainment.

It was then - at her lowest juncture, her weakest breath - that the strength of her ancestors surged through Grandma Ellen's dormant veins and empowered her to relieve her ushers of their duty. For she possessed everything needed to do what was required of one in her position: the Matriarch of the Mahu, the Priestess of the Congregation, the Keeper of the Stones.

The beacon in that hour of cecity was that scorched oval on the cobblestone that mixed with the taunting stench of gas. Both demanded credit for a job well done.

Grandma Ellen stepped out of her shoes. With cold, bare feet, she brushed away the carpet of carnival debris. Amongst the trash, she unearthed the dearest of treasures. A few shreds of Orrin's coat, the collar of his shirt, and the makeshift turban he had worn to protect his head. She buried these pieces of her grandson in her bosom - sealed with a smile of sadness and serenity.

A lily in the desert.

It was here that Grandma Ellen hugged herself as she lowered onto her knees and hummed a tune beneath her breath - a tune that was older than the shadows where she kneeled, a tune that possessed the power to slow the ticking of time. Somewhere around mid-verse, Grandma Ellen proceeded to crawl directly over the place where Orrin's soul had departed, and slowly kissed the ash.

> *Nifunulie mimi.*
> *Nifunulie mimi.*
> *Nifunulie mimi.*
> *Nifunulie mimi.*
> *Nifunulie mimi.*

She mourned to the moon. After about five minutes of silence, her attention shifted to a drainage gutter that was at the edge of the sidewalk, just to the left of where Orrin had fallen. With the urgency of a bride who lost her wedding ring, Grandma Ellen raked through the gutters with the tips of her fingers until it was finally revealed.

Bloody, yet it glistered and glimmered.

Bloody, yet it glittered and gleamed.

Yet bloody.

Nevertheless, she picked up and held the 1968 commemorative doubloon and the gold string of beads up to the heavens as the sky poured tears upon her face. For thirty minutes she kneeled in the downpour with the doubloon high above her head as Pananie, Martin, Willie, and Gary watched in fear through the back window of the truck.

"Ninataka upatanisho! Ninataka upatanisho! Ninataka upatanisho!" She blew to the moon, kissed the doubloon, then fell silent. Then the rain stopped. Then she rose to her feet in all her glory, power, and strength. Grandma Ellen turned to face Martin with the doubloon around her neck. The radiant doubloon that the Captain's wife had gifted to Orrin at the start of the parade, the one that gave him so much joy and expectation . . . Grandma Ellen took sole possession of it. Only then did the four men step out and walk over to the rear of the truck to get a closer look at the relic.

"I have found what I came for and there is only one thing left to do."

"Tonight?" Pananie asked.

"Not tonight, but in thirty moons. Now if you would be so kind as to bring me back to the hospital. My only remaining grandson is in need of healing, and I am a healer." She walked back to the truck and climbed inside without any assistance.

Once everyone was back in the truck and Pananie shifted into drive, Grandma Ellen turned a half-shoulder to the house on the corner and uttered a settled goodbye.

"Not even a cup of water was offered out of any of these homes on Burgundy Street, but as sure as this doubloon is around my neck, so too will I grip the necks of the guilty in due time."

CHAPTER 22

March 28, 1968

E ven in broad daylight, he couldn't escape the nightmares. Somehow his mind always came back to that night, that young man, and that flambeau. Thirty days ago, his integrity had died on Burgundy Street. That night, he had assimilated into something unrecognizable; something bankrupt of character and foreclosed of morals.

In more ways than one, he wanted to go back to that night and make it right - and not submit to the advice of Attorney Morris Igelhart. If only he could return to Mardi Gras night . . .

It had all happened so fast. One minute a young kid was leading his float through the night with his flambeau, and the next minute, he had covered his nose to escape the intolerable stench of burning flesh. Like the nightmares, there was no way of escaping that smell - or the way the kid's brother cried for help - all of which he had observed aboard the Captain's float.

Jack McGowan watched every day as Morris Igelhart took victory laps around their headquarters, overjoyed at the success of his legal strategy - the story was buried with the young man.

As far as Jack McGowan was concerned, there wasn't anything to celebrate, even if the Krewe of Ares had escaped all liability.

Unbeknownst to Morris Igelhart, Jack hid a cutout of Orrin Toussaint's obituary inside his desk, and every day since it was published in the newspaper, he read it at the top of the morning. Every family member that Orrin left behind, Jack McGowan committed their names to memory. Even his girlfriend, Bridgette.

Jack reclined in his champagne-leather executive chair with his legs resting on the corner of his desk. On the other side of his desk was Attorney Morris Igelhart, mouthing one muted word after the other, but all Jack could think about was contacting Teresa Toussaint and telling her the truth about Burgundy and St. Phillips.

He wanted to confess it all. He wanted to tell the world how from his vantage point on the float, he had watched the men pop the trunk of a blue Buick and run through the crowd with a can of gas. Not only did he see it all, but he also heard it all - the entire altercation. He knew Orrin was innocent of everything he was accused of, including setting himself on fire, but it was Igelhart who re-wrote history.

It was also Igelhart who had suggested that the krewe could save money on police detail by reducing the number of officers on Burgundy Street from twelve down to two lone rookies.

If only I hadn't listened to that asshole.

"Jack, I think if we make a move now, we have a shot at convincing the city that we should roll first next Mardi Gras. We have to get that a.m. time slot - that accident last month is just what I need to make my pitch to the city council," Attorney Morris Igelhart said. Jack was a million miles away.

"Hello, Jack McGowan! Hello! Is anybody home?" Attorney Igelhart yelled through his cuffed hands like a megaphone. "You didn't hear a word I said. What's bothering you, bud?"

Jack removed his black wingtip Oxfords from his favorite ottoman and adjusted to the center of his desk. "How do you sleep at night?"

"Pardon me?" Morris removed his glasses.

"I know it's your job and all, but how do you do it?" Jack asked with his head tilted slightly left and his eyes compressed. "How do you represent someone you know is guilty?"

"Well, the way I see it is, my personal opinion as it relates to a client's guilt or innocence is irrelevant, the only thing that -"

Jack cut him off. "When you know deep down that this motherfucker is lying, and he is guilty of everything the District Attorney has charged him with, how do you sleep at night knowing you helped him walk?"

Morris leaned back in his chair as his lips fluttered in exasperation. "Oh, now I know what has your panties in a knot. That Negro kid."

"His name was Orrin Toussaint!" Jack McGowan screamed like a drill sergeant.

"I meant no disrespect, the accident -"

"It wasn't no got-damn accident, Morris -"

"But it had to be!" Morris stood and leaned in. "for the sake of Ares, for the sake of our plans to beat out Rex as the King of Mardi Gras, for your political future . . . it had to be."

Jack stood over his desk and met Morris nose to nose. "They murdered that kid in cold blood. And you helped them get away with it."

"I did no such thing! I protected this organization, I protected you - I did my job!"

"You helped them walk!" Jack accused.

"AND SO DID YOU! YOU ARE JUST AS GUILTY - SO CUT THE SHIT!" Attorney Morris Igelhart yelled, showering Jack in a spit storm.

A reluctant knock on the inner glass of Jack's office door ended the round and sent both fighters back to their corners.

"Yes, Suzanna, what is it?" Jack readjusted his tie.

Suzanna Dauterive was a slender woman a year or so past the age of thirty. She was the daughter of the previous Captain, Danny Dauterive, who the members had grown tired of and voted out. Suzanna was a political concession Igelhart had convinced Jack to sign on in exchange for the votes needed to become Captain. But Jack didn't trust her because he didn't trust her dad. Thanks once again to Igelhart, he was stuck with the outcome.

Jack noticed that Suzanna's normal blonde perkiness was, for some strange reason, replaced by a reddish hue of agitation. As she stood there with half of her body in the door frame and the lower half in the lobby, he quickly figured it out.

"Sir, there's a Negro woman in the lobby, and she's not leaving until she meets with you."

"Oh, really?" Igelhart replied.

"Yes! And I have tried everything to get her to schedule an appointment, but she refuses. Would you like me to call the police?"

"No. No, don't do that. What's her name?" Jack inquired.

"She wouldn't say."

"I'll just have to get her name once she makes it back here. Send her on back—"

"Sir, are you sure? I can have the police here in the time it would take her to make it to the parking lot."

"Suzanna, I appreciate your concern, but I think I can handle myself. And besides, I have this puny shrimp attorney with me - I think the both of us together should be enough to handle it should things get physical. Send her on back."

Moments later, Suzanna made a full body entrance into his office and used her back as a doorstop. From down the lobby came a slow, rhythmic tapping on the floor from a walking cane.

Tat.

Tat.

Tat.

Tat.

Tat.

Through the open door entered an old woman of medium height that neither one of them recognized. She approached determined and persistent, wearing a white satin scarf around her neck. At first, Jack took her for one of the cleaning ladies who helped with their Mardi Gras ball, but her face lacked the cordialness of a housekeeper, nor did she brandish that customary counterfeit smile.

In an all-white dress, white shoes, and matching purse, the woman entered Jack McGowan's office and only stopped once she was front and center in the room. The skin on her face was glossy and smooth like plastic. Her hair was covered with a white satin wrap, and she wore no visible jewelry on her fingers, ears, or neck.

Attorney Morris Igelhart offered her a seat in the available chair next to where he sat during his meeting, but she refused. She stood, so Jack stood, as did Attorney Igelhart. With the cue from Jack, Suzanna left the room and quietly closed the door.

Jack extended his hand. "Hi, I am Krewe Captain Jack McGowan, and this is Krewe Attorney Morris Igelhart. I understand you have an urgent matter you would like to discuss with us. For starters, may we ask your name and what is this about?"

"He wasn't a homeless kid, he came from a good home - not too far from here on Louisa Street," she replied.

"Ma'am, please pardon me for interrupting, but as Chief Legal Counsel for the Krewe of Ares, I have to ask whether the purpose of this meeting is to discuss a legal matter. If so, then it would be more in your best interest to have your attorney contact me directly." Morris extended his business card.

She looked down at the card for a brief moment, then refocused on Jack McGowan.

"Attorney Igelhart, Captain McGowan, this is not about a settlement. I need you to understand a little bit about the young man that you told the press was a *homeless street kid*. Other than lying to me about marching as flambeaux, that boy never got into any trouble. He'd never seen the inside of a jail a day in his life. Orrin Toussaint was on the *honor roll* and was selected as one of fourteen students from Carver High to desegregate *Francis T. Nichols High School -*"

Attorney Igelhart cut her off. "Ma'am, I am - we are - so sorry for your loss, but our organization had nothing to do with that accident."

"HA! You know damn well that wasn't no accident," she growled.

Grandma Ellen reached into her large purse and placed the burnt portion of Orrin's shirt collar on Jack's desk. Still reeking of smoke and burnt flesh, still stained with blood and ash. Then she reached into her purse a second time and retrieved a smutty pouch tie-wrapped with Orrin's identification band from the morgue. Jack and Igelhart both became instantly fixated on the white pouch.

"I didn't come here to ask for money." Her voice lowered to deep threatening tone. "What you're looking at is one of the pants pockets from my grandson - he died with 120 dollars in each one of his pockets. I came here today to return this money."

"Ma'am, there is no need for that, and there is no way we would accept this money," Jack McGowan said.

"We buried my grandson in the clothes he wanted to wear in the talent show. What a wonderful funeral service it was. Even his little singing group did a special song for him. A beautiful poem by his girlfriend that he planned to marry."

Jack waited for a break in her address to express his devastation. "As Captain of this krewe; please grant me this opportunity to offer our condolences . . ."

"I will do one better than that. I will grant you twenty-four hours to get those reporters back out here and set the record straight: That my grandson was murdered by the boys from Chalmette." Her pointed finger threatened Jack like a samurai sword. "You will also apologize for referring to him as a homeless kid. Not only that, but you will demand that NOPD re-open the investigation into the first-degree murder of Orrin Toussaint."

"Ma'am, I am afraid what you're requesting is out of our control, it has already been ruled an accident. I think a better place for you to make your argument is down at DA Garrison's office," Morris Igelhart suggested.

"I will accept nothing less than what I have demanded—that is the only atonement for the shame you have brought on my family."

"Mrs. Chauvet? Am I correct?" Jack asked.

"Yes. Mrs. Ellen Vieux Chauvet, wife of the late Jean Pierre Chauvet, grandfather of Orrin Francois Toussaint."

"As Captain of Ares, I am prepared to -"

Attorney Igelhart cut him off. "I am sorry for your loss, Mrs. Chauvet, but we can't - nor will I allow - Mr. McGowan to do what you're asking. We are one of the most reputable Carnival organizations in the city of New Orleans; therefore a press conference like the one you're requesting is not in the best interest of the Krewe of Ares. We cannot agree to that. I will, however, give you some time to reconsider a confidential cash settlement, but that is our final offer." For the second time, Igelhart offered his card. "Thank you, Mrs. Chauvet, for stopping by." He extended his arm toward the door.

Jack wanted to confess everything he witnessed that night, but once again, he yielded the right of way to Igelhart. Even if it meant the guys from Chalmette got away with murder.

"As my attorney said, we are willing to discuss a very generous cash settlement, but unfortunately, that is all we can offer," Jack said while extending his hand again.

Grandma Ellen allowed his hand to hang for five seconds before she removed one of the white satin gloves she wore. With her right hand, she shook in the traditional manner of two businessmen. Then she squeezed. With her teeth, she pinched the tips of her left glove, removed it, and clamped her hand down on his wrist like a pair of vice grips.

"Wewe ni gerezani! Wewe ni gerezani!" And then a third-time. *"Wewe ni gerezani! You are the atonement.* You, and all that is connected to you. You have until the unborn returns and the glass shatteres to repent to my family. AMUN is now lord over you and your soul."

Mrs. Ellen Vieux Chauvet, the wife of the late Jean Pierre Chauvet, blew peacefully in Jack McGowan's face as she released his arm. Immediately, his knees buckled like folding chairs and he fell to the floor in the space behind his desk. Attorney Igelhart rushed around the desk to assist him as Grandma Ellen collected her white satin glove off the floor. Before departing, she untied the white scarf around her neck to reveal the doubloon his wife gave Orrin. That doubloon was the last thing they saw of her as she gracefully tapped her way back down the hall.

Tat.

Tat.

Tat.

Tat.

Tat.

Grandma Ellen was gone, but not the pain in his wrist. Jack opened his right hand, and inside he saw black soot, as if he had just carried a charred log. His eyes felt as if he'd endured a sandstorm - then came the coughing and sneezing, followed by a flu-like fever . . . all in a matter of ten minutes.

"Suzanna, please get a medic over here ASAP!" Igelhart yelled down the hall as he helped Jack over to the sofa. It took the ambulance about twenty minutes to arrive. With each passing minute, Jack McGowan's condition deteriorated. Once they arrived at Touro Hospital, Jack was admitted with a debilitating fever that afflicted his entire body.

By the time his wife arrived with their two boys, Craig and Steven, Jack McGowan had been moved to intensive care, where he remained for three days - unresponsive.

It took three days before the doctors at Touro Hospital could give Helen McGowan a diagnosis and get her signature on the release forms required to perform an emergency surgery. Her husband needed a partial hepatectomy to remove a rapidly growing tumor on his liver, and the surgeons didn't have a minute to spare.

Jack McGowan became a liver cancer patient that day, and he now had until the unborn returned and the glass shattered to undo what was spoken over his life and the lives of all those connected to him.

ACT II

CHAPTER 23

Amarah swept the last of shattered glass from the picture frame into a dustpan while her mother grew ever more fixated on the tawny-colored articles that were once hidden behind the photo.

Flambeau Carrier Burned Alive, Another Severely injured. Times-Picayune, February 28, 1968, Ash Wednesday Edition.

Marci sat next to Trent on the couch and shared a view of the old newspaper clippings. She could tell that the article was placed in the frame with care by someone who wanted it hidden, but never wanted to forget. As they continued to read the article, a couple of names appeared in the fourth paragraph that caused Trent to snatch the article from Marci. *Orrin and Earl Toussaint.*

There was something about the name *Earl Toussaint* that rang familiar to him; something quite recent, something vivid. It was then that a name on an ID badge for Tou Brothers Movers slowly came into focus.

"No way! No way!" Trent said in disbelief as he stood with the article. "There is no damn way this could be -"

"No way what could be?" Marci interjected.

His hand covered his mouth as he muddled through his fingers. "One of the movers, the older gentleman with the burns on his arms . . . He introduced himself as Earl Toussaint. Earlier today, that same guy stormed out of the house after coming in contact with this picture.

"You mean the picture that crashed to the floor for no apparent reason?" Marci confirmed as she held the picture to his face. "This picture?"

Trent took hold of the photo. "Yes, the one with the flambeaux carriers." He held it up to the light. "Marci, that picture took Earl to a very dark place. One minute he was joking that I could move in with him after we discovered your broken dolls, and the next minute he was across the street, emotional."

"So, he knew you broke my dolls?!" Marci's neck and cheeks turned red as a jar of strawberry jelly. "So, he helped you hide the evidence?"

Trent wanted to kick himself for bringing up the dolls again. "No Marci, he simply offered me a place to stay. That's all. It was my idea to hide the dolls, but I am sure there is a connection to this photo," he attempted to redirect.

It was then that Amarah flipped the picture over. There it was - inscribed on the back:

Ares Starting Point: A great photo I took of a wonderful young man who marched as a flambeaux - his name is Orrin. How blessed are we to have them.

"Dad, it appears this picture was taken by Grandma Helen at the start of the parade, and if Earl ran out the house after viewing this picture - that could only mean that guy in the picture is his brother."

"Who died as a result of the fire that night," Marci concluded as she turned to Amarah. "Could you give us a minute alone, please?"

"Sure Mom, no problem," Amarah replied. "This flambeaux business is starting to creep me out anyway." She snapped the dustpan to the broom. "I just need something to drink, and I'm headed upstairs."

Once Amarah left the room, Marci turned to Trent and lowered her voice to a discreet tone. "Trent, you don't think it's strange how this picture - of all the other pictures - just fell off the wall? I think something in this house is trying to convey a message to us."

In a whisper, he replied, "Marci, I think you're reading too much into this. Pictures fall off the wall all the time . . ."

Trent agreed with his wife, but at the same time, he did not want to express any concern within earshot of Amarah. He hadn't told Marci about the unusual happenings Aunt Frieda had shared with him - or about how the nurses reported that they also heard his father's voice late at night. He chose to remain in denial and blamed the shattered picture frame on the drafty old house.

"Trent, your mom took this picture. Earl saw this picture. What are the chances of a 1968 reunion like that taking place in this living room? A young man died in a parade that your father was the captain of, and by some freak coincidence, you hired his brother to unpack the moving truck. The other kid mentioned in the article is the same Earl Toussaint, and you know it - so cut the bullshit, Trent."

"Goodnight, Mom. Goodnight, Dad," Amarah called as she skated to the staircase with a handful of lemon cookies and a chilled glass of milk.

"Goodnight, Amarah," Trent and Marci replied.

Only once he heard Amarah walking down the second floor walkway did Trent continue his downplay of Marci's concerns. "Marci, I see where you're going with this, but I still think you're overreacting."

"Overreacting, my ass," she huffed through tight lips. "I heard your mother talking to your *FATHER* - consoling him, telling him it wasn't his fault. I am convinced that your father died thinking whatever took place in 1968 was his fault, and now in some strange way, all of these events have come full circle. And you've never wondered about any of this?"

Trent interjected. "Marci! Everything you've just said took place in 1968 - I wasn't born then!"

"Trenton, I know that! You were born in 1971, but you can't tell me you never overheard one conversation about the night that kid died in the parade?"

He stood from the sofa and walked over to the wall in front of the empty spot where the picture had hung undisturbed for decades. On the left side of the picture was a photo of a float themed after the television show *Gunsmoke*. On the float, wearing cowboy costumes, were his brothers Craig and Steven. To the right of where that photo hung was a picture from the 1968 Krewe of Ares Mardi Gras Ball, which captured Jack McGowan, Helen McGowan, Aunt Frieda, and Attorney Igelhart. Next to Ingelhart was another man who Trent did not recognize. They all held up a toast of cheer - all except his father.

"Growing up in this house, running up and down these stairs, I passed this picture a million times and never wondered who any of these people in the photos were because my family was in the parade business. I overheard thousands of conversations about parades - but never once did I hear my parents discussing a kid that burned alive."

As he spoke, Marci read the article repeatedly - shaking her head in astonishment and disgust each time. "Okay Trent, I will give you the benefit of the doubt that you were oblivious to all of this, but now you know. And now we're here. You have dragged us into this with no plan or clue. If I had known any of this before packing up my life in Bristol and my children, I would not be here right now."

"Is that so?"

"Yes! At least I would still have my dolls you destroyed and then tried to hide. Trent, hiding the truth is the same as lying and if I discover that you . . ."

"Marci, I fucked up, and I am sorry about the dolls - I am - but please don't make it seem like I have a pattern of hiding the truth from you. I get that you're angry, but that's not fair, and you know it."

"Not fair?" Marci whipped her hair to the left. "You know what is not fair? The fact that I am twenty hours from everything I know and love, and you have the audacity to lecture me about what's fair! New Orleans is not fair! This creepy fucking house is NOT FAIR!"

Trent returned to the west pole of the sofa and took a slow seat. "Look Marci . . . this has been a long and stressful day for both of us. I think a good night's sleep would do both of us a ton of good. If you like, we could continue this conversation in the morning, but I am tired."

"And so, the conversation is over?"

"Marci, please . . ."

Marci stood from the east pole of the sofa. "I will give you tonight - because of the move - but trust me, we will continue this conversation in the morning as soon -"

Marci was suddenly interrupted by singing.

> *Cupid draw back your bow*
> *And let your arrow go*
> *Straight to my lover's heart for me, for me.*

Trent heard the singing too. It was followed by the continuous sound of someone coming down the stairs. A few moments later, his mother reached the last step of the staircase. As if on a cloud, she entered the living room dressed in a pair of loose-fitting jeans, a blouse that was rolled up at the sleeves, and sunshades tucked under a large-brimmed sun hat. Before proceeding to the kitchen, she paused in front of Trent and Marci.

"Trenton, why did you come back here?" Helen asked with a face full of confusion. "I didn't want you to come back here - now your father is very upset and worried. He says she's coming for you, too - she will be here shortly."

"What lady?" Trent asked his mom.

"The one who made your daddy sick. Why did you come back here?"

"Mom, I was gone too long, so I came home to help you. So that we could spend more time together and you could enjoy your granddaughters." Trent took his mother by the arm. "It's much too late for gardening, Mom, but I am sure Zoe and Maggie would love to help you plant whatever you like this weekend. Let's get you back to bed."

Like shaking off an unwanted touch from a stranger on a bus, his mother pulled away from him. "She called you back here, didn't she? This evil, this is all her doing -"

"Mom, I came back to take care of you. Let's forget this talk about a lady - there is no lady. Now, up to bed you go," Trent said as he reached for his mother's arm, but she pulled away again.

"*That woman in white*, she's real. She called you back here because we're out of time. I tried everything to protect you, but we're out of time. That's why she called you back here."

"Mother, a 'woman in white' didn't call me back, I came on my own to be with you." He reached for her arm again. It was then that Trent realized he hadn't administered her evening meds, so he concluded that was the reason for her behavior. "Mom, let's head back up to your room where Marci will help tuck you in for the night."

But Helen pulled away again and bolted for the kitchen, where she retrieved paring blade from the counter rack that held an assortment of cutting knives. Once Trent made it to her, she turned. With a stiff arm, she pointed the knife at his face. Trent froze in place while Marci looked on from a few paces behind.

"Mommy, listen to me," he said in a calming voice. "I need you to hand me that knife before someone gets hurt." He outstretched his arm as he inched closer to his mother. "Mom, please hand me the knife."

"She has come for you, and I will not let her take you like she took your father . . . and Craig . . . and Steven."

"Mom, no one has come for me -"

"SHE HAS COME - THAT HIGH PRIESTESS BITCH - YOUR FATHER SAID SHE'S COMING!" Helen yelled at the ceiling, frantically searching from corner to corner as if she expected someone or something to drop down from the sky. That's when the house slid into darkness. With nothing more than a column of light from the streetlamp outside protruding through the kitchen window, the only visible thing was the blade she brandished.

"I told you she has come for you, but I will not let her win! DO YOU HEAR ME? YOU WILL NOT TAKE MY LAST BOY!" Helen McGowan screamed in defiance.

Trent watched as his mother stabbed at the ceiling with all her might, over and over again, trying to kill someone he could not see. Suddenly the lights switched back on. Trent leaped for the arm that held the knife and unclutched her grip from the handle. Once the knife fell to the floor, Marci recovered it while Trent cradled his exhausted mom in his arms and carried her up the stairs.

After Trent and Marci administered Helen's p.m. meds, she gradually calmed, and Marci redressed her for bed. With the recommended dosage flowing through her veins, Marci held her as they rested against a plush upholstered headboard.

Marci brushed Helen's long strands of gray as she drifted in and out of consciousness. While conscious, Helen reached for her husband. While out of consciousness, she begged the woman in white to spare the life of her remaining son. Helen carried on in that manner for another ten minutes before she finally dozed off to sleep.

From the doorway, Trent turned to get one final glimpse of his mother as she rested peacefully in her bed. It was then that he made eye contact with Marci and noticed that her face had sunken into deep concern. Trent knew Marci, and he knew part two of their conversation was going to resume the moment they made it back into the bedroom, but for now, she appeared more concerned for his mother. After Marci turned off the light, she waited for her husband in the hallway. Trent reached for the doorknob to pull it closed. It was then that he heard his mother's weak, shaky voice make one final plea.

"Trennnnton. Trennnnton. My dear boy, Trennnton."

"Yes, mother, I'm still here."

"Please do not go to that parade. Please don't take my grand-babies. Please don't go."

CHAPTER 24

In the hush of the night, Marci soaked up to her neck in steam as she gazed into yesterday - back to la-la-land, back to Bristol. Just to the right of her, within arm's reach, was a glass of red wine. Next to the wine was her razor, and next to her razor was her cell phone. But Marci was in no mood to shave her legs, chat on the phone, or sip her favorite merlot because her urgency to escape 1524 Toledano Street was overwhelming. If she couldn't escape in the fullness of her body, then the limitless boundaries of her imagination would have to suffice. For now.

Marci turned sideways in the tub and allowed a multitude of random thoughts to flow freely through her mind - some reasonable, some irrational, and some as gray as a stormy day. One thought suggested that she spend the night wrapped in the warmth of the water, but that thought was pushed aside by the idea of sinking under the water forever, which was disrupted by a competing thought of who would care for her daughters?

But it never failed; whenever she reached her peak of pressure or the summit of what she could process, Marci would always hear the voice.

Like a breeze so soft it tickled the lobes of her ears, the voice spoke to her and also imposed on her. As her anxiety increased, the voice became more demanding and assertive. The voice was consistent - it said she should leave here, leave this world . . . because to leave was the way to escape it all. The old, persistent voice was born the night before Marci's prom, when she decided she'd rather die than watch a guy she loved more than life dance with a girl she'd known since kindergarten. As she sat in the tub that night holding the wooden handle of her father's J.R. Torrey straight-edge razor, the voice spoke to her for the first time. *If you kill yourself then it will ruin their perfect night.*

He never loved you. He betrayed you. You gave him every-thing he asked for, and he still betrayed you. You don't have to go through this. Drag the blade from left to right and then lie back in the tub. I will be with you. Trust me, the voice coaxed.

"Okay," Marci replied as the blade touched her skin. "But wait, I must write a goodbye note to my parents . . . and my sister."

There's no time to write a note - no one cares about you. Marci, it's time to go, your heart is broken beyond repair. Don't you want the pain to stop?

"Yes, I want the pain to stop. It hurts so bad," she wept.

Then do it - do it now!

At the exact moment the sharp razor pricked her skin and three drops of blood dripped into the water, Evie blew into the bathroom unannounced.

"Marci guess what?" Evie danced in excitement "I have great news! I got you a date. I got you a date. I got you a DATE TO THE PROM!"

"I don't want to go. I don't care about the prom," Marci said as she secretly lowered the blade into the water along with her partially slit wrist, hiding both in the suds.

Back in present day on Toledano Street, Marci reached for her glass of wine. Without warning, the voice returned.

Marci, you are miserable. This is not the life you wanted. This is the life Trent wanted. Aren't you tired of sacrificing for him? What happened to your dreams? Marci, you died a long time ago—but you forgot to kill yourself. Trent doesn't love you - he needs you, and he's selfish. That's all this marriage is and ever will be. Pick up the blade Marci; I will help you. Trust me.

Marci placed the glass of wine on the floor and clutched the razor. Tears began to race down both sides of her cheeks as she held the blade at eye level. The thought of leaving her daughters with Trent was so heavy, but she started to do as she was told. In that brief moment, her life was cut and pasted into the following morning when Trent would awaken to find he'd slept alone. Then, once he entered the bathroom to relieve himself, he would discover her in a bloody tub, cold and afloat. She felt he deserved to see her afloat.

Marci, instead of your wrist, I suggest you place the blade under your neck and cut from ear to ear. It will hurt a little at first, but trust me - it will be over before you know it. Do it, Marci. Do it now. Let's leave this place. There is no way Trent will stay in this house after he discovers you in the morning. He will move the girls back to Bristol where you can still watch over them. I promise.

Marci placed the blade directly under her jaw and slowly closed her eyes. Millimeters from the blade, a vein pulsated as her breathing and heart rate increased. Her lungs begged for more oxygen as hyperventilation disturbed the calmness of the water. The voice was right; she was miserable and grieved to be back in Bristol. She hated giving up her business, and she hated New Orleans. Though she tried her best to present an image of strength and resolve in front of her girls, deep down, she agreed with the voice. The best way to get her daughters back to Bristol was to obey the voice - once and for all.

Marci gripped the handle of the blade and pressed against the pulsating vein. That's when she heard a familiar tune—a tune that always made her smile. It was "Head Over Heels" by the Go-Gos - it was Evie calling.

Don't answer it.

"I must - it could be important."

You must finish - don't answer it.

"I have to, if only to hear her voice one last time. I must."

Marci placed the blade on the floor and grabbed her cell phone. On the other end was her little sister; the closest person to her and the only person she trusted unconditionally. "Hi, Evie, what has you up this time of night?"

"Umm hello, what do we do every night at this same time?"

"I know, I know, our alone time."

"And it will not change now that you're in New Orleans. Speaking of which, I have been waiting all day for you to call me."

"I'm sorry about that, it's been a crazy day, and to top it off, Trent shattered my dolls."

"NOOOOOO! Not the dolls!"

"Yes, in a million pieces. But that's not the worst part. He tried to hide the evidence."

"Oh Marci, I am so sorry."

"But there's more - so much more . . ."

"I can't see anything being worse than Trent breaking your share of Mommy's doll collection, so please share."

Marci leaned forward to replenish the hot water, then reclined back in the tub. "It's his mother. I think Trent underestimated her condition - she has full-blown dementia. The severe type that requires around-the-clock medical care, to the point that I feel the best place for her is an assisted living facility. I don't feel it's my place to suggest it -"

"A nursing home? It's that bad?"

"Way past bad. I should have never moved down here. Trent should moved alone, for up to six months - long enough to get a grip on this situation. Why did I go and pack up my daughters?"

"Because you wanted to keep your family intact - so don't beat yourself up over it. As much as I miss you and my three angels, I respect the big girl move you made to keep your family together. That was a great example for your daughters . . ."

"But there's more . . ."

"More? As in additional things gone wrong?"

"I think this fucking house is haunted!"

Laugher blared in Marci's ear as she took a sip of wine.

"Haunted? Like ghost haunted? Like *Casper*?"

"Yes, but it's my father-in-law. The man is still in here. Trent's mother is having these conversations with his dad regarding an incident that took place in 1968 during a parade."

"Wait. What? A parade in 1968? Marci, are you drunk?"

"No, not yet at least." Marci took another sip of her wine. "In 1968, a young man died in the parade, and something about his death has Helen freaking out. Like, the last thing she said to us before I tucked her in for the night was: *Do not take the girls to the parade.* It's just bizarre."

"Marci, Helen was married to Jack for over sixty years, and with her condition, I think it's to be expected that she would have hallucinations."

"That's what I thought originally, but I think something else is going on here. It's his dad. He's in this house, and the fact that we're here has disturbed him. I need you to do me a favor and put your journalism degree to work."

"And research symptoms of dementia?"

"No, I need you to research Orrin Toussaint. He was the kid who died in the parade. Find out what happened - because I think it would explain what's going on with Trent's mother and the spookiness of this house."

"I will do one better than that - not only will I research it for you, I will present my findings to you in person!"

"In person? You're coming?"

"Yes, that's why I called!" Evie smirked. "I want to help you and the girls get settled in, so I took a one-week vacation."

"Wait, Kevin gave you an entire week off the desk? But I thought next week was the kick-off of your fall ratings period?"

"It is, and that's why I told him I will be reporting live from

Mardi Gras. You can pick me up at New Orleans Airport on Friday, and we can spend the next four days enjoying Carnival."

"That's great that you're coming, but Trent's mother insisted that we avoid the parades."

"Marci you said it yourself; she is far worse than you thought. I am coming, and we're going to enjoying our first Mardi Gras together. My photographer is flying in on Monday, so that settles it - we're going.

"Well, that settles it. I was planning to register the girls in their new schools on Friday, but I guess I can knock that out in the morning and pick you up on Friday instead."

"And don't tell the girls I am coming - let's surprise them."

"I agree, seeing you is the only thing that will cheer them up. The only problem is when it's time for you to leave . . . Lord help me."

"Just leave it up to me, I got this - see you Friday!"

"See you Friday, Evie - love you."

Marci ended the call with her sister, and also ended her conversation with the voice. Once again, Evie had given her a reason to live - at least for another week.

CHAPTER 25

The following morning, a comforting aroma snaked its way up the stairs, under the door gap, and into Marci's nose - the scent of Colombia on a wintery morning. The fragrance of life. Suddenly perturbed by the silence in the room, Marci patted underneath and across her cotton-stuffed comforter in search of the remote, but to no avail. Trent's inability to sleep without the background noise of the television had morphed into a shared habit. On some nights, it was the lullaby of infomercials that protected her from terrifying dreams, the voice, and her mental reenactment of the day she had discovered her parents wrapped in each other's arms, lifeless.

They had both slipped away peacefully in the night as they slept, lulled to eternal rest by soothing carbon monoxide. That's how Marci had discovered her parents two years ago. Without the pleasant distraction of a Time Life offering of songs from the 1970s or a retracting garden hose infomercial, the playback of the episode starring her mom and dad would recur every night - and this morning, the television was silent.

Abandoning her search for the remote, Marci followed the scent of Colombia to the kitchen where her eyes came into focus on Aunt Frieda and Trent. They were both seated at the table, caressing large white mugs that were filled to the rim.

"Good morning, darling," Aunt Frieda said as she placed her mug on a small saucer and stood to embrace Marci. "How did you sleep?"

Marci's eyes flashed over to Trent. "Could have slept longer if not for the -"

"The TV," Trent added. "Sorry sweetie, once I heard Aunt Frieda at the door I freaked out, thinking it was my mother making a break for it. I turned it off before I left the room without thinking," he said as he walked over to kiss her on the forehead.

"How is she, anyway?" Marci asked as she took a seat at the table.

"She's still in bed, sleeping like a baby," Aunt Frieda said as she poured Marci a cup of coffee. "But all hell is about to break loose the moment she gets the news."

Marci made eye contact with her husband as his cup tilted toward his lips. "The news? What news?"

"Well . . . Trenton shared the experience you had last night, and I feel horrible that on your first night in New Orleans, my sister had a major episode. It has happened before; she goes off the deep end talking to Jack like he's sitting right here at this table, but the hallucinations are normally due to variations in her medication." Aunt Frieda placed a coffee cup in front of Marci with a sterling silver kettle of creamer.

"Variations in her medication?" Marci asked.

"It seems every time some pharmaceutical rep came in swishing in a little mini-skirt offering the latest and greatest pill, Dr. Brooks would switch up Helen's meds. I asked him several times not to change her medication, but he tells me: *The only way to know for sure what's working is to slightly change it up every so often*," Aunt Frieda explained as she blew across the top of her coffee.

"Then Dr. Brooks better switch her back immediately, because he must have prescribed the drug from hell - she nearly sliced me in half last night," Trent said. The conversation went silent for a moment.

Marci's eyes followed Aunt Frieda's blank stare through the kitchen window, across Toledano Street, and to a two-story wooden white house. Under the street-facing balcony, a carved sign swung in the February breeze and greeted all who entered. *The Morials Welcome You*. The house appeared just as old as the McGowan home, with the same gray trimming on the columns, but minus the brilliantly wrought iron fencing that was love at first sight for Marci.

Returning her eyes to the confines of the kitchen, Marci couldn't help but notice Aunt Frieda's floral printed head scarf. It was tightly pulled to the back of her tampered silver hair and tied into a stylish knot in the front. The skin on her face was absent of a single wrinkle, but the same wasn't true of the skin beneath her chin and neck. Aunt Frieda sipped her coffee with the grace of a starlet as she sat with exemplary etiquette. Marci still found her aura quite intimidating and luminous, even though Aunt Frieda was exceptionally welcoming and warm. Across from her, Trent's blank stare traveled back into the living room and stopped short of the wall where the picture frame had fallen and glass shattered across the floor.

Trent resembled Tom Cruise at every stage of life, and though Marci never told him, his face was part of the reason she'd married him. During their eighteen years of marriage, she had developed a unique talent for reading his thoughts by using two indicators: the tension in his bottom lip and the creases in his forehead. If his forehead was wrinkled, he was lost in a sea of thought. If he bit down on his bottom lip, that was a clear sign of suppressed agitation. This morning, the cornrows were present above his brow. Tom Cruise had set sail. Marci was still pissed at Trent from their conversation last night, but once again, she placed her concerns in the garage of their marriage.

"So, what is it about this news that she will find so upsetting?" Marci asked in an attempt to bring both of them back from a distant place in their minds - back to the kitchen table and their fragmented comments regarding Helen McGowan.

Trent cleared his throat. "Her doctor is recommending we admit her for a few days - just long enough to get her levels balanced out again. The only problem is, Mother hates the hospital and will raise all kinds of hell." Trent took another sip of his coffee. "But after last night, I agree with Dr. Brooks - she has to be admitted."

"What time is your mother's appointment?

"It's set for ten o'clock," Trent said as his eyes returned to the wall at the base of the stairs.

"The reason I ask is because Evie informed me last night that she took some vacation time next week, so she's flying down to surprise the girls."

"Oh really?" Aunt Frieda placed her cup on the table and half-turned toward Marci.

"Yes, I will pick her up at the airport on Friday morning . . ."

"Wait . . . I thought you were registering the girls on Friday? Do you need me to pick her up instead?" Trent interjected.

"I'm registering them today, so it's not a problem." Clutching her mug tightly, Marci took a sip. "And please do not tell the girls. It is a surprise. Evie would also like to experience her first Mardi Gras and is very much looking forward to the parades this weekend."

As soon as she finished her sentence, Marci noticed that Aunt Frieda and Trent's eyes connected for a few seconds, as if they wanted to say something but couldn't decide who would go first. Aunt Frieda went first.

"Please wait until we get Helen admitted to the hospital before you make any mention of going to the parades this weekend. For some strange reason, any mention of a parade is her trigger."

"I gathered that from the incident last night - she appeared concerned. In fact, it was the last thing she said after I tucked her in." Marci took another quick sip of her coffee. "Do you think this paranoia is also a symptom of the inconsistencies with her medication?"

"Perhaps," Aunt Frieda said as she stood from the table walked over to the sink. "However, I noticed that right after Christmas, her symptoms started to worsen. Not just the delusional conversations with Jack, but also the way she becomes agitated the moment she hears or sees anything associated with Carnival." With teary eyes, Aunt Frieda stared down into the sink. "It's so hard seeing her like this, because Carnival was always her favorite time of year. She loved it more than Christmas or Thanksgiving. And now she's scared to death that something is going to happen - something terrible."

Aunt Frieda walked toward the stairs, then froze in motion. "Trenton, what happened to the picture that was hung right here?"

"Auntie, that's the part of the ordeal I mentioned this morning on the phone. The *something strange* part. Remember?"

"That's right. Oh well, maybe all the moving up and down the stairs jarred a few things loose. This house hasn't had this many people walking through it since the repast dinner for Jack." She touched a photo of Jack McGowan from 1968 - one that hung directly next to the frame that had shattered. "I'm headed on up to get your mother together for her doctor's appointment." Aunt Frieda said as she gripped the banister railing. "We'll be down in a few."

"Aunt Frieda, if you need a hand I would love to help," Marci offered.

"I got it, Marci," Aunt Frieda replied. "Our daily one-on-one works better than Dr. Brooks' cocktail of pills." With that, upward she went, steadily, as if she expected the stairs to give way beneath her feet.

Marci slowly osculated to her husband, who continued to gaze into the living room long after his aunt was out of view. Marci spoke in a soft voice. "Trent, you know as well as I do that once Evie arrives, we're going to those parades - with you or without you."

"I know."

"So, you haven't changed your mind about taking us?"

"Marci, I haven't changed my mind," Trent said as he walked over to the kitchen sink. "It's just . . . I have never witnessed my mother so adamant - so serious - about avoiding a parade. That is what makes this so out of the ordinary - and believe me when I say my aunt spared you the details. My mother was obsessed with this particular time of year; she loved it. B-But last night . . . there was something in her eyes that was deadly serious. I don't think it was dementia . . ."

Marci interrupted. "So you feel she had a moment of clarity just as it relates to a parade?"

Right before Trent could reply, the *pitter-patter* of little feet and bouncing pigtails raced across the living room. Seconds later, Zoe crashed into Marci with her usual big hug and waved good morning to her daddy. Only once Zoe pulled away did Marci release her hug. Then, she supported Zoe by the arm as she climbed onto a chair.

"So, what will it be this morning . . . cereal or egg sandwich?" Marci asked.

Gazing upward with a finger on her temple, Zoe replied. "Fruity Pebbles, please."

"Then Fruity Pebbles it is," Marci said as she made her way to the refrigerator.

"So, how was your first night in New Orleans? Did you have a dream you would like to share?" Trent asked.

"It was awesome," Zoe said with both arms extended wide and high. "I had the best night's sleep ever . . . but I don't remember my dream."

"Well, that's okay, just as long as you had a good night's sleep. I appreciate you being a big girl for Daddy last night and helping put away those boxes." Trent held his hand up for a high five.

"Because I am a big girl - and Maggie is a crybaby boo-hoo."

"She's not a crybaby, she just misses Aunt Evie, her friends, and our old house - that's all."

"Daddy, after breakfast, can I play in the backyard in the doll-house Grandpa Jack made for me?"

"Maybe later, Zoe. I'm taking you and your sisters to view your new schools this morning," Marci answered.

"But Mommy, Maggie said we don't have to go back to school until after Mardi Gras. It's not Mardi Gras."

"Zoe, we're only going to visit the school then we're coming right back," Marci said as she placed the bowl of cereal on the table. "And if you continue to be a big girl, then we can play in the dollhouse together once we get back. Okay?"

"You promise?"

"Yes Zoe, I promise."

"Mommy, can my new friend play in the dollhouse with us?"

Marci looked at Trent, but he shrugged his shoulders.

"Your new friend?" Marci asked. "Zoe, when did you meet a new friend?"

"Last night. She likes to tickle my feet under the covers."

"Zoe, are you playing make-believe again?"

"Nope, she's not make-believe, Mommy, and I like her a lot. She's a lot of fun," Zoe said as she slurped her cereal.

Marci returned to her chair and proceeded to reason with Zoe. "Since you have been such a big girl, your new friend can join us in the dollhouse, but only this once. Do we have a deal?" Marci extended her hand to shake.

"Yes, we have a deal." Zoe paused her slurping long enough to make the deal official.

"Am I invited too?" Trent asked.

"Yes Daddy, you're invited too."

"Seems we're having a guest over," he chuckled. "So, does your new friend have a name?"

"Yes, but it's a secret," Zoe slurped. "She made me promise not to tell."

"Well, those types of promises are only for kids your age - it's okay to tell Mommy and Daddy," Marci assured her. "So tell us, what is your new friend's name?"

"If I break a promise, then doesn't it make me a bad person?"

"Zoe, if you tell your parents that doesn't make you a bad person - it makes you an honest person," Marci said.

"So tell us, Zoe, what's your new friend's name?"

The slurping paused again. "This morning, my new friend said I could call her Grandma Ellen."

CHAPTER 26

Marci came to a rolling stop at New Orleans International Airport and there she was - the most familiar face she had ever seen in her life - her little sister, Evie. In an instant, her mind reeled back to their old grade school in Newtown, back to those precious mornings walking to school together with their mom following a few paces behind. On some days, their mom would intentionally walk a block behind them, as if preparing Evie and Marci to walk hand-in-hand through the many neighborhoods of life. It worked.

That was all before their father's promotion from local bureau chief to managing editor for the *Hartford Courant* newspaper headquartered in Bristol. As Marci strolled past the waving arms of the airport traffic cop, she greeted him with a friendly smile. She missed her dad - even though most of her childhood was spent talking to him on the other side of a newspaper. The life of an editor had consumed her father. Even at the breakfast table, he read through a fresh bundle of the morning edition before jetting off to work on autopilot - to inspect more newspapers.

Marci parked a boomstick away from where Evie waited at the edge of the pickup curb, but Evie didn't notice - she was

distracted by a wife and kids who ran into the arms of a returning Marine. Marci chuckled because her sister was every bit of
their father. She could sensationalize an empty closet; she had
his nose for news. Marci, on the other hand, was their mother in
the sense that she appreciated the slower pace of life, minding
her business, collecting antiques, and treasuring memories fro-
zen in old photo albums.

Marci lowered the passenger window. "You couldn't make it
one week without me?" she called as she popped the tailgate of
her truck.

"Correction: I couldn't make it one week without seeing my
nieces," Evie said as she slung her large suitcase in the rear car-
go area and closed the hatch.

"Hey, keep it moving!" an airport traffic cop yelled at Marci.
"You got my lane backed up!"

"Yes, sir," Marci replied as they drove away.

"Why didn't you bring my girls?" Evie asked.

"Because they have no clue you're here."

"So none of them wanted to take the ride with you this morning?"

"Not at all. I told them I was headed out to get their school
uniforms and supplies, and all three declined my invitation."

"School uniforms," Evie shuddered with a puke finger in
her mouth. "I'm sure Amarah feels like you have crushed her
world."

"You know her well, but Maggie is worse than the other two
combined."

"Trust me, I know," Evie said as she unzipped her carry-on
bag. "I have received text messages from Maggie every day
since you arrived, begging me to come get her and telling me
how much she hates the new house."

"Not Zoe, she loves the house."

"Has Amarah . . . warmed up any?"

Marci exhaled in exasperation. "Amarah feels like I have
moved her into the nursing home from hell."

Evie removed her iPad from her carry-on bag. "Trust me, I am aware of that too - she calls me at least four times a day. *Nannie, please can I live with you? Nannie, I'd rather die than live down here. Nannie, why are my parents destroying my life?* And on and on and on."

"That's Amarah. Everything is personal."

"But have you tried to get her to see the big picture?"

"Evie, the only picture that matters to her right now is the picture of her boyfriend, who happens to live in Bristol. In her mind they will go off to college together, graduate, buy a home far away from me, and live happily ever after." Marci checked her rearview mirrors before merging right at the I-10 split. "Her entire world is centered on this one boy. Justin, Justin, Justin." Marci pumped a fist in frustration.

"But did she steal it, or did she get it honestly?"

"Whatever Evie . . . I was nowhere near Amarah's level of boy-crazy."

"Marci, you were boy-crazy level 120! When Pus-Face Carlton dumped you before the prom, you cried every day and all day. You didn't eat. And you hid in the bathroom for hours. All those tears wasted on *Carlton*. God, he was ugly."

"He wasn't ugly!" Marci fired back.

"And that is the same thing you used to say whenever I called him Pus Face," Evie threw her head back in laughter. "How quickly you've forgotten. Don't you remember the days Pus Face sat between your legs in the bleachers with his head tilted back while you applied acne cream to his lumpy face?!" Evie cringed.

"It wasn't that bad."

"And there's your proof that Amarah didn't steal it!" Evie laughed. "Now that I think about it, I don't ever remember you washing your hands after popping his bumps . . ."

"I hate you!" Marci laughed.

"As I said, Amarah got it honestly."

On the straightaway, Evie became distracted by the NOLA

skyline and the emergence of a large, silver oval known as the Louisiana Superdome. Like a child approaching Disney World after a twelve-hour drive, Evie's eyes could hardly take it all in as she rubbernecked through the passenger window. "So, this is New Orleans?"

"Yes, it is."

"I love it already," Evie whispered.

"In many ways, it reminds me of Bristol. It's very old and full of culture, but there's no place like home."

Evie's eyes rolled from left to right. "Marci, cut the bullshit - you're living in a town famous for something called Mardi Gras, whereas I just left five inches of snow. Please spare me."

"Speaking of New Orleans, were you able to pull up anything on the Krewe of Ares and the kid who died?"

Evie sat up quickly. "That's what I was about to share before you got on the subject of your first love - Mr. Pus Face."

"Evie, you brought up Pus Face . . . I mean Carlton. I haven't thought of that asshole since high school," she lied.

"Sure you haven't, but anyway, I contacted a Mormon friend of mine whose mother is an expert genealogist, and she was a miracle worker . . ."

"Wait - you contacted Mormons in regards to an incident in New Orleans?"

"Yes, her name is Mrs. Susan Young."

"You contacted the Mormons . . . of Utah?"

"Yes, Grasshopper."

"Why?" *She's so smart it makes me sick.*

"If you would have taken journalism like I begged you to, then you would have the answer to that question," Evie said as she tucked a lock of sandy blonde hair behind her ear. "I would have you know that the Mormon Church is obsessed with gene-alogy. As a result, they have compiled a database stuffed with the genealogy of millions of Americans."

"But why?"

"Apparently they believe in this concept called the *Eternal*

Family, so the purpose is to link the current dots back to their ancestors. From what Mrs. Young explained, the Mormons believe that their earthly status is carried over once they transition into heaven. And so, they keep track of all of their Mormon relatives and all of ours. They even collect genealogy data on descendants from Africa. So, I asked Mrs. Young to track down everything she could find about the Toussaint family in New Orleans, which freed me up to do a comb-through of the local news archive from that day."

"Well . . . did Mrs. Young discover anything interesting?"

"Did she ever!"

"Like what?" Marci asked as she struggled to keep her eyes on the road.

With her index finger, Evie slid through notes on her tablet. "I should really charge you a fee for this - it's just that good."

"Evie!" Marci yelled. "What did she discover?"

"I'm considering doing an investigative report about what we've discovered, so you may have to wait until it airs . . ." Evie snickered.

"EVIE!"

"Okay, okay, I guess I will tell you, but first I need to send you a PayPal invoice."

"Evie, I swear to God . . ."

"Welllll . . . Mrs. Young discovered an ancestor whose name was listed on a deed as *John Boy Nebneteru*; I'll refer to him as Neb . . . it's a lot easier to say. It appears Neb and his two daughters were sold in New Orleans at a slave auction in a section of town called Algiers in 1786. They lived and worked on a plantation there until 1820, when they were freed by their owner - a guy name Henry Behrman."

It was then that Marci pulled to the side of the road on Carrollton Avenue, because she wasn't familiar enough with New Orleans to drive and listen to Evie at the same time. Once the car was in park, she turned to face her sister. "Tell me more."

"Here's where it gets interesting. Not only were Neb and his two daughters freed, but so were all of the slaves on the plantation - a total of 180 slaves."

"I wonder why," Marci pondered. "Did Mrs. Young give a reason why so many slaves were freed during a time when many Africans were in bondage?"

"No. No reason was given, but most of them were shipped back to a region in West Africa now known as Sierra Leone. Those who remained in New Orleans were able to maintain their status as Free People of Color. One of Neb's daughters, who decided to make New Orleans her home, was named Kuhani Nuia. Kuhani Nuia gave birth to a daughter name Kuhani Azizi, who gave birth to Kuhani Lakicia, who gave birth to Kuhani Nalah in 1909."

"Why were all of their first names Kuhani?" Marci asked.

"Great question - I asked Mrs. Young the same question, and she explained that it is a common custom for tribal families to continue a name if the origin of the name is either traced back to royal ancestors or the leaders of a religious order. Mrs. Young seems to feel that this continuation was due to a religious succession."

"But I am not following . . . how is this connected to Orrin Toussaint?"

"Well, Kuhani Nalah married an immigrant from Haiti, and after their marriage, she gave up her Kuhani name and took a traditional name."

"Another name?" Marci asked. "Why would she change her name?"

Evie made eye contact with Marci for the first time. "According to Mrs. Young, on the paperwork filed with the State of Louisiana, the reason given for the name change was *abdication*."

"Abdication, as in King Edward VIII abdication?"

"Yes, whatever power or authority she possessed was abdicated and passed onto another family member instead."

"I totally get it, but who did she abdicate to?"

"I'm still waiting on Mrs. Young to email that part."

Just then, Marci's cell phone rang. It was Maggie asking for McDonald's. After a quick stop through the drive thru, Marci and Evie arrived at 1524 Toledano Street and quietly entered the home. Once inside, Marci called out for the girls.

Maggie was the first to bobsled down the stairs, and the first to scream. "AUNT EVIE!"

CHAPTER 27

Trent ended his transfer interview with a handshake and a *welcome aboard* from NOPD Chief Jonathan Bolton. Due to his nearly twenty years of experience as a white collar crimes detective, Trent was only required to take a policy and procedures class at the police academy before resuming his career of investigating embezzlers. As soon as he shut the door of his Audi A6, he received a call from Dr. Brooks.

"Hi Trent, it's Dr. Brooks, did I catch you at a good time?"

"Perfect time, I was just about to head your way to check on Mom."

"You may want to make that visit later this evening because I need to run a series of tests on her today."

"A series of tests? What for?" Trent's face collapsed into his hand as he braced himself for the bad news.

"Tests to help me understand the strange utterances I over-heard during my observation time last night and this morning."

"Utterances?" Trent asked as his seatbelt clicked.

"Yes, I have several patients with symptoms similar to your mother's, therefore I'm quite familiar with hearing bits and piec-es of conversations, but last night, your mother . . . sh-she . . .

engaged in a full conversation with someone. A man."

"Oh that, in her mind . . ." Trent searched for an explanation. "My aunt says she's been reenacting old conversations, but after her evening meds it typically stops," he downplayed.

"Trent, I heard him."

"Who?"

"Your father, *Mr. McGowan.*"

". . . Dr. Brooks? I don't follow."

There was no answer - only silence.

"Hello, hello? Did I lose you?"

"Y-yes Trent, I am still here."

"Did I hear you say you overheard my mom in a conversation with my dad?"

"Just as coherent as this conversation. I heard a male voice and your mother's voice from the other side of a privacy curtain. At first, I took the voice for one of our orderlies, but when I pulled back the curtain, it was only your mother kissing an invisible someone goodnight. Trent, I know this sounds crazy, because it feels crazy to say it, but I heard him."

"Dr. Brooks . . . I don't know what to say," Trent replied. "Were you able to determine the nature of the conversation?"

"It was about not allowing the grandkids to attend a parade, and someone named Evie headed to New Orleans to take her grandkids to a parade. She appeared very worried about the kids attending that parade."

"Wait, she said Evie? Dr. Brooks, are you sure?"

"Yes, very sure, because her words were crystal-clear. The male voice notified her that she must get home quickly. Trent, we had no choice but to sedate your mom, because shortly after that she became irate - determined to walk out of the front door of the hospital."

Trent wanted to tell Dr. Brooks about the incident in the kitchen last night and how he was nearly stabbed to death by his own mother, but he held it all in. *They will only pump her full of more drugs - like a pharmaceutical lab rat.* At the same time, he wanted his mother to get better so she could enjoy her grandkids, but after last night he didn't feel safe with her - and he couldn't even think about leaving her in a room alone with his girls.

"I plan to run several tests on her throughout the day, so later tonight might be a better time to visit."

It was painful to hear, but Trent believed Dr. Brooks. His observations of Helen's conversations with his father were identical to the stories the home health nurses had told Aunt Frieda. The fact that his mother knew that Evie was in New Orleans was all the proof he needed - his mother was inflicted with something far more critical than dementia. Something paranormal.

"And Trent, there was one more thing."

"Yes, Dr. Brooks?"

"The male voice I heard constantly apologized for his wrong-doing, and kept saying that if he had the chance to do it all over again, he *would have restored their honor.* I am not sure where that fits in, but I just wanted to make you are aware of it."

Trent thanked Dr. Brooks and informed him that they would come to visit tomorrow - that way, he'd have the space he needed to treat his mother. After the call ended, Trent's thoughts immediately switched to his children and the text Marci had sent him during his call with Dr. Brooks.

Maggie just said there's a parade starting at 6 p.m. and Evie would like to go.

Trent looked at his watch - the time was 6:10 pm.

He tried to call Marci.

No answer.

CHAPTER 28

When Trent arrived home, he noticed that Marci's car wasn't in the driveway. Every call he placed ended in a voicemail asking her to wait for him. Don't go. Let's talk about this first. But it was too late - the house was empty, and his fear was confirmed with a simple sticky note on the refrigerator:

Taking the street car to see the Krewe of Babylon - join us.

Trent immediately ran up the stairs to his gun safe, grabbed his Glock with an extra clip, and bolted back to his car.

The Krewe of Babylon parade was one of those old, nighttime Carnival parades that started around St. Charles and Washington Avenue and continued to Canal Street. Night parades in New Orleans always drew huge crowds, especially the parades that rolled the weekend before Mardi Gras. With Fat Tuesday only four days away, tonight was no exception. Louisiana Avenue and Baronne Street was as close as Trent could get to St. Charles, so he parked his car and hiked the two blocks to the starting point of the parade. It was only once he arrived on St. Charles Street that he finally received a call from Marci.

"Hello!" Trent answered in a tone of disconcerted relief. "I have been trying to reach you for nearly an hour."

"I'm sorry, but with all the noise down here I can't hear myself think, let alone hear the phone!" Marci yelled above the crowd noise.

"Where are you?"

"We walked down near a roundabout circle with a tall monument in the center, but we're still on the street called St. Charles."

"Okay, I know where you are. Stay right there, and I will come find you!" Trent yelled.

Once the call ended, Trent slid his phone into his coat pocket and adjusted his conceal carry holster. With his brown leather biker jacket zipped up to his chin to block out the frigid air, Trent made his way to St. Charles and merged into the rip current of parade-goers traveling alongside the floats at a maddeningly slow pace. He tiptoed above the crowd to gauge his progress, but the monument area known as Lee Circle was still several blocks away.

Directly in front of Trent was a compressed group of teenagers who migrated together for safety. They showed zero interest in what the Krewe of Babylon had to offer. Like wildebeest treading across a shallow river, they moved with great caution - trapping Trent at the back of their herd. It was not so long ago that Trent moved through Carnival crowds with a similar pack of friends, showing no interest in parade souvenirs - only there for the opportunity to group chat with packs of girls from Ursuline Academy and Sacred Heart High School.

To his left were shoulder-to-shoulder storefronts that made their living along St Charles Avenue. To his right were three rows of begging arms pleading for beads. In the middle of it all was Trent - inching along slower than the guy who sold cotton candy from a basket cart. After thirty minutes of walking, he arrived at the place his wife had described only to spot his family on the opposite side of the street, pressed against the NOPD

Barricade.

Trent only managed to penetrate up to the second row of the crowd - parade crowds in New Orleans don't take kindly to people skipping in them - but he did manage to get close enough to see his family clearly. Trent looked on as Marci, Evie, and his daughters gleamed with joy after every passing float. He watched as Marci searched the oncoming crowd in both directions for him - unable to hear her cell phone, unable to see that he was directly across the street. *Come on Marci, take out your phone and call me*, he telepathically suggested. After about ten minutes, it worked.

"Hello? Hello? Can you hear me?" Marci asked.

"Yes, I can hear you!" Trent yelled.

"Are you near us?"

"Yes, I am across the street from you - look straight ahead." Trent waved his arms.

"I see you! Can you cross over?"

"Not until there is a break in the parade - only then will the police officer allows me to cross the barricade. Just enjoy the parade, and I will wait here until then."

With each passing float and walking jazz band, he watched his wife and her sister enjoy their first Carnival parade in New Orleans. He saw the same joy and excitement in the eyes of Zoe and Maggie, but not Amarah. She appeared less interested in the parade and more captivated by texting Justin. Though Trent hated the sadness that had glazed her eyes since the family relocated to 1524 Toledano Street, he did feel a sense of accomplishment in putting distance between his daughter and Justin.

The Krewe of Babylon was now on their thirtieth float with ten more to go when Trent noticed a group of Babylon members trailing the float on foot. Like ambassadors of joy, the members interacted with the crowd and posed for selfies with screaming toddlers. Suddenly there was a pause in the parade - the only pause of the evening - and the perfect opportunity for Trent to cross the barricade. Just as he was about to cross, he noticed one of the Babylon members taking a picture with Evie. The woman handed each one of them a bead accompanied by a hug - all except Amarah, who stepped back into the crowd to avoid the gesture of kindness. So, the lady handed Amarah's bead to Marci.

From across the street, Trent was disappointed with Amarah for how rudely she'd treated the kind member of the parade krewe and decided he would address her ugly disposition once they made it home. As he hurdled across the barricade, he saw Zoe leap into the woman's arms and give her a huge hug - followed by another group selfie taken by Evie. Right as Trent made it to the other side of the street, the parade started up again and the kind woman continued moving through the rest of the parade. Marci and Evie stuffed their beads into Maggie and Zoe's bag just as Trent grabbed hold of the barricade in front of them and hurdled over to the other side.

"Hi, Dad," Amarah greeted him, dry as crackers.

"Daddy, you made it!" Maggie exclaimed in excitement.

"Daddy, look at all the beads we caught!" Zoe added.

"Well hello, Mr. McGowan!" Evie yelled over the crowd as she leaned in to hug him. Then, without warning, she slapped him on the shoulder.

"Ouch!" Trent burped in laughter. "Why the abuse?"

"Because you took my girls!" Evie laughed back. "How dare you take my girls from me?"

"So, in other words, you miss me."

"Not you - just my girls."

Marci interrupted. "What about me?" She pointed inward. "He took me, too."

Evie yelled in her direction, "I have had two lifetimes of you - but he took my three angels!" She slapped Trent again. "I have come to take back what's rightfully mine."

Trent leaned in to kiss Marci, but she only offered a cheek. Since the argument about the dolls, their marriage was only back to about forty-five percent, which equated to no sex, pecks on the cheek, and functional dysfunctionality to keep the kids from getting alarmed. This was Day Four of the icy treatment, and Marci wasn't showing any signs of returning back to lovey-dovey. She stood next to him as if he were a friend of the family, or someone she use to know, yet she was very cordial. To make matters worse, the couple directly on the side of Trent couldn't stop kissing and discreetly groping each other, while Trent and Marci interacted like a couple in a Michael Bolton video.

Suddenly, the blast of blaring sirens distracted Trent's attention from his distant love, and just like that, the last float in the Krewe of Babylon parade rolled past. They were completely out of beads, so they waved and blew kisses while a few on the second level of the float toasted the crowd with a can of beer in between sips. Directly behind the float of intoxicated members were twelve horseback NOPD officers and several sanitation crews, who did their best to clean the blanket of litter that was left behind.

As a rite of passage, Trent made Zoe and Maggie carry their bags the entire two-mile hike back to Marci's Honda Pilot. After a short drive filled with recollection and laughter, they arrived home around 10:30 p.m. - still excited, yet tired and hungry.

"Aunt Frieda dropped off a pot of gumbo this morning. I'm about to warm it up and I'll have it ready in a minute," Trent said as the rest of the family raced to one of three bathrooms throughout the house. The first to rejoin Trent in the kitchen was Marci, who took a seat at the table and allowed the silence between them to reign for five minutes before clearing her throat.

"So . . . how did the interview go today with Chief Bolton?"

"It went well, and after a policy and procedures course, I will join his detective squad in about two weeks."

"That's wonderful."

"And . . . how did you enjoy your first Mardi Gras parade?"

"Trent, it was amazing - I only wished I would have brought the girls down here sooner. Maggie and Zoe loved every minute of it, but Amarah . . ."

"Yes, I know, I saw it all from across the street. I have never seen her so distant and detached from this family. I plan to have a word with her before she goes to bed. I saw how rude she was to that krewe member who handed you guys beads. Amarah's nasty attitude was uncalled for."

"I agree," Marci nodded. "Totally uncalled for."

"Other than Amarah, how was everything else?" Trent asked as he stirred the chilled pot of gumbo.

"Everything else was fine until . . . until . . ."

Trent turned from the gumbo pot. "Until?"

"Until Zoe continued to call the little old lady who gave us the beads *Grandma Ellen*."

"Grandma Ellen?"

"Yes, she said, 'Grandma Ellen, you promised me you would come, and you're here.' Then she leaped out of my arms into the lady's arms, as if they'd known each other for years. It was really weird."

Just as Trent was about to inquire further, Evie entered the room staring at her cell phone, scrolling with a thumb. "Marci, guess who replied back to me when we were at the parade?"

"Who?" Marci asked.

Mrs. Young."

"Who?"

"Mrs. Young, the genealogist I told you about this morning."

"Yes, yes, now I remember. So what did she say about the name change?"

"The what?" Trent asked. "Name change?"

"I will explain it to you later - but I asked Evie to do some research for me," Marci reassured Trent before turning back to Evie. "After abdication, what was her new name?"

"It appears that she changed her name from Kuhani Nalah to Ellen Vieux Chauvet."

It was then that Marci took a step toward Evie. "Grandma Ellen."

That's when Trent also made the connection. "Wait, wait, hold up; you don't think the woman from the parade is the same woman Zoe has been interacting with? That's ridiculous."

"Evie, please pull up your pictures from the parade - quick!" Marci said breathlessly.

Trent and Marci looked over Evie's shoulder as she scrolled through all the pictures from the parade on her phone. She finally stopped on the group photo taken with the lady Zoe had referred to as *Grandma Ellen*. With great haste, the three ran up the stairs to Zoe and Maggie's room, where they found the two girls seated on the floor sorting out all their beads and cups from the Krewe of Babylon. Marci called Zoe out into the hall where Evie lowered her phone.

"Zoe, do you know this lady in the picture?" Marci asked as she pointed.

"Yes, I know her."

"And how do you know her, Zoe?" Trent asked.

Zoe pointed in the direction of her pink My Little Pony bed, which sat alongside the wall. "Because she likes to play tickle. But Grandpa said I shouldn't play with her. I don't think he likes Grandma Ellen."

CHAPTER 29

Maggie stood at the top of the staircase listening as hard as she could to the conversation in the living room, but the *Tonight Show* band made it extremely difficult. She knew her parents and Aunt Evie were hiding something in their voices. *But what?* From the second step down, Maggie bent her body as much as she could without blowing her cover.

Why are they talking about Zoe's imaginary friend? Who is Orrin? Maggie wondered as she strained her ears to hear every word of their private conversation. She could tell something was wrong by the quiet way they spoke - it's how her parents always spoke when something was wrong - but the television made it impossible to decipher. Then she heard what sounded like a suggestion to have Zoe see a doctor. *But Zoe isn't sick.* The longer the conversation went on, the more bits she collected, but none of the pieces snapped together regardless of the rotation. *Whoa, Grandma is in the hospital.* That part she heard clearly.

"What are you doing?" Amarah asked as she headed to the hallway bathroom.

"Shhh, Shhh!" Maggie waved Amarah into the bathroom.

"What did Mom tell you about evesdropping on her conversations?" Amarah asked with an arm full of toiletries.

Facing Amarah with her arms folded, Maggie snapped, "Mommy also said don't have sex until you're married - did you listen?"

"You snooping little *rat!*" Amarah snarled. "Stay out of my phone! Do you hear me? *Stay. Out. Of. My. Phone.*" Amarah stomped her way into the bathroom and slammed the door.

Glad she's gone.

Maggie resumed her effort to gather as much intel as she could from the summit in the living room, hoping to hear any indication of the family moving back to Bristol. Needing to get closer, Maggie softly placed her foot on the third step from the top but the stair screamed in pain - as if she were a three hundred-pound football player.

Her cover was blown.

The conversation fell silent.

The only voiced she heard came from the *Tonight Show.*

Then her mother appeared at the base of the staircase with tight eyes and cheeks full of hot air.

Maggie immediately about-faced and ran back to her room. From the middle of her bed, she watched as Zoe canoed across the floor on a river of beads. After a few minutes ticked away, Maggie concluded that the conversation in the living room was extremely important, because her mother didn't tear way and chase her back to her room.

Why were they talking about Zoe's imaginary friend?

Who is Orrin?

"Come play with me - play with me!" Zoe begged.

"Not now Zoe, I am trying to figure out what's going on downstairs."

Zoe grabbed a handful of beads, tossed them in the air, then tried to catch them. "Maggie, let's play parade. It's fun, come on."

"No Zoe, and I am not helping you clean up this mess."

"Then I will ask Grandma Ellen to help me."

"Zoe, please stop with this Grandma Ellen crap - *she is not real*," Maggie tried to reason. "If you keep this up, Mommy is going to take you to the doctor, and they will give you a shot."

"But I like Grandma Ellen; she's nice to me."

"Zoe, do you want a shot?"

Zoe ran over to the window. "*No. No. No.* I don't want a shot in my arm. It will hurt. Really bad."

"Then you have to stop bringing up Grandma Ellen. Okay?"

"Okay," Zoe said sadly. "But if I can't play with Grandma Ellen, then will you play fashion show with me?"

"Not tonight, Zoe, maybe tomorrow. I'm tired."

"But I have no one to play with," a teary voice replied.

"Okay, okay - stop crying, we can play fashion show for a little while."

One by one, Maggie and Zoe placed the beads around their necks and pranced over to the vanity mirror where they struck their poses for an audience of two.

"Girls, the gumbo is hot and delicious - come and get it," their father called out from the kitchen.

"What's gumbo?" Zoe asked.

"It's like spicy soup with crabs floating on top," Maggie said in a quiet voice. "I sniffed it in the refrigerator this morning. It looks yucky."

"I don't want any gumbo," Zoe whispered back.

"I think I will have a peanut butter and jelly sandwich. What about you?"

"I think I would like a peanut butter and jelly sandwich too," Zoe whispered back.

Maggie poked her head out their bedroom door. "Mom, can you fix us peanut butter and jelly sandwiches instead of gumbo?"

"Are you sure, Maggie? It's really delicious."

"Yes Mom, we're sure."

"Okay, give me about ten minutes."

Maggie turned back to her room to find Zoe holding a sparkly string of bead in front of the mirror. "Wow, that one is different," Maggie said. "Can I see it?"

"No, because there's more like it in that pile over there. We got five, I think - go get your own."

Maggie searched frantically but could not find any beads similar to the string Zoe wore. However, she wanted one - desperately. Zoe's string of beads was different from all the other plastic throws. It was heavier, like one of the expensive necklaces in their mother's jewelry box - the necklaces they were forbidden to touch because half of them once belonged to their late grandmother.

I'm going to update my profile picture wearing that beautiful necklace . . . all of my friends in Bristol will wish they were here.

"I am wearing this one to bed," Zoe said as she placed the radiant beads around her neck.

"Zoe, come help me find more - you said there were other beads just like the one you have, but I can't find any," Maggie called out as she continued her frantic search, but Zoe ignored her.

"It's beautiful; it is so beautiful," Zoe said as she viewed the string of beads in the moonlight.

Frustrated, Maggie shuffled back over to where Zoe stood in the window and read the doubloon in her cuffed hands. "*Krewe of Ares 1968* - I must have it," Maggie craved.

"*Krewe of Ares 1968*," Zoe mimicked. "You are so beautiful. *Yes, I will. Yes, I will.*"

"Zoe, are you okay?" Maggie asked, but Zoe was preoccupied by the doubloon.

"I will never take it off," Zoe murmured in a low, airy voice.

"Yes, it is beautiful, and I want one. Zoe, help me find one . . . please."

"That which you seek is here," Zoe replied.

"Zoe, you're starting to freak me out - just hand it to me because I have looked in every pile and can't find one exactly like yours."

"In my pocket, you will find what you're looking for," Zoe said.

As Maggie drew closer, she could hear what sounded like deep, raspy whispers coming from outside their bedroom window, but she figured it was just the wind circling the house. As Zoe had instructed, Maggie slid her hand inside Zoe's pants pocket and retrieved a string of beads with a dazzling doubloon attached. The same one that had captivated her little sister. The same one that suspended her little sister in time. To confirm that it was the exact doubloon, Maggie read the circular inscription again - *Krewe of Ares 1968.*

"Put it on, Maggie, hurry. You have to see how it sparkles in the moonlight - it's beautiful. It's so beautiful."

Ignoring her inner voice that said *call Mom because something is wrong with Zoe*, Maggie placed the beads around her neck, then walked over to where Zoe stood in the moonlight. The hue of the doubloon was so bright that it transformed the white latex walls into an incandescent rouge. Suddenly, a warm surge traveled from her toes up to her head, giving her the feeling of flying through the clouds. Her skin tingled as if the feet of a million ants were marching to and fro, and around, up, and down her entire body. But nothing mattered. No one mattered. To Maggie's touch, the doubloon felt like a beating heart in the hands of a surgeon. She could not take her eyes off the doubloon, nor could she focus on anything else. Then she heard the deep, raspy whispers.

Maggie listened, then she replied.

Yes, I will.

Yes, I will.

Yes, I will.

CHAPTER 30

Marci poured two cups of milk and placed them on the sides of two paper plates that each held a peanut butter and jelly sandwich. After opening several cabinet drawers, she finally located the one that held the utensils, and but all she could find was a butter knife. It was then that she remembered the violent confrontation with Helen, and how Helen had nearly killed her own son. *That's right . . . I hid all the knives on the top shelf in the hallway closet - the one where Trent hid my broken dolls.* Just the thought of the dolls caused a flare-up of anger deep inside of her, but Marci did her best to suppress it.

She sliced one sandwich diagonally, then sliced the other into four squares and topped both with a handful of grapes. Next, a teaspoon of Nestle strawberry syrup was added to the cup next to the four squares - Zoe wouldn't drink her milk any other way. In the living room, Evie was nearing the end of her recap for Trent, who'd asked very few questions - as if he already knew most of what she'd discovered.

Walking past where Evie and Trent sat on the sofa, Marci called out to her daughters from the base of the stairs. "Zoe and

Maggie, your sandwiches are ready."

On the end table at the edge of the sofa was an old article that had been hidden behind the photo of the flambeaux carriers, but this wasn't the one she'd read the night the picture frame shattered on the floor. It was Orrin Toussaint's obituary, dated March 2, 1968. Unfolding the clipping, Marci panned down to surviving family members, and that's when she read aloud the same name Evie said aloud in the conclusion of her recap to Trent: *Ellen Vieux Chauvet.*

"It's the same woman. I am sure of it," Marci said as she sat in a narrow space between Evie and the armrest of the sofa. Suddenly, she began to feel the rumbling of an eruption inside of her ribcage. The anger she'd suppressed in the kitchen ignited again at the thought that Trent had relocated her family to New Orleans, to a house filled with so many questions, to his father's past sins that had somehow now fallen on her baby girl.

"My child is interacting with this woman; it must be the same woman that has been tormenting Helen. Now she's tormenting my entire family," Marci said as she slouched deeper into the sofa and gazed two thousand miles away to the perfect life she had in Bristol.

"Marci, are you sure Zoe has been interacting with a person named Grandma Ellen? Zoe has a very vivid imagination . . . it could be a coincidence."

"It's no coincidence." Marci sat up and peered across her sister at Trent. "What are you hiding?" She shot-putted off the sofa and slowly paced to where he sat. "What is the real reason you dragged us down here?" she growled.

Trent looked up at her. "Marci, why are you acting as if this is the first time Zoe has ever played with an imaginary friend? She had several fake friends back in Bristol."

Marci leaned in. "But her imaginary friends were always kiddie friends - or bunnies, or little fucking fairies! Not the grandmother of a kid who died in your father's parade," she said through tight lips in an angry, muffled voice.

"Marci, I know as much as you do . . . I walked into this with *you*."

"That's bullshit! I heard your mother say to her husband that it wasn't his fault. What wasn't his fault, Trent?" Marci demanded, inches from his nose.

Evie cleared her throat and spoke in a non-combative voice. "The cover-up."

"What cover-up?" Marci asked while she remained focused on Trent.

"Well, considering the time period, there appears to have been some sort of cover-up regarding the death of Orrin Toussaint," Evie answered.

"Evie, I didn't read anything in that article that gave the impression of a cover-up. The young man was a flambeaux carrier . . . they twirl kerosene lanterns, his lantern killed him, it was an accident," Trent reasoned.

"But I can prove it wasn't his flambeaux lantern that killed him . . ."

"Look Evie, this is stressful enough," Trent snapped. "The newspaper article I read was open and shut about how the kid died, and my father didn't have a got-damn thing to do with it. The last thing I need for you to do is to drag in conspiracy theories."

"*Don't holler at my sister*!" Marci snapped back. "It's your fault we're in this mess."

"I need both of you to calm down and hear me out . . . the information I have didn't come from researching the *Times-Picayune* archive," Evie said.

". . . Which means you're inserting your own facts. If the reporter on the scene reported that it was an accident, then I accept that as fact and everything else as speculation," Trent argued.

"But the *Times-Picayune* wasn't the only media source on the scene that night," Evie snapped back at Trent. "There was also a publication called Jet magazine, which sent reporters down to cover the bussing of black students to white schools. It appears they also witness reported from the scene after the fire." Evie walked over to Trent and Marci and handed Trent her iPad.

Jet Magazine, April Issue, 1968
NEW ORLEANS, LA - Even the passage of the Civil Rights Bill could not protect a Negro teen in New Orleans from getting lynched on Mardi Gras night, and those who ruled his death an accident are just as guilty as the murderers who casually walked away from the gruesome scene. A member of a group known during Carnival as flambeaux carriers was burned alive when two white men doused his torch with a flammable substance, causing flames to quickly engulf his entire body. Orrin Toussaint, age sixteen, was pronounced dead an hour later at Charity Hospital in New Orleans as a result of injuries suffered during the fire. Martin Robichaux, an eyewitness (and best friend of the victim), told a reporter from Jet magazine that he witnessed the men burn Orrin Toussaint alive. Jet reporters discovered the following day that the Captain of the Krewe of Ares not only witnessed the lynching of Orrin Toussaint but may have hindered the investigation by providing a false statement to New Orleans Police. Jet has also discovered that the Krewe Captain who provided the statement which contradicted Martin Robichaux's eyewitness account was Jack McGowan . . .

Marci watched as Trent handed Evie the iPad and slowly headed for the front door.

"Trent, if I discover that you knew this all along . . . I am leaving your ass down here! Do you hear me?" Her threat followed Trent through the front door all the way to the porch swing. As her fiery eyes stalked Trent, two sandwiches and two full glasses of milk came into view.

"Maggie and Zoe, come down here and eat these sandwiches you asked for!" Marci yelled up to the second floor from the base of the stairs.

"Marci, I am so sorry. I was going to reveal that once we were further along in our discussion, but, but . . . Trent accused me of adding facts to a story, and you know -"

Marci clipped her sentence. "I know how sensitive you are about facts - you are the reincarnation of Dad. I also knew you would get to the bottom of this, because my husband has developed a bad habit of lying through concealment. *First my dolls and now this.*"

"Marci, I am not trying to make an excuse for Trent, but I had to dig to unearth this story. Maybe . . . just maybe, he had no clue about the cover-up surrounding Orrin Toussaint's death."

"Evie, what you're saying very well could be the case . . . but right now I have major trust issues with my husband and this house."

"Marci, there's more. I found that article online and in the comments section, people who knew the Toussaint family called it a cover-up by the Krewe of Ares and seemed to take great offense that your father-in-law mischaracterized Orrin Toussaint as a homeless kid." Evie took her sister by the hand. "All I am saying is maybe Trent doesn't know this part of the story - so cut him some slack."

Marci allowed Evie to have the last word for now as she headed up the stairs to Maggie and Zoe's room. When Marci entered the room, she found Maggie and Zoe standing in the window, preoccupied with their beads. She reminded them again that their food was waiting on the table, but they never acknowledged her. Stepping over the piles of discarded beads from the Krewe of Babylon, Marci stood at their backs.

"I said, your food is on the table, now hurry downstairs and eat. After you eat, take your baths and let's all call it a night."

"Isn't it beautiful?" Zoe asked Maggie.

"Yes, it is . . . the most beautiful thing I have ever seen," Maggie replied.

"Girls, I understand this was your first Mardi Gras parade and you're excited about all the beads you caught tonight, but it's late. Tomorrow there is another parade that rolls during the day, and we plan to catch that one as well. Now go eat . . . and then prepare for bed."

"I'm not hungry," Zoe replied.

"Mommy, you can have my sandwich; I'd rather stay here," Maggie added.

"MAGGIE AND ZOE, TURN AROUND AND FACE ME . . . NOW!" Marci demanded, but neither of the girls moved.

"This is so pretty," Zoe said.

Losing her patience, Marci grabbed both girls by the shoulders and forced them to face her anger. "I don't know what's going on with you two, but I have had enough. You asked for those sandwiches, and you will eat them. Have I made myself clear?"

"What's going on in here?" Amarah asked from the hall as she dried her hair.

"Your sisters are so excited about the beads they caught at the parade that they seem to have lost their appetites."

"That parade tonight was okay, but it wasn't all that," Amarah said.

"That's because you didn't see the parade," Marci said. "The entire night, you texted! Evie flew all the way down here to spend time with you, and you didn't say a word all night to any of us other than Justin. And you were so rude to that little old lady who handed you those beads," Marci added, completely forgetting the Grandma Ellen connection in her moment of frustration with her daughter.

"But I didn't want the beads - I was over it by that point."

Half of Marci's body faced Zoe and Maggie while the other half twisted toward Amarah. "When someone is showing you kindness, you show your gratitude," Marci spoke through her index finger. "Do you understand me?"

Amarah huffed. "Yes."

"The next time someone is offering you a gift and you act that way, you can say goodbye to that cell phone until you graduate and buy your own with your own money. Do you understand?" Marci scolded, then half-turned back to Zoe and Maggie.

"Well excuse me if I am not as impressed by some stupid parade," Amarah countered.

"Have I made myself clear?"

"YES!" Amarah groaned as she stomped her way down the stairs.

That's when a gentle little voice caught Marci's attention.

"Mommy, I have a gift for you." Zoe said. Marci looked down to see Zoe handing her a string of beads with a doubloon attached. "Mommy, will you wear it so we all can be alike?"

"Zoe, I am too tired to play with beads. I promise to play with you in the morning. Take your butts downstairs and eat."

"But Mommy, you just told Amarah that we are to be polite to people who show us kindness."

"Maggie, I am aware of what I said . . ."

"Zoe is showing you kindness right now, please take the beads and put them on."

"Please, Mommy," Zoe said with a pouty lip that her mother could never resist.

"Please . . ." Maggie joined in.

"All right, all right, I will wear the beads." Marci quickly removed the beads from Zoe's fingers and raised them up to her head. The doubloon dangled in the center of the beads.

The Krewe of Ares . . . Hmmm, how did we get beads from the Krewe of Ares? Marci wondered for a moment.

Maggie took Zoe by the hand and walked toward the door. "We're waiting for you, Mommy."

Marci stretched open the beads and slid her head inside. As soon as the doubloon came to rest on her chest, she felt it - a euphoric rush from the tips of her toes to the crown of her head.

"*It is so beautiful.* The most beautiful thing I have ever touched."

Her body felt like she had been wrapped in a thick, warm blanket that soothed away all her concerns and worries. Her eyes could not blink, not even for a second. The doubloon was the most beautiful thing she had ever seen in her life. Marci held the doubloon up to the light. Then suddenly, she began to hear a different type of voice - an unfamiliar voice that whispered.

"It is I, Kuhani Nalah, and you have entered into the congregation of Mahu." Marci nodded her head. "*Utamtii kuhani mkuu* - You will obey the High Priestess," the whisper instructed.

"*Ninamtii tu*," Marci replied. "I will obey only you."

Zoe and Maggie walked back to the window to join their mother, and the three of them resumed the intimacy of the doubloon. They were still standing at the window, enraptured, when Amarah returned from the kitchen.

CHAPTER 31

Amarah didn't invest much effort in trying to figure out why her mother and sisters were gazing silently out of the window. In fact, she stood outside of their door less than a minute before trotting back to her room. Amarah was in love with Justin - outside of that, very little mattered. And it wasn't that he was her first sexual experience, or even her first boyfriend - in Justin, she had discovered the power of compatibility for the first time. He liked what she liked, and his preferences were also her favorite things. That's why they talked for hours on end; they could believe it themselves.

Earlier that evening, shortly after the start of the parade, Justin said something to Amarah that gave her life:

I'm coming to see you.

That was all it took to confirm in Amarah that their love wasn't just another corny Disney Channel sitcom, but a love worth fighting for and waiting for. *He's coming to see me* is all she could think about when Aunt Evie tried to engage her in their normal chatter as if New Orleans were normal; just a family vacation that would end on Ash Wednesday.

He's coming to see me was all Amarah could think about

when the elderly lady approached with the annoying elation of a clown - the one who offered a hug and a string of beads.

What could matter more for a woman stricken with amaurosis than to suddenly regain her sight? For a man held in a cocoon of paralysis to revisit his favorite fishing pond? An expectant mother well into her forties to hear the heartbeat of a child she never thought was possible? Those five little words were so intoxicating, so potent, so stirring to Amarah that she never asked when he was coming or how. Neither of the two unknowns tugged at the arteries of her heart like that simple sentence: I *'m coming to see you.* Those five little words provided the sustainable breath that allowed her to be miles away from Justin, yet still submerged in him. The moment she came up for air, she inhaled again.

I'm coming to see you.

As the parade rolled by, Amarah recited his words out loud, just to feel a part of him in her mouth like a deep, passionate kiss. Helplessly enraptured in the only person that mattered, her private recital didn't end until the parade ended. That was the reason she'd appeared distant tonight. She missed his Prince Harry smile, his Prince Harry lips and hair.

"I never meant to distract you, but I figured that was the best time to tell you. I couldn't go another week . . ."

"Justin, it wasn't that type of distraction - more like I wish I were with you rather than at a parade."

"Soon you will be, even if it's just for a day . . . being away from you is killing me."

"I die every night, and only come back to life when I hear your voice in the morning."

On the side of her bed that was furthest away from her door, in the absence of light, Amarah burrowed under her blanket and blew kisses to Justin in real time. He kissed her back. The privilege of being able to see each other every night wasn't lost on them. Video chat was their coping mechanism, whereas distant lovers of yesterday only had handwritten letters, and if one could afford it, the occasional phone call.

"Aa-choo!"

"God bless you. That cold is really kicking your butt."

"But it's still not going to stop me from coming. Not even the flu will keep me from you another day. I will be there Sunday. I am coming to see you - *I promise*."

Those five words again, followed by two more, created an echo in her heart: I promise. They hadn't lasted a week before one of them hatched a runaway plan to see the other. Amarah knew that Justin would often spend entire weekends at gaming tournaments, and she knew he could sneak a flight to New Orleans and make it back to Bristol before his nine p.m. curfew.

"Justin, you know how bad I want to see you, but your eyes are running, and your nose sounds stuffy. You don't sound like you're in any shape to travel. Let's put it off a week to give you time to beat this flu."

"Amarah, I will be there Sunday, and that's final - okay?"

"If you say so." Right there, she fell even deeper in love.

"Before we say goodnight, how is your grandmother?"

"I'm not sure. She's still in the hospital, but my dad hasn't given us an update." A sigh of hesitation. "I should ask him in the morning. Maybe go see her . . . I guess?"

"I think you should visit her. Maybe we should go to med school and be the first husband and wife team of doctors to discover a cure?"

"I get it . . . you're afraid it's hereditary, and if you marry me one day, I will whack out on you," Amarah giggled.

He smiled back. "Even if I am unable to discover a cure, I would love you no less."

"Even if I had dementia?"

"Yes."

"You better." Her lips pressed softly against the screen of her cell phone. "Hold on . . . don't hang up. I think Maggie has just tiptoed into my room."

From under her blanket, Amarah listened as strips of oak in

the wooden floor mashed like piano keys with each person who entered her room. "Maggie and Zoe, get out of here and close my door," she called out from under the blanket. "Maggie and Zoe! Leave now."

But the silence was just as thick as the darkness. Losing her patience, Amarah shifted in her bed to face the door, and with the urgency of an aged tortoise, her head slowly emerged from under the blanket.

Three glowing circles were all she could see. They provided just enough light to help her locate the switch on the reading lamp. With more light than before but still very little, Amarah saw her mother and sisters standing in the center of her bedroom.

"Amarah."

"Yes, Mom?"

"I wanted to tuck you in before they go to bed."

"Mom, I will be seventeen next month, no need to. Thanks, but no thanks." From under the blanket, Amarah heard Justin's laughter.

"That's just it, sweetheart, we were once so close, and each night ended with a hug before you fell asleep. I miss the closeness I once had with you."

"Mom, I still feel close to you, but I miss my life. I hate New Orleans, and Bristol will always be my home."

"And that's the other reason I wanted to come in here and talk to you." Her mom moved closer to her bed. "I am thinking about letting you go back to Bristol with Evie. Seeing how sad you are is really breaking my heart."

Amarah sat up on the bed. "Mom . . . really? This isn't a prank?"

"It's not a prank. When Evie boards her plane, you will sit next to her."

Amarah ejected out of her bed and bear-hugged her mother. "Mommy, thank you, thank you, thank you!"

While Amarah trampolined in her bed and danced around the room, her mother and sisters stood motionless - stone-faced silent - but Amarah never noticed. "And Dad agreed to it as well?"

"Yes, you father has agreed that it's best for you to live with Evie."

"Mommy, I love you so much. Thank you. Thank you." Remembering her video chat with Justin was still live, Amarah dropped to her knees and searched the bed for her phone. She raised Justin up to her face. "Did you hear that?"

"Yes, yes! I heard every word. *Oh, my God. Oh my God.*"

"This means I will see you in . . ." Amarah counted on her fingers. "Saturday, Sunday, Monday, Tuesday is Mardi Gras, Aunt Evie is leaving Wednesday . . . In as little as *five days,* we will be together. Not for a day - but forever."

"Amarah."

She asked Justin to hold on. "Yes, Mommy?"

"To celebrate, we brought you a gift."

"A gift? This is turning into the best night ever."

It was then that Zoe stepped forward and stood in front of the nightstand that held Amarah's reading lamp. It only then did she realize that her sisters weren't coming with her - she was going back to Bristol without them. Suddenly her cell phone sneezed: *aa-chooo awh-choo aa-choooo.* All it took was hearing him sneeze to remind her that she was moving back to Bristol, and her sisters would just have to adjust and get over it. Justin was all that mattered.

Amarah crawled over to the edge of her bed and sat on the side, where her little sister waited patiently to hand her a gift.

"This is for you."

"Zoe, that is so sweet of you. When I get back to Bristol, I will send you a picture of myself wearing it, so you'll know I'm thinking of you." Amarah took hold of the beads and opened her nightstand drawer.

"Can you please put it on now, like Mommy and Maggie?"

"Not tonight, Zoe, only because it's bedtime, and the beads could get tangled in my hair, but I promise you I will wear it tomorrow."

"But she is showing you *kindness*," Maggie said.

In that instant, Amarah's eyes intersected with her mother's, and she remembered the argument in the hall - the one about being grateful. For the first time in years, she felt a smidgen of guilt for the selfish way she'd treated her family. Amarah closed the nightstand drawer and opened the beads wide enough to slide her head through.

"My beautiful daughter, from this point forward, no matter how far you go, this doubloon is a reminder that we will never part - we love you," her mother said with a warm smile.

"I love you too, Mommy, and Maggie." Amarah turned back to her baby sister, whose nose she honked. "And you too, little Zoe."

"Goodnight, Amarah," they said in one voice.

"Goodnight, and thanks for my gift." Her family turned to leave the room - but didn't go far.

The moment the beads were around her neck and the doubloon rested on her chest, she felt it. A new love - one more powerful than the love she felt for Justin. A new hunger - one more intense than the longing she'd had two minutes ago. A new soul to replace her old soul. A corporeal soul. An all-consuming soul.

"It's beautiful. It's so beautiful," Amarah said as her lips pressed softly against the burgundy doubloon. "This is the most beautiful thing I have ever held." All four doubloons started to pulsate and contract in perfect sync with Amarah's beating heart. Then came the whispers.

"Yes, yes, I will obey you."

It was then that Marci and Maggie followed Zoe out of the room and back to the window where they first held the doubloon. Amarah lifted her phone to eye level where Justin could see her clearly.

"Amarah! Amarah? What's going on?"

"Justin, if you come here, I will kill you," a scratchy voice said.

"Amarah? What's happening?

Amarah powered off her phone and headed to her sister's room, where she joined her family in the window under the light of the moon. From outside the door, a voice soon called out to them.

"Oh, there you are . . . Marci, when you're done tucking the girls in, can you join me for a glass of wine? Mrs. Young just sent me another email regarding Orrin Toussaint."

"Certainly, we will be there in a minute."

CHAPTER 32

A unt Frieda's gumbo was better than he remembered. Trent was overjoyed that she was the type of aunt who overcooked, because he planned to eat gumbo every day until he scraped the bottom of the pot. With the last of the dishes put away, Trent switched off the light in the kitchen and allowed the green numbers on the microwave some alone time. It was 11:47 p.m.

Leaving the kitchen, Trent rescued the remote from the abyss of the sofa cushions and powered off the TV. Just as he placed his hand on the old familiar banister ball, his cell phone demanded attention.

"Hello?"

"Hi, is this Mr. McGowan?"

"Yes, it is - to whom am I speaking?"

"Mr. McGowan, this is Rene, I am the charge nurse at Touro Hospital. The reason I'm calling is because a woman is here to see your mother, but her name is not on your visitor's list. So, as part of the hospital's visitation procedure involving patients in your mother's condition, we have to get your permission before allowing her to visit."

"Rene, thank you so much. The only person other than immediate family who asked to visit my mother was Mother Bauman from Ursuline Church, but she's coming for morning prayer. What is the lady's name?"

"I know Mother Bauman well; this lady wasn't Mother Bauman."

"What is her name?"

"Just one moment, Mr. McGowan, while I confirm."

Trent could still hear the nurse because she never placed him on mute. *"Ma'am - Ma'am? Where did she go? Did anyone see the little old lady that was just standing at the front counter?"* The panic in her voice quickly reached full max. "Mr. McGowan, I need to call you back!"

"Wait, please! Before you go, did that lady give her name?"

"Yes, but I only have the first."

"What is it?"

"I believe she said Ellen. I have to call you back."

When the elevator doors opened directly in front of the nurses' station, it was in a state of complete chaos. Trent looked down the hall in the direction of his mother's room and saw that the police had completely roped off the hallway with crime scene tape. He immediately sprinted down the hall toward his mother's room, outpacing the charge nurse and an NOPD officer.

It was like one of those stressful dreams where the more he ran, the longer the hallway became. As he ran, more and more hospital and police officers tried to roadblock his path toward Helen's room. They were unsuccessful. Tearing through the crime scene tape, Trent crashed into three detectives and four uniformed officers.

He tried to get through the blockade, but the officers made it impossible - his mother's room was a crime scene. Rene, the nurse who had called him on the phone, was in the next room from his mother's getting consoled by her co-workers. She was the one who found Helen McGowan.

One of the detectives recognized Trent from his visit to head-quarters yesterday, and advised the other cops to release him. Trent entered his mother's room and saw a body in the bed covered with a sheet.

"Are you sure, Detective McGowan?" one of the officers asked.

Trent replied with a nod. The officer nodded, cast his eyes toward the floor, and lifted the sheet.

There she lay, with the center of her forehead crushed, and a crescent moon splatter on the back wall. The murder weapon was a brick - like the type used two hundred years ago in French Quarter home construction. Dark orange fragments of brick mixed in with the fresh blood on her pillow and congealed into a sandy paste. That's when Trent noticed his mother wearing something that wasn't around her neck when she was admitted - a string of Mardi Gras beads. Leaning in to get a closer look at the beads without contaminating the crime scene, Trent noticed that the beads were gold, with a doubloon the color of blood in the center.

"*It says Krewe of Ares 1968*," the detective said. "What gets me is the attending nurse who bathed her said that beads weren't there when she left the room. I think our suspect may know more about these beads. Like a calling card." The detective continued to take notes. "For what it's worth, your mother was sleeping when she was attacked, and probably never knew who or what attacked her. For what it's worth. Detective McGowan . . . we will give you a moment alone with your mother. You are one of us now, and we will catch the monster who did this. You have our condolences."

The moment the officers stepped out into the corridor, Trent collapsed in front of his mother's bed and wept at her feet.

We should have listened to you . . .

CHAPTER 33

At the end of the second floor hallway, Evie stepped out of the guest room snuggled in a pink bathrobe with her damp butterscotch hair twisted up in a large pink towel. In one hand was a tall glass of Booker Fracture and in the other was her phone, open to the in-depth emails from Mrs. Young. There was a total of five emails in all, sent two hours apart. Evie could tell from the sheer quantity of content that Mrs. Young hadn't focused on anything else since their initial conversation - her jaws were locked like a pitbull around the suspicious details surrounding the Orrin Toussaint murder.

The first room she passed on the right was Amarah's - it was empty. The second room on the right was the hallway bathroom that still bellowed steam from her shower. Hanging on a section of the wall between Amarah's room and the bathroom was a picture of Trent's father and three other men. At the base of the photo was a little bronze plate that read:

From left to right: Krewe Attorney Morris Igelhart, Krewe Treasure Ralph Fuller, Krewe Vice Captain Danny Dauterive, New Krewe Captain Jack McGowan.

Evie leaned into the photo and recognized two of the men

from the WWL-TV archive video of the night Jack McGowan gave his statement.

Morris Igelhart.

Ralph Fuller.

According to the bronze plate, the picture was taken December 15, 1968 at the Krewe of Ares Headquarters. Engraved on the final line in a large bold font was *CONGRATULATIONS TO OUR NEW CAPTAIN*. The next room on the right was the room Trent's parents once shared. Directly next to it was Marci and Trent's new bedroom. The door was partially closed, so Evie knocked a few times before she peeked inside - it was empty. The next room on the right was Maggie and Zoe's. Evie opened the door to find Marci and the girls all huddled in the light of the moon, too preoccupied to notice her.

"There you are. Marci, I know it's late, but as soon as you tuck the girls away I have to show you this. You will not believe it."

There was no reply, no acknowledgment; not one head turned in Evie's direction. Evie tried several more times to get their attention, even speaking to each one of them individually, but it was as if she were a Ghost of Christmas Past watching a family she once belonged in. It wasn't until Evie clicked on the light that she got a response. Not in words, but in one single motion. They all turned to face her - with eyes the color of molten lava. Once they faced her, Evie started to notice the reason they'd ignored her in the dark - the florid burgundy doubloons.

"Hmm, what's going on in here?" Evie was rattled with concern. "Marci? Amarah? Hello! Your prank has failed - the gig's up, you guys." Evie's voice was the only sound in the entire house; even the wind that howled like wolves fifteen minutes ago had suddenly fallen asleep. "Marci, what's happening? Why won't you guys talk to me?"

The first to leave the room was Maggie, who walked past Evie without and glance and continued down the stairs, followed by Amarah. The next to leave was Marci. The thought entered

Evie's mind to block the door and force Marci to explain what was going on and why no one would speak to her, but the scowl on Marci's face was as an angry prune - a frown Evie hadn't seen in the thirty-eight years she'd known her sister. Marci continued into the hall and down the stairs. The last to leave the room was Zoe, who appeared just as angry as the others, and equally as silent. Evie followed Zoe down the stairs where she noticed the front door was open, so she followed Zoe onto the porch. Once outside, Marci, Amarah, and Maggie waited for Zoe on the sidewalk. Before Zoe stepped down off the porch, she turned and spoke to her aunt.

"The unborn has returned and the glass has shattered. At this time, the atonement does not involve you - leave here and return from whence you came," Zoe said as she clutched an additional doubloon in her hand.

The glass of Booker Fracture that Evie had eagerly anticipated slipped from her fingers. Like the photo of the flambeaux carriers, it shattered on the floor. After Zoe finished speaking, she continued through the front gate and joined her mother and sisters on the sidewalk. Evie watch as her sister and three nieces continued in a single file line down the pavement. Evie sprinted up to her room to change her clothes and retrieve her cell phone off the charger on the side of her bed. Then she ran outside to follow her family. From a block away, Evie struggled to keep them in sight while she repeatedly dialed Trent. After about a mile of left and right turns, they finally stopped and stood shoulder-to-shoulder on the sidewalk in front of a yellow single-story wooden house.

To avoid detection, Evie crossed to the other side of the street and hid behind the bed of a Dodge Ram truck. There she crouched in a pair of sweatpants, a pink robe, black flats, and freeze-dried, matted hair. Like four mannequins without a window to call home, her sister and nieces just stood there. After about five minutes had ticked away, it was Zoe who knocked on the door of the yellow house. No one answered. Zoe continued to knock, but no one answered. The knocking continued past midnight until someone inside switched on the porch light and peeked through a portion of the venetian blinds.

A very disheveled and confused lady answered the door and waved them inside, but they ignored her invitation. Instead, Zoe handed the lady the beads she'd carried, and the elderly woman received the gift with great appreciation. Evie watched as her sister and nieces encouraged the lady to place the beads around her neck. After a minute or so, she honored their request.

Evie observed the lady as she became instantly smitten with the same doubloon her sister and nieces wore. The woman who had answered her door with extreme caution moments ago now walked out into the street and held the doubloon high as an offering to the moon. Marci, Amarah, and Maggie stood stiffly on the sidewalk as Zoe kept a close eye on her from the porch. At first, the doubloon flickered in a sporadic pattern, but a front of fear blew through Evie when she observed the lady's doubloon sync with the others - like a singular living organism. As if instructions had been spoken in a frequency only those with a doubloon could hear, the woman fell in line on the sidewalk and stood shoulder-to-shoulder with Marci.

Zoe stepped off the porch, touched each doubloon, then led the group down the street - deeper into the night. With trembling fingers, Evie reached into the large pocket of her housecoat and made another attempt to reach Trent. The call went to voicemail again. *I must get back to the house and get Marci's car.* As Evie peeked out from behind the Dodge truck, a little voice threatened her life.

"If you follow us and Aunt Frieda . . . I will kill you," Zoe asserted.

CHAPTER 34

T he charge nurse sobbed. "I took my eyes off her for a second to call Mr. McGowan, and she was gone. It wasn't even one minute, and she was gone," the charge nurse sobbed. "Who would do something like this to a sweet little old lady?" she asked the lead detective.

"Rene, I know this is hard for you and I thank you for your cooperation. How many cameras cover this hallway?"

"Two, I believe."

"And both are working?"

"I believe so . . ."

"That's all the questions I have for now . . . after I interview Helen McGowan's son, I will pass by your station once more to view that video."

To those in his homicide unit, he was known as Key. To everyone else, he was Lead Detective Keenan Encalade, a fifteen-year veteran of the homicide division. His mother hated his job, his wife Irnessa threatened to leave him if he didn't find another job, and his father took a knee in prayer every time his son clocked in for another night shift. Key was the oldest of four boys. He'd followed his father into law enforcement right after graduating from St. Augustine High School, as did his brothers.

The voltage in Detective Encalade's handshake was enough

to jump a Nissan Sentra if you had the cables. In his off time, he competed as a professional body builder, a sport he hoped would soon retire him from the department. His mood was artificially stimulated lately, ever since Chief Bolton had added his favorite muscle-building supplement, Sustanon 250, to the list of banned substances for officers. To make up the difference, Keenan took two Adderall capsules a day, two large salad-bowl servings of sugar grits, five Quarter Pounders from McDonald's, and chased it all down with six raw eggs.

With the face of actor Idris Elba attached to the body of an MMA fighter, Detective Encalade looked like a better fit for the NFL draft than a cop on the NOPD Homicide Squad, but he loved his job. And he was simply the best at solving murder cases. His approach to the murder of Helen McGowan was the same as his approach to many of the other murders he had investigated - up until the moment he spoke with Trent.

"Let's start from the beginning," Detective Encalade told Trent once they were both seated for their interview at the nurses' station. "Did you mother have any enemies?"

"Hmm. Hmm. No . . . well, maybe." Trent shared as much as he knew about Grandma Ellen.

"Let me get this *shit* straight - you believe that whoever murdered your mom has something to do with those Mardi Gras beads around her neck?"

"Yes, I am convinced of it."

"But according to the research your sister-in-law Evie is conducting, this Ellen lady died in 1971?"

"I know this sounds crazy, but . . . yes."

Hot blood pumped through Detective Encalade's veins like a pressure washer. His ink pen stopped in mid-sentence for the first time since he arrived on the scene. The sugar grits and Adderall had just collided in his brain, and the volume on his deep voice lowered to a very serious tone.

"Listen up here, Detective McGowan. We're in the same line of business, you and I, and you know as well as I do that you haven't given me a *got-damn thing* I can go off to catch the motherfucker who killed your mother." With a stiff finger, Encalade jabbed Trent in the chest. "Now stop bullshitting around and tell me what the *fuuuuck* is really going on." Encalade's voice lowered even deeper. "I am asking you again - who in the fuck would want to smash your mother in the head with a mother-fuckin' brick?"

"I told you all I know. The only person my mother was concerned about was -"

"Ellen, the woman who died in 1971? That's what you're giving me?"

"Yes. I mean, no . . . I-I don't know what to think anymore. All I know is my life was going along normally, then my Aunt Frieda asked me to move back here from Bristol because my mom's condition was worsening -"

"The Alzheimer's?"

"Yes . . . the Alzheimer's."

"And your mother warned you that this Ellen lady was coming?"

"Yes."

"And Ellen arrived exactly when your mother said she would arrive and started terrorizing the fuck out of y'all on Toledano Street?"

"Yes . . ."

"Other than your wife, Evie -"

"My sister-in-law Evie . . . my wife is Marci."

"Sorry about that . . . can Marci back up these claims?"

"I think so . . . I am not sure. We were all trying to put these pieces together when the nurse called me tonight."

Encalade flipped back over two pages of notes and did a single-breath recap. "But you say your youngest daughter is the only one in the family who has seen this Ellen woman and identified her on Evie's cell phone because they took a group photo tonight at a parade with a woman who has been dead since 1971 and the person who warned your mother that Ellen was pissed off about the death of Orrin Toussaint in 1968 was the Krewe Captain of that parade . . . Jack McGowan?" Detective Encalade took a deep breath.

Before Trent could confirm, a voice spoke from behind Detective Encalade's enormous muscles.

"I heard it too."

Encalade turned to see a doctor in a high-beam white lab jacket; he extended his hand. "And you are?"

"Doctor Terry Brooks, I am Mrs. McGowan's primary care specialist. I just received the news and made it up here as fast as I could." Just on the other side of Dr. Brooks, two orderlies arrived to transport Trent's mother to the medical examiner.

"So you heard Mrs. McGowan described a woman named Ellen . . ."

"Chauvet. Her name is Ellen Vieux Chauvet." Dr. Brooks produced a notepad with the correct spelling of her name. "The reason why I am so sure about this woman is because we discovered early on in our testing that Helen was terrified of her. She said Ellen Chauvet, the *woman in white,* put a curse on her late husband Jack - she said it happened after Ellen visited the Krewe of Ares office a few weeks after Mardi Gras in 1968. From her random utterings, we concluded that after the woman left his office, Jack became deathly ill - nearly died from liver failure. According to Helen, her husband was the picture of perfect health until Ellen grabbed him by the arm. Since then, her husband and two of her sons died of liver cancer. My staff and I researched this incident, and Jack McGowan was indeed admitted on that exact day at the exact time Helen mentioned. If Trent would permit it, I could make those records available to you right now."

Though he was doubtful that any of what he heard was true, Encalade remained true to his creed to follow the evidence and see where it leads. "Even though this shit is way out there, I need to hear those recordings. Trent, do I have your permission?"

"Yes, you have my permission to view her entire medical file, as well as any files pertaining to my father and brothers," Trent answered without hesitation.

Just as Detective Encalade was about to depart, one of the transport orderlies called out for him with great urgency and panic. He quickly arrived in Helen's room, followed by Dr. Brooks and Trent McGowan. Detective Encalade immediately yelled down the hall for one of his uniformed officers. "Get the crime scene photographer back in here!"

The orderlies had discovered it when they moved Helen's body from the bed where she was murdered to the transport gurney. In a place where not even the most seasoned detective had thought to look, a message was left for Trent. It was written in his mother's blood on the bedsheet.

A doubloon will find you -
Ralph Fuller
Morris Igelhart
Bill Diliberto
Danny Diliberto
Trenton McGowan, the Unborn who has returned.

Exasperated, Detective Encalade asked everyone to clear out for the crime scene photographer - the message on the bedsheet and the bloody brick would require more man hours than he'd originally estimated.

"Wait . . . you're kicking me out, too? I have twenty years of experience on the force - let me help you solve this," Trent pleaded.

Encalade stared up at the ceiling for a moment, then looked back at Trent. "I appreciate the offer, but . . . no, thank you."

"Why not?"

"Dude, your name is the last name on that list. If there is a speck of truth to any of this bullshit, you better run . . . and pray, because Dead Grandma is pissed *the fuck* off."

CHAPTER 35

D etective Encalade radioed a patrol car in the area of 1524 Toledano Street to establish a protective detail. "Well Mr. McGowan, I can't put out an APB for a ghost, but just to be on the safe side, I will have a car parked out front until I can get to the bottom of this. If you see or hear anything else, here's my card." The detective walked away still facing Trent. "And I will need Evie's phone number. I plan to visit your mother's home in the morning."

It was then that Trent realized he had forgotten his cell phone in the car, so he hurried to the elevator. The scene at the nurses' station was just as chaotic as when he arrived. A vortex of police and overwrought hospital administrators converged on the entire floor seeking witnesses. Suddenly, there was a *ding* of the elevator. Once the doors opened, a news crew nearly trampled him as they raced to the story. When Trent arrived on the first floor lobby, he was frustrated to see another news crew racing for the same elevator - someone had tipped them off. After getting grilled by Detective Encalade, he was in no mood for another interview.

Once inside his car, Trent noticed that he had seventeen

missed calls from Evie and one text from Marci. Not sure why Evie would call him so many times consecutively, he figured it was probably best to return her call first, so she could break the news to her sister. Evie answered on the first ring.

"Evie, it's Trent . . . is Marci around?"

"Trent, *oh my God, oh my God* - where have you been? I have been trying to reach you for well over - "

"My mother is gone."

"Gone where? Did someone check her out of the hospital? How could she just leave?"

"What my mother feared finally happened. She killed her."

"Killed who?" Evie asked in a horrified voice.

Trent wept. "Evie . . . someone murdered my mom tonight."

"WHAT?!" Evie screamed.

"I received a call earlier tonight—I'm just leaving the homicide investigators at the hospital."

"She's really gone?"

"Yes . . ." he sobbed. "I am the last McGowan left."

"Trent, I am so sorry . . ."

"Is Marci near you? I may need you to break the news."

"Trent, that is why I've called you repeatedly. Something is wrong. Something horrible is going on. When I walked into Zoe and Maggie's room, I found all four of them - in the window. Mesmerized by those doubloons." Evie when on to explain what happened at Aunt Frieda's house.

"So you have no idea where they are right now?"

Evie started crying. "Zoe told me that if I followed them, she was going to kill me."

"Zoe said that?"

"Trent, it wasn't Zoe. I mean it was, but it wasn't. She appeared to be the leader of it all - they followed her. They disappeared into the fog of the night. *Trent, it was horrible* . . . please come home. We need to find them."

Trent accelerated down St. Charles. "Evie, I am on my way. Lock the door and do not let anyone in - including Marci and my daughters. Somehow Ellen is behind this, and now she has control of my family. I will explain more when I get there."

CHAPTER 36

Trent arrived at 1524 Toledano Street to find Evie sitting on the porch swing wrapped in the comforter from the guest bedroom. Every light in the house beamed and all the drapes were drawn - not even on the side of the house could he find one dimly lit area. Trent could see the trauma in Evie's eyes as he pulled into the driveway. Once he arrived inside the gate, the only distinguishable sound was the squeaking of the bolts that held the swing.

"*Thank God,*" a breathless voice exclaimed.

Trent barely made it onto the porch before Evie ran to him and wrapped her arms around him, like a child frightened of a sinister closet. "Trent my heart grieves with you."

"Thank you, Evie," he said as they consoled each other through the front door. He walked Evie over to the sofa, then darted up the stairs to a locked foot chest that contained his armor gear. After strapping on his bulletproof vest and throwing a black leather jacket over the top, Trent chambered his Glock .45 and slid it into a hip holster.

"Ready to ride?" he asked as he ran down the stairs.

Evie grabbed her purse and cell phone while Trent turned off the lights. As soon as he locked the door, an NOPD patrol car assigned by the lead detective parked in front of the house. Trent asked the officer to join in the search for his family instead of guarding an empty house. The officer agreed, and both cars accelerated away from 1524 Toledano Street.

"Trent, it's the beads from the parade, I am convinced of it," Evie moaned in a voice filled with sadness.

"I plan to kill them and free my family."

"I am not sure if it's that simple. The beads have taken control of them; their minds and bodies."

"Anything from Marci? A call or text?"

"All of them left the house without their cell phones."

"This is not good."

The streets were damp and quiet, even the area surrounding the French Quarter. The city that was known for a party felt eerily lethargic that night. With no particular place to go and all night to get there, Trent cut through a cloak of fog that slinked across the levees, which only allowed a few feet of visibility. While sitting at the red light on Rampart and Canal Street, Trent's phone rang.

"This is Trent."

"Detective Encalade here, sorry to bother you, but I just finished viewing the video and wanted to have a quick word."

"It's no bother. In fact, we're out searching for my family as we speak," Trent placed the call on speaker so Evie could listen in as the light turned green.

"And we're going to do everything we can to find them."

"So, what did you get from the video?"

"So . . . yeah . . . hmm. I viewed the video, and there was a woman at the desk who fit the description. An elderly African American woman with a large black purse and a cane. She stopped at the nurse's station, then walked down the corridor to your mother's room."

"How long was she in my mother's room?"

"That's the part I can't answer . . ."

"Why not? You viewed the video . . . what was the exit time stamp?"

"There wasn't one."

"Excuse me . . . ?"

"The video doesn't capture her leaving the room."

"But-but I just left that room. She wasn't there."

"How do you think I feel right now? She entered but never left the room. At first, I thought there could have been a glitch with the security camera, but after viewing the second camera from the opposite end - she never exited that room. This shit . . . is crazy."

"Now you have witnessed firsthand what I was trying to explain - something dark and evil killed my mother."

"When you figure out how to kill it - please teach me. I still need to interview your sister-in-law, please let her know."

"She right here, and it's confirmed."

"Thanks. By the way, I have eight cars out tonight searching for your family. The moment I hear something, I will ring your phone."

"Detective, thank you so much . . . for everything."

After making a right on St. Phillips Street, Trent headed north through the French Quarter on Frenchmen Street - no sign of his family. It was then that Trent had an emotional breakdown.

"This is all my fault. I should have never dragged my family down here. I didn't want to be alone. I have never been alone." Trent punched the ceiling of the SUV. "The moment I find my family, we're getting the fuck out from down here and never coming back." The steering wheel took the brunt of his grief as he tugged and pounded the center airbag.

"Trent, this is not your fault, your mother needed you . . ."

"Evie, it's my fault. In less than a week, I destroyed my family. Marci was probably going to leave me anyway."

"Trent, I know my sister - she is loyal to a fault. Marci wasn't going to leave you. Yes, your life was going to be a living hell for a while because of her dolls, but she wasn't going to leave you. If we're going to find them, I need you to stay with me - we have to think and focus. I have something I need to share that might help us understand what's going on. Pull to the shoulder when you can."

Trent drove through the intersection of Poydras and St. Charles Avenue and parked on the narrow shoulder of the road across from old Gallier Hall. Evie took a deep breath and turned to face him.

"Trent, it's pretty clear now that Ellen Chauvet is seeking revenge for your father's role in the cover-up of her grandson's murder. Before all hell broke loose tonight, I waited for my sister to tuck in the girls so I could share this email with you guys," Evie started to sob.

Trent reached across the center armrest to comfort her. "It's your turn to be strong."

Evie wiped her eyes. "Orrin Toussaint wasn't her only grandson - his brother is still alive and well. His name is . . ."

"Earl Toussaint, owner of Tou Brothers Movers."

"Yes, the picture on the wall was taken by your mother at the start of the parade. Marci filled me in on what happened the day you moved in."

"That is why he became so emotional."

"Yes, that's why . . ."

"But why would he help us? It's a miracle he didn't seek his revenge that day."

"And that's why we have to find him . . . we have to speak with him first thing in the morning. Trent, Earl Toussaint is our only hope."

Trent sighed and nodded. After driving around for a seemingly endless span of time, mostly silent and seeing no signs of his family, he and Evie decided to call it a night and drove back to the empty house on Toledano Street.

The next morning, while Evie conducted her portion of the

interview with Detective Encalade, Trent searched through his contacts for Earl's phone number. Just as he was about to press dial, there was a knock on the front door. Both Trent and Detective Encalade drew their guns and waved Evie up to the second floor. Trent peeked out the window but didn't see a car in the driveway - it was then that he switched his pistol out of safety mode. Then came another knock, but Trent couldn't identify who was at the door from his vantage point. "Who is it?" he called out.

"Trenton, it's me - Dr. Morial from across the street."

Dr. Morial was a medical examiner, and a neighbor Trent had known all his life. Trent and Detective Encalade holstered their weapons and opened the door to a very puffy eyed, swollen-nosed woman who had been very close to his mom.

"Trent, I saw her last night . . . no warning at all. Not my Helen . . ." Dr. Morial hugged her way into the house.

"Thank you, Dr. Morial; I am still in shock . . ."

"I know baby, I know." She finally spotted Detective Encalade on the other side of the door. "Oh hey, Keenan; I thought that was your car."

Detective Encalade reached over to hug her. "I didn't know Mrs. McGowan was your neighbor."

"Yes, she was, Lord bless the dead. When my husband bought this house back in 1973, the people around here treated us so nasty - half of them put their houses up for sale the next day. But not Helen. She walked across the street holding Craig by one hand, Steven by the other, and you on her hip. She welcomed me and we have been the best of friends since. Lord, who would do something like that to the sweetest person in this city?"

"Dr. Morial, that's why I am here early this morning. We will catch the person who did this."

She hugged them both before heading for the door. "I will get out of your way, just wanted to let you know I am finished with our side of things and the report has been emailed to Homicide. Trent, if you need anything, you do like you used to do - just cross the street and come on in. You hear me?"

"Will do, Dr. Morial."

She waved and started to close the gate at the same time.

"Dr. Morial, I thought this was your last year - you change your mind about retiring?" Trent called after her.

"Trent, I done retired twice. They called me back each time, but this is it. I have nine months to go." She blew a kiss from her porch.

At the kitchen table, Trent could see that Evie and Encalade had already resumed their interview, so he seized the opportunity to dial Tou Brothers Movers. The phone rang for a few seconds, then a female voice answered. After a brief hold, the call was passed through.

"This is Earl, what can I move for you today?"

"Hi Mr. Toussaint, this is Trenton McGowan. You unpacked us earlier this month." There was a pause. "I think you know why I'm calling . . . My family is in danger, please help me -"

Click.

Call time: 1 minute 37 seconds.

CHAPTER 37

March 9, 1968

T he last of the funeral attendees offered their final hugs and condolences before they moseyed out the door. The funeral for Orrin Toussaint was about as sad as everyone expected; a death that devastated the entire community. To accommodate all who wanted to attend, the service was held in his high school auditorium. That day, the auditorium was packed from wall to wall with Teresa's late husband's side of the family, the Toussaints, Grandma Ellen's Chauvet side of the family from as far away as Sierra Leone, the Desire and Florida housing project communities, and numerous students from Carver High School.

Also in attendance at the funeral were reporters from Jet magazine, who attended the funeral as part of their ongoing coverage into what they reported as *The Lynching of Orrin Toussaint*. The story of what happened that Mardi Gras night had become a national story, thanks to the two *Jet* reporters who interviewed Martin at the scene.

The highlight of the day was the NOLA Hearts featuring

Bridgette Banks. With the permission of Mrs. Banks, for just that one moment in time, Bridgette paid tribute to the love of her life the best way she knew how - through song. Bridgette stood onstage like Gladys Knight in an all-white dress while the three remaining members of the NOLA Hearts provided her background and perfect harmony. At Grandma Ellen's request, there was no eulogy - only Orrin's favorite songs followed by words of reflection from friends and family.

Someone who wanted to be there, but preferred to stand outside, was Orrin's big brother Earl Toussaint. Still heavily bandaged from his arms up to his neck, his physical appearance answered any and all questions regarding the closed casket that held Orrin's remains. And then there was Orrin's mother Teresa. During the moments in the program when one singer replaced another or one speaker was replaced by another, in the silence of those interludes, everyone in attendance could hear the totality of Teresa's sorrow. Though no one would allow it, Earl just wanted to be alone - at the funeral and home.

After returning home from the cemetery, Earl lay across his bed reading the letter from the Orleans Parish School Board - the one that notified his mother that Orrin would have to attend Francis T. Nichols High School, the high School Grandma Ellen didn't trust. It reminded him of yesterday, when they had worked through the dilemma of whether he should attend Grambling or the University of Southern California. Just as Earl was getting settled in that memory, he heard the familiar tapping of a walking cane coming in his direction. Since Orrin's murder, Earl had avoided being alone with his grandmother, but now he was cornered in his room and could not avoid her any longer.

"You know why I am here, don't you?"

"Yes, Grandma, but I still don't want to talk about it."

"Sometimes we have to do those things that we don't want to do . . . for the sake of our family. You do know that, right?" She took a seat in a chair on the side of his dresser.

"Grandma, I don't want it."

"I don't think you have much choice in the matter at this point. Having Orrin allowed you to pass on this responsibility, but they murdered my grandson. They will pay severely - with no mercy for what they did to Orrin and for the pain they inflicted on our peaceful family - but in the meantime, we have to get you prepared. Do you understand what I say?"

Earl sat up. "Grandma, I don't want it! Why can't you pass it to Uncle Donald? I'm your grandson, but he is your only son."

"You know the reason why I cannot pass it to your uncle; he abandoned his duty when he allowed that pastor to baptize him. And it was your grandfather who picked you long before your uncle - it was as if he knew Donald was not fit for such an honor. You were the original chosen one, until your grandfather dreamed that it should be passed to your brother."

It was then that Earl's mother overheard the conversation from the hallway. Teresa charged into the room in rage. "Momma, you will not do this - enough is enough. The dirt hasn't even settled on my son's grave. Couldn't this wait?"

"Teresa, this doesn't have anything to do would you . . ."

"That's where you're wrong, Momma . . . it has everything to do with me. I have just buried one son, and Earl is all I have left!"

"I raise these boys while you clean toilets for white folk. How dare you speak to me like that?"

"You help to raise them! The days of you bossing my children around . . . I mean my son . . . are over."

Grandma Ellen raised one finger above her head. Immediately, Gail Narcisse and Vesta Mae, who had been peering in from the hallway, took hold of Teresa's arms and escorted her to the living room, kicking and screaming.

"Earl, the knowledge and authority that have been handed down to me derive from generations upon generations of honorable servants of Amun. It has been my honor to follow the truth as instructed. You know my soul cannot rest unless I pass the gift of Nebneteru on to you - it is not mine to keep."

"Grandma, if I accept it, then I have to give up football. I have already lost my brother, and now you want to take the only thing I have left?"

"I know how much you love football, but you will love reigning as High Priest more than anything else in life. It is an honor to reign as High Priest, and it is the least that we can do to pay our respect and gratitude. We have no one else."

"Grandma, I just want a normal life - I don't want to control souls, I don't want to control the dead. I just want to control my life."

"You're not normal! You are in the line of succession, and you will do your part. Before I leave this Earth, you will do your part."

It was then that Teresa broke free from Grandma Ellen's handmaidens and ran down the hall. "Earl, grab your medication and let's go."

"Teresa, you will not take him out of this house!"

"Earl . . . grab your things, and let's go."

"Earl, you better not take one step toward that door."

Gail Narcisse and Vesta Mae blocked passage to the front door - even if she wanted to, Teresa could not make it to the front door. The only other exit was the back door on the other side of Earl's bed. Teresa ran to the door and opened it. "Earl let's go. My mother's responsibility is not yours, nor are her burdens. Come with me, we are leaving here tonight."

Just as Earl stood to follow his mom, the door slammed shut - followed by the clicking sounds of windows locks. From outside, Teresa struggled to twist the doorknob, but it was airtight.

"Grandma, please stop. Please stop, Grandma . . ." Earl stammered.

"You have been chosen; I will not allow you to escape your responsibility . . ."

Grandma Ellen stopped abruptly when they all heard muffled wails coming from the other side of the house. They all turned and looked in the direction of the door she had cut in the middle of the shotgun home.

A few seconds later, Bridgette staggered through the door with a face full of tears - tormented by heartache, trembling from bereavement.

"Bridgette, how long have you been over there?" Bridgette didn't answer at first. "Bridgette, how long have you been over there?" Grandma Ellen demanded to know.

"So is that the reason why Orrin would never come to church with me?"

Earl took the liberty. "Bridgette, we're not allowed to step foot in the worship facilities of any religion. That is how my Uncle Donald disqualified himself - I was next in line. My brother wanted to tell you, but he couldn't. We're not even allowed to speak about our beliefs."

"Is this voodoo?"

Grandma Ellen erupted into laughter. "We were in existence five thousand years before voodoo was a thought. Since the rule of the pharaohs of Ancient Egypt," she asserted with a chest full of pride. "Bridgette, this doesn't concern you anymore, you can go on home now."

As soon as she spoke, Grandma Ellen's handmaidens stood to help her execute her will.

"Mrs. Narcisse, you are a part of this as well?" Bridgette asked in confusion. "Your daughter is my best friend. She never mentioned any of this."

Gail Narcisse took a long, hard swallow, then proclaimed in firm voice, *"Sisi tu hutumikia amri ya zamani ya Amun."* Then Gail walked over to Grandma Ellen, lowered to her knees, and kissed the tops of her feet. *"Tunatumikia tu Kuhani Nalah."*

"Mrs. Narcisse, I-I don't understand - what are you saying?"

"She said we only serve the ancient order of Amun under his High Priestess Kuhani Nalah."

Tears fell off both sides of Bridgette's face. "And who is this Kuhani Nalah?"

"Sweet, precious child . . . I am Kuhani Nalah."

"And my Orrin was in line to replace you?"

"Yes."

From the backyard, Teresa continued to bang on the door while Earl did as he was told and remained seated. Vesta Mae went to Kuhani Nalah's bedroom and returned with a red candle and the picture of Jean Pierre Chauvet.

"And all of you belong to this?" a bewildered Bridgette continued to inquire.

"And so do I," Pananie said as he entered the crowded doorway and joined Gail Narcisse's tribute. After they recited a full litany of honor, with the traditional responses, Pananie and Gail assumed positions on the left and right of Kuhani Nalah as she returned to her chair.

"Bridgette, it's like this - you can plan and plan, but things don't always go as planned. It was my husband, Jean Chauvet, who said Amun the Keeper of Souls came to him in a dream and ordered the succession to fall upon a male successor. Once, it was Earl. Then, it fell to Orrin. It was arranged for Orrin to marry Phyllis, because Gail is a fifth-generation and Orrin is a fifth generation, and from those two the power over trapped souls would continue. Then came you, and then came Martin, so Gail and I figured you and Orrin would break up on your own, but . . ."

"Orrin and I fell deeper in love, then Martin and Phyllis fell deeper in love."

"And then they murdered my grandson in the street like a dog." Grandma Ellen turned back to Earl. "I cannot force you to reign, but to deny this gift will cost you something you cherish. I'm asking you for the last time - will you serve?"

Earl could still hear his mother banging on the door, pleading with him to reject his grandmother. In tears, Earl approached his grandmother, took hold of her right hand, and wiped his tears. "Grandma, I love you and always will, but please pass on your authority to someone else, because I am not qualified."

Suddenly, Grandma Ellen's voice rumbled the walls like a

thunderstorm. "What do you mean you are not qualified?"

Earl kissed her hand six times. "Grandma, we never told you, but the week after Uncle Donald was baptized into the Christian faith - so was I."

Suddenly, the door that had slammed shut thirty minutes ago swung open with a force that cracked the wall paneling. Grandma Ellen's walking cane pointed the way. "GET OUT, NOW! TERESA AND EARL, FROM THIS DAY FORWARD, WE ARE STRANGERS! GET OUT OF MY HOUSE, NOW!"

Earl gathered his medication and book sack, then he obeyed his grandmother for the final time. Anger traveled around the room like a Northern breeze.

"Gail, go send word to the family that we are in dire crisis. We are in danger of losing our authority over the souls," Grandma Ellen commanded.

"Bridgette, let us walk you home," Earl said from the doorway.

Just before Bridgette reached the darkness of the backyard, she suddenly stopped in the center of the doorframe. She turned and called out, the backdrop of the night behind her.

"Grandma Ellen, you can have Mrs. Narcisse cancel those phone calls to your followers about the succession crisis."

Grandma Ellen leaned forward on her cane. "Young lady, what did you say?"

"I said, you can tell Mrs. Narcisse to cancel all those phone calls, because you no longer have a succession crisis."

"And why is that, Bridgette?" Grandma Ellen asked in a shoo-fly tone of voice.

"Because I am pregnant with the successor."

CHAPTER 38

All throughout the office were balloons celebrating her fiftieth anniversary. There was a *Happy 50th Anniversary* cake, and a huge *We're going to miss you* card that had collected signatures from everyone in the office. The only problem was, she wasn't quite ready to go.

Even Mrs. Mackie couldn't believe how fast the years had flown; it felt as if she'd blanked five decades into the future. This company was the only company she'd ever known, and only an exceptional few could relate. Over the years she had seen it all, heard it all, and could do it all, because fifty years was a lot of time to master a craft. To put it simply, Mrs. Mackie was the best. The best at what, you might ask? She was the best Parade Organizer, Executive Assistant, Float Designer, Doubloon Designer, Costume Designer, Membership Manager, and Public Relations Director in the City of New Orleans . . . but she never wanted the title of Captain.

As Mrs. Mackie reclined in her chair, she pondered if today was really her last day. She didn't really have an answer, despite the fact that she'd announced over a month ago that she would retire today. *And if I retire today, where will I sit tomorrow?*

Over the years, she'd changed hats many times, but she never changed desks. Her desk had a name, and a gender: She was Hagatha - the old hag, for short. It was the same dry-rooted desk she sat in on her first day, with a few new hinges here, a few nails there, and a few bottle caps underneath to keep the old hag upright.

Oh Hagatha, stop worrying. If I retire today, then you're retiring today.

Her husband, Fred Mackie, had long since retired from the post office, and for the past ten years had encouraged her to hang it up so they could spend months on end indulging in European vacations. She never had kids, but her desk was her surrogate child - and she never wanted to experience the separation anxiety of leaving her bundle of joy behind.

Over by the copy machine, several employees gathered around her husband as he flipped through old albums from her archive. After about an hour, they created a quiz show where they competed to name previous kings and queens. Mrs. Mackie wasn't allowed to play. One of the new hires in the office sat in a chair next to Hagatha and asked Mrs Mackie, "Who was your favorite krewe captain?"

"Jack McGowan," she replied without a second of hesitation.

". . . And who was the most difficult captain to work for?"

"My father." Without a second of hesitation.

She finally made her decision around eleven-thirty a.m. - Mrs. Mackie was officially retiring. Deep down she knew it was time to go - time for one of the young ladies in her office to become the new Mrs. Mackie, even though the current Mrs. Mackie had the endurance to go another ten years without a sweat. Mrs. Mackie gazed at the young woman who sat on the edge of her desk, tanning in her rays, absorbing all she could in the precious time that remained.

How are they ever going to grow into their roles while I'm here?

It was time to go. From her desk, she finally managed to get her husband's attention. Then, she tossed her purse around her shoulder and stood in front of Hagatha. *Oh, Hagatha, stop that pouting. Fred will come back for you in his truck.* Every employee ran to the window to watch Mr. and Mrs. Mackie walk through the parking lot, load the car with all her gifts, and drive away.

It took less than two minutes for them make it home, and another ten minutes for her husband to haul in all her gifts. Mrs. Mackie plopped across her bed, stared at the ceiling, and sailed through a sea of memories. Inside of her purse, her phone vibrated with a text message. She reached into her purse absently to check.

Mrs. Mackie, members from the Krewe of Zulu and Rex have delivered more gifts for you.

She held the phone to her heart and released a sigh of appreciation. After a soft kiss on the lips, her husband departed to get Hagatha and her additional gifts. *Old Hag would look great in the sunroom; the light should serve her well.*

For a brief bit of time, Mrs. Mackie experienced a spike in her heart rate; a sudden case of hyperventilation at the realization that she was home alone, in the middle of the day, with nothing to do. But medicinal thoughts of her husband of thirty-eight years soothed her sudden anxiety. Thoughts rolled across her mind of how he'd stuck by her side during those dark days of infertility, how he'd reassured and calmed her . . . It was then that she noticed the large card from her office - the one signed by all her staff. She read each signature and note with delight, mentally placing a face with every name - even the young lady who'd sat on the edge of her desk.

Her nostalgic voyage was briefly interrupted by the sound of a tap on the tile floor in the foyer of her home.

"Honey, did you forget something?" Mrs. Mackie called out. No one answered. She listened as the sound that started in the foyer started to approach from the end of the hall that connected to her bedroom.

Closer. Louder. Steady.

Tat.

Tat.

Tat.

Tat.

Tat.

It took a while for Mrs. Mackie to register why the sound was familiar, but her recollection never failed her. *How is that possible?* Her sciatic vertebrates cracked to an upright position as she inched toward the bedroom door. That's when she saw her . . . and that walking cane.
    That woman in white.

CHAPTER 39

When the call came in, Detective Encalade ended his interview with Evie and Trent and hurried a few blocks over to 7903 Freret Street. On the corner was a white single-story house with a large oak tree and a white wrought iron fence. Encalade entered the house and greeted three of the officers who'd arrived first at the home of Fred and Suzanna Mackie.

"What we got, fellas?"

An officer taking pictures of the foyer area turned to face him. "Key, it's a bad one. Haven't seen one like this since I joined the force."

"That bad, huh?"

"You will see, simply follow the yellow tape road."

Encalade was in no rush to view his latest victim; experience on homicides taught him that the body could wait, but the crime scene couldn't. From the foyer, he could see the buzz of Crime Lab at other end of the hall, but something more intriguing than the victim caught his attention. On every wall in the house, as far as his eyes could see, hung Mardi Gras-themed portraits. All were hung in reverse chronological order. Each one of the portraits was eleven-by-seventeen inches and professionally matted in a mahogany frame. Each was framed with a title card at the base.

The first picture on the left side of the hallway captured the King and Queen of Ares in 2017 as they led a royal court precession into the Grand Ball. The photo to the right of that displayed a Queen and her debutants from 2010. The third picture showed the 2010 King and Queen that year as they promenaded the ballroom. As Detective Encalade continued down the hall, he encountered a familiar name at the Captain's Table during a ball in 1975. Seated at the huge circular table were eight previous Captains of the Krewe of Ares, along with their wives. On the title card at the base, Detective Encalade read the names:

Jack & Helen McGowan 1968.

Detective Encalade couldn't help but notice how stiff Helen's face was in the picture as compared to the faces of the other wives. Not only did she have that look that said *get me out of here,* so too did Jack McGowan. It was then that Detective Encalade remembered the liver cancer that Jack was mysteriously stricken with - the sickness his wife felt was induced by a visit from Grandma Ellen. The last picture in the row of photos was one of Jack McGowan standing next to Suzanna Dauterive.

"Well hello, Mzzz. Sexy!" Detective Encalade grinned as he admired the woman in the picture with Jack McGowan.

"You may want to say that a little louder so she can hear you - she right over there," his partner, Detective Seals, suggested.

"Over where?"

"Look down . . . Now to the other side of the room." Detective Seals then redirected Encalade back to the photo on the wall. "She's waiting for you over there," he called as he hurried down the hall.

"Where are you off to?"

"You didn't hear? I guess not . . . you leave your radio in the car again?"

"Dammit!"

"There's been another homicide on Esplanade and Burgundy. Chief told me to stay until you arrived. Something about *you've been up twenty-four hours* or something. Anyway, after you're done here, Chief said go home and rest!"

"Machines don't need sleep!" Detective Encalade yelled as Detective Seals exited the home.

Kennan Encalade was two feet into the bedroom where he heard a female voice threaten him. "If you take another step, I will crack you in the head with this fucking camera!"

"Teri, my bad, my bad . . . geez."

"I am tired of saying the same shit over and over - do not step foot in my crime scene without proper gear! Why is this so hard for you? Huh? Why?" Lieutenant Teri Moore, Head of NOPD Crime Lab, demanded as she wrapped the strap of her Nokia camera around her fist.

"Okay, give me a second to step back in the hall and remove my shoes." Encalade removed his left shoe, then the right.

"You want me to fuck you up?" she charged at him. "You think I won't fuck you up, huh? You are the most forgetful detective I have ever seen."

"Teri, I have been up for twenty-four hours. I forgot."

"I don't give a fuck. You contaminate my crime scene, I will fuck you up - we clear?"

Encalade took Teri's threat seriously and slid down the tile in his black dress socks. He padded out the front door to his patrol car to retrieve his radio and a pair of disposable shoe covers. He couldn't let her know, but Teri's words cut deep - he'd been struggling with his short-term memory for the last six months. He would forget everything, like stepping into the shower with no washcloth, grabbing his laptop with no cord, and carrying a gun with only three bullets in the clip because he constantly forgot to restock after leaving the gun range.

When he reentered the house, he walked back to where Teri was finishing up.

"So, the victim's full name is Suzanna Dauterive Mackie?"

he asked her.

"Yes, and her husband is Fred Mackie. He's out back with Detective Gloster."

"Okay."

"Hey, Key?"

"What, Teri?"

Teri snapped the last of her pictures and headed for the door. "What's her husband's name?"

"Teri, chill . . . please - I've been up twenty-four hours, okay?"

"Well piss on me in the morning." Her hands moved to her hips and her eyes rolled to the left. "You forgot just that fast, didn't you? Didn't you? I keep telling you to lay off those steroids. First to go is your nuts - then your memory. Now that I think about it, you can't remember shit as it is - which means your nuts have already shriveled up." She laughed her way down the hall. "See you at the next one - *Mr. Prunes.*"

"Bye Teri . . . with your aggravating ass." Detective Encalade was happy to see her clear out so he could finally have the entire crime scene to himself. Kennan Encalade and Teri Moore had graduated from the academy together and remained joined at the hip because he went into homicide and she specialized in forensics. Teri reminded him of Niecy Nash from the sitcom *Reno 911*, only taller, and louder. Very loud. She had recently married and divorced all in a span of ninety days. When Encalade asked her what caused her marriage to fail so quickly, her response was, "Dude kept *playin* with me." Lieutenant Teri didn't mean playin in a good way - she meant he constantly disrespected her. Whenever she asked him not to do something, he did it anyway.

Now, where was I?

Detective Encalade stood over the body of Suzanna Dauterive Mackie and he knew at first glance what he was dealing with: a very personal motive. Someone was determined to send a clear message to the people connected to the victim - You're next. Her top and bottom lips were ripped off her face, her eyes were gouged, and she was bleeding from the neck. Kneeling down for a closer view, he saw it - the same doubloon from the Helen Mc-Gowan crime scene. Detective Encalade took a few pictures of his own so he wouldn't have to ask Lieutenant Teri, then headed out back to interview her husband.

When he arrived in the sunroom, Mr. Mackie was being consoled by two men who introduced themselves as his brothers. Detective Encalade gave Detective Gloster their secret hand signal to indicate that the person being interviewed was no longer the primary suspect. Detective Gloster excused himself, leaving Detective Encalade alone to interview the grieving husband.

"Hello sir, I am Detective Encalade . . . and your full name? I just need to get it exact on my report." He realized he still couldn't remember her husband's name.

"It's Fred Mackie," one of his brothers answered.

"Look, I have talked to three of you guys already . . . why are you not out there looking for the son of a bitch who killed my Suzanna?" Fred wept into his palms.

"Sir, I know this is a difficult time for you. Please believe we will do everything possible to catch this killer, but first I just have a few questions and I will be out of your way."

"Ask whatever questions you need to ask to catch this asshole who killed my wife. If I hadn't pressured her to retire, she would still be alive," Fred mourned.

"Mr. Mackie, how close was your wife with Jack McGowan?"

"Her old krewe captain?"

"Yes, sir."

"They were very close . . . he helped her get her foot in the door . . . did more than her father did, that's for sure. Her father used all five of his daughters to gain power. Old man Dauterive forced her to take that job."

Detective Encalade flipped back ten pages in his notes. "Did she ever talk about a kid who died during a parade in . . ."

Fred Mackie cut him off. "1968. Orrin Toussaint. Yes . . . at least once a week. Not as much about the kid, but mainly about his grandmother."

"That's who I'm referring to."

"My wife started having these really bad dreams about five years ago after Jack died. She told me he would come to her during those dreams."

"Did she describe the dreams?"

"Just the other night, my wife woke from a bad dream. She told me all the pictures in the house had fallen to the floor and shattered. For her, it was the worst dream ever. She continued to say *we're out of time, the woman in white is coming . . .*" Fred collapsed in the arms of his brother.

Encalade gave Fred a few minutes before he continued the interview. "Did you know Helen McGowan was murdered?"

"No, I didn't. Do you feel there is a connection?"

"Sir . . ." He forgot his name again. "Your wife has beads and a doubloon on from the Krewe of Ares 1968 - did she have these beads on earlier today?"

"No . . . a 1968 doubloon? That year was a very bad year - and she wouldn't be caught dead wearing a doubloon from 1968."

Detective Encalade held his cell phone at an angle so Fred could view a close-up of the doubloon. "Sir, I have reason to believe the person who killed your wife is also the person who killed Mrs. McGowan."

"Like a serial killer targeting people who work for Ares?"

"Yes and no." Detective Encalade showed Fred the close-up view of Mrs. McGowan's doubloon from his cell phone. "I believe the people who were members of Ares and knew of the details surrounding the murder of Orrin Toussaint are the targets. That appears to be a very small group. How your wife plays into this, I am not sure - but I will find out."

It was then that Detective Encalade's radio chirped.

"Come back."

"Detective Encalade, I need you over here at the scene on Esplanade."

"Roger that."

"Please hurry."

"Ten-four."

CHAPTER 40

The plan was simple: Have Evie lure Earl to a storage facility for an estimate on the cost to move three large units from New Orleans to Baton Rouge. Once he arrived, Trent would plead for his help in locating his family. What Trent remembered about Earl was his genuine compassion, and his Good Samaritan kindness to help someone in need. Trent was extremely desperate, and failure wasn't an option. They had to convince the surviving grandson of Ellen Chauvet to help in the search for his family and free them from her control without getting killed in the process.

The meeting time was set for noon, because Earl was on an office relocation job just up the road in Mandeville and was willing to meet on his break. Trent hadn't come up with the plan - he was too busy wallowing in a gutter of self-pity and defeatism to conceive a caper so daring. Luckily for him, he had an unlikely partner in this crisis with just as much skin in the game - her sister Marci was her only next of kin. It was Evie who picked Trent up off the floor of despair.

"If you won't come with me to the location in Slidell, then I will go alone, but I will not sit here while waiting on the police to find someone who doesn't know they're lost," she'd told him. Evie had stopped just short of calling him a coward, but she didn't have to - her eyes said it loud and clear.

And with that direct challenge, Trent regained his composure and realized that his only chance of any reunion with his family was going to come through Earl Toussaint and Detective Encalade. And so, he waited in a strip mall parking lot across the street from Move It Now Self Storage, making sure Evie had a full view of Marci's cherry red Honda Pilot. He lowered the windows to allow the chilled air to slap his face and toughen his senses; to become one with his environment prior to what was sure to be a heated confrontation. Next to his car, two guys devoured foot-long po-boy sandwiches while debating an upcoming college football championship game. The aroma of their cheese-drenched, hot, sausage sandwiches took him back to a time when his father had taken him and his brothers to Domilise's Po-Boys and Bar on Annunciation Street.

Trent also remembered his parents arguing that day. They argued through dinnertime and throughout the night, resuming their argument during breakfast the following morning. His mother had barged into his father's office one day unannounced only to discover that his usual gatekeeper—the one who screened all his calls, typed all his memos, and tended to all his administrative needs - was not at her desk. Rather, she was in his office, on a couch, under her husband. His mother never left his father over the affair with Suzanna Dauterive, and his father never divorced his work wife - only with his death did they part. The troubles in his parents' marriage were sealed tight inside the walls of 1524 Toledano Street. To Trent, his dad was still the greatest father in the world, and his mother was the embodiment of unconditional love. Just the scent of a short-lived po-boy sandwich evoked memories so vivid he could still hear his brother's voices, the sound of the wooden floors when his father entered the home, and the call of his mother's voice when it was time for dinner.

Ellen Chauvet has taken everything I love, but it ends today.

The rumbling of a white, twenty-eight-foot cube truck slowly crawled into the parking lot. The side of the truck displayed the words *Tou Brothers Movers* in large black letters. The truck was quickly followed by a text message from Evie announcing the obvious:

HE'S HERE!

Trent watched from across the street as Evie exited first and stood at the rear of the SUV. She wore form-fitting jeans, and had given her hair the day off in a ponytail hidden under a denim baseball cap. Though there was a freeze warning advisory for people, plants, and pets, Evie only wore a deep purple insulated vest with a yoga shirt underneath.

Earl walked over to her with a huge smile and a handshake that started from the moment his feet touched the ground. Trent could hear the faint sound of *Have we met before?* and Evie's reply of *I don't think so*. He watched as Evie excused herself to retrieve her cell phone - that was his cue to move into position. Evie pretended that her phone had slid between the driver's seat and the center console, which gave Trent just enough time to cross the street.

"And . . . got it," Evie said as she finally recovered the phone.

"That happens to me all the time. They make these phones so paper-thin these days. When it happens to me, I have to pull over to the side of the road. Every single time."

"Sorry about that, and I won't keep you much longer because I know you're busy with another job, but I just wanted to ask you . . . Well, he wanted to ask you . . ."

"Hello again, Mr. Toussaint."

Earl's full-tooth smile vanished the moment he turned and saw Trent McGowan standing there with his hand extended. Earl scowled, first at the hand that waited patiently, then at Trent. Earl shook Trent's hand and walked past him to his truck. "Good day."

"I know why you ran out of the house that day and needed a moment," Trent called after him. Earl opened his truck door and slung his clipboard across the cabin. Just as he placed his foot on the lift step, Trent continued. "I know your little brother's name, and the truth about what happened to him." Earl's chin slowly came to rest on his neck.

"Earl, I know what they did to Orrin and how they covered it up. It was wrong, and it breaks my heart to know my father was involved. Earl, my mother was murdered yesterday, but shortly before her death, some of her last words were those of my father, Jack McGowan. He regretted everything that happened - even from beyond the grave he has expressed remorse. I wasn't even born at the time, but in less than twenty-four hours, I've lost my mother and I can't find my wife, my kids, or my aunt."

Earl removed his foot from the lift step and half-turned to face Trent.

"Earl, you offered me a place to live when we opened that box and discovered those broken dolls. I don't know you personally, but I know your heart. Please Earl, help me find my family."

"I can't help you."

"Why not?"

"Because no one can help you." Earl started to close the distance between them. "It's not up to me. What's happening to you and your family was put in motion in March of 1968 and your father, the Krewe of Ares, and everyone involved had more than enough time to make this right. Trust me when I say that I am truly sorry this is happening to you, but it is your turn to feel the pain we felt."

"B-But I had no part in his death. Earl, my wife and kids are innocent -"

"MY BROTHER WAS INNOCENT!" Earl yelled as he removed his coat and sweater and stood in the icy wind with exposed skin. "Look at me . . . I was innocent. Look! Do you see what that fire did to my innocent skin as I tried to save my innocent brother? These injuries robbed me of my scholarships and any hope I had of playing college football. My brother was all I had, and he was innocent too." Earl collected his clothes off the ground.

Evie all but elbowed Trent out of the way. "Mr. Toussaint, Marci is my sister . . . she is my only sister. My parents are gone, and she is all I have left. If you can't help Trent, then please help me. Your grandmother gave my nieces some doubloons. They put on the doubloons, gave one to my sister, and within a matter of minutes, the entire family fell under a spell. Please, Mr. Toussaint, I am begging you . . . how do we break the curse of these doubloons?"

Earl chuckled through clenched lips. "We were a very quiet family - didn't start no trouble, mainly kept to ourselves. The authority that was passed down to my grandmother was a gift she'd carried all her life. She never had to use it until my Aunt Vesta Mae's sons were lynched . . . followed by my brother. You see, it's not the doubloons," he said as he zipped his coat. "It could be anything. A hat, some eyeglasses . . . When we were purchased during slavery, the master's smoking pipe became the point of contact that controlled his soul. That's why he freed all my ancestors and sent them home in style."

Earl approached Evie. "It's not a voodoo curse, because then anyone could help you as long as they had a remedy or a dead chicken or whatever the fuck they do. Those doubloons you mentioned will only respond to the voice of one person, and unfortunately for your family, that person is my grandmother. Sorry, but there isn't anything I can do or say to help you."

With that, Earl climbed into his truck and filled the air with exhaust and the loud knocking of his diesel engine. An ear-piercing *chirp* warned all in the surrounding area that his truck was backing out onto the street. It was then that Evie ran to his truck, climbed up the left step, and held onto the same chrome bar Earl had used to climb into the cabin.

"Roll down this window!" She slapped that glass repeatedly. *PACK, PACK, PACK.*

"Lady, I am asking you to please get off my truck."

"No." Evie's eyes filled with distress.

"If you don't get off my truck now, I am calling the police."

"Earl, you leave me no other choice - I have to find my sister! You cannot leave us like this. Please!" she screamed over the warning chirp and the diesel engine. "My youngest niece is only six years old. Please! I am begging you . . . please help us."

Suddenly the warning chirp ended and the loud knocking fell silent. Earl sighed and looked down at Evie. "It's called Mahuism, the orthodox wisdom of Amun. It traveled here with my ancestors from West Africa, by way of Egypt. There are a lot of rules involved because Mahuism is the knowledge of the pyramid priests who prepared the pharaohs for the afterlife. We are descendants of the tribe responsible for guarding the souls of the pharaohs and their servants. We are the Keepers of the Souls. Look, that's all I know . . . because I never wanted to know more than that. That's why my grandmother passed it onto my brother. Orrin was in the final prep stages to become High Priest when he was murdered that night - that is why what you're witnessing will get worse before it gets better."

"So, what can we do? Earl, there has to be something. Anything?"

"There is one who knows more than I do. I doubt if she will talk to you, but it's worth a try." Earl hastily wrote a name and address on a sheet of paper and handed it to Evie. "Here is her address, but you better move fast because she hates Mardi Gras and spends the week in Oakland. Now if you would excuse me . . . I have to job to finish."

"Thank you . . . thank you!" Evie called as Earl backed onto the street and drove away.

Trent frantically ran to Evie's side. "Evie, I just received a text from Detective Encalade. He says there has been a sighting of Marci and the girls and we should meet him at 934 Esplanade Street . . . ASAP."

"Oh my God, let's go." Evie handed Trent the slip of paper from Earl. "I will be right behind you, let's go."

Trent ran across the street to Marci's car, and both vehicles raced to the I-10 West headed back to New Orleans. Only once Trent reached the Twin Span bridge over Lake Pontchartrain did he unfold the paper from Earl.

Bridgette Banks: 2300 Louisa Street.
Tell her Cap sent you.

CHAPTER 41

I t only took them thirty-two minutes to make it from Slidell to Esplanade Street in New Orleans. Locating the house required little effort due to the overwhelming police presence. Plus, the yellow taped-off section directly in front of the residence made it stand out like a sore thumb. Evie continued to follow Trent until he located a place to park - which ended up being three blocks south of Esplanade. It was a struggle to keep pace with Trent because Evie just couldn't take it all in - the stunning historic architecture was overwhelming. For three city blocks, she journeyed back in time to the 1800s, passing brilliantly painted Creole cottages, elegant, elevated Center Hall with its masterful landscaping, and two hundred-year-old shotgun doubles with roof-supporting molding - handcrafted works of art. It was there, on the 1600 block of Dauphine Street, that Evie fell in love with New Orleans. At that moment, she wished for more than a one-night stand or a kiss in passing - she wanted a romance for the ages.

They arrived at 934 Esplanade Street winded from anticipation and hoping for the best. Detective Encalade had just closed the trunk of his patrol car when Trent called out to him. The detective quickly waved them under the crime scene tape.

"You made it faster than I thought."

"We headed your way as soon as I received your text," Trent's lungs required a breath in between each word.

"Your timing is perfect . . . I just stepped out for a moment. Forgot to snap on my vest."

"Text said there had been a sighting of my wife and kids?"

"Not all of them, but three of them for sure. Follow me, right this way."

Evie trailed Trent as he trailed Detective Encalade up two steps, across a narrow wooden porch, and into a marvelously decorated home. The living room was a vintage world of antiques, both French and English. The antique furniture and sculptures were placed on top of import rugs under lamp lighting of the softest touch, and arranged to display the uniqueness of every individual piece. Even the sofas were works of art - like the smoked leather, tufted, English Chesterfield, placed back-to-back with an identical sofa and a single-seat wingback chair. The Chesterfield guided the way to an exquisite wooden dining room table, which was surrounded by chairs that appeared too expensive for sitting. Past the dining room, Detective Encalade stopped in an area that had been converted into a study, with plush love seats for lounging and a large flat-screen television that sat on top of a mahogany buffet table.

Detective Encalade offered Trent and Evie a seat on the sofa that faced the television and grabbed the remote. "I invited you here because I believe I've found a link to your mother's murder, and to another body we discovered when I left your home this morning. A woman by the name of Suzanna Mackie."

"I'm sorry Detective, but that name doesn't ring a bell."

"Her maiden name was *Dauterive*."

"Ms. Dauterive from the Krewe of Ares - my dad's old secretary? Was murdered?"

"Yes, with a doubloon around her neck—the same one from your mother's crime scene."

"Detective, what about the sighting of my sister and the kids?" Evie asked impatiently.

"Yes, I'll get to that part, but first I need to make you aware of a few developments since I left your home this morning. We have just issued arrest warrants for Marci McGowan, Maggie McGowan, and Zoe McGowan . . ."

"WHAT?" Trent leaped to his feet. "Arrest warrants?"

"Upon arrest, I will charge them with first degree murder."

"Who have they allegedly murdered?" Evie interrupted.

"Not allegedly - the security cameras in this home captured the moment they entered and murdered Mr. Danny Diliberto. We identified them from the missing person photos you gave me. Also, a doubloon was also discovered around the neck of Danny Diliberto."

"Detective, the images this video has captured are not of my wife and kids - in the sense that something has them acting strange . . . like a spell. I assure you, there is an explanation for this. My wife never hurt a fly . . ."

As they spoke, Evie searched through her notes for *Diliberto* - she was sure it was a name she'd recently encountered. It wasn't until she revisited the article from the archive of *Jet* magazine, at the very bottom of the comment section, in the very last entry, that she found her answer.

10/02/2008 - NINTH WARD FREDDIE: Those Diliberto brothers got away with murder, but God don't sleep.

"Detective Encalade, I think there is a possibility that this Diliberto guy was connected to the murder of Orrin Toussaint," Evie broke in.

"I suspected that too, which is why requested a thorough check of his arrest record, but I found no prior arrest - only an instance when he was detained and released."

"And released? On what day did that occur?" Evie asked.

Encalade flipped a page of his notepad. "At 10:50 p.m. on February 27, 1968."

"Mardi Gras night," Evie replied.

Detective Encalade pressed play on the remote, then stood to the side as the security footage appeared on the television. After thirty seconds or so, Evie and Trent moved in for a closer view.

"Zoe . . . no," Evie soon whispered.

"Marci, no . . . no . . . no, Marci!" Trent's hands covered his mouth.

CHAPTER 42

Home of Danny Diliberto
Security Footage — The Previous Night

I didn't want to do it - didn't want any part of it - but that *got damn* Bill. And this drinking. That's all I seem to do now is drink, it helps me get away from it all. The dreams, even the daydreams. I can't stop thinking about that night no matter what I do or how old I get - and I'm seventy years old. I am seventy, with no one . . . just this house from Grandma and a bunch of regrets. Look at me. Sitting on the edge of my bed with an empty bottle of vodka on the floor and a glass half empty in my hand. Alone. How did I get here? That got damn Bill, that's how.

CAM 1: FRONT DOOR
CAM 2: LIVING ROOM
CAM 3: PATIO
CAM 4: STAIRS
CAM 5: MASTER BED - I would call him a son of a bitch . . . if we didn't share the same mother. And my mother wasn't a bitch - she raised us right. But Daddy? He was a hateful dog.

He was the devil, and we were innocent boys until he poured all of his hate inside of us. I never took no offense in *blaccckk peopppllle* - African Americans - or whatever the fuck they're called today: they were always friendly to me. Friendly to all of us, but my dad hated them as much as any man could hate. And for what reason? It had to be Grandpa Diliberto—he never cared for The Niggers, as he called them. Told us all those stories about how they use to hang 'em at the end of the workday when the Army Core of Engineers was building the industrial canal. Said it was the only way to keep food on the table . . . is to chase the niggers away, because they take all the jobs from decent folk. But how do you fault a man for trying to feed his family . . . even a nigger?

Then there was that time when Daddy and a few of his drinking buddies accused those *blaccckk* boys of kissing on those white girls from Jackson - when it was the white girls kissing on the boys. Beat them something awful - even made us watch. I can still hear Daddy today as he beat that boy in the head with that bat.

Dis is how you treat a nigger when you catch his putting his black nigger's lips on one of our women. Boy, do you understand?

Yes, sir, Bill said.

My brother and I were just kids - should have been home watching the Ed Sullivan show. But not us - no, no. We were at the foot of Canal Street over by the ferry watching our father and his friends strap those three boys to that train track. We went home after that - never knew if they freed themselves or not but that's when the drinking started for me. *Gluuug, glug . . .*

Then that Mardi Gras night and that double date . . . Why do I think about all of this? Why do I go back to those places in my mind - why can't I drink in peace? Why do I always drink? *Gluug.* Now I remember . . . to forget about it.

I was standing right there when Shelly-Ann Parker started asking that flambeaux boy all those nosey questions, one after the other. I heard she had a thing for colored boys back then - my cousin Francine said she even slept with one before and she liked it - but I never told Bill anything about what I heard. Maybe I should have? Maybe that flambeaux boy would still be living today. I wish I could drown myself in this glass . . . I would. Then Bill went to showing off and everything and he came up with the idea of running down here on Esplanade by Grandma's house and headed straight to the garage.

Bill handed me the can of gas, but it was only half full. There were two other gas cans in the garage, so we emptied them all into the ten-gallon can - filled it up to the top. At first, I wasn't sure what Bill was up to but, I should have known something terrible was fixing to happen when he asked our dates to wait on the porch until we got back.

Then we found that flambeaux boy again. *Why did I do it? I could have said no, but I didn't.* I helped my brother lift that can up real high, and gas rained down on that flambeaux like Hurricane Betsy. I never looked back, and I'm glad I didn't. But I never left the corner of St. Phillips & Burgundy Street. I'm still out there all these years later because I did everything Bill told me to do like a jackass - never even put up a fuss. Bill showed more concern about the gas that spilled on the sleeves of his Chalmette High letterman jacket than he did for the boy he set on fire. I need another drink . . .

CAM 1: FRONT DOOR
CAM 2: LIVING ROOM
CAM 3: PATIO - *The back door opens. A woman enters the screen portion of the patio and kicks in the back door.*
CAM 4: STAIRS
CAM 5: MASTER BED - My trusty Bombay Sapphire will have to finish me off for the night - gin never lasted long in this bedroom. The strangest part of the night was when the police officer put us in the back of the car. He said we fit the description of the two white males in their late teens or early twenties who doused the flambeaux carrier with a flammable substance; we were in the back of that police car in front of my grandmother's house shaking like to bowls of Jell-O. That when my grandmother - God bless her soul - told those officers:

My grandsons never left this porch - they have been out here courting these young ladies all night. I would have you to know

*that my brother is Judge Leander Perez, and if you don't release
them from the backseat of that car, I will have you fired tonight.*

Yes, Mrs. Diliberto, and I apologize for the confusion, that
young police officer said. He couldn't have been on the job no
more than a week. What was his name . . . Officer De . . . Officer Debruce? That's it. Officer Doug Debruce. He had us in the
backseat of his car, and we walked free as birds - after killing an
innocent boy.

But that's what rich grandparents are for . . . I guess? What do
I know? Fuck it, I need to refill this glass.

CAM 1: FRONT DOOR - *The front door opens. Two little
girls enter the front room of the house.*
CAM 2: LIVING ROOM - *The woman who entered from
the patio is now in the living room.*
CAM 3: PATIO
CAM 4: STAIRS
CAM 5: MASTER BED - But that was my grandmother,
flexing her political muscle to get her way. She later confessed
on her deathbed that she saw us in that garage filling up that
gas can—she even told the newscasters who were a few blocks
up the street that a colored boy accidentally set himself on fire.
She knew we did it—and still helped us get away with murder.
Now I live in the same house . . . she left it to me because she resented Bill for getting me involved in trouble. My grandmother
use to say Bill had a demon in him like our daddy, but I was
the wholesome side of the Diliberto family. Grandma, you were
right about a lot of things, but wrong about that—all of us Diliberto men have the same demon.

CAM 1: FRONT DOOR
CAM 2: LIVING ROOM
CAM 3: PATIO
CAM 4: STAIRS - *The woman and the two girls slowly walk
up the stairs and continue to the master bedroom.*
CAM 5: MASTER BED - But hey, fuck it . . . what happened
in the past is the past. That's what my ex-wife use to say before
she grew exhausted with my drinking, and rode off into the sun-

set with half of my inheritance. *Glug* . . . but that gold-digging bitch didn't get my house - we fought her ass tooth and nail. This house had been in the Diliberto family for nearly two hundred years, and it will remain for another two hundred. Glug Glug . . . Bill Diliberto, *fuck you*. Did you hear that, Bill, I said fuck you, I am not coming to see you in the nursing home. I hope you die in there with a pamper full of shit stuck to your ass, you hear that, Bill?

In his old age, he all of a sudden found Jesus—my ass. He is the same Bill that poured that gas on the kid, he is the same Bill that got me involved, he is the same Bill that when Daddy told him to kick that colored boy in the face who they tied to the tracks . . . Bill kicked until his pants were bloody. *Glug* . . . If I am going to hell, then you're going with me. Do you hear me, Bill - *FUCK YOU!*

CAM 1: FRONT DOOR
CAM 2: LIVING ROOM
CAM 3: PATIO
CAM 4: STAIRS
CAM 5: MASTER BED - *The bedroom door opens* . . .

As Danny Diliberto paced and staggered in the front of his bed barking obscenities at the ceiling, the bedroom door slowly opened behind him. Danny turned to see a woman and two girls standing in his bedroom, each with a bright, pulsating doubloon in the center of her chest. After a stare-off of twenty seconds, Trent and Evie witnessed the exact moment the attack took place: After Zoe pointed, Maggie leaped across the room and crawled up Danny Dilberto's body. He fell to the floor with Maggie wrapped around his face like an octopus with tentacles outstretched. With two fingers, she stabbed through both his eye sockets. With her teeth, she tore his lips and spat them across the room. As Danny Diliberto squealed in pain for help that would not come, Marci stood over him.

"His name was Orrin Toussaint, anointed heir of the High Priestess. We have a message for you before you die: The High Priestess says your life is only a portion of the atonement for the murder of her heir. *Maneno yako, macho yako, na nafsi yako imetolewa kwa Kuhani Nalah."*

With stiff fingers, Marci stabbed Danny Diliberto in the throat and watched as he drowned in his blood. After he took his last breath, Zoe lifted his head just enough to slide on the doubloon. Evie's hands covered her mouth as her sister, Zoe, and Maggie exited the front door of the house and walked into the fog. She noticed that the murder of Danny Diliberto was carried out exactly one hour after they converted Aunt Frieda.

FRONT DOOR OPEN
FRONT DOOR OPEN
FRONT DOOR OPEN
FRONT . . .

CHAPTER 43

Detective Encalade pressed the red power button, and from the share menu, he sent a copy of the file to his email. Behind him sat Trent and Evie, smothered in a cloud of disbelief and shock. No questions, no comments, no objections . . . just silence. The kind of life-changing silence when you know you will never be the same once your brain completes the reboot process. Trent and Evie sunk into the sofa with their brains stuck at twenty-three percent.

"As I said in my text, your wife and kids have been sighted, but now you understand why I waited until you got here."

"Yes, that-that is my wife and two of my daughters, but-but . . ."

"Mr. McGowan, I know this is hard . . . like you, I am a husband and a father of three girls, but there isn't anything you can do until we apprehend them for these murders."

"*Murders?* There was only one person in the video - what other murders are you charging them with? Trent protested.

"Well, there's this one for sure . . . and your dad's old secretary . . . what is her name?"

"Suzanna Dauterive Mackie," Evie inserted.

"Yes, Mrs. Mackie, and if I don't get to Bill Diliberto, Ralph Fuller, Attorney Morris Igelhart, and last but not least on the McGowan Kill List is . . ."

"Me."

"Winner-winner, chicken dinner. You're on the list, and from the way they took out Diliberto, I have made arrangements for you to hide out in the safest place I know."

"Where is that?"

"Jail."

"In jail," Evie asked incredulously.

"Yes, jail," Detective Encalade patted his pocket for his keys. "Yes jail, at least until we can apprehend them. Until then, you're next."

"Detective, I understand that you have to do your job, but the woman in that video is not my sister - or my nieces. They're being controlled . . . like a spell. You have to believe me," Evie pleaded.

"Hey, guilt or innocence is not for me to decide. Basically, I am the taxi cab to jail - how they get out of jail is why you pay the lawyers."

"But Detective, you watched that video more than once, I'm sure, and in the last two minutes, my sister spoke a language I have never heard before."

"I was going to say the same thing; my wife isn't bilingual. I have no clue what she said, which is further proof that this Ellen Chauvet . . ."

"Ellen Chauvet died in 1971 -"

Evie cut him off. "Detective, that's true, but . . ."

Detective Encalade was done. "Ellen Chauvet died in 1971. ELLEN. CHAUVET. DIED. IN. 1971. That video you just watched is proof that will convict in court. We have no other suspect - just Marci McGowan and her bad-ass kids!" Encalade yelled at Evie and Trent. "Until I see proof of another suspect in action - other than your sister and her bad-ass kids - I don't want to hear this shit about a DEAD GRANDMA!" Encalade patted his pockets in a full circle. "Where in the *fuck* did I put my keys?"

"Hey Encalade, we're done upstairs, but transport said they're backed up - you have to babysit this body until they get here," Teri called as she opened the front door.

"No. No. NO! I am going home and getting some sleep - it's your job to sit with that body until the coroner's office arrives. I am not staying."

"I'm sorry . . . did you get the impression I was asking you something? I am telling you I'm leaving. You go work that out with Diliberto - maybe y'all can play Uno or something, I don't give a fuck. I have a nail appointment in ten minutes. Hey, hey, baybay!" Teri laughed all the way to her van.

Keenan Encalade sighed. "McGowan, you can take my offer, or you can wing it out here on your own. It's up to you, but after I get in touch with the coroner's office, I am headed home and getting some rest. Take a few hours and think about it."

"We will do just that, and thank you for the offer," Evie said as they headed for the door. Just as Trent was about to grab the doorknob, it swung open. It was Teri, stomping her way towards Encalade.

"I just cancelled my nail appointment," she said as she held up his car keys. "You left these in the trunk! Take your tired, forgetful ass home . . . and go the fuck to bed." Teri slapped the keys into his hand and pointed at the front door.

CHAPTER 44

When his Crown Victoria pulled into the driveway, the time was 8:05 p.m.. Seated at the kitchen table was his wife, Irnessa - pissed off. She loved Kennan, but she was tired. Kennan had been gone for almost two days. What she understood very clearly was that he loved his job and was very passionate about taking care of his family. Was she couldn't understand was how a man could love his job more than his wife, and even worse, as much as he loved his kids.

In the center of the table was a brown sugar bowl shaped like a heart; a random gift from Kennan once upon a time. He'd delivered it to her job with balloons. The bowl had been filled with her favorite treat - hot pralines from his mother.

The card inside the bowl had read: *You are my brown sugar.*

Once she'd devoured all the candy, Irnessa discovered that her bowl could hold five pounds of sugar. *How perfect.* Every time she poured her husband a cup of coffee, the bowl flirted with her.

I used to be his brown sugar.

Nevertheless, Irnessa always made sure her bowl was filled to the top with sugar as a symbol of her love for Kennan - but she was tired. Neglected. Lonely. *I shouldn't have to compete with the police department for his time and attention.* Irnessa wanted her husband exclusively, and tonight he would have to decide.

When Kennan entered the kitchen, she wanted her disappointment to be the first thing he saw - and it was. Though she would not admit it at the moment, her favorite part of the day was watching her man walk through the kitchen door. He was so sexy to her with his Hershey's chocolate skin hidden under his bulletproof vest - when he remembered to wear it. Irnessa loved his fitted button-up shirt and how his triceps bulged on the sides. She also loved his shoulders, his smile, and the feel of his calloused hands across her mocha skin. It was his coming through the door that got her every time. It always made her forget the reason she was angry, and it was about to happen again . . .

Strong Irnessa: Stop looking at him like that, that's how he breaks you down. Put your courtroom face on.

Weak Irnessa: But damn he's fine . . . don't listen to her.

Strong Irnessa: Kennan been fine, you should be over it by now. It's time he got his priorities in order, and you should be at the top of that list.

Weak Irnessa: You should be on top of some dick . . . fuck the dumb shit.

Strong Irnessa: Girl, remember what we rehearsed . . . you are sick of how he's treating you. Tired of Kennan putting you last.

Weak Irnessa: But I want some dick on this table . . . bend over and pull that robe to the middle of your back, and none of that bullshit she's saying will matter.

Strong Irnessa: DICK CAN WAIT - we have to address these issues! Get your mind off dick and focus. Act pissed off! Roll your eyes and fold your arms.

Irnessa resembled actress Angela Bassett, with a lighter complexion. She wore her hair in a short cut that was easy to finger-comb and go. Her daughters and her law practice only allowed her enough time for one trip to her stylist a month.

Weak Irnessa: *Maybe it's weight gain?*

Strong Irnessa: Girl, your weight is irrelevant. Remember when you were as skinny as that vacuum cleaner? Kennan was still gone nineteen hours a day. Stick to our plan, and end every sentence with *YES INDEED* - that always pisses him off. Show Kennan, you're sick of his bullshit.

Weak Irnessa: *Don't listen to her. At the end of the night the goal is some dick from your hussssssban. Not pissed off soft dick - happy hard dick . . . Okaaaaay!*

Kennan circled the table to kiss Irnessa, but she only offered a cheek. "Are you serious? I can't get a real kiss?"

"Do you feel you deserve a real kiss?"

"Here we go . . ."

"Then let's go. Kennan, today is Saturday - you left out of here Thursday night . . ."

"I am working back-to-back murders, but you know that already." Kennan pressed start on the microwave, where a steak laid over some jambalaya patiently waited for him.

"So, were you successful in saving the world, Superman? Have you leaped enough tall buildings? Stopped enough locomotives? Have you rid New Orleans of all its crime? Is the city safe?"

"Irnessa, I am not up for this shit - I am not up for it. I have been awake for almost forty-eight hours, and I just want to take a shower and go to sleep. I'm tired."

"So, you own all the rights to tired . . . guess I don't have the right to get tired. Everything is about you. You are never inconvenienced when it comes to this marriage."

"Nessa, can I please eat my food, take my shower, and go to bed?"

"A shower and go to bed?" She stood over him as he held his

fork above the jambalaya.

"Yes!" his voice boomed off the kitchen cabinets. "Eat, shit, shower, and shave . . . if that's all right with you?"

Weak Irnessa: Stop fussing . . . he didn't come home for this . . .

Strong Irnessa: Keep it right here, shit getting serious now. Is he complaining about food and a shower? It's time for you to list a few of your complaints.

"Well, I want a husband with a normal job, who works normal hours, who can remember that he has a wife at home!"

"Nessa, I am going to say this one time and one time only." Kennan towered over her like a black Hulk. "I am not a normal man with a normal job! If you wanted a normal man who worked normal hours, then you should have married the dude who cuts our grass. I am not that man."

Weak Irnessa: We're going to be dickless tonight, tomorrow, and next week. The Young & the Dickless.
Strong Irnessa: What the fuck did he just say? Wait . . . what?
Weak Irnessa: Bye dick, see you later, don't forget about me . . .

"So, you feel you have a right to tell me who I should marry? So, you're Super Cop and Match.com? You'd much rather I hook up with the gentlemen who cuts our lawn than consider my concerns?" Irnessa shoved his plate of food to the floor.

Strong Irnessa: That's my girl! Now slap him in the face for disrespecting you!

"So, am I to take our girls and go out and find someone who would have us? And care for us? And love us?" Her fist balled so tight her knuckles cracked. "Is that what you're saying to me?"

Strong Irnessa: That's it Mrs. Irnessa Encalade - we need clarity from this motherfucker!

Kennan stared at the moist steak on the floor as if he were at a funeral. He flexed up from his chair and huffed hot air in her face.

"So, what, you're going hit me? Huh? Then hit!"

Strong Irnessa: I wish he would lay a hand on you . . .

"You didn't have to knock my plate of food on the floor!"

"Kennan . . . fuck your food." Her eyes and head rolled beneath his chin. "The next time you say some dumb shit like that, you better think first because I'm fully capable of replacing you with that lawn guy!"

"Whatever, Nessa - I'm going take a shower. You can fuss with yourself." Kennan walked past Irnessa and flicked her off without the bird.

"So, you're just going to walk past me as if I don't matter? You can work forty-eight hours - only getting paid for twelve - but you can't give me twenty minutes of your time?"

Kennan continued to walk away. "Well, maybe lawn dude has twenty minutes for you."

"You fuuuucka!"

Weak Irnessa: *I guess we can take off the cute drawers - we ain't getting a piece of dick tonight . . .*

In a fit of rage, Irnessa Encalade grabbed her brown sugar bowl and pitched it. At her husband. With all her might. Kennan only made it to the third step of the staircase before the bowl ricocheted off the back of his head, knocking him out face forward. Unconscious, he snored on the stairs.

Weak Irnessa: One day you will listen to me - maybe once you're single again. Kennan walked past you to prevent another argument around the kids. He walked past you because he was tired and had no energy to argue. He walked past you hoping to deal with it in the morning, after sedative sex to help him sleep. Kennan is your husband - why can't you respect the peace?

Back in college, Irnessa was the pitcher for her softball team, so she knew how to pitch a fastball over the plate. She also knew in that instant that her marriage just hit a new low. For years, she'd prepared herself for the day when Kennan would come home and take out the frustrations of his job with a backhand slap to her face, but she had just become her worse fear -she was the first to commit domestic violence.

After a minute of napping on the stairs, Kennan finally managed to sit up. "What just happened?" he asked while feeling the back of his head. "Why is there sugar all over the floor? Why is the back of my head bleeding?"

Weak Irnessa: Guurrrl, lie! You better lie to him. Tell him he was so tired he slipped down and busted his head wide open. And you tried to save him. Maybe we can still get some dick?
Strong Irnessa: Shut up!

Though her trembling hands, Irnessa covered her mouth up to the bridge of her nose while her eyes spoke every thought that scurried through her mind.

I just hit my husband. I just hit my husband with a bowl in the back of his head; I could've killed him. I could've just killed the only man I have ever loved, and the only man that has ever loved me. What is happening to me? What am I becoming? I can't believe I hit him with a fucking sugar bowl. My mama told me never hurt the ones you love, and never discipline my children in anger. I have just hurt the one I love.

Tears raced down her cheeks. *Oh my God, I cannot believe I hit my husband. He's not going to hit me back. No, because he's not that kind of man, but it looks like I'm that kind of woman. He's probably going to leave me because all I've done for the past week is look for reasons to fight. I'm about to lose Kennan, I know it. I'm about to lose my husband. There is no way he's going to forgive me for this. There is no way.*

At the top of the stairs, her daughters Jarah, age sixteen, Emma, age twelve, and Layla, age eight, came to investigate.

"Hey Daddy, I didn't know you were home," Jarah said. "Whoa! You're bleeding from the back of your head!"

"Grossss, Daddy, your head is bleeding," Layla chimed in.

"Girls, go back to your room," Irnessa pointed.

"But why is Daddy's head bleeding? Daddy, did you get shot in the head at work?" Layla asked.

"Daddy slipped on the stairs. GO TO YOUR ROOM NOW!" Irnessa demanded.

"I slip on those stairs all the time and never bust my head like that," Emma murmured as all three girls turned around and disappeared upstairs.

A fragile voice of panic consumed Irnessa's thoughts. *Should I express how sorry I am? I doubt if he'll accept my apology right now. Should I hug him and tell him how much I love him? Then again, he probably will never allow me to touch him again. Keenan is going to leave me - I can feel it. His lip is still bleeding, but he's not wiping it. Maybe I should wipe? Or maybe he's letting the blood drip intentionally. He's forcing me to see what I've become. If he leaves me, I deserve it. That was dumb, Irnessa - dumb!*

With conscience-stricken eyes, Irnessa watched as Kennan struggled to his feet, placed one hand on the banister, and continued up the stairs. Irnessa followed him.

"Kennan. Kennan, I'm sorry, baby." Kennan paused and listened. "I'm so sorry, I didn't mean to . . ." Kennan shot her a look. "Kennan, you know I would never intentionally hurt you

. . ."

"You just did . . ."

"I think the cut on the back of your head is deep and will require stitches." She let out a guilt-ridden sigh. "I may have to take you to the ER - you're losing a lot of blood. The entire back of your shirt and the collar are bloody. Kennan, I am so sorry! Can I take you to the ER?"

There was no reply from her husband as he wobbled to the bathroom. Once Keenan made it to his bathroom, he unbuttoned his shirt and removed his bulletproof vest. "I can't believe you hit me," he said while applying pressure to his head with a cold towel. "I can't remember shit as it is . . ." Kennan winched in the medicine cabinet mirror.

On the back of his neck was a one-inch cut that bled continuously. In her hand? A cup of ice and a towel. In her eyes? Tears. She placed the ice in the towel then twisted tight to form an ice pack. She then applied the ice pack to the laceration on the back of his head and pressed. As she stood there pressing the ice firmly against the hemorrhage, Irnessa started to pray.

Lord, please. Please, Lord . . . stop this cut from bleeding. Lord, please forgive me for hitting my husband, I didn't mean to do it.

After about five minutes of continuous pressure and ice, the bleeding finally stopped. Irnessa was grateful to God. Kennan gazed into her remorseful eyes while she stared back at him. The mirror served as a mediator, one that reflected the accumulated miles in their long-distance relationship, miles too far to travel in one night. But her prayer had been answered - the bleeding stopped.

"Keenan, I'm sorry, please forgive me. Please forgive me. I don't know what came over me, but I should never have hit you, especially since you have never raised your hand to hit me. Please forgive me."

Keenan continued to gaze into her eyes through the mirror, but said nothing.

Irnessa walked out of the bathroom, collapsed across her bed, and buried her face in the pillow.

Weak Irnessa: *Sniff . . . Bye, dick . . .*

CHAPTER 45

February 4, 1968

B ridgette could hear Mrs. Banks moving from room to room like a drill sergeant on the first day of boot camp. Her thunderous voice threatened anyone who walked too slow or took too long in the bathroom, and in between her threats, she sang hymns. The sound of James Cleveland's "The Lord Is Blessing Me Right Now" forced its way into every room, whether you liked the song or not. Protest about James Cleveland, and Mrs. Banks would assume you had the devil in you, because *no saved Christian would take issue with James Cleveland.* In the Banks home on Sunday morning, there wasn't much time to eat, dress, or ease into day unless you were burning up with fever. That morning, Bridgette was burning up.

"Bridgette, I know you're not still in that bed." Mrs. Banks held an iron-pressed crimson and white choir robe in one hand and a pair of Hanes coffee-colored nylon stockings in the other. "Didn't I tell you twenty minutes ago to get out of that bed? Ola Mae already in her robe already and you're still in the bed. Get out that bed and get ready."

"Mammmma . . . I -*on* feel-good," Bridgette whined.

"What's hurting you?"

"My head and my back . . . and I feel cold." Bridgette waited for her mom to run the standard test that confirmed whether she was really sick or faking it.

"Child, you're burning up with fever." Mrs. Banks hurried to the medicine cabinet "Forget about church today. Don't need you infecting all of us." Bridgette's mom returned with a large teaspoon and a bottle of Vick's Formula 44 cold medicine.

"I keep telling you and that hard head Ola Mae to stop walking around on this cold floor barefooted. That's why y'all stay sick. But I am not sitting with you all day in Charity Hospital - not today, devil." Mrs. Banks twisted the top off the bourbon-colored bottle. "Sit up and take this." Her mom administered two spoons to Bridgette. "I will leave some chicken noodle soup for you on the stove, and make sure you have slippers on your feet when you go in that kitchen."

"Cough, cough . . . Okay, Momma. *Cough, cough, cough."*

"The devil is busy. Let me get out of here."

The Banks family made their weekly mass exodus out the front door in their Sunday best, loaded into her father's station wagon, and cruised their way to church. Little did Mrs. Banks know, the only thing Bridgette was burning up for was Orrin. The old hot water bottle across the face trick had worked again. Bridgette had decided the previous night that Orrin's wait was over - she was going to make love to the love of her life for the first time. After peeking out the front door to make sure her parents were gone, she ran to the phone and called Orrin.

"Hello?"

"Cap?"

"Yeah?"

"Why do you always have to answer the phone?"

"Who do you want? Orrin?"

"Not you! Can you hand him the phone, please?"

"Orrin, pick up the phone - it's Bridgette."

A few seconds later, Orrin answered. "Good morning, my love . . . You woke up with Big O on your mind?"

Bridgette had no time for small talk. "Get over here now and take the fences."

"Huh?"

"Pound cake . . . NOW!"

"You baked some pound cake . . .?"

"Right now, and it's hot . . . the back door is open."

CLICK.

Bridgette hung up the phone, grabbed her purse, and ran into the bathroom to change. In her purse was a pair of red panties she'd hidden from Mrs. Banks. Orrin had made a promise that he would never pressure her to have sex, but they had decided that moment she was ready, the code was *hot pound cake*. Bridgette knew it wouldn't take Orrin long to hurdle the six backyard fences that separated their homes. As soon she strapped the red panties on, she heard him opening the back door.

The bathroom was less than twenty feet from the door, so she timed his entrance and staged herself like a gift-wrapped present. She wore only those red panties. He saw her. If she could have taken a picture of Orrin's expression when he saw her nearly naked for the first time, she would have - Bridgette watched the air leave his lungs. With one foot behind the other and a finger inviting him to follow, Bridgette led the way to her bed. Once there, she lay back on her elbows and waited for him to undress. Orrin's clothes tore off his body as he eased himself over her and pulled her blanket over the top.

"I love you, Bridgette."

"Do you promise you will marry me."

"I promise . . . as soon as we graduate, you will be my wife."

"Pound cake?" he asked

"Yes . . . pound cake," said in a soft voice.

CHAPTER 46

Five Weeks Later

The walk from Grandma Ellen's house after the funeral felt like the longest mile, but there was no way around it - Bridgette had to tell her parents she was pregnant. When a young lady has to inform her parents that she is with child, it could play out as a moment when the family suppresses their disappointment and rallies in support - or, it could turn instantly combustible. Bridgette anticipated the latter. Not only was Bridgette pregnant, her mother was the General of the Holy Police; known to pass sharp judgment on other pregnant teenagers, and their parents, without care or compassion. She never seemed to have a single thought that it could happen to one of her daughters.

Of Stella's daughter, Janice, Bridgette's mom said: *"The reason why that girl got pregnant is that Stella was too loose with them - I knew it was a matter of time."*

Of Caroline's daughter, Stacy, Bridgette's mom said *"I knew when Stacy's hips started getting wide she was fast. I said to myself, somebody must be touching on her - I knew it was a matter of time."*

Of Bertha's daughter, Bonnie, Bridgette's mom said: *"That Bonnie had the nastiest little walk in New Orleans. Twitching her little butt like it had a price tag - I knew it was just a matter of time."*

And now, Bridgette was pregnant.

Earl and Teresa walked Bridgette right up to her screen door. Once they arrived, Teresa held her by the curves of her shoulders. "You are carrying my grandson; we are family. I wanted to walk you all the way to your door, so you will know that I'm with you tonight, and from this point forward. Just so you know, I got my own place on Bartholomew Street - I secured it last week because I had a feeling things with Momma were coming to a head - and you're welcome if you need a peaceful place to raise your baby. Okay?" Bridgette nodded her head, then slowly entered the house.

Once inside, Bridgette called for her mother from the living room and took a seat in the center of the sofa like a guest. Every joint in her body trembled with gut-wrenching fear. Her arms folded across her belly as she tried to cover the ears of her child from the rejection she expected. Her mother blocked the light from the kitchen as she approached the living room from down the hall wearing a bathrobe and shower cap.

"I was just about to send Ola Mae down there to get you. How are they holding up down there?" Mrs. Banks asked.

"As well as to be expected, I guess." In that instant, she nearly changed her mind about announcing her pregnancy.

"That's good to hear; it's going to take a while before they come to terms with this. You may want to give them some space and let them grieve. Seeing you will remind them of Orrin."

Bridgette looked up at her mother. "Momma, there is something I need to tell you."

"About the funeral today?

"No."

"Then what is it? I have a hot tub running."

"Momma, I don't know how to say this . . ." The tears started to flow. "I am sorry -"

"You don't know how to tell me what?" Mrs. Banks turned and yelled down the hall, *"Ola Mae! Turn my water off."* She turned back to Bridgette. "Now what is it that you don't know how to say?"

Intense trepidation bent Bridgette forward in her seat. "I-I . . . am pregnant."

"You're what?!"

"Pregnant."

"For who?"

"Orrin."

A gawk of confusion. "Bridgette, are you sitting on my sofa in my house telling me that you are pregnant? For Orrin? Is that what you're telling me?"

A flash flood of tears. "Yes, Momma."

"Are you sure?"

"Yes, Momma."

"When was your last period?"

"January. The nurse at school gave me the test yesterday."

The pressure started to build. "Hmm, hmm." Mrs. Banks paced from the door to the dining room table and then back again, skiing with her arms, talking over the top of Bridgette. "You mean to tell me, after all I have done for you, after all the time I spent teaching you right from wrong, you would do something like this to me?"

"Momma, I'm sorry. I never meant to . . ."

Mrs. Banks grabbed a fist of Bridgette's collar and bra strap and forced her to stand. "How could you do this to me? Huh? HOW COULD YOU? HUH?"

"What's going on in here?" Lawson Banks entered the room, followed by Bridgette's sister, Ola Mae.

"Tell your daddy what you told me. Tell him."

Bridgette fought to pull her words together. "I-I am . . ."

"If you don't say it loud . . . I will slap the lips off your face."

Her mother tightened the noose around the back of Bridgette's neck. "Tell your daddy what you told me - look him in the face and say it." Mrs. Banks dragged Bridgette by the collar into the dining room and stood behind her. "You were woman-ish enough to do it, so don't cry like a child - SAY IT AGAIN!"

"Daddy I . . . I am pregnant."

Her dad didn't say a word.

It was then that Mrs. Banks moved to Bridgette's side. "Where did you have sex?"

"Momma, I said I was sorry. I am sorry . . . please."

"Down by Ellen? Is that where you got pregnant?"

". . . No, Momma."

Mrs. Banks raised a backhand. "Where did you have sex? If you don't answer me right now . . ."

"Here . . . we did it here."

"You had sex in my house? You had sex in my . . . house?" Mrs. Banks never gave Bridgette a chance to confirm before she rammed her backward into the china cabinet, shattering the exterior glass. "YOU HAD SEX IN MY HOUSE?" Mrs. Banks's fingers locked around Bridgette's neck as the glass from the china cabinets sliced into her lower back.

"That's enough now!" Mr. Banks pried his wife's hands off of Bridgette and freed his daughter to breathe. "All of this hum-buggin ain't making things no better. Let's have a seat and talk this out." Her father shielded Bridgette from Mrs. Banks and returned her to the sofa, where he continued to stand guard.

With one hand on her hip, Mrs. Banks pointed at her husband. "I tried to tell you about that Orrin boy, but you was too caught up in his singing to see what was going on. I tried to tell you we need to stop him from coming around, but you . . . you said I was too hard on them. You said I needed to give them some air to breathe - well, I hope you're happy now!" Mrs. Banks slipped by her husband and charged at Bridgette again on the sofa. She pounced on her daughter like a lion, slapping, punching, and driving Bridgette's face as deep into the seat cushions as she could. It was a struggle for Mr. Banks to separate them.

"Momma, I'm sorry. I'm sorry, Momma. Momma, please stop!"

"I knew it was going to be you. How dare you bring shame on this family?" Mrs. Banks screamed. "You picked up all those whorish ways from hanging around with Phyllis!" She paused as if faced with a grave decision that was hers alone to make. "Well, this baby will never see the light of day. I am setting an appointment for the clinic in the morning . . . do you hear me?"

"Momma, no!" Bridgette yelled.

"You think you're going to bring a baby in here and we have to care for it? That baby will never see the light of day!"

"Betsy . . . you listen to me good." Her husband moved in with a sharp finger. "There's a lot that goes on around her that I stay out of because I let you handle it . . . but I'll be damned if my daughter is going lay on a table just because you're afraid of what the church folk are going to say."

"Then she's going live in Pine Grove with my sister. Her and Sylvester will be more than happy to raise that baby - but she's not walking around here pregnant."

"Momma, noooo!" Ola Mae screamed. "Don't send my sister away, Momma."

"My daughter is not leaving this house, and you are sure as hell not throwing her away in Pine Grove, Louisiana." Mrs. Banks charged across the room at Bridgette again, but this time Lawson Banks grabbed her by the collar and drove her into the loveseat. "I have never put my hands on you, but you touch my daughter again and I swear to God . . ." Lawson held Betsy's gaze as he released his grip, and she grudgingly sat upright.

"Well, it's my house, too - she can't stay here!"

"Betsy, she's not going anywhere! Bridgette is the same age you were when I crawled through your window in the middle of the night. I guess you're so holy now that you forgot."

"She's not staying here."

"Yes, she is."

"We will see."

Suddenly, Mrs. Banks stormed to Bridgette's room, and Bridgette could hear her mother violently snatching all her clothes off the hangers and tossing them into the hallway. Then, with an arm full of clothes and some on the floor which she kicked down the hall, Mrs. Banks opened the door and started to throw Bridgette's belongings out of the house. With every load she tossed outside, more neighbors stepped out onto their porches to watch. Every time she entered the house to get another load of Bridgette's clothes, her father and Ola Mae collected all her things from the fence, sidewalk, and lawn and brought them back inside. The cycle continued for nearly an hour.

While her mother continued the eviction in front of an audience of neighbors, Bridgette stood from the sofa and slowly made her way out onto the porch, devastated and humiliated. It was then that she noticed Orrin's mother standing in the middle of the street waving for her. Bridgette ran to Teresa and collapsed into her arms.

"My mother is throwing me out because I refused to have an abortion or give my child away. I want my baby - it's all I have left of Orrin."

"Bridgette, you don't have to do either. Like I said, I have prepared a peaceful place for you whenever you're ready. I heard all the commotion and came back to bring you there now if you like."

Bridgette looked over her shoulder at the scene of her mother pitching clothes outside, and quickly made her decision.

"My mother has kicked me out of her life . . . let's go."

CHAPTER 47

Today was the second day Evie had made two attempts to reach Bridgette - once in the morning and then again in the evening - but no one answered the door. The only person she saw nearby was an older man who had converted the front of his house into a mechanic shop, and Evie could tell he was never short of customers. Yesterday, he had been under a Dodge minivan that appeared to eat him up to his waist. Today it was an orange Chevy Camaro with thick tires and a black stripe up the middle. From under the hood, he teetered with a part as he tried to bolt it to the engine - something to make a fast car even faster, Evie concluded. The hood provided the perfect acoustics as he bellowed a song in a clear, vibrant voice.

Oh, what the hell, Evie thought as she approached the mechanic in hopes he could provide her with information on the best time to speak with Bridgette. The embroidery on his navy blue shirt introduced him as *Fred*, so that is how she addressed him.

"She used to be. She used to be my girrrrrl, she used to be my girrrrl. Ask me how I know . . ."

"Excuse me, Mr. Fred, I have a family emergency and desperately need to reach Ms. Bridgette. Is there a better time to reach her?"

Fred never lifted his chin to acknowledge her. "Sugarrrrrr, sugar . . . sugaaaar . . . sugga . . ."

Evie could tell she was interrupting his favorite part of the Ojay's "She Used to be My Girl." Both of his arms where positioned in the engine compartment like a midwife waiting patiently for a miracle. His beard was the same color as the grease on his arms, his shirt, and the brow of his face. From the porch came one soulful seventies tune after the other, and Evie could tell each song took him to a special place. In between the street and the paved sidewalk was a strip of grass where he laid a pack of Camel cigarettes and a pint-sized bottle of Thunderbird. Evie waited for a reply, but the only sound was the clicking of his wrench as he winced in frustration. She conceded defeat and started to mosey to her car.

Suddenly he spoke. "What type of family emergency?"

Evie about-faced back to the open mouth of the Chevy. "It's my sister and her daughters. Cap said Bridgette could help me . . ."

"Help you with what?"

"A-A situation involving Grandma Ellen." Suddenly, she was afraid to tell Fred the whole truth out of fear it would sound ridiculous. How do you tell a stranger that a woman who died in 1971 is haunting your family and has taken control of them? How do you tell someone it all started with a parade in 1968, a flambeaux carrier, and a doubloon?

"So, your family emergency is involving Ellen Chauvet?"

"Yes, so you know her?"

Wrenching a bolt with all his might, "I have lived on this block all my life." He grunted as the bolt finally turned.

"So, you know Ellen . . . as in what she is capable of?"

"You could say that." With the final bolt secured, Fred reached for his towel, which was just as greasy as his shirt, and wiped his hands. "For you to come to this block and knock on that door tells me that someone in your family . . . has done something they need to make right."

"And that's why I need to see Ms. Bridgette."

"So . . . this is connected to Orrin Toussaint?"

"How did you know?"

"Like I said, I have lived in that house right there all my life." He pointed to a single-family home that appeared to have been elevated after Hurricane Katrina. This neighborhood on Louisa Street was blocks away from where the levees broke the day following the storm, but though it was north of the industrial canal, nearly every home had flooded.

"Well . . . Cap told me to reach out to Bridgette. She might be willing to help."

"Cap told you that? For real?" He clapped the pack of Camel cigarettes about ten times in the inside of his hand before he opened the pack.

"Yes." Evie opened her hand to reveal a strip of paper from Earl Toussaint.

"*That jive-ass Cap* didn't tell you that Bridgette don't stick around for Mardi Gras?"

"He did." Evie looked discouraged. "She vacations in Oakland?"

"That's right . . . and I saw you each time you rolled through, knocking on her door and praying. I knew then it was something serious."

"*Mr. Frrrred*, my car drives better than when I bought it. *You da man!*" a woman in a Nissan Maxima yelled out her window in a high-pitched voice.

Fred lifted a stiff fist into the air and nodded. "I am still waiting on that pah-cone candy you promised me."

"Oh . . . don't *worry*. You will have twelve pralines today! Love you, Mr. Franklin." The grateful customer made a left turn out of view.

"Sorry about that . . . now what was I saying?"

"About Ms. Bridgette leaving . . ."

"That's right. I watched you for two days, but I try to mind my business. Bridgette left on Thursday—and she's not coming back until Thursday.

As Fred spoke, a cigarette dangled out of the corner of his mouth, but it never fell - not once. This puzzled Evie. The cigarette was very distracting. He only touched it once in a while, when he squeezed it between two fingers to put emphasis on a sentence like that *jive-ass Cap*. Then Evie became distracted by his periodic sips from the pint of Thunderbird. It was nearly empty, but Fred displayed no signs of being intoxicated. Not even a wobble in his step. Not even a stumble or an incoherent word - as if the pint of whiskey was a noon-day soda.

"Then can you answer this - Grandma Ellen was the head of a religious sect and now my sister . . ."

"Got one of those curses on her ass, huh?"

"Yes, if that's what you call it. A doubloon. She is controlling my sister and her kids through those doubloons."

"I grew up with the Toussaint boys - as a matter of fact, Orrin was the lead singer of our group back in the day called the NOLA Hearts." Fred eyes focused in on a light pole a few feet away. "We harmonized some good music under that pole."

Evie looked over her shoulder at the pole, then back to Fred. "So you were friends with Orrin?"

"I was friends with Orrin and Bridgette. Her daddy left her that house after Ola Mae moved to Oakland. I remember the night she told her mother she was pregnant for Orrin. Mrs. Banks acted a complete ass that night - a lot of people stopped speaking to her because of it. The pastor even fired her as choir director."

"Because her daughter got pregnant?"

"Not at all - she was fired because of how she handled the situation. Embarrassing. I still remember it like it was yesterday. But God had Bridgette, because Orrin's mother took her in and everything worked out find from there until . . ."

Evie waited patiently as Fred lit another cigarette. "You were saying?"

"Until the baby turned three. They had a birthday party for him over there in the park. Mrs. Banks got jealous because the baby called Teresa *Grandma*. Then, all of a sudden, she wanted to see the child, but Bridgette wasn't having it. Bridgette only allowed her father and her sister Ola Mae to spend time with her baby. Once that baby turned three, everything fell apart. Ola Mae ended up moving to California a few years after she graduated. She and Cap were together for a while when we were growing up, but after Orrin's death and the mounting tension between the two families, their relationship fizzled out. It was sad to watch. Soon after Ola Mae left home, Mr. Banks divorced Mrs. Banks. He never forgave her for the night she threw Bridgette out of the house."

"That's pretty tragic . . . but why would Earl request that I meet with Bridgette?"

"I don't know, maybe she knows something about how all this works because of what happened at the church on Christmas Eve 1971, when Ola Mae was still living at home and the Banks's were still trying to make their marriage work. I was there. I saw it all," Fred said as he greeted another honking customer with a stiff fist.

Wanting to get as much information as she could before another happy customer rolled up, Evie pressed, "Fred, please tell me what happened on Christmas Eve 1971."

"Shit hit the fan . . . and knocked the fan out the window."

CHAPTER 48

Christmas Eve 1971

O n some days, it was best to simply take the phone off the hook - Mrs. Banks would call just that much. Each call started the same way, with continuous apologies for the first two minutes, then accusations that the Toussaint family had turned Bridgette against her by using voodoo. Each time, Bridgette would explain that she was not under a spell, but she needed more time to heal. The night Mrs. Banks threw her out the house - her words and the way she was attacked - was still a recurring nightmare that had played out in front of the entire neighborhood. Bridgette needed more alone time, more space between her and Betsy Banks, and more distance from religion.

It was the shame that Bridgette couldn't escape. Her pregnancy started with a very obvious belly early on - that is how she finished her eleventh-grade year. Unfortunately, the kick-off to her much-anticipated senior year was the second-to-last month of her pregnancy; her son was delivered on October 22, 1968. There was nowhere to hide from the rumors of the night she was evicted, or the pointing and cruel chatter that ended the moment she was close enough to hear the ridicule of her classmates. Every pregnant teenager Mrs. Banks had nailed to a cross, and every mother of a teen girl Mrs. Banks had indicted as unfit, made sure Bridgette was shamed one hundred-fold in retaliation.

As Bridgette wobbled through the halls of Carver High, only a few people had compassion, and that compassion came from former teachers and friends of Orrin, not the packs of girls who indulged in the irony of her humiliation. And then there was the loneliness, brought on by the loss of Phyllis. Bridgette didn't blame Phyllis, because she knew the source of it all. Gail had banned Bridgette from calling or visiting - not because she was pregnant, but because she had refused Grandma Ellen.

No one was allowed to refuse Grandma Ellen.

With each birthday, the tug-of-war between the two grandmothers intensified to the point that Teresa prohibited both from visiting her home. Bridgette's son became a trophy coveted by the grandmothers, and both refused to accept no for an answer. Bridgette wanted her son to know both families and spend as much time as possible with her father, who was more than willing to fill in for Orrin when needed. And that was the crack Mrs. Banks needed to get in - if not by a foot, then at least by a toe.

While she waited for a Social Security approval for her son, Bridgette secured a weekend job working at McDonald's. She always made sure to alternate her schedule around Teresa's work week so there was always someone available to babysit. It all went well until one day when Bridgette's manager scheduled her incorrectly, which left no one available to babysit other than her dad. Her father was overjoyed to watch the baby for the entire day if need be. That morning, Lawson Banks arrived at Teresa's house at seven a.m., as they had agreed.

"Dad, I don't have a problem with Momma holding my baby, but she is not allowed to take him out of the house. This cold air makes his asthma that much harder to manage."

"Not a problem, he will sit on my lap like always and watch

TV," Mr. Banks assured her.

And with that agreement in place, Mr. Banks dropped Bridgette off at work and headed home with his grandson.

"Here is another cup for you," Mrs. Banks said as she placed the coffee on the table and toted her husband's empty mug to the kitchen.

In the living room, Lawson Banks sat in front of the television bouncing his grandson on his lap while sipping hot coffee with no sugar and no cream. Lawson had affectionately nicknamed his grandson *Lil' O*, because the toddler resembled Orrin from every angle and loved to sing nursery rhymes. In Bridgette's old room, Mrs. Banks sprayed the last mist of water on the dress she intended to wear to church. After that, she slipped into the powder blue dress, fastened on some black heels, and waited for the perfect time. She knew her husband was addicted to freshly brewed coffee, so on this particular morning, she delivered one after the other to the living room. Then she waited.

The child was so precious. Such a bundle of joy. Betsy couldn't forgive herself for the way she'd treated her daughter and her unborn grandson the night Bridgette broke the news. It wasn't that she didn't want grandkids - nothing could be further from the truth. She had, however, wanted a different experience for her daughters. She didn't want her daughters to experience the ridicule that came with out-of-wedlock pregnancies. She didn't want her daughters to experience the fall from grace of being a good girl yesterday, ghetto trash tomorrow - all for making the brave decision to carry the baby to full term.

Lord, I suggested that Bridgette have an abortion. How could I?

Years ago, when Betsy Banks told her mom she was pregnant, her mother's reply was, *I hope the Negro you fucked has a place for you to sleep.* Lawson's father had immediately converted his garage into a one-bedroom apartment so she could have a place to sleep. To her horror, Betsy Banks found that she was, in fact, her mother in every sense - including the abuse she'd vowed never to emulate. Despite her vow, she was a carbon copy.

Her mother had never displayed affection.

Her mother had been swift to administer tough love.

Her mother had used religion as a mask, and Betsy forced her daughters to wear that same mask.

In the horrific parenting failure that was Betsy's mom, Betsy was the sequel - not in the way she provided for Bridgette and Ola Mae, but in the way she loved. Unlike her mother, Betsy was remorseful. And even though Bridgette didn't receive it, she did offer a heartfelt apology several times over the past three years and begged her daughter for forgiveness - but only when she was praying alone in her room, or silently at church. Her mother, even when dead wrong, would never apologize. To make matters worse, Teresa was spending every day with her grandchild. For Betsy, to hear her only grandson call Teresa Grandma whenever she held him tore her up inside - it wasn't supposed to be this way. Surely, Ellen and Teresa had used voodoo on her daughter and grandson. Betsy was convinced.

Like most other people in the neighborhood, she'd heard the rumors about Ellen's husband and how he could heal a child by painting their picture. She'd also heard about how all the white men who tied Vesta Mae's sons and nephew to the train tracks died in car crashes - all decapitated by automotive machinery within one year of the funerals. Betsy had heard rumors from her mother about how Ellen controlled the souls of dead men; how she could transfer spirits, how the souls obeyed her, and how she had power in her touch. She also knew that Ellen wanted her grandson to take over their religious cult . . . and that was something she was determined to stop.

Betsy Banks looked at the clock. It was nearing her time to leave if she wanted to park next to the pastor and enjoy her favorite pew. She sent Ola Mae out to the car to warm the engine. Once she heard Ola Mae crank the station wagon, Betsy made her way back to the front of the house with another cup of hot coffee. That was cup number five, to be exact. She placed the steaming cup on the table, where the aroma of beans could penetrate his nostrils and trigger the reaction she'd waited for all morning.

"Betsy, before you go, could you hold Lil' O one second? I have to piss like a racehorse."

When Lawson Banks exited the bathroom, Betsy and his grandbaby were gone.

She could feel life oozing out of her body like the torturous drip of her kitchen faucet. Ellen knew Time was not her ally or her friend; rather a sub-prime lender who preferred foreclosure over forbearance. Grandma Ellen sat at her kitchen table with barely enough strength to open a loaf of bread. She was known to cook every day, all day . . . but those days had gone by. The one room in the house that was guaranteed to be an unlimited source of warmth during the winter was as cold as a morgue this morning. *The dead have no use for stewed chicken and rice, or a chocolate cake perfectly iced,* she thought. Her fire-breathing stove was as chilled as the pane of glass in her kitchen window; the window that aligned with Mrs. Dorothy's kitchen. Her kitchen was just as cold. No Dorothy.

Ellen could still hear snips of conversations they'd had over the years about their husbands, children, grandchildren, and great-grandchildren. Their lives were parallel in that they became neighbors when their husbands returned from the war, parallel in how they loved to cook, and unfortunately, parallel in how they became widows within months of one another. Grandma Ellen gazed into Mrs. Dorothy's window. A deep sigh added to the draft in her bleak and bitter kitchen. Time had foreclosed on the life of her kitchen buddy - and now she was on notice.

Orrin was gone, Earl was gone, Donald was gone, and Teresa never bothered to confirm whether she was dead or alive.

Where are all of the people I fed?

Where are all of the strangers I gave shelter?

Where are my children and why have they forsaken me?

This wasn't how it was supposed to end. Not like this - not alone with no family, only servants who were obligated to serve. Grandma Ellen shook her head and let out another deep, labored sigh. Despite everything, she had to fulfill her duty and reestablish the line of succession. Little mattered outside of that quest. If she failed, then Ellen would be the first to fail since the Purge of Akhenaten in Egypt, dating back to the period known as the New Kingdom. Ellen would have welcomed death by a thousand snakes over leaving her earthly body without an heir. She also was charged with avenging the death of the one she'd anointed - her grandson, Orrin Toussaint. In the accomplishment of that task, Time was far more gracious, and extended her the liberty to redeem the atonement from the other side.

She also had to convince Bridgette to raise Orrin's son in the wisdom of Amun - if only Bridgette would lend her an ear. Without Bridgette's baby, all was lost - unless there was, of course, a child offered up with blood. However, there was no such child available. It was Bridgette's baby or nothing. Ellen was out of time.

As she dozed in and out of conscious thought at the kitchen table, Grandma Ellen was suddenly awakened in the thralls of panic and dire urgency. She quickly reached for her trusted walking cane and squeezed her fist around the handle. Utilizing her entire daily allotment of strength, she made her way to the wall-mounted phone that sat on the side of her refrigerator and called Gail Narcisse.

"Gail, Gail, please get over here now," she huffed on the phone.

"I will be right over. Did you fall again?" Gail worried.

"No, it's worse than a fall." Her breath was heavy. "Pick up Vesta Mae and come quick."

Once Ellen hung up the phone she made her way to the front door, not even taking a detour to grab her overcoat. As soon as she stepped foot on the porch, she could see Gail whipping around the corner with Vesta Mae in the passenger seat. They helped Ellen into the back of Gail's extra-long Plymouth sedan and raced to Galvez Avenue, where they made a quick left. Once they arrived, Gail parked in the middle of the street. With the assistance of Vesta Mae, she helped Ellen to stand. Per Grandma Ellen's request, they assisted her to the center of the street, where she instructed them to lock hands with her hands.

"It is time to fight . . . as we know to fight."

Lawson Banks needed a ride and he needed one quick, so he ran next door and knocked on the door of his good buddy and neighbor, Leo Franklin. Leo's son Freddie answered the door.

"Merry Christmas and a Happy Birthday to me."

"Happy Birthday, Freddie, please call your father. It is an emergency."

Freddie stepped out on the porch and pointed at his father's pickup truck. "He's probably sleeping under there."

Lawson turned to see the legs of Leo Franklin protruding out from underside of the pickup truck and hurried over to wake him. His wife always joked that her husband slept better under a truck than next to her in bed. Leo was a mechanic for Bill Watson Ford. He worked six days a week, and on his lone off day, he tried to fix the family vehicles in between naps.

"Leo. Leo. Wake up, Leo. I need your help, buddy."

"Hold up, hold your horses," Leo said as he rolled himself out from under the truck.

Leo allowed Lawson to drive as the three of them bolted toward Second Baptist Church of God in Christ; they made good time in the process. In less than ten minutes, Lawson crossed the Claiborne Bridge and made another left on Tennessee Street. From a block away, Lawson could see Vesta Mae and Gail escorting Ellen to the front of her car.

"Hey, is that Ellen?" Leo pointed. "Why Ellen out here in all this cold with no coat on?"

"Why is Grandma Ellen standing outside of the church instead of going in?" Freddie asked.

"Don't do it, Betsy . . . don't you do it," Lawson whispered.

"Don't do what?" Leo wondered.

Lawson came to a rolling stop behind Gail, who parked in the church parking lot next to the pastor's pink Cadillac. Lawson hadn't attended service for well over three years, but he was very familiar with all the cars in the parking lot, and knew that the church was wall-to-wall packed. No surprise, since Christmas Eve had fallen on a Sunday. Lawson asked Leo and Freddie to wait in the truck as he approached the front door of the church. Nearing the steps beneath the door, he heard Grandma Ellen call out in a loud voice:

"Amun nipe nguvu zako, Amun nipe nguvu zako, Amun nipe nguvu zako. Amun, give me your strength."

"Lawson, if I were you . . . I would step back," Gail advised.

No sooner did Lawson back away from the door did a gust of wind nearly knock him off his feet as the two wooden doors blasted off the church. One flew to the east of Grandma Ellen, and the other to the west. The entire church turned to see her standing in the street, staring down Betsy, who stood behind the pulpit of the church near the baptism pool. They needed no coaching or convincing - all the congregation members quickly found the exits on both sides of the church. Some knocked down others, some hurdled the pews to the back of the church, but no one exited the front doors. Grandma Ellen was at the front door.

It took the church less than two minutes to vacate, leaving the pastor standing in the baptism pool waiting for Betsy to hand him her grandson. Bridgette's baby was decked in the traditional baptism attire - all-white garments, with a white scarf tied around his head. Lawson could hear his grandson screaming from outside the church, so he ran through the scrambling congregation and entered through a side door.

"Betsy . . . don't hand my grandson to that pastor," Ellen warned.

"You practice the devil's religion." Betsy inched to the edge of the baptism pool. "Last week, your son Donald told me that if I can get him baptized, then you can't use him. That's all I needed to know. My grandbaby getting baptized this morning. He will not be a part of your devil's religion."

"Devils religion? Ha! There isn't a religion in the history of your God that has spilled more blood than Christianity. We've burned no one alive for heresy, nor have we taken a single dime to build temples of idolatry. We've attacked no one - but once attacked, we end all conflict." Ellen freed her hands from Vesta Mae and Gail. "It is in your best interest to hand my grandson to your husband. If you do, I will spare your life."

"I will not," Betsy said as she leaned to place the child into the pastor's outstretched arms. Before he could take hold, Ellen clapped her hands one time. Suddenly, the pastor grabbed his chest and cried out in agony. He lost his footing and slipped under the water, in full cardiac arrest.

"Your pastor is drowning," Ellen said. "Betsy, don't make me hurt you, too, because I will if you try to baptize that baby. Set the baby down and save your pastor, but you will not do both."

Lawson watched as the pastor suffered a heart attack while fully submerged in the baptism pool. He wanted to help, but feared Ellen. Soon, the pastor's agony ended. He no longer held his chest or flopped about at the bottom of the pool. Betsy watched her pastor of twenty years take his last breath. Her anguish echoed across the empty church as she looked down at his lifeless body.

Ellen made one final demand. "Betsy Banks, set the baby down. I will not ask you again."

Lawson ran to the pool. "Betsy, hand me the baby."

"No."

"Betsy, hand me the baby, please!" Lawson pleaded.

"She cannot have our grandbaby, Lawson." Betsy's left foot entered the pool. "I will baptize him myself."

It was at that moment that Ellen placed her left hand on her right wrist and started to twist. As she churned on her wrist, Betsy Banks's head started to turn as if she were looking over her shoulder, as if someone were trying to break her neck." Betsy cried out in pain.

"Betsy, hand me the baby. She will kill you!" Lawson begged his wife.

It wasn't until the vertebrae in her neck could give no more that Betsy Banks handed the screaming child to his grandfather. Once Lawson was clear of the baptism pool, Ellen released her wrist. Betsy fell forward onto the chairs in the choir stand and wallowed on the floor in pain.

Lawson walked up the middle of the aisle to the front door with Lil' O wrapped in his coat. "Ellen, I-I am bringing him to my daughter, that's all. I have no dealings with this church anymore. Please allow me to pass."

"Betsy is to never lay hands on my grandson again."

"Ellen, if you let me pass, I give you my word—she will never touch him again."

With that vow, Lawson was allowed to pass. He ran directly to Leo's truck. After a short drive back over the Claiborne Bridge, they pulled up to Teresa's house just as Bridgette was unlocking the door. Lil' O had stopped crying, and was suddenly in a playful mood again.

"Hmmm, Daddy, why is my son dressed all in white?"

"Bridgette, I will explain it later," Lawson said as he handed Bridgette her son, who was babbling to himself merrily, and ran back to the truck. "Just lock the door, please! I need to check on your mother - I will be right back."

CHAPTER 49

E vie had discovered the best archive she could have ever asked for - the memories Fred shared with her left her astonished. *If I ever decide to write a book about Orrin Toussaint, then Freddie Franklin is all the resource I need.* She now had a better understanding of the High Priestess, but she still needed to know how to free her family from the doubloons. And then there was the pressing issue of the arrest warrants. The massive manhunt was on to apprehend her sister and nieces for first degree murder. And then there was the video proof of their guilt . . . and the realization that her nieces were killers - unwilling, but killers nonetheless. Evie could tell Fred was ready to return to soulful solitude, but she still needed answers.

"I will get out of your way soon, but please tell me, how do you think Bridgette can help me?"

"I couldn't tell you." Fred tossed the empty Thunderbird bottle in a large, black garbage can. "Bridgette and Orrin's mother remained close until the end . . . Teresa died a few months ago." Fred reflected on his lifelong neighbor as he lit another cigarette. "What a sweet lady."

"Sorry to hear that. Do you think Bridgette knows how to free my family from Ellen?"

"If anyone would know, she would." Fred opened the driver's door of the Camaro and sat inside. "Just a word of advice: Bridgette will talk a hole in your head until you bring up 1968 . . . that was a bad year for her."

"I know it was. Just awful."

Fred looked in the rearview mirror of the Camaro. "So, what's up with him?"

"Oh, that's my brother-in-law, Trenton. It's his wife and kids who are affected by this."

"Then why isn't he the one chasing down Bridgette?"

That question had never entered Evie's mind. "It's been a hard week for him . . . he also lost his mother."

"I hear you, but if Ellen had my wife and kids, then I would be in this conversation instead of chatting it up on my cell phone . . . I'm just saying."

Evie had noticed it, too. The entire time she interviewed Fred, Trent was preoccupied on his cell. *Who is he talking too?*

"Fred, thank you for everything . . ."

"I smoke Camels."

"I will make a deal with you." Evie wrote her number on a piece of paper. "If you can get Bridgette to call me, I will show up with three cartons of Camel cigarettes."

Fred extended his grease-stained hand. "You have a deal."

"Deal." Evie gladly shook it.

As Evie and Trent drove away, Trent visibly deflated. The more she spoke, the more distant Trent appeared. Evie suggested that they go to the NOPD safe house where Detective Encalade had finally agreed they could stay when he realized they weren't going to take him up on his jail offer. There, they could regroup and come up with another plan. It was going to take longer than she anticipated to speak with Bridgette. Evie could tell that it was only the driver's side door that prevented Trent from falling out of their moving vehicle; the hopelessness of not being able to find his wife, kids, and Aunt Frieda had taken its toll. Adding to his bewilderment, the city morgue had called earlier this morning and asked if he'd made funeral plans for his mother. There were no funeral plans, no plans to rescue his family, and no place to call home without potentially getting murdered. Trenton McGowan was a wanted man. Of no fault of his own, his life had collided with the wrath of Ellen Chauvet.

Making use of the quiet drive to the safe house, Evie powered up her tablet and flipped through all her copious notes. She scrolled back to the start of it all - the night they attended that parade against the wishes of Helen McGowan. *We should have obeyed Helen.* She sighed at the retrospect longing. The call from the morgue had also caused her to reflect on the night Helen was murdered, and the words Detective Encalade had discovered written under her body.

A doubloon will find you -
Ralph Fuller
Morris Igelhart
Bill Diliberto
Danny Diliberto
Trenton McGowan, the Unborn who has returned.

Evie became transfixed on the *Unborn* part. Then there was Attorney Morries Igelhart. "Trent, do you think if I contact the Krewe of Ares, they could help me locate Morris Igelhart?"

"You don't have to contact them; I think I may have his number." Trent slid through the menu of his cell, then handed Evie the phone.

"Seriously Trent - you've had his number the entire time?"

"I last spoke with him at my father's funeral. I'm pretty sure his number is the same."

"I'm sitting her wracking my brain while you're in a cloud somewhere. We're not working as a team."

"Evie, I gave you the number . . . let's just move on."

"Once you get your head out of your ass, then we can move on!"

"My head is not in my ass . . ."

"Then why haven't you thought to call Attorney Iglehart? He was your father's best friend. Why does it feel like I'm doing all of the thinking and all of the work?"

"Evie, cut me some slack!" Trent accelerated towards an intersection that had a red light. "I have lost my entire family - all of them. I have no one. So, excuse me if I am not in a talkative mood."

"Well that makes two of us - Marci and the girls are all I have. Do you plan on stopping for this red light or should I roll the window down and jump out?"

Trent stopped only feet short of sliding into the intersection of Elysian Fields and Claiborne Avenue. At the light, Evie glanced down at Trent's phone and entered Attorney Igelhart's number into her own. Before handing Trent his phone, she secretly viewed his call log, It was then that she noticed that shortly after they arrived at Bridgette's, Trent had received a call from Marci. *What the actual hell is going on?* The phone slid out of her hands - her nerves were rattled. She wanted to mention it right then and there, but decided to gauge how long it would take him to share such pertinent information.

I understand he is dealing with a lot and trying to process it all, but I am giving him until we arrive at this safe house before I rip his fucking head off for not informing me that he has spoken with my sister. We're in this together . . . aren't we?

"Trent, I would like to place a call to Igelhart. Maybe he remembers something from a conversation with your father?" Evie wondered, but Trent was miles away. "Trent, did you hear me?"

"I'm sorry, could you repeat that?"

"I asked your opinion about Morris Igelhart. I say we contact him. Maybe he can help." Evie tried to cap her pressure valve again, but it was a losing battle.

"I can't see how it would hurt. Sure . . . call him."

314 / TJ SPENCER JACQUES

The pressure leaked. "How about you call him?" she growled. "Attorney Igelhart doesn't know me, he knows you."

"I will make the call once we get to the safe house."

"How about we make the call now and ask if he could meet with us, because this is an emergency!"

"Evie . . . I'm not mentally there right now to speak with Igelhart or anyone else."

Evie pushed her belongings off her lap to the floor of the car. "I can't do this with you . . . I can't."

Trent pulled into the driveway to the safe house, but Evie noticed she was the only one exiting the car. He seemed anxious for her to get out, but she didn't. She decided to try a calm approach.

"Trent, what's going on?"

"With what?"

"You."

"Nothing."

"Trent . . . I know you have been in contact with my sister today." Evie returned to the passenger seat and scowled. Trent avoided her eyes. "She called you. That's who you were on the phone with when I was interviewing Fred. Tell me what's going on . . ."

"They need me," he replied in a stoic voice. "They have been set free from the doubloons and are waiting for me. We're going to be a family again."

"Waiting for you? Where?"

"At home." Trent placed the car in reverse. "Marci asked me to come alone."

"And just like that, you're going?"

"Yes, that's my wife."

"Trent, those calls may have come from Marci's phone, but that wasn't my sister."

"Evie, I heard her voice. Marci explained everything to me; it's over. She asked me to come home."

"Trent, listen to me; I am not sure what was said during that conversation, but it's not that simple. Let's call Detective Enca-lade . . ." Evie started to dial.

"No!" Trent slapped the phone out of her hand. "No police, Marci made me promise. We're going back to Bristol - today. No need to get the police involved anymore."

"The police are already involved," Evie said as she leaned forward to retrieve her phone. "Do you think they're going to simply allow you to move them back to Bristol as if these mur-ders never happened? Trent, you're having a moment right now, but you have to listen to me . . . do not go to that house."

"Evie, please step out of the car . . . my family is waiting for me."

"Trent, your name is on the kill list. You saw that video of Danny Diliberto . . . how Maggie chewed his face. Look at me . . . that wasn't your little girl or your wife who slit his throat. That was Ellen Chauvet using your family to settle a score. If you go to that house, they will kill you."

"Get out of my car, Evie."

"Trent, I will not let you do it."

"Get out, now."

"No . . . they will kill you."

At first, Trent tried to push Evie out of the car, but she leaned over him and held onto the steering wheel. Once he pried her fin-gers off, she held onto the headrest of her seat. Finally, Trent ran around to her side of the car and dragged her out. The sound of rubber threading across the pavement filled the air as he backed out of the driveway and darted away. Evie searched her purse for the keys to Marci's car while she flipped through her recent calls. She backed out of the driveway and hauled ass after Trent. After a seemingly endless chorus of rings, Detective Encalade finally answered his phone.

"Detective, help, please!"

"What is it?"

"Trent received a call from Marci asking him to meet her on Toledano Street, but it's not her, it's Ellen. If he goes there, they will kill him. Can you meet me there?"

"On Toledano Street, you say?"

"Yes . . . please hurry."

"I will have some units there in five minutes, but I can't get to you right now."

"Detective, if you come then maybe you can talk some sense into him. Please!"

"Evie, I can't . . . not right now. But I will meet you there later."

"Why can't you come now?"

"Because I have just arrived at another murder, and this guy is also wearing a doubloon."

"Krewe of Ares?"

"Yes . . . a burgundy doubloon from the Krewe of Ares 1968."

CHAPTER 50

When the call came in, Kennan and Irnessa Encalade had just loaded up the girls in her red-tinted Cadillac Escalade, but it was too good to be true. They would have to attend the Krewe of Bacchus parade without Daddy. As he kissed his daughters on the forehead and his wife on the cheek, Kennan noticed that none of them complained. It was almost as if they expected his cell phone to ring with another murder, so they'd lowered all expectations of Daddy. That's the part of it that stung him the most - the appearance that it didn't matter if he was in the truck or not. From Bullard to the Poland Street exit on I-10, Kennan drove on the side of them making funny faces at Laylah as she giggled uncontrollably. Jarah and Emma ignored him. He wondered how long it would be before Laylah ignored him, too. Kennan loved his job, but he hated what his job was doing to his family - he was so tired of kissing three sleeping daughters late in the evening, only to kiss the same sleeping beauties at five a.m. and stagger back to work in a haze of red and blue lights.

I am a full-time dad and an absent father . . . how is that even possible?

Kennan Encalade lived in both realities.

It was a little after four p.m. when he arrived at the old St. Margaret's Nursing Home on 6220 Charters Street to find six patrol cars, the fire department, and the local news crews already on site. The nursing home was a single-story facility laid out in the shape of a rectangle, and it was the last two units on the corner that were receiving the most attention from the fire department. As he approached the charred portion of the building, he noticed that all the resident patients had been evacuated, and none of the rooms were marked off with crime scene tape.

So why was I dispatched? I don't see a dead body.

Detective Encalade stood outside of the two saturated rooms and saw what appeared to be a typical cigarette fire, set by the typical sleepy smoker. Confused, he shrugged his shoulders at a firefighter who was inspecting the area for hotspots. *Why did they call me in on my off day for a nursing home fire?* Kennan entered the next room over that was unscathed, and that's when he spotted the familiar crime scene tape. His homicide squad was huddled at the rear of an EMS vehicle, and Detective Seals was in the center of the huddle. That's not a good sign. Kennan hurried for the nearest exit and seconds later, he stepped under the yellow crime scene tape like a heavyweight fighter entering the ring. He quickly approached his partner, Detective Seals.

"Something better be dead and stinking to call me in on my first off day in a month. Point it out," Kennan said to Detective Seals. "Why is the back of this EMS vehicle covered by a white tarp?"

"Detective Encalade, *come on down*, you're the next contestant on *Shit Ain't Right.*" Detective Seal waved his arm like Bob Barker. "It's just another mutilated guy with a Krewe of Ares doubloon around his neck from 1968 . . . what's your opening bid?"

Encalade opened the tarp and before his eyes could process the scene, his nose detected the foul stench of roasted flesh. The odor came from a burnt guy on the gurney. Kennan forced his eyes to look into the face of the rotisserie victim only to see emptied eye sockets, no lips, and fire-resistant white teeth. His head was absent of hair, and his entire body appeared evenly cooked except for his feet and hands, which were charcoal-black. Hanging off his body and embedded in his grilled muscle tissue were shreds of gray pajamas and a blue bathrobe, on his finger was a wedding band, and around his neck hung a doubloon from the Krewe of Ares 1968. Once Kennan spotted that doubloon, he knew why he was called in on a beautiful off day.

A third body with a connecting link just escalated these cases to the serial killer side of the court.

Just as he was about to close the tarp, he noticed that the right arm of the victim appeared to be extended out from his body, but his line of sight was blocked. Just as he placed his foot on the step bumper to get a closer look, he heard her voice.

"If you step in the back of that vehicle I will fuck you up . . . I promise you." The usual threat from Lieutenant Teri Moore.

"Teri, I need to see the other side of his body . . ."

"And people in hell need ice water."

"But, but I . . ."

"But, but, my ass," Lieutenant Moore said as she snapped pictures from the driver's seat, facing the rear. "Get your protective gear or get fucked up. You-heard me?"

"I'm out of foot covers . . . okay. How about you shoot me a picture to my cell?" a frustrated Encalade replied.

"How about I shoot you in the ass? You have protective gear, but you forgot it—again.

"Teri . . ."

"All right, all right! Sent, you should have it. If you had to remember to snap on your dick, you wouldn't piss for eight weeks."

"Bye, Teri."

"And fuck you too."

Just as Kennan closed the privacy trap, his cell phone alerted him to two new text messages with images. The first one he

320/ TJ SPENCER JACQUES

opened was a fuck you from a well-manicured middle finger, and the second image showed the right side of the victim's body. Kennan held his cell phone horizontally to allow the image to expand in portrait view. That's when he saw it, written in blood: *The unborn has returned.*

He knew Trent was the unborn, *but why was his family playing the role of the executioner?* Suddenly, his cell phone alerted him to another text message with an image. Kennan opened the picture thinking it was another prank from Teri, only to see a group photo of his wife and kids at the parade, followed by, *Wish you were here.* His family was less than five miles away, but it felt as if they were in Des Moines, Iowa. Kennan slid the phone in his pocket and sighed. *If I don't apprehend the McGowan family . . . I will not have a family.*

Kennan walked over to Detective Seals, who was herding a group of news crews back on the other side of the yellow tape. That was a mistake - he should have waited for Detective Seals by the EMS. He was instantly swarmed by cameras.

"Detective Encalade, do you have any suspects?"

"Detective Encalade, can you confirm reports that all three victims were found wearing the same doubloon?"

"Detective Encalade, why hasn't there been a press conference?"

"Detective Encalade, why hasn't Chief Bolton requested the help of the FBI to catch the Doubloon Serial Killers?"

And just like that, the killers were given a collective name, and Encalade knew their homicide department had less than twenty-four hours before national news outlets flooded New Orleans again with bloodthirsty media crews. On cue, his phone alerted him to an incoming call. It was from Chief Bolton. He sent Chief Bolton to voicemail.

"Hey Seals, this guy have a name?" Encalade asked as they walked back to the EMS vehicle.

"Yes . . . it's Bill Diliberto, a resident of Chalmette. Detective Gloster confirmed that his brother was Danny Diliberto."

"Brothers. Murdered two days apart. The exact same way." Encalade did not want to entertain the idea that these murders were connected to Orrin Toussaint, but the evidence was becoming too hard to ignore. Friday evening, he had reopened the Orrin Toussaint case and assigned it to Detective Gloster, who was one hundred percent certain he could close it with Bill and Danny as the perpetrators. After Danny Diliberto's murder, he had also ordered around-the-clock security for Morris Igelhart, Ralph Fuller, and Bill Diliberto.

"There should have been an officer on site, did he see anything?" Encalade asked Detective Seals.

"The officer on watch said he witnessed an older lady standing on the sidewalk waving at Mr. Diliberto through the window."

"Waving, like *hello?*"

"No, waving like *come outside and play*. Then, a younger woman joined the older lady."

"So, two women stood outside of his window and tried to persuade the victim to come outside? Did he?"

"According to the officer, after a while, Bill closed the shades. The officer thought that was the end of it. That's when the fire alarm sounded, and the staff evacuated all the patients. As a precaution, the EMS was called."

"So, he wasn't burned in his room?"

"Nope, not a scratch. Bill Diliberto walked out of the nursing home, crossed the street, and watched his room burn from right over there according to the nurse."

"If the victim evacuated the building, how did he get so crispy?"

"A better question is where."

"Byron Seals, you better not say it . . . you better not!"

"In the back of that got-damn EMS vehicle," Detective Seals confirmed. "One second the nurse said Diliberto was standing next to her, and the next second he was gone. She searched the crowd for him, and that's when they saw black smoke seeping out the EMS truck. When the firefighters opened the back doors, there he was - lit like a gas stove." Detective Seals shook his head in disbelief.

Detective Encalade patted all his pockets and searched the ground around the EMS truck, but he couldn't find it. The more he searched, the higher his blood pressure soared. If he couldn't find it, he was doomed. *Maybe it's in the car?*

"Hey, where are you running off to?" Detective Seals called after him.

"I can't find my notepad!"

"Oh no, not the notepad. You're doomed!" Seals laughed.

"You got jokes today? I'll be right back - I think it's in my car."

As Kennan made his way through the crowd, he received another incoming call - this time from a number he had recently saved as Evie - *Suspect's Sister*. He listened to a distraught Evie explain how she was following Trenton McGowan because Marci had asked to meet him. What Encalade didn't share with Evie is that he'd been keeping the McGowan house under surveillance since Saturday by two officers on the second floor of the Morial residence.

"I will be there shortly - right now I'm in the Lower Ninth Ward, which is on the other side of town from you . . . not to mention the Krewe of Bacchus is rolling as we speak. Traffic is a mess, and I am short a few officers, but I will be there. And by the way . . . I need to speak with you."

"About?" Evie asked.

Encalade searched his car for his notepad. "It's the strangest thing. One of my patrol officers said he spotted who I believe was your sister Marci and Trent's Aunt Frieda outside of St. Margaret's Nursing Home, stalking the victim."

"Who was the victim?"

"Bill Diliberto. When he refused to come outside, it appears they may have set a fire to force him out. Once outside, he died of very suspicious circumstances."

"Did you say the name of the nursing home was St. Margaret's?

"That's correct."

"Is there a Catholic church nearby?

"The nursing home is connected to the Catholic church."

"Then Fred was right . . ."

"Right about what? Who's Fred?"

"The reason they forced Bill Diliberto outside is because they can't step foot inside a church!"

"Well, you may want to get Trent to a church, because he's next."

As Detective Encalade entered the wrought iron gate at 1524 Toledano, he could hear what sounded like a rolling argument traveling from room to room inside the house, similar to the fight he'd recently had with Irnessa. His wife still hated his work hours, but after knocking him unconscious with the sugar bowl, there hadn't been one argument - just a lot of sex in the kitchen. Not since their early twenties had they had so much sex. *It's like her temperamental inner voice was muted while a kinder, softer voice was amplified.* Whatever the reason, Kennan loved the New Irnessa, and her seductive text messages were all the encouragement he needed to get him home by seven p.m. The time now was six p.m., and his notepad was nowhere in sight.

Evie opened the door and was very relieved to see Detective Encalade, but Trent wasn't. While Evie held the door open for the detective, Trent stood by the wall at the base of the stairs, holding a family photo of his parents and brothers. Evie sat down on the sofa in front of a coffee table with several cell phones laid out on top. It was then that she handed over Marci's cell phone as proof that Marci had called Trent.

"There was a call from this phone placed to Trent's phone four hours ago," Evie said.

"When you arrived today, this phone was in the same place you left it?" Detective Encalade asked.

"Yes, we stayed in the safe house yesterday. Today is my first day back since Saturday."

"So you believe Marci made the call?"

"There's no other explanation, but when we entered the house . . . no one was here."

Immediately, Encalade wondered why his officers hadn't alerted him of Marci's visit. Across the street was his best surveillance crew; two retired officers who enjoyed working detail and trailing suspects. The Sky Squad, as he'd branded the team, never dosed off on assignment and was recently recognized by the U.S. Marshals for its assistance in apprehending a record numbers of fugitives. *Surely my Sky Squad would have detected some movement?*

"While we wait them out, I have a few additional questions for you, Detective McGowan."

Trent remounted the picture and turned to face Encalade. "Yes, ask whatever you like."

"When you spoke with your wife earlier today, did she provide an explanation for these murders?"

Trent appeared hesitant to speak. "Not really."

"Not really?" Encalade dug deeper. "What may not seem like a lot to you could be just what I need to bring your family in safely. Trenton, you know how this works - you're one of us. Please share what you two discussed."

"When I asked her why they killed Danny Diliberto, she started speaking in a foreign language. Words I have never heard her use before. But she spoke this new language so fluidly. So effortlessly . . ."

"It's the ancient Mahu dialect."

"Excuse me?"

"The language you heard was ancient Mahu. The translations are largely undocumented. My partner, Detective Seals, said his mother once spoke the same language. When he watched the Danny Diliberto footage, he detected a word here and there."

"Marci has never spoken in Mahu or anything like that. When I asked her to repeat it in English . . ." Trent slid into thought.

"Trent, stay with me . . . what did she say?"

"She-she said that she was *so happy* that I decided to move back to New Orleans because I was the unborn. I don't have a clue what that means."

"It means the events of 1968 predated your birth - but Ellen Chauvet gave your father until the time you moved back home to retract what was reported regarding the death of Orrin Toussaint."

"How do you know this for sure?" Evie asked

"Because in my line of work, I have learned to never show my hand at the beginning of the round. I watched three hours of recordings from Dr. Brooks's sessions with Helen McGowan. She said it as clear as a sunny day. When Ellen Chauvet held Jack McGowan by the arm, she gave him until the *unborn* returned to make things right. He didn't. You moved home two weeks ago. And that's how we got here."

"So you believe us?" Evie asked with a voice of full excitement. "You now believe that all of this is out of character - downright extreme behavior - for my sister and her daughters and Aunt Frieda? So, this has to be the work of Ellen Chauvet!"

"I wouldn't say I am completely sold on the idea, because the evidence only points to the same five individuals. Having said that . . . I do have a better understanding of the motive."

"But Detective, my sister didn't have a motive to kill these people." Evie stood at the other end of the coffee table. "You said it just a minute ago, she's only been here two weeks. Everything that has taken place is all part of a personal vendetta, but the involvement of Aunt Frieda, my nieces, and Marci - with no motives for any of them - classifies these murders as random killings. You can't have it both ways, Detective. You have to acknowledge the influence of Ellen Chauvet."

"Now you're starting to sound like Detective Seals with all this stuff about superpowers and some high priest who has control over souls. He swears by it."

"Because it's true," Evie argued. "Whether you believe it or not, it's true." It was then that Evie opened an email she'd received an hour ago from Mrs. Young. The subject of the email: *The Commandments of Mahu.*

Scribe 9: A nyumbu (human host) is under the authority of

the High Priest until an atonement is made - only then can they be released. Only through a relic can the High Priest join a host to a soul from the Realm of Sinar. If the relic is removed without atonement, the host will die. The High Priest sets the atonement.

Suddenly there was banging on the front door, followed by the twisting of the doorknob, then the opening of the door. Encalade gripped his gun - the one with three bullets in the clip - while Trent moved closer to the door. In ran Dr. Morial from across the street. She ran straight into the arms of Detective Encalade.

"Kennan, it's awful, so awful!" Dr. Morial's legs gave out.

It was very difficult for Kennan Encalade to keep his composure. In his entire career, he'd never witnessed anything so barbaric, so vile, inflicted on a member of his fraternal brotherhood. Both members of the Sky Squad had been murdered. They were stripped naked, and the top layer of their skin was scraped away. *They were skinned alive, perhaps?* Definitely -dissected across the abdomen. Both officers were positioned on the floor with their hands bound by their own intestines and their mouths stuffed with their own intestines. No eyes, no lips. No life. Only the crowns of their heads touched. Their bodies were arranged in a line, with their own intestines arranged like an arrow tip. Kennan's eyes followed the tip of the arrow, and to no surprise, it was aimed at 1524 Toledano Street.

"Rest in peace, retired Officer Steve Copeland. Rest in peace, retired Officer Doug Debruce."

CHAPTER 51

L ieutenant Teri Moore had to pause after every photo; it was too difficult to capture Steve Copeland, her old precinct boss, in such a mutilated state. It felt like only yesterday when she was ordered to report to him right out of the academy, and he took her under his wing. A little smile appeared between the tears when Teri reflected on how Captain Copeland would always give her a hard time about uniform pants he felt were too tight. *Teri, those pants remind me of blood pressure cuffs.* To this, she would reply, *Your belly is overdue for a C-section.* All the officers would laugh and hug their way out the door, including Lieutenant Teri Moore and Captain Steve Copeland.

Standing just inside the door were Detective Encalade and Detective Seals, watching from a distance, respecting her space.

"This shit real personal now, Kennan . . . for real." A snap of the camera and then a sniff.

"Yes it is, and I will bring an end to this if it's the last thing I do," Kennan promised.

"Copeland didn't deserve this . . . no human deserves this. What's the deal with these people? How do we stop this shit?" A snap and two sniffs.

"Teri, that's what we're trying to figure out." Kennan tried to look away but couldn't. "They were doing me a favor."

Teri handed Kennan Officer Doug Debruce's surveillance camera. "Everything you need to know about how it went down is there - just hit play." Another sob and a sniff. "Do me a favor and view it somewhere else. I can't listen again."

Detective Encalade and Detective Seals sat in a patrol car and pressed play on the camcorder. For the most part, the video only captured mundane day-to-day life in the 1500 block of Toledano Street. A letter carrier carried a large postal bag from porch to porch, a door-to-door salesman from a local cable company ambled the block, and a meter checker from the water board strolled through to check the meters - just a typical morning. Encalade fast-forwarded the camera to eleven a.m., and that's when he noticed three individuals standing in the second floor window. From across the street, Doug Debruce saw the glowing doubloons flashing like a No Vacancy sign.

"Steve, wake your ass up, we have action across the street," Kennan heard Doug say to his partner.

"What the hell is that they're wearing?" Copeland asked. "Mardi Gras beads?"

"Hey, take a look at the kitchen window . . . there's the aunt."

"Keep an eye on them while I call the calvary. It looks like we have them all in one place," Debruce said.

As soon as Doug Debruce stood to radio in an update, Copeland called to him. "Hey, get back over here, buddy, the front door just opened. Isn't that the youngest one . . . what's her name?"

"It's Zoe," Debruce answered.

"Why is Zoe alone . . . on the porch?"

Doug grabbed his binoculars and honed in on Zoe. "Holy shit; she looked right at me."

"No way," Copeland dismissed his partner.

"I am telling you . . . she looked right at me when I zoomed in. She knows we're up here."

"Doug, there is no fucking way that little girl can see us through these surveillance shades. We can see her, but she can't see us."

"Well if that were true, why is she about to cross the street?"

Encalade and Seals watched the screen as Zoe crossed the street and looked up at Doug and Steve from the pavement. In her hand was a piece of sidewalk chalk. She looked down from the window and began to write.

"Dude, you're freaking out for no reason," Officer Steve Copeland said. "She's looking for somewhere to draw. My grandkids mark up my entire driveway every weekend with that chalk. Wait until I catch the Bozo who invented that shit. I will kick his ass - and make him pressure wash my driveway."

Slowly, Zoe's hand wrote in the penmanship of a six-year-old, in bulky red letters. In the wide view, the camera recorded the other four family members in the window, where they stood perfectly still with their eyes focused on the second level of the Morial residence.

"SHE WROTE MY NAME—HOW IN THE HELL?!" Doug started to freak out on camera. "HOW DOES SHE KNOW MY FUCKING NAME? HOW?" The mic on the video camera recorded the sound of Doug chambering his weapon.

"Holy mother of God," Copeland said as he watched Zoe complete her writing. When she was done, she left the view of the camera and stepped onto the Morial's porch. In big bold letters, Zoe had written a personalized message for Doug Debruce:

HI DOUG. THE DILIBERTO BROTHERS ARE DEAD. YOU'RE NEXT.

Upon reading the message, Steve joined Doug in chambering his weapon. "SHIT, THE DOOR IS OPENING!" he soon screamed to his partner. Then, everything on screen devolved into hysteria. Detective Encalade and Seals listened to the gunfire and screams, one explosion and wail after the other, and winced as they witnessed their fellow officers' destruction. During the chaos, Marci, Amarah, Maggie, and Aunt Frieda never left the window.

The video camera soon captured Zoe as she skipped her way down the porch steps. She turned to wave bye-bye to the second floor, then skipped back across the street. The officers who had detained Danny and Bill Diliberto in 1968, but released them shortly afterward, joined the brothers in the afterworld - killed by a six-year-old named Zoe McGowan at the request of the High Priestess.

CHAPTER 52

It was around eight o'clock that evening when the last of the police officers left the Morial residence; only news crews and Detective Encalade remained. Evie was exhausted from interviews. Normally she would have loved a scoop on a story this big, if only the people committing the murders weren't her immediate family - her only sister, Trent's aunt, and her precious nieces. Due to recent events, Evie had taken leave of absence from her job; she knew Marci was going to need her well beyond Mardi Gras. New Orleans was her new home for the foreseeable future.

Evie watched through the blinds as Detective Encalade and Chief Bolton concluded the last press conference. She sent Encalade a text to stop by before he left the Morial's, and he soon gazed in her direction and waved. As he entered the gate, Evie could see the heavy weight of grief on his face. The loss of Steve Copeland and Doug Debruce on the same day ignited a wave of heartbreak that crashed into every officer on the force. The whole department was unified in sorrow.

"Detective Encalade, I've said this several times today, but I am so sorry for your loss. My heart is truly broken." Evie and

Encalade embraced.

"It's been a tough day all the way around, and to add to it, the FBI jerks are breathing down my back, and I can't find my little notepad."

"Oh no, is there anything I can do to help?"

"Can I copy your notes?"

"Not a problem, I would love to help in any way I can."

Encalade placed his hand on the doorknob. "I wasn't sold on this Ellen Chauvet theory, but I just watched a video of a six-year-old who possessed the strength of two grown men. Evie, I owe you an apology."

"Detective Encalade I appreciate that so much. All my research has confirmed that we are battling something supernatural that has the power to turn normal people into killers. To bring an end to this may take something just as powerful."

"I agree. Does eight a.m. work for you for notes?"

"Not a problem . . . goodnight, Detective."

"Goodnight."

To her dismay, Trent had returned to the wall. He held the same picture as before. At that moment, Evie realized Trent was absorbing all the blame - but she blamed Ellen Chauvet and those who had botched the investigation into the murder of Orrin Toussaint.

Evie walked over to Trent and stood behind him. "Trent, I'm sorry for yelling at you. This entire ordeal has me so frustrated."

"No need to apologize, Evie, it's my fault." Trent held the McGowan family photo to his heart. "Marci was right, but I didn't listen. And now . . ."

"Trent, this is not your fault—there was no way you could have known about a meeting that took place in your dad's office in 1968 . . ."

"But I am the unborn who set these events in motion."

"That's true, but it was Ellen who eliminated your options. Can't you see that?" Evie tried to reason. "Coming back to New Orleans was the right thing to do because Ellen was tormenting your mother. And I am not minimizing the symptoms of dementia, but I think Ellen played a major role."

Trent reached for a photo of Marci and the kids, which had been placed on a nearby end table. "I miss my wife. I have never been apart from my daughters. We're leaving New Orleans . . . as a family." His tears landed on the picture frame. "Why didn't I listen to her? I was so afraid our marriage wouldn't survive the distance. I should have listened to Marci. I destroyed my family," Trent wept.

"Trent, there is still a chance we can bring them in safely. A slight chance is better than no chance at all. We have to fight for what we love, and if you love your family as much as you say you do . . . then we have to fight." Evie fist-bumped the wall. "Tomorrow when Detective Encalade comes, we need to have our game plan and the first thing I . . ."

Trent cut her off. "I am not going with you tomorrow."

"Why not?"

"I am not leaving this house . . . I am waiting for my wife. When she returns, I will be right here."

"The only way we're going to beat Ellen is if we stick together."

"Marci said Ellen released her."

"Then why isn't she here right now? Ellen is luring you into a trap!"

"I didn't listen to her the first time, I will not make that mistake again."

"Trent, they will kill you . . ."

"They love me . . . we are a family."

Evie clutched a fist of her hair in frustration. "Take tonight and think about this . . . please."

"If I can't live with them, then I don't want to live without them."

"Trent . . ."

"Goodnight, Evie."

CHAPTER 53

24 hours until Mardi Gras

What the morning sun lacked in warmth, it over-compensated for in brilliant rays that radiated the historic character and spirit of New Orleans. At the Canal Street Ferry, no one complained about the icy breeze that traveled the levee south to the Gulf of Mexico. Why not? Because they had arrived filled with desire.

And lust.

And great expectations.

And the anticipation of pleasure.

At this time tomorrow, at this exact hour, the ecstasy of Carnival would cast away all stress and worry, for this was the time of year when New Orleanians tossed tension like beads and discarded troubles like cheap trinkets. Today marked a revival of joy and a renewal life, love, and laissez les bon temps rouler (let the good times roll).

It was Lundi Gras morning. The annual arrival of the King of Rex across the Canal Street Ferry was well underway. For those who savored the pageantry of Mardi Gras, the Monday morning arrival of King Rex was a must-see tradition, and one that Detective Encalade knew Morris Igelhart would not miss. The King and Queen of Zulu and the King and Queen of Ares were arriving to toast the King of Rex. Evie and Encalade made their way through a crowd of mostly tourists and continued to the passenger boarding level of the ferry dock.

THE GOAL: Recruit Attorney Morris Igelhart to the coalition to defeat Ellen Chauvet.

THE PLAN: Wait until after the King of Rex is toasted by Zulu and Ares, then ask Igelhart for his support.

PLAN B: Run.

Encalade and Evie arrived at the passenger boarding level just the King of Rex received the keys to the city from the mayor. Encalade couldn't help but notice Evie's excitement as she tried to take it all in. Once the toast was completed, they snaked through the onlookers until they located the Ares Delegation. In attendance for Ares were several previous captains and lifelong board members.

"Okay Evie, I have done my part, it's your go," Encalade said.

Her part was to locate Igelhart in the crowd; a task she was overqualified to perform. On her tablet was an extra photo of him from a recent tribute dinner. "That's our guy right there, second to the end, on the left." Evie held the iPad so Encalade could confirm.

Morris Igelhart was a polished man with a molasses beard that fooled no one. He reminded Encalade of John Goodman from *Roseanne* in his build and expression. Encalade could tell Igelhart didn't share his passion for the gym, and the custom-tailored jacket he wore only accentuated his neglect. Just as Detective Encalade was about to approach him, Igelhart stepped in front of the Ares delegation to make another toast.

"Ralph and I joined Ares in 1966. Two years later, our best buddy, who is in heaven smiling down, became the longest-serving captain of our club. Jack, old buddy, I hope we have made you proud . . . *to Jack McGowan*." The members lifted their wine glasses in a toast to the late captain. "Ralph, get your ass over here!" Igelhart wrapped his arm around the neck of Ralph Fuller as he approached the mic. "Kelsey and Rhonda, I remember when you two were little maids and dukes in this krewe . . . the fact that I will see you roll tomorrow, on Mardi Gras, as the King and Queen of Ares, has me overjoyed beyond measure. *To Kelsey and Rhonda.*"

With that final toast, Attorney Igelhart concluded the Krewe of Ares's Lundi Gras festivities on the river. It was then that Detective Encalade moved in and pounced.

"Hello, Attorney Igelhart . . . I am Detective Encalade, and this is Evie Haggerty. Could we have a quick moment of your time?"

"Is this about our police details? I am not the one to see for that; our Queen is your lady."

"No sir, but if we could have a word with you in private, I can explain how you could help us."

"Well, anything I can do to assist New Orleans's finest, count me in." Igelhart followed Encalade and Evie to the ground level. Once there, he turned to face Encalade. "And how may I help you, Detective?"

"It was interesting to hear you mention former captain Jack McGowan; he's part of the reason I need to speak with you."

"Really . . . you need to speak with me . . . about Jack?" Igelhart said with a muddled face.

"Yes, you sat in a meeting some years back . . ."

"Detective Encalade, I have sat in over five thousand meetings . . . far too many to recall one in particular."

"But I think you will remember this one . . . it was held shortly after Orrin Toussaint was burned alive during the 1968 parade," Evie inserted.

"That's my cue; this conversation is over." Attorney Igelhart turned to walk away.

"They will kill you next!" Encalade called out. "You're next!"

Attorney Igelhart froze in motion as if someone had clicked

an off switch. He faced north as if he'd heard his name whispered on Lake Pontchartrain - as if he wanted to visit a vintage store-front on Canal Street. As if he knew this conversation would happen one day. The warp speed of a memory immobilized him and left him retained in recollection.

Detective Encalade closed the distance. "If you want to see Kelsey and Rhonda Fuller reign as King and Queen tomorrow, then I advise you to hear me out."

"Detective, do you have a wife and kids?" Igelhart faced Encalade with a ghostly expression.

"Yes, I do . . ."

"In your line of work, could you think of anything that is worse than death?" Igelhart asked.

Encalade pondered for a second. "I cannot think of anything worse than leaving my wife without a husband, and my daughters without a father to protect them."

"The anticipation of death, perhaps?" Igelhart said in a theater voice. "I know I'm next . . . I've known for some time, but she's toying with me. Like a cat that has stumbled upon a lame rat. She could gulp me at any moment, but she toys with me. She chuckles at my fears. I'm tired."

Evie entered the dead space between the two men. "Sir, she has control of my sister and nieces . . ."

"The Doubloon Killers?" Igelhart asked.

"For lack of a better name . . . yes. You are the only living person from that meeting with Mrs. Ellen Chauvet. Is there anything you remember that could help us end these killings?" On Evie's tablet was a picture of Marci, Trent, Amarah, Maggie, and Zoe, which she showed to Igelhart.

"It was all my idea—that press conference. Jack, God bless his soul, simply said what I told him to say. To admit Jack witnessed that lynching would have placed Ares in a negative light. We were rookies. Wet behind the ears. We learned on the job. We figured it out after the mistakes. How we handled the Toussaint kid was a mistake. It was my mistake, but Jack never forgot that kid." A puddle formed in the lids of his eyes from tears that re-fused to fall. "I was with him when he took his last breath . . . he never let me forget it."

"In the moments before Jack McGowan passed away, did he say anything to you? Anything at all that could assist us?" Encalade asked.

"He said *make it right.*" Igelhart turned to walk away again. "It's too late to make it right with Ellen . . . so I have made it right with my maker. Good day and good luck."

ACT III

CHAPTER 54

Ash Wednesday
8:05 a.m.

E ven though he had a key to their home, Ralph blew the horn in ten-second intervals for no other reason than to annoy the hell out of his only child, Kelsey. After the third honk, Rhonda peeked her head out of the door with a face full of sleep and confirmed what Ralph already knew - they were running late. Normally it would drive him crazy if someone requested a meeting time and then arrived late, but not today. Today, their annual tardiness was forgiven. After all, they were the King and Queen of Ares, and Ralph was Captain.

Unlike so many other captains, Ralph ran uncontested and was voted in unanimously; some even called it a miracle. But it made perfect sense to the entire organization following the death of Jack McGowan; if Igelhart was Jack's right-hand man, then Fuller was his left. Literally. That night in 1968, when the flambeaux carrier was burned alive in the middle of Burgundy Street, it was Ralph Fuller standing next to Captain Jack McGowan during the news coverage when the official statement was released. It was also Ralph who'd initially suggested the reduction of police officers on the tail end of the route - the section that ran through the French Quarter. And yes, it was Ralph Fuller who approved the dollar amount for the settlement that Ellen Chauvet never requested or wanted.

All the current krewe members remembered from that horrible night was that the entire ordeal soon faded from public interest. Things at the Krewe of Ares headquarters soon returned to business as usual. Ralph loved his role as Captain, but now the time was near to pass it on to his son Kelsey, who had just completed a successful reign as King. *What better way to secure his nomination?* Ralph strategized. *I will announce my retirement tomorrow, and when Kelsey returns from his vacation, he can run for Captain.*

Rhonda was first out of the house. She strolled over to the car holding a carry-on bag, She was followed by Kelsey, who already appeared winded. Ralph and Kelsey stuffed the last of the luggage in the back of his Mercedes CLS550 and shuttled to the airport.

"Dad, have you spoken to Mom yet?" Kelsey worried.

"No, I haven't, but she's facing a monumental challenge right now, I'm sure of it. But your mother is strong," Ralph assured of his ex-wife.

In his mind, they would grow old together, and after their last Mardi Gras, they would float to heaven in each other's arms. But it wasn't to be; they ran out of love long before they ran out of life. They found themselves single again at the worst possible age, yet they remained friends. In Ralph's rearview mirror, Kelsey and Rhonda were conjoined at the lips. *I used to have a woman who kissed me the same way Rhonda kissed Kelsey.*

The kiss ended just as he came to a stop in front of the Southwest Airlines passenger drop-off. With the urgency of a racecar pit crew, Ralph and Kelsey unloaded the compressed luggage in the trunk and waved as the airport traffic officer whistled.

The drive back to his Marigny neighborhood was as smooth

and effortless as a monorail, especially since most of the residents were still asleep or hung over from Mardi Gras. Once inside his home, Ralph brewed a strong cup of coffee and spent the next hour online, searching for as much footage as he could find of his son Kelsey as the King of Ares. His moment of joy was interrupted by a gentle knock on the door - a very unexpected guest, but very familiar.

"And to what do I owe this visit?" Ralph said as he welcomed his ex-wife in and assisted her with her coat. He pressed his nose into the curve of her neck - Dior Miss Dior. She took a seat in his tufted leather wingback chair, statuesque in a form-fitting, auburn, velvet skirt topped with a flowing wool sweater. She looked too perfect to touch. So, he admired from across the room. "Can I get you some coffee? It's your favorite brand."

"No, thank you . . . maybe tomorrow."

"How about forever?" he wished.

"Let's take it one cup at a time."

"Your son just asked about you. He's worried."

"Once he lands, I will check in."

"Wish you could have sat in the viewing stand with me yesterday, it was amazing . . ."

"I wasn't with you, but I was there . . . and Kelsey looked marvelous." Seductively, she crossed her legs. "And that Rhonda . . . she embodied the elegance of Buckingham Palace."

"I missed you . . . a lot," Ralph said.

"It appears you have adjusted fine without me . . . look at this place."

"Oh, quit," he brushed off her attempt to minimize his loneliness. "I am nothing more than an old jar of wax without a wick. You were the light of my world, you know."

Ralph studied her every move; every flinch of her hand, every puck of her lips. He searched for a sign that she wanted the same for them - a renewal. Another tall glass of passion, with a pinch of lime and two straws. Another long sip of each other, another chance to indulge in her, savor the taste of her skin . . .

"How did we drift apart?" he asked as he walked to the wing-back chair and took a knee. Her boots were crocheted and blended flawlessly with her skirt. Her food had hooked him and her intelligence had kept him, but it was her idiosyncratic style and the jazz in her walk that made her irreplaceable. Ralph rested his head on her lap and daydreamed as his hand enjoyed the curves of her knee-high boots from her favorite designer, Yves Saint Laurent.

"I was such a fool to let you walk out of my life. Too stressed out to enjoy what I had in you. Then I retired, life became simple . . . but you were gone. I was such a fool."

"In the mind of the curator, even the most exquisite work of art eventually fuses into the background. That is, of course, until it's moved, or stolen . . . or both," she said as she groomed his metallic hair with her fingers.

"But I never stopped loving you . . ."

"But you stop noticing me, Ralph. Everyone noticed me but you. And don't get me started on that Jack McGowan. But my husband? My curator? Unfortunately, Ralph, I dissolved into the background of your life."

Ralph looked into her eyes. "I never knew you felt that way."

"I just wanted you to want me as much as you obsessed over that business."

"But what about now?" His head returned to the pillow of her lap. "Let's try again—a new start. You can rent your place out and move back here. Let's give us another go at it. What do you say?"

"Ralph, as much as I love you . . . I can't."

"Why not . . . ? Isn't that the reason for this visit?"

"That's not the reason . . . we can never go back and rekindle something that was broken." Her soft strokes through his hair turned into scrapes and scratches on his scalp.

"Ouch!" he protested.

"Ralph, you're out of time."

He moved within inches of her lips. "We still have so much

life to live, why do you feel we're out of time?"

"I said you. You are out of time."

"Frieda, I don't understand . . ."

"Maybe this will help you understand." Frieda reached inside of her wool sweater and pulled the burgundy doubloon from underneath. Ralph's eyes stretched to the fullest capacity as he mumbled the embossed words.

"Krewe of Ares 1968."

"The High Priestess sent me to collect your portion of the atonement."

Ralph fell and slid across the mahogany floor. Suddenly, Frieda clawed through the air and saddled him. Ralph was paralyzed with fear and hypnotized by the illumination of the doubloon. He watched her eyes change from autumn brown to the tint of raw liver. Gone was the fragrance of Dior, that succulent, sweet scent he wanted to inhale forever. Now he struggled to breathe, because her body reeked of rigor mortis. That's when she licked his neck from his collarbone up to his ear. Her tongue raked like at rusted Brillo across his sensitive skin.

"What's the matter, Ralphie boy? *Is the thrill gone already?* Kiss me, Ralphie . . . one last time. Kiss me goodbye." A high pitch sucking sound squealed from Frieda's puckered lips.

"Please, please Frieda!" He begged for his life. "What can I do to be forgiven? Please tell me, I will do it . . . anything!" Ralph cried out as Frieda leaned down to his ear and whispered.

"Five minutes ago, Rhonda and Kelsey took their last breaths in a romantic hotel room in Vegas." Frieda gave Ralph a rough kiss on the lips. "The moment you opened that door, you were . . . *wewe ni nguruwe kwa ajili ya kuchinjwa.* You were swine for the slaughter."

First, the eyes, because he was a witness.

Then the lips, because he was silent.

Finally, the throat, to release the soul to the Realm of Sinar.

Ellen Vieux Chauvet (Kuhani Nalah) and her line of succession control who enters or leaves the Realm of Sinar.

CHAPTER 55

E vie sat at a desk in the safe house, lost in her worried thoughts. The safe house had all the amenities of home, minus the windows and live plants. What Detective Encalade referred to as a safe house was nothing more than the fifth floor of the NOPD headquarters, which had been converted into hotel rooms. The internet was awesome, the food was better than the best restaurant in Bristol, and she was permitted to scroll through the NOPD archive on the sixth floor. *If not for the current crisis . . . I could live here forever.*

Putting her comfort and security aside, Evie worried about Trent, who was still over on Toledano Street. Her last conversation with him was yesterday, but he'd abruptly ended the call. His position hadn't changed, and his grief drowned all his concern for his own safety. Trent was determined to see his family, even if that one visit would ultimately cost him his life. So, he'd sat in the house all through Mardi Gras waiting for them. Last she'd heard - no news.

Strangely, Evie received no word of any murders - or any nefarious activity at all - happening on Mardi Gras day. Evie had assumed that everything would come to a head yesterday, but the parades went off without a hitch. She saw the smiling faces of the parade-goers from the event coverage on the safe house television, and other than a few drunk and disorderly individuals, everything seemed to be going smoothly. *Perhaps Ellen sees Mardi Gras as a day of mourning, a day to honor Orrin's memory.* Whatever the reason, Evie was glad for the twenty-four-hour respite from the madness.

Suddenly, Evie's laptop made its signature *gling*. She looked and found an email from Mrs. Young. The subject line read, *The Only Way*. Evie scooched closer and began to read.

Hi Evie, As you know, I am still knee-deep in research on this Mahu religious sect you're dealing with. Here's what I have discovered. This particular belief system is older than Islam and Christianity, and the only real record of it was found in an archive in Tanzania, but I hit the jackpot. Here it is in a nutshell.

Like I explained in my previous email, the knowledge you're up against derives from the postmortem priests who prepared Egyptian pharaohs for transition into the afterlife. The moment a Pharaoh died, the High Priest of Amun performed rites over his body for three days. His purpose was to collect the soul of the ruler as it left his body. His duty was also to store that soul until it was time for it to reunite with the Pharaoh. This knowledge was so hidden and powerful that there was only one priest who stood guard over the souls at a time. This is why the congregation of Mahu practices royal succession.

Mahuism has many followers around the world, but the Orthodoxy of Mahu only has one High Priest or Priestess at any given time. It looks like you've just discovered the true nature of Ellen Chauvet. The only way to stop the murders now is to give her what she originally requested. I've attached all the information I could find on the Pillars of Mahuism to this email, to give you a better idea of what you're dealing with.

From the information you've given me, it looks like your only hope is Igelhart.

P.S. Trenton is next if he's not dead by now.
Hurry.

As soon as she finished reading the email and looking through the attachments, Evie called Detective Encalade as she slipped on her shoes and grabbed a jacket. With her purse strap across her torso, she sprinted to Marci's car. Kennan Encalade didn't answer on her first attempt, so she dialed repeatedly.

"Thank God, you answered," Evie said in between deep breaths. "I know how to bring this to an end!" Her voice was filled with excitement and panic.

"Evie, that's good news, but your sister and her bad-ass kids have struck again, and . . ."

"Again?"

"Yes, again. I am at the beginning of the process. I'll call you . . ."

Evie cut him off. "But I know how to snap them out of this, it's all right here! It's Igelhart. It may be a long shot, but we have to get him to apologize. If we can't get Igelhart to apologize, she will continue to kill people affiliated with Ares. When Ellen grabbed the arm of Jack McGowan, that act was a declaration of war, but one of the pillars of their faith states that *The High Priest or Priestess cannot declare war in the presence of repentance.*"

"Evie, I just made a second attempt to convince Igelhart to help us - the guy is a stubborn asshole. He says that he is tired of the dreams, and everyone he loved is already dead. We need to look at other options."

"Detective, there are no other options."

"Then I guess the Krewe of Ares is royally fucked."

Just then, Evie received an urgent call. "Detective, I have to take this . . . I will call you back."

Evie ended her call with Detective Encalade and quickly switched to the other line. It was Fred Franklin.

"Fred! Hello! Did you hear from Bridgette?"

"Yes, she called me, and you need to get here quick. If you want to save your family, we have an appointment to keep."

"An appointment? Fred . . . what did Bridgette say? Can I talk to her?"

"She won't talk to you, she doesn't want to get involved, but she did tell me where and when shit's going down."

"I don't understand . . ."

"If you want a chance at stopping this, just get here now."

As she drove, a million questions swirled in Evie's mind. *Why won't she talk to me? I guess it's understandable, but this is an emergency! What's going to happen? What's this appointment? How does Bridgette know what's going to happen? Is she involved?* Evie forced herself to take several deep breaths. She started wondering about Bridgette's son, the one who was supposed to be Ellen's heir. She realized Fred had never mentioned where he was or what happened to him. So, she stopped the baptism, but what about the child? Is he still the successor? Is he even alive? *Obviously, Ellen Chauvet is still the High Priestess, even in death, so what happens to the succession?* Evie had a world of questions, and no answers at all. She decided to focus on the mission at hand and ask Fred what he knew later.

Ten minutes later, Evie pulled up to Fred Franklin's house on Louisa Street. Fred was already out in his yard waiting for her. As soon as she put the car in park, he opened the door and hopped in. "Let's move," he called, his voice grim.

"Where are we going? What's this appointment? What did Bridgette say?" Evie frantically asked as she backed the car out of Fred's driveway.

"No time to explain, but in a nutshell, she told me when Grandma Ellen is coming to collect, and she told me where. We have to get to your sister and brother-in-law's house. But first, we have one stop to make. Someone who might be able to help."

"Who?" Evie asked, forgetting her other questions in a rush of adrenaline.

"Morris Igelhart."

The initial investigation at Ralph Fuller's house was in the process of wrapping up when the city morgue arrived to remove his body. Detective Seals, who had ridden with Detective Encalade to the scene, was held up on a call with Las Vegas Homicide. Meanwhile, Encalade's phone indicated seven missed calls from Evie, four missed calls from Chief Bolton, two missed calls from an unknown number, and one missed call from Irnessa. He'd figured it was best to start with Irnessa and work his way to Chief Bolton.

"Hi sexy, I just noticed I missed your call."

"Oh, my," Irnessa said with an air of shock. "Calling back within the same hour . . . I'm impressed."

"Well, you know, your *milkshake* brings this boy to the yard."

"Damn right!" she blushed. "Anyway . . . what are you in the mood for -"

He jumped in quick. "On the table again, you on your stomach, your legs closed again, in the -"

"For dinner!" she giggled. "What do you want for dinner? Because the girls requested pizza, and you're not going to like the pizza they ordered. Gross."

"Don't worry about me - I am on Mandeville Street in the Marigny neighborhood. I can grab a hot sausage sandwich from Gene's Po-Boys."

"Are you sure, honey? It's no problem for me to whip up something."

"I'm sure." Then his voice lowered to level Barry White. "But I do want that milkshake."

"Since you have been such a good boy . . . I will have the milkshake waiting for you, but I want a hot sausage."

"You want a sandwich, too?"

"No . . . I want your *hot sausage.*"

"Keep talking that gooooood talk to meeee . . . see you in an hour." Kennan Encalade ended the call with every intention of ending his shift. He no longer wanted to chase dead leads late into the night if his shift ended at six o'clock. If he did have to chase an active lead, he decided he'd do his best to arrive home within an hour of the action. "Now, what was I about to do?" he forgot.

Detective Seals finally ended his call. He walked over to Encalade in disbelief and frustration. "The Doubloon Killers have taken their show on the road. Two active investigations in two different states."

"How bad is it?"

"Kelsey and Rhonda Fuller were mutilated like our victims." Seals collected an item off Ralph Fuller's desk. "By the way, your suspicion was correct . . . Ralph is his Kelsey's father," Detective Seals affirmed as the city morgue removed the body and rolled it into the van.

"I knew it. If you are a member of the Krewe of Ares and connected to this Orrin Toussaint murder, you're next."

"From the looks of it, the family members are also getting caught up in this bloody vendetta." Detective Seals entered the kitchen and returned with a slice of king cake and a glass of milk. "I know why the chief is trying to reach you."

"That's what I was about to do . . . I need to return his call."

Seals stuffed the cake in his mouth and washed it down with the milk. "No rush . . . because he just took us off this case and turned it over to the FBI."

"I can't say I am surprised."

"Same here."

"There goes my promotion to a white shirt." Encalade shrugged his shoulders. "No sweat off my back. The FBI can have this case. I haven't been to the gym in four days. Let's lock up this place and call it a night." He searched the room keys to lock the front door. "I think Fuller is in the morgue with the keys in his pocket," he laughed. "I can lock the deadbolt and exit out of the back door," he said as he followed Seals to the front door.

Detective Seals stopped a few feet from the front door. "I almost forgot to tell you . . ."

"What's that?"

"*Hakuna mtu anayekataa kuhani mkuu.*"

"What?"

"*No one declines Kuhani Nalah.*"

Without a second of hesitation, Detective Seals turned, aimed his pistol at Detective Encalade, and shot him at point-blank range. Kennan Encalade fell to the floor in a cloud of gunpowder smoke. As he lay on the floor dying, his last visual before everything went black was of an older woman all in white, standing on the sidewalk supported by a walking cane. At the same time, he briefly saw Detective Seals reaching inside his shirt to pull his doubloon front and center.

"I am the grandson of Gail Narcisse," Detective Seals said as he retrieved the front door keys from his pocket and entombed Detective Encalade inside.

Trent sat in the living room in 1524 Toledano Street and waited for his wife and kids to come home. He had barely moved from his spot on the couch in two days. He'd missed all the Mardi Gras parades yesterday, and completely forgot about seeing the Fullers reign as King and Queen of Ares. None of that was important now. His sole focus was on reuniting with his family.

He'd heard the warnings loud and clear, but in his mind, there was no way Marci and the girls could kill him. After all, he was their loving father. With the speed of a text message, his mind traveled back to 1978, when everyone he loved was alive. A time when he and his brother played hide and seek indoors. A time when his mother roamed from room to room cleaning behind them, complaining how she couldn't get any help from his father. His mind traveled forward to Christmas in 1984, when the presents under the tree consisted of Rubik's Cubes, Transformers action figures, an Atari, a giant Tyco Racetrack with extra cars, and a Michael Jackson doll in the red zipper jacket. The doll was for Trent. He sighed. That was the love he wanted his family to experience in his parents' home—the warmest house on Toledano Street.

But it wasn't to be.

The house was as cold as a heart that refused to pump, and as dark as the last rites of the dying. His childhood home at 1524 Toledano was cold, not because the heating unit had failed, but cold because of the absence of laughter. His tears freeze-dried before reaching his chin at the thought that he hadn't heard any member of his family laugh since they moved from Bristol - not even a giggle. Nor had he made love to his wife.

"Why, Dad?!" Trent screamed to the heavens. "Why did you do this to us? To your grandkids . . . to your wife? It's all your fault. Do you hear me, Jack McGowan? Their blood is on your hands! Show yourself to me . . . take responsibility for this mess you made. Face me . . . reveal yourself!" Trent howled into the darkness. There was no reply from his father, only the barking of a golden retriever as his owner strolled along the pavement. Only the hum of the empty refrigerator. It was then that Trent returned to the wall full of portraits. One by one, he smashed them all. He slammed them to the floor with emphasis and anger. Not a single frame survived the massacre. Once the wall was bare, Trent collapsed on top of the carpet of glass and continued to mourn the loss of his family.

Suddenly, Trent heard the sound of someone entering the house from the back door. He staggered to his feet, bleeding from his arms and hands. The floor was like walking on an ice skating rink, but he continued to the hall. He wanted to see his wife as she walked through the door.

"Marci, is that you? Is that the woman I love . . . the mother of my beautiful daughters?

Tat.

Tat.

Tat.

Tat.

Tat.

With relentless determination, the trusted old walking cane propelled her forward to a meeting that was scheduled fifty years and one day ago to the hour. To the minute. To the exact second the soul departed from her grandson, the heir to ten thousand years of wisdom. The one chosen as an ark to carry the souls of the kings, and every High Priest who had ever served the Amun Priesthood. Kuhani Nalah had come to collect the final payment with interest from the last McGowan standing - the unborn, Trenton McGowan.

There she stood in the middle of the room with a knitted face, sullen eyes, and a mouth full of sharp daggers. Trent's eyes peeled away from Kuhani Nalah when the wrought iron gate shut with a bang. Then he heard footsteps on the porch and the twisting of the doorknob. He withdrew to the furthest space in the room; the portrait wall. Seconds later, Zoe, Maggie, and Amarah entered the house. They blocked him in; there was nowhere else to go.

Cupid, draw back your bow
And let your arrow go
Straight to my lover's heart for me, for me
Cupid, please hear my cry
And let your arrow fly
Straight to my lover's heart for me.

The singing was coming from the upper left part of the house, where a doubloon lit the staircase - Aunt Frieda descended one single step after the other. As she stepped, she continued to sing. Trent's family forced him to the center of a blockade, wrapping him in a gust of icy wind. The last person to enter the room was Marci, who appeared to move on a cloud from the pitch black of the dining room, all the way through the kitchen, and into the living room where she fully blocked her husband from escaping. Trent's eyes searched for a familiar face, but there were none - only strangers with jaws filled with rage, rouge-stained teeth, and clothes drenched from the fulfillment of a prophecy.

"Marci, you asked me to wait for you . . . so I waited. You said it was over and we could move back to Bristol," his voice shivered. "Marci, it's me . . . your husband. Maggie, Zoe, Amarah . . . it's Daddy."

Marci and Amarah parted shoulders, creating a doorway that led Kuhani Nalah directly to Trent. He appeared as a caged fox.

As soon as she entered the crescent, Trent watched her take several deep breaths. Then, she handed her walking cane to Marci. Kuhani Nalah never made eye contact with Trent. Instead, she searched through him to a place far beyond Toledano Street. Then she called him, to kneel beneath accountability.

"You can come forward now," Kuhani Nalah demanded in a groaning voice. "Come on, let's make this quick."

Trent's eyes panned the room in terror; he searched for the one she conjured. He wondered who it could be. He didn't have to wonder long. As per Kuhani Nalah's request, the guest soon entered the room. He made his appearance through the wall just to the right of Trent, above a section of floor covered with shattered glass.

Jack McGowan stood in the midst of the blockade; he had answered her call.

For ten silent minutes, Kuhani Nalah and Jack McGowan spoke to each other in a frequency Trent could not detect. Through their eyes, they exchanged they their deepest disdain. Trent also saw hurt and anger in the eyes of his father - emotions he was never allowed to see as a child.

"I wanted you to be here to experience what it feels like to lose everything, to feel what I felt, to carry an eternity of anguish." Kuhani Nalah took a step closer to Jack and scowled at him defiantly. "I wanted you to experience what it feels like to have a soul that can't rest. Have I made it plain?"

"Yes, you have," Jack replied with a heavy heart.

"Are you ready to watch your last-born child die slowly as I stand here and wait for his soul to ooze out of his throat?"

"Seems like I don't have much of choice, do I?"

"Fire or eaten? Those are your choices for your son. Pick one."

"I choose life."

"Death is the only option for Trenton McGowan." Thunder rolled throughout the house. Suddenly, ancient hieroglyphics appeared on every wall. Hieroglyphics from the Land of the Kings, followed by the rhythm of the Ivory Coast, and the east-blowing winds that raced from Tanzania across the white sands of Sierra Leone. From beneath the floor arose a suffocating stench of turpentine. It quickly that filled the room. It was the turpentine that preserved the innermost parts of the kings. The aroma of cedar oil came next, to cling to the soul. Then came the substance needed to transport the soul.

Above Trent's head, droplets of mercury started to rain down. The silver-colored substance was reserved for Trent - regardless of where he shuffled, it followed him from up above.

"Kuhani Nalah, you are in authority over roho za wafu, the souls of the dead, but you are also under the authority of the Amun Priesthood and what is written!" Jack McGowan called out.

Suddenly, the glass in the window pane next to Trent began to shatter. The first to enter the house from the other side of the shattered pane was Evie. She was quickly followed by Fred Franklin and Morris Igelhart. It was then that Jack McGowan walked over to the place where the glass had shattered on the floor. There, he picked up an envelope that was nested in the glass - it had finally hatched from behind a photo.

Jack turned to his friend. "Old buddy, could you do me the honor of reading something I prepared fifty years ago?" With trembling hands, Igelhart opened the envelope, unfolded a time-tanned letter, and began to read it out loud.

April 4, 1968

To All Members of the Media:

This most recent Mardi Gras, I had the very unfortunate experience of watching a young man by the name of Orrin Toussaint burn to death at the corner of St. Phillips and Burgundy Street. The lynching took place during a parade rest. That is when I witnessed two white men pour a flammable substance on Orrin Toussaint, thus setting him on fire. I will never forget that night as long as I live - or the way he cried for his grandmother over and over, or the smell of his flesh. Orrin was an innocent victim of a hateful attack that ended with the loss of his life and the attacker escaping the arms of justice.

I would have you to know that Orrin Toussaint was mischaracterized by the Krewe of Ares as a 'homeless kid' who was not authorized to be in our parade. That statement was false, and I take full responsibility for the release of any and all false information pertaining to the death of Orrin Toussaint. Not only was Orrin authorized to participate in the Krewe of Ares as a flambeaux carrier, but here is a photo my wife took of him, posing with her mother at the beginning of the parade.

I am requesting that the New Orleans Police Department reopen the investigation into the death of this fine young man - by any angle reviewed, this was first degree murder. To the family of Orrin Toussaint, on behalf of the Krewe of Ares, myself, and my family, I ask for your forgiveness. My office is standing by to support you through this difficult time of bereavement.

Sincerely yours,
Jack McGowan
Captain and CEO, Krewe of Ares

Once Igelhart finished reading the letter, Jack McGowan stepped forward. "I wrote this letter on April fourth, and I was fully prepared to give it to you, but then another tragic event took place on the same day." Igelhart handed Jack McGowan the letter. "On April 4, 1968, just as I dialed the local news station to request a press conference, news bulletins flashed across the television in my office. Dr. Martin Luther King, Jr. had just been assassinated in Memphis. And so, I put it off. I am truly sorry. According to what is written in the articles that govern the actions of the High Priestess, you cannot wage war in the presence of repentance."

Kuhani Nalah nodded, then added, "The same articles gave the High Priestess the authority to set the price of the atonement."

"Kuhani Nalah, you have left only one of my children, and as we speak, the mercury is raining down on him. I have repented." Jack stepped forward and offered the letter he wrote in April of 1968. After what felt like a month, Kuhani Nalah received the letter as payment on the atonement and reached for her walking cane. Only then did she fix her eyes on Trent, who was covered in a shower of quicksilver. He struggled to keep the mercury out of his eyes and mouth, and when Evie tried to help him, it was Jack McGowan who shoved her away. Slowly, Kuhani Nalah approached Trent with the letter still clutched in her hand. Under the steady flow of metallic liquid, Kuhani Nalah handed down her judgment in a malignant voice.

"Toleo lako inashughulikia tu."

Then, Kuhani Nalah summoned those who wore the original doubloons. One by one, she snapped each golden string of beads. The last doubloon removed was the first to obey - Zoe McGowan. It was then that Fred stepped out of the window onto the front porch. He leaned back in the window and whispered, "Evie, my part is done. Six cartons . . . okay. I'm out."

To all those who served, Kuhani Nalah offered her gratitude. *"Ulifanya vizuri.* You served well.

With all five doubloons in hand, Kuhani Nalah slowly waved the palm of her hand from left to right. Then, she closed her fist. Five souls immediately left the five bodies who once wore the burgundy doubloons. Lifeless, they fell to the floor. Hollow. Only then did the mercury ceased to rain on Trenton McGowan. Without so much as a word, Kuhani Nalah, once known as Grandma Ellen, departed the way she entered, followed by a listless Jack McGowan.

Tat.

Tat.

Tat.

Tat.

Tat.

Zoe McGowan.
Maggie McGowan.

Amarah McGowan.
Marci McGowan.
Frieda Fuller.

Rest in Peace.

EPILOGUE

It's been three years since the curse of the burgundy doubloons collided with my life, but I don't blame the city - not in
the least. I have decided to invest my best effort in moving forward, and so far, that decision has blown away the storm clouds.
These past three years have allowed me the wonderful benefit of
opening the sunroof of my life and basking in the brighter days.
And yes, I still grieve over the loss of Marci, Amarah, Maggie,
Aunt Frieda, Helen, and Zoe, but when I told myself I was moving forward, my words became flesh. I took my first step. I like
to refer to that point in my life as my emergence - when I accepted my new reality, my current hour, I hiked a trail of maturity
that prepared me for the emotional uncertainties of tomorrow.

Grief is a hole in the wall.

The second step in my entrance was acknowledging the debilitating magnitude of losing a loved one as intimate as a child,
a spouse, a lifelong friend, a lover, or in my case, Marci and my
nieces. Their untimely deaths, plus my parents' sudden demise,
were three years apart. That equated to seven bucket-sized holes
in my walls that I tried to ignore . . . but they couldn't be ignored.
My holes required immediate attention, and I was forced to de-

360 / TJ SPENCER JACQUES

cide if I was going to repair the holes, or relocate and run from them. I decided to confront and repair them.

The third step of my emergence required that I lower my expectations of this word called healing. In doing so, I fortified my entrance. I realized that healing from my holes is a fictitious ideology, because things will never be the same going forward, nor should I be. Losing people who were essential to my daily life should bring about major changes as I adjust to the empty space they once occupied. The intimacy I share and receive requires me to expand my walls, because intimacy requires an intimate place to bond. I also decided to welcome new people into my life, and with each passing day, I expand my space.

And I love the intimacy of New Orleans!

It didn't take long for me to make 1524 Toledano Street into a home. I refuse to allow the stigma of the house to win. It was a ton of work, but I upgraded the lighting, repaired the AC unit, added a much-needed coat of paint throughout the house, and did a landscaping makeover that proved to be a facelift for the entire neighborhood. Our home is now intimate, warm, nurturing, and inviting. One of the new invites into my intimate space has become a little too comfortable and has overstayed his welcome. The doctor said he would give the little guy one more week to enter the world on his own; my baby is currently eight days overdue. I love him already, and every time I feel him kick or hear his heartbeat on an EKG, I expand my space.

When I finally settled on a name, I was afraid that my husband wasn't going to like it, but to my surprise, he loved my suggestion. He said I was *a woman after his own heart.*

I blushed like he was my first boyfriend. "Then it's official, we will name him Orrin."

But that's my husband; he's very agreeable when I need him to agree. *What more could a girl ask for?* Even when I suggested an intimate wedding, he planned it on my favorite beach in Destin, Florida - on my birthday, with four friends in attendance. It was beautiful. To my surprise, the adjustment from dating to marriage was a lot easier than I anticipated. In fact, once I got over the awkwardness, we quickly became an authentic couple. And when Trent discovered that this overdue baby was a boy, every morning since has been paradise on Toledano Street.

If there is one thing I would like to get a better grip on, it's the nightmares. It's the same annoying nightmare at least once a week, and always at three a.m. Lately, the dreams have become more frequent, but my clinical psychologist said life-changing events beget anxiety, and anxiety begets recurring fears that run wild in my subconscious mind. I have shared my dream with Trent, but he agreed with Dr. Neem Mohammad, it's the anxiety of being an expecting mother - but here's where we disagree. I don't feel anxious, nor am I freaking out about the baby . . . but I am freaking out about this dream.

In the dream, I pick up Fred, and we're hauling ass to Attorney Igelhart. It came as quite a shock to me, but Fred handles all the mechanical services on the tractors that pull the floats in the Krewe of Ares parade. The Krewe of Ares hasn't had one tractor breakdown during the parade since Fred started working for them. Now that I think about it, that horrific incident in 1968 happened because a float broke down . . . twice. But I digress. Igelhart apparently feels highly indebted to Fred for keeping the parades flowing smoothly - his guilt over 1968 built over the years, so Fred has quite a bit of influence over him. Who knew? So, I pick up Fred, we drive to Igelhart's house, and Fred tells him to *Get his ass in the car and go help those people.* No lie, this part of the dream happened in real life three years ago. Then the dream skips to the part where Ellen whispers to Trent; then it skips to my delivery of six cartons of Camel cigarettes to Fred. Same dream, every time.

Ellen walks up to Trent and whispers:
Toleo lako inashughulikia tu!
Toleo lako inashughulikia tu!
Toleo lako inashughulikia tu!
It's bothering me, and I am my dad - I will not rest until I

know. Maybe Mrs. Young has found something? I emailed her about this months ago, but so far, she's come up with nothing. However, I'm confident in her abilities. Over the last three years, she has become the only expert on the Mahu religious sect, and she's been a big help on my manuscript. Yes, I have decided to write about it, and Trent agreed with me on my title: *The Unborn* by Evie McGowan. I think McGowan is the perfect name for an author . . . then again, I'm biased.

The baby just kicked. That was a really hard kick that time - I better ask Trent to load my maternity bag. Today could be the day. I just sent him a text . . . marching up those stairs all day with this belly is brutal on my lower back, but Trent is the greatest husband in the world. He's so understanding and patient. And yes, sometimes I do wonder if Marci approves, but I would like to think that she would. After the funerals, Trent was the only person I could talk to about the doubloons, and I was the only person who understood what he was feeling. So, we clung to each other. I decided to extend my stay in New Orleans . . . and then it happened. We kissed. From the first kiss, we have been inseparable. Once we totaled up all the insurance policies, there was enough money to for us to retire early and for me to pursue my dream of becoming a full-time author. Once a major publisher accepted my first manuscript, I became the family business, and Trent helps me develop my cop characters. Oh . . . I just received an email from Mrs. Young. It's late - already 8:38 p.m. I wonder why she typed *Worried* in the subject line?

Evie, I've researched the quote you sent, finally got some matches, and I'm a little uneasy to say the least. If this phrase is exactly what you heard that night Ellen Chauvet came to visit, then we need to have a conversation today. Below, you will find the phrase and the translation.

Mahu Dialect   English Translation
Toleo lako inashughulikia tu. Your offer only covers you.

Evie, my question is, what was offered and when was it offered? Like I said, after you speak with your husband, call me.

Sincerely worried,
Mrs. Susan Young.

Evie, I got your text - do you feel like today is the day? my husband just texted back.

I am feeling a lot of movement . . . low movement. I think you should load the bags. I don't feel like this is a false alarm.

Your offer only covers you; I must know what that means. So many thoughts are racing through my head right now. I plan to call Mrs. Young once we get settled in the labor and delivery ward, but I must ask Trent about this offer. Here he comes with my bags.

"Trent, I need to ask you something, it's related to my dream."

"You mean the dream about Fred and the cartons of Camel cigarettes?"

"Yes, but my question is not about the Fred part of it, but rather the . . ."

"Wait, we're having this conversation right now? We can't talk on the way to the hospital?"

"Yes, we can, but I need to know something, and it has me puzzled. I am asking for five minutes. Could you please have a seat, so we can confront something that has the potential to punch holes in our happiness?"

He sat the bags down with a thump and deflated on the furthest end of the sofa. This is one of those times where I am mindful not to confuse patronizing with agreeable. It's obvious he doesn't value what I have to say right now, I have never seen him act this closed-minded. Since I read the email from Mrs. Young, three questions have spontaneously combusted in my mind - I need an answer to all three right now. Would you look at that . . . he does resemble Tom Cruise, but the *War of The Worlds* Cruise, not *Top Gun. Evie McGowa*n . . . what are you doing? Do you know? Breathe . . . Breathe . . . I have to focus; my mind is all over the place. Focus, Evie. Focus!

"Trent, I have been thinking considerably about hereditary illnesses, and I noticed that all the men in your family died from liver cancer. We assumed it was Ellen making them sick, but then you would be sick too, so we dismissed that as a horrible coincidence. However, although your father lived longer with his condition, but both Steven and Craig died before the age of thirty-five. You just turned forty-seven, with a perfectly healthy liver. How is that?"

"Beats me; I figure my brothers drew the genes from my father's side while I hit the jackpot on my mother's side. Nothing to see here."

My husband normally says nothing to see here whenever he would like to quickly move onto the next topic, or to kill the conversation altogether. Like when I asked why he had a two million-dollar life insurance policy on his mother. *Because it would have paid off some bills*, he said. His father left Helen debt-free with a house that was paid in full. *But I digress, stay focused. Next question.*

"Trent, when Ellen Chauvet whispered in your ear, do you recall what she said?"

"Evie, that was three years ago, I couldn't tell you."

"That's interesting, because she spoke directly to you, the same as she spoke to my sister—who could also understand her. Interestingly enough, I hear the words in my dreams and thanks to Mrs. Young . . ."

"Let me guess, she researched it for you and discovered some nonsense about offers or whatever." He cut the distance between us in half, and his voice lowered to the level of a hostage negotiator. "Evie, I thought we were moving forward; leaving the past in the past. Why are you dredging this up?"

"That Mrs. Young is something special; a real master of facts. Her reply to me mentioned something about *the offer only covers you*. And you just mentioned the word *offer*, but that could be a coincidence, I guess." I reached for my cell phone on the coffee table, and my husband rushed to assist me. "I need to notify the hospital that I am coming in tonight - they have this wonderful text notification that expedites the check-in. I love it."

I didn't text the hospital. I just texted Mrs. Young SOS.

"Here is my last question, and then we can leave. My parents raised us in the Presbyterian church, and I would like the same for our son. I noticed that this . . ."

"Evie, I don't know about that, I don't think we should force religion on our kid. Religion is something very personal, and I'd rather we wait until he's of age and let him decide."

"And what age do you consider of *age*?"

"I am thinking at least eighteen . . . at least."

"So, I can't attend church with my son until he's eighteen?"

"Evie, everything you ever wanted, I went along with it whether I liked it or not. On this one thing, can we not fight over it?"

My cell phone just alerted me that I have a text.

I paused for a moment and reflected on his position. "You're right, you have made my transition seamless, and I agree that we shouldn't fight. Especially not now. Perfect timing . . . a text reply from the hospital. I have been admitted, and they are standing by," I lied. The text was from Mrs. Young, notifying me that she was standing by.

Before Trent reached for the bags, I took hold of his hands and pulled him close. "I have a feeling that after tonight, our lives will never be the same. I'm prepared to welcome this little fellow into our family, and I am sorry about all the questions. Becoming a mother has me hypersensitive about every little thing."

"Evie, sweetheart, it's okay." He kissed me on the edge of my hairline. "I totally understand and am looking forward to welcoming our little man into the world."

"If you don't mind, as I am sure it will calm my nerves while we're joined hand-in-hand, could you lead us in the Lord's

Prayer?" I closed my eyes and waited for the *Our Father* part. I waited. And I waited. It never came. I opened my eyes and all of a sudden, his nostrils were flaring, and the skin under his neck and earlobes had turned tomato-red. His breath felt like the heat from a broiler. This was not my husband; this was someone else.

"You couldn't leave well enough alone; you had to keep picking and digging and snooping!"

He had revealed himself. "Trent, what did you offer Ellen?"

He released my hands and gripped me by the wrists. It hurt. "A better question is not what I offered Ellen, but what I won in the process . . . I won life." He inhaled for five seconds then exhaled, inhaled for five seconds then exhaled. Each time, he became visibly more intoxicated with evil and darkness. His pupils dilated; he was under the influence of wretchedness - he'd swallowed a dose large enough it looked like it could consume him.

"I won. I am alive."

"Trent, you are hurting me!" I screamed. "Either answer the question or let-let me go!"

"All right, is that how you want to play?" he said in the voice of a privateer at sea. "Let's make this quick, because the baby will be here soon." He released my arms and started to unbutton his shirt. "When? One year before we moved to New Orleans. My father didn't let me grow up ignorant of the curse upon our heads, after all. Why? To meet with Gail Narcisse before she passed away. What was offered?"

It was then that he pulled from his shirt a relic I thought I would never see again. A burgundy doubloon. I started to back away and run, but then I heard the sound of someone entering the house from the back door.

"I offered you, and this baby, as the final atonement."

Tat.

Tat.

That's when I saw her—dressed in all white with a black walking cane. Kuhani Nalah was here for my baby.

Tat.

Tat.

I had nowhere to run. My back was against the wall, and my water just broke.

Tat.

Oh no, oh my God . . . She came for my Orrin . . . they're going to kill me.

Just as I realized the full consequences of my ignorance, Kuhani Nalah snatched me by the crown of my head and dragged me up the stairs. Trent had my cell phone, so there was no one I could call. He didn't lift a finger to help me, but I still held onto a grain of hope that he would. Instead, he came up behind me and spoke in the Mahu tongue in my presence for the first time. Fluently.

"Ninawasilisha mtoto huyu kwa kuhani mkuu Malipo kwa ukamilifu. I present this child to Kuhani Nalah as payment in full," my husband's words stabbed me in my back.

"No, Ellen! No! Stop, please stop, I'm begging you! You can't have my son! Help me . . ." I screamed as a river of life streamed from my womb to the bottom of stairs and formed a puddle. My husband stood in the puddle. "Trent, I thought you loved me!"

Those were the last words I spoke to him as Kuhani Nalah neared the top of the stairs. Suddenly, I heard bongos coming from one of the bedrooms, and I smelled the thickening fumes of turpentine.

At the bottom of the stairs stood the man I thought was in love with me - but he never loved me, or Marci, or Helen, or even his daughters. We were simply vessels he used to get to his true love. Tonight, it became crystal clear that Trenton McGowan only loves *Trenton McGowan.*

THE END

As a lifelong citizen of New Orleans, I wanted to write something entertaining for those who love this beautiful city. I set out to answer the worst possible What If for people who love Mardi Gras: what if one of your kids caught a bead at a parade – and a spirit was attached to that bead? Burgundy Doubloons was the answer to that question, and I hope you enjoyed it.

Thank you for reading Burgundy Doubloons, it was challenging to write but in the end prove to be very rewarding. Growing up in New Orleans I grew exhausted with the typical adaptations of my city, many torn right out of the voodoo movie stereotypes: for that reason, I created Grandma Ellen. In many ways, her character was familiar to me, because she embodied the spirit and personality of my very own grandmother: Mrs. Mary Jacques.

If you would like to know what happens next, please visit my website, and I will keep you posted on future releases. Once again thank you for your support, this novel was my audition to earn a place on the shelve of authors you love, I hope after reading Burgundy Doubloons, you have made room for me.

Please visit my website https://www.tjnovels.com/

Thank you

TJ Spencer Jacques

GEAUX TIGERS!

www.ingramcontent.com/pod-product-compliance
Lightning Source LLC
Chambersburg PA
CBHW050911250626
47155CB00001B/196